The Holy Grail War
Hedgehog

By

Armanis Ar-feinial

Disclaimer

This is a work of fiction. Any portrayals of real people, living or dead, businesses, or events is strictly coincidental.

ISBN: 978-0-578-95637-4

Acknowledgement

Cover Design by Jeff Brown Graphics

Editor: Aimee Hill with AJ Editorial Services

And of course, Mayling for your Epic critique work!

And the many numbers of test and beta readers to tone out the details.

For a Stand-alone reading experience, skip chapters 3, 5, 6, 8, 13, 14, and 19.

Triggers: If you require trigger warnings, any warnings, if there are any, will be in the last page of this book.

Dedication

Dedicated to those who gave all.

Dedicated to those who were discarded.

Dedicated to those we left and abandoned.

"For there to be peace, any at all, we must remove all manner of humans from the equation."

~Administrator Colton.

Table of Contents

Prologue: The Flames of War

~The monsters and demons aren't hiding in my closet or underneath my bed: I'd be fortunate if they were that far away. No, they are all running amuck inside my head, and they're relentless!

It was supposed to be a training exercise, nothing more. But on that day, a war hero walked into his own execution. Guns roared, and the engines revved. Bullets fired from all directions, striking metallic debris of crashed helicopters and planes. Blood painted the desert sand of Nevada crimson, and limbs were sprawled over the sand mounds. Humvees were blown to pieces. Many of those Humvees still had bodies in them, the rotting carcasses were wreathed in flames as their arms hung out the windows, blood dripping down into the sand like oil. Ghost, in his black fatigues and caviar, smelled the putrid rotting of flesh, and he heard the buzzing of flies as they roamed above the corpses littering the desert. His limbs were heavy, and his body hot with the oppressive scorching wind and pelting of sand.

Ghost ducked behind the bags of sand, his heart pounding. He knew his brain was searing these images into the back of his mind, never to be forgotten should he miraculously make it out alive today, but did he want to? He covered his hand with his mouth as Slithers, Ticker, and Butcher crouched to the side, hiding behind the sandbags. The gunfire finally subsided. Slither's bloody hand covered her mouth as she stifled a cry, knowing that even the slightest sound would give away their position to the Americans. The Americans they swore to protect and fight for! Did they?

Ghost took several measured breaths. His heart pounded, trying to free itself from its fleshy prison, doomed to die. He cursed to himself, swearing under his breath, his right hand trembled, his finger coming dangerously close to the trigger, ready to fire into the scorching hot sand. Words rattled inside his mind like an echo chamber.

Treason.

He felt the ground around him suddenly tremble, just like his hand did. He stifled a gasp. He jerked his head upwards, still covered by the sandstorm. Humvees rolled over the dirt of the desert, driving on the roads and shifting the sand around its tires. The Humvees drove past, and he was allowed a moments rest, just a moment. No telling when the helicopters would soar overhead and ping his location. *What is happening? I don't understand any of this!* He thought to himself.

"Time to go," he said, his eyes scanned the horizon, while peering his head just above the sandbags.

"Ghost," Butcher's face was grave, her hands trembling at her side, her teeth gritted. "Why did we do nothing? They are dead because we did nothing. What did you do?" She turned her head to him, her blood-stained hair swinging in the air as she snarled at him.

"I did nothing. You did nothing. They did nothing." He replied, knowing full well, and bearing the guilt of killing the four that were down there. That was *his* fault. *I let them die!* As always, whenever lives were lost, his heart felt weaker, being restrained by those imaginary lines that occasionally, if by accident rose up to the surface of his skin. The guilt swept over his chest and his heart felt like it was bleeding inside. "You and I both know, none of us were making it out alive tonight. These last few moments are going to be the most defining moment in our time. We were born to live and die in obscurity. But we need to go. We—we'll see them again before the night is over; on the other side." A tear escaped his eye, "But damn it all, we are blowing up Area 51, and taking every last one of those sons of bitches with us. That will be our legacy, and perhaps they'll learn their lesson to not repeat this mistake ever again." *We were just unlucky. That's all. We were just thirty-two monsters who got the unfortunate short stick.*

"Ghost! That is not enough. We need to do more than just—"

Bang!

Ghost saw a flash in the distance. The bullet howled, whistling in the air. He immediately turned to face Butcher, knowing the trajectory of the bullet, he was filled with a sense of dread, and he opened his mouth to scream, but nothing came out. Butcher was next, and then there would be three. He winced as the flashing bullet grazed his cheek. His heart raced as the shot missed him, and his pupil watched the bullet in front of him, spinning as it soared through the air. He was in a daze, not knowing how the sniper knew they were here, watching the firing squad. Or was he watching all along?

The bullet penetrated Butcher's eye. Ghost's brown eyes opened wide as he gasped. Blood sprayed all over the place as she was knocked down with the bullet shards entering out the back of her head. Fortunately for her, though blind in one eye now, and in excruciating pain, all the shards miraculously missed the brain. Ghost blinked as the blood sprayed.

Ticker ducked down immediately, pulling out his barrett M82, relaxing his grip. His eyes aimed down the barrel of his rifle. His rifle swiftly swayed as he surveilled the sandy horizon for the sniper. He found the sniper; the bright reflection of the scope got his attention as the sniper was taking aim again. His trigger finger curled around the trigger. The trigger clicked back, the rifle shot immediately, and flared the end of his barrel. The round reached the sniper's cover, forcing the sniper to pick up his rifle and hide at a different location.

The gunfire was so loud, that it nearly deafened Slither's ears, who covered them with both of her hands, her face grimaced and tears streamed down her face. Her limbs trembled, and her eyes were gaped open. Her brown hair drippled blood on the ground from her sides. Ghost heard the ringing in his ears, just like everything else, hand-me-downs for earplugs.

Butcher cackled a raspy laugh, her voice cracking. "Pain. It hurts. Ghost, it hurts! Isn't it great! I can feel pain." Her tone became soft. Her arms and fingers trembled and her other eye wide open. She set one hand over her wounded eye, and blood seeped through the cracks of her fingers, she took several deep breaths. "Did they—did they feel it too?" She sat up and ripped off a piece of her sleeve and wrapped it around her eye. "I bet I look dashing.

"Damn it all. We can't sneak back there then." Butcher struggled to get to her feet and drew her MK16. "You said it. We are not getting out of this alive. Not one of us. I'll buy you time. After tonight, we're gonna make sure they know never to mess with Task Force Seven again! After all, there won't be a Task Force Seven."

Butcher jumped out from behind the sandbags and latching onto a flash grenade, tossed the black cylinder, she closed her eyes. The grenade made a deafening explosion with bright white lights with the soldiers nearby. The noise deafened more ears as she aimed her rifle down, firing at the temporarily blinded soldiers, staggering over their own feet, some stumbling for cover behind sand mounds. Soldiers further away started firing upon her, bullets pelted her limbs. As if on instinct, she pulled out a smoke grenade and dropped it at her feet. "RUN DAMNIT!"

Ghost, Ticker, and Slithers immediately turned around and sprinted away from the execution zone. He could hear the rapid gunfire from the distance. He could hear the whirring of helicopter blades in the distance with his overly sensitive ears. He must stay focused on the mission, ignore the fact that this was the last time he would see Butcher again.

***

The remnants of Task Force Seven rushed at their inhuman pace, kicking the sands with their strides, which shrouded behind them. The sand got into their boots, heating their feet. Area 51 was not far from them, the base which kept so many people away successfully would be penetrated and devoured from within with the rage that filled what remained of Task Force Seven.

It was at this time, much closer to his objective did Ghost picture Butcher lying dead, faced down on the scorching sand, blood streaming out of her body after being pelted with bullets aplenty. He pictured she died with a defiant smile, a fake one, but perhaps this one in his mind was genuine. He heard the whirring of the helicopters and felt the rumble of the ground with tanks and armored vehicles with heavy machine guns mounted on them driving in this direction. What remained of Task Force Seven departed with such haste they couldn't hide their tracks. *It's okay. It's okay. Nothing is going to change tonight. We are all going to die, and I have accepted it. Butcher, I'll see you soon.* Ghost blinked his eyes and tears streamed down it, and his face cringed as he stifled another childish cry.

"Ghost," Ticker said from the front. "Do we have a plan, or am I just blowing a hole in the front?"

"This was supposed to be a training exercise, I don't have time for briefing. Just get in, kill everyone, blow the hull and we go down into the facility to blow it!" Ghost snapped. "Nothing about any of this is normal! Maybe with this distraction, we can make it."

Slithers never took her eyes off the horizon in front of them. "Don't hide it, Ghost. Don't give us hope where there is none. There never was. That promise was bullshit."

"We can't blow it up if we're dead, now can we," Ghost replied angrily. "Ticker, Slithers, switch. Ticker, while you're running, I need you to prep that bomb. We won't have time to do it when we get there."

Ticker let out a deep sigh as he shook his head, his brown hair dropping crusted blood, slowing down to let Slithers pass him. "If I screw up, we're going to be dead before we started."

"You're the best at it. I trust you," Ghost frowned. "We're dead anyway, what difference does it make."

Ticker sneered, "Those might be the last words you ever say."

Ghost saw Ticker swing his rifle over his shoulder and pulled out a large black device out of his satchel, which was just marginally larger than a claymore. The device had blue, green, and red wires of various thickness, attached to numerous knobs. Underneath the device was a metal magnet. Ticker moved some of the knobs and turned them. He shifted the wires around, moving them around the knobs and into various tubes inside the device. Ticker was meticulous, no one knew bombs better than he.

***

Ghost saw the chain linked fences with guards stationed around, walking back and forth, patrolling the perimeter, the strobing lights swayed in the distance from the sentry tower. The soldiers patrolled in their camouflage gear: their charging American flag patches on their shoulders, something Task Force Seven was forbidden from ever wearing. After all, they were never considered soldiers; their side arms holstered with singular shot rifles aiming down to the ground. There were some unarmored Humvees resting about with drivers inside, and other soldiers moving heavily reinforced crates onto trucks. Their eyes seemed to scan the perimeter and horizon.

Ghost knew area 51. He knew of all the experiments and weapons development, but one thing they never invested in, was security. *I guess Task Force Seven was all they ever needed!* Rumors and all that kept the common person out, and quite frankly, the absurd rumors of harboring aliens kept enemy interest in the classified air force base low, surprisingly, but there would be no more wars for a while, Ghost made sure of that.

I can't afford mistakes; however, I can't afford the time necessary to prevent them. But nothing about this damn training exercise would be considered normal. We are all that's left. Ghost thought to himself as he considered his options.

"Slithers, kill 'em," he ordered from behind, raising his rifle, his eyes barreled down the iron sights.

Ghost noticed, before he looked onward to something else, Slithers sighing heavily and shaking her head. She was exhausted, he knew that. They all were. Fighting these wars for years was finally taking tolls on them, but *this* battle, or training if they want to call it that, this was taking an entire toll on them mentally, killing soldiers with faces they recognized. Ghost heard the sound of her rifle firing several controlled shots. They found their target's heads, blood sprayed out of their bodies as they collapsed onto the ground. The ruckus of gun fire soon followed in front of them as the loud alarms went off.

Ghost lobbed a grenade swiftly out to the fence. It shattered the foundations hidden underneath the gates, forcing them open. Soldiers swarmed out the buildings. Their eyes already aimed down their holographic sights, training their aim on Task Force Seven. Slithers slipped through and made a beeline to the left, dodging behind a building. Ghost moved in front of Ticker as he laid down suppressing fire. His heart jumped as bullets came for him. The temperature dropped, red veins covered his eyes; the bullets fired, they appeared to slow, he could track their trajectory, moving his body to avoid being hit in anything vital. The bullets pelted his arms and legs, but none were of a high enough caliber to sever him. Ghost knew these soldiers never saw *real* war, and their weapons were inadequate to the likes of him, *a monster.*

Ghost felt the wounds, the warm blood trickling down his legs. He felt the lead penetrate his body like needles and tore through the other side, spilling more of his own blood behind him. He felt the temperature drop around him as Ticker finished his calibration behind him, but what he could not feel was pain. Yes, they even took that away from them. From all of them. *Butcher, what does it feel like?*

***

Slithers rushed behind another building, shooting other soldiers who were distracted with Ghost and Ticker on the entrance. She tossed a flash bang in front of her as she dodged behind the cover of some wooden crates. The crates were not ideal, the bullets could shred the crates, sending debris, splinters and ballistic fragments; sparks emitted from the crates upon impact.

Bright white lights emitted from the black cylinder as it exploded, blinding the soldiers nearby, some of which ducked, attempting to find some cover. Slithers breathed out, jumping over the crate; aimed down the barrel of her rifle, swiftly pulling her trigger, gunning down the disoriented soldiers, bullets penetrating their chests as they fell. Reloading, she jumped behind a crate where another soldier was down. He swiftly moved up, and to fortunately for Slithers, he was in perfect melee range. He swung his rifle at her. She blocked the stop with her own arm, hastily pulled out a knife. The blade impaled his throat, she twisted the knife, rending his neck. She ran behind the last line of defense, and up towards the sentry towers, aiming up high, and unloaded into the sentries pushing on the alarms for more soldiers to come up from down below.

Slithers fired upon the last line of defense from behind, the remaining soldiers were immediately killed as bullets penetrated their bodies from numerous directions.

Ghost raised his hand and dropped it, motioning to Ticker to follow him as he ran to Slithers. "Slithers, turn that damn alarm off!" Slithers went to the sentry towers, climbed up the ladder, and shortly after Ghost saw her in the tower, the alarm stopped. "Ticker, plant it right here!" Ghost pointed to the ground where there appeared to be a barely noticeable crack in it; with some sand which blew over their feet, the sand itself poured ever so slightly into the crack. He knew this much larger door, was for much larger machinery. This would be the best point of entry, after all, every unfortunate soul down there already knew trouble was coming. He glanced over to Ticker and pointed at the crack. Ticker took out the device and attached heavy duty magnets on the bottom, planting it upright over the door. Ticker flicked a switch, and a red light turned on. Ghost exhaled deeply, taking just a moment to reflect on the magnitude of what he was doing, and taking a moment to realize this was going to be the closest thing to a funeral they would ever get.

"We'll wait," Ghost said with panted breath. "We'll wait until they get here."

The remnants of Task Force Seven pulled corpses together behind a building, about fifteen meters from the explosive. Ghost took an arm from one of the corpses and cut it open, pouring the blood over his face. The three of them pulled together some smaller crates in front of the body of corpses. Ticker and Slithers followed his example as they hid underneath the bodies, their eyes open, watching.

They all took measured breaths, allowing their heart rates to finally slow down as they hid underneath the mass of bodies. They had been racing ever since the first shot was fired, and none of them remembered how long ago that was. *Three days? A month?* None of them had any sense of time anymore. They hadn't slept since it started.

Time had passed. Ghost couldn't tell how much time, but he knew it was long enough for the *enemy* to regroup from Butcher's efforts, but they took far longer than necessary. Ghost assumed security below was waiting for further orders before coming up from their little foxhole. Perhaps, General Snells assumed that the modest force at Area 51 would hold them off long enough for an appropriate response. One thing was for certain, General Snells was coming for them, and he never left a stone unturned. Ghost knew this from working with him for the last decade and a half.

They certainly took their time getting here. Ghost saw the soldiers walking on the premise, he saw their gazes and their heads turning, looking over the carnage. He saw their eyes always aiming down the barrel of their rifles. Their faces were grimacing and cringing with the stench, but there was one thing different about these soldiers than the rest of them: they had clean faces, as if they weren't out today, or on leave and coming back from leave to see all of their friends dead, and who else to blame for that than them, Task Force Seven. These soldiers had a *black* eagle patch on their shoulders.

Ghost's eyes scanned from underneath the arm resting over his head, trying to get a count of these *black eagle* soldiers, many of them were hiding behind parked, armored vehicles, their sights trained on the corners of the buildings, places where Ghost would normally hide for cover, but not against this foe. He heard the whirring of the helicopter blades coming closer, dusting the sand off the perimeter, and into Ghost's face. He closed his eyes and continued to listen to heavy boots clamor on the metal plates covering the ground. There was that one thing that truly concerned him. *Where is that damned sniper!*

Ghost had no choice but to carefully listen to the number of footsteps taken, counting with each pace as the rapidly approaching steps were now faster than their beating hearts. It was impossible to discern where *precisely* they were. But they likely marched down the middle as he suspected they would, right to the device. He knew too well. He counted their footsteps. Right when he thought them to have passed over the device: "Ticker," he whispered.

Ticker needed no more words. He pulled out the remote in his side pocket and pushed the black button.

The device started whirring. The light blinked red repeatedly. The soldiers who were right in front of the device saw it, glanced down swiftly and stepped backwards, "It's a trap!" one called. *Boom!* The explosion was like a small hurricane, blowing flames and debris in all directions. The soldiers immediately caught in the blast were now black, unrecognizable husks. Others were flailed into the nearby buildings and other objects, snapping their bodies, limbs were strewn over the vicinity. Ghost could hear the bones cracking and crushing underneath the tremendous velocity and sudden halting of their respective trajectories, at least those that landed closer to him. Outside by the armored vehicles, the soldier's eyes gaped open in a daze. Immediately, they retrained their aim at the vicinity, looking for movement for whoever remained from Task Force Seven.

"NOW!" Ghost cried out.

The remnants of Task Force Seven jumped from underneath the bodies, sprinting towards the explosion where the door into the bowels of Area 51 lay. They were more refreshed and confident, firing at the armored vehicles. They were right there, by the hole.

Slithers jumped down, throwing a dazed soldier off the internal catwalk into a burning heap as molten metal seeped from the opening, melting through to the bottom of Area 51. Ghost was a few steps in front the hole, and Ticker followed behind him.

Bang!

His heart raced again. His eyes shifted behind the armored vehicles to the flash. *Sniper. You, again.* He could see the bullet flying right towards him. The bullet was too close for him to dodge it. *Good-bye.* He closed his eyes, welcoming the precisely aimed bullet.

Thwick!

Ghost eyes opened. Blood sprayed across his face. In front of him was an arm, severed by the shot. He swiftly looked to his right, and Ticker was in front of him. The ballistic fragments scattered as they struck Ghost's arms. He now knew the round of the sniper: a .50 Cal. Barret. Ghost saw Ticker pulling out a satchel with his other arm.

"Take this. Quick." He looked at his arm, pouring blood out of his like a faucet, his other arm trembled as his body began to feel the effects of rapid blood loss. Ticker breathed deeply, shaking his head, "I can't get you much time. But damnit! I'll try." Ticker kicked Ghost into the hole, and he charged towards the armored vehicles. It was not long before the roar of gunfire continued, drowning out the screams.

Ghost landed on his feet, following Slithers down the steel grated walkways. His calculations were correct, the damage done here was more than enough to send the soldiers on the upper levels to their untimely demise and sending significant disarray to everyone else.

The guards down here were disheveled, looking in every direction, not going to their battle stations, not knowing where everything was. Many kept their hands on top their heads, limping to their next location, while others were laying on the ground, covering their wounds with their hands, trying to keep themselves from bleeding out. *Perhaps if they didn't rely on us too much, they might have a chance down here. We carried your burdens you little shits.* Ghost and Slithers descended to the second level.

Ghost sucked in the air through his teeth, stifling a whimpered cry. *And then there was only two left.* He knew it was time but that didn't make this any easier. He raised his rifle, firing with Slithers at the disorganized men below. Their corpses littered the ground, and their blood painted the walls. They made it down three more levels. The stench of gunpowder filled the air.

Red lights from the alarms flared, and the buzzing pierced their ears. This level was more open, and the soldiers were more organized, preparing barricades and riot shields. There was reinforced steel for cover, even Ghost and Slithers' rounds would not pierce them. Soldiers held their ground behind cover. "Slithers, take right!" he pointed right. She went to the right, firing at the shield walls, keeping the soldiers behind cover as Ghost strode to the left.

Ghost took a deep breath, his lungs and body filled with an unnatural energy. Yet, it felt natural, like the natural essence of humanity. This *essence* passed through his body, and he suddenly felt refreshed as black veins protruded on his skin. He felt the temperature drop, his hair sticking on ends as he *passed through* the barricade, behind their iron defense. The soldier's eyes stretched open, and their trigger fingers trembled as he opened fire behind them. These soldiers immediately turned around and shot through Ghost. Slithers flipped over the other side, crossing her fire with Ghost's line of sight. The soldiers were a disorganized mess as they started shooting in random directions. Their fire was immediately suppressed, their bodies strewn behind at the reinforced steel cover. Their blood made a large pool at Ghost and Slithers' feet. Ghost's black veins receded back into his body.

"One more level," Ghost said. "One more level, and we're done."

Bang!

A shot came from above. His eyes opened wide before hastily spinning around, aiming his rifle to the top of the catwalk, from which, stood a single marksman. Ghost pulled the trigger of his rifle, and he felt uncontrolled kickback into his shoulder as the bullet ripped through the marksman. The walls were painted with blood. Suddenly, Ghost realized that the shot was not aimed for him. Turning around, he looked at the worse thing he could imagine, Slithers, and suddenly, he knew pain.

She smiled as tears streamed down her face; she covered the wound with her hand. Black blood spilled through the cracks of her hand like the inside of a sinking ship. Ghost had enough medical training to assume the bullet struck the liver. She leaned against a wall, breathing heavily. He bolted over to her, pulling out a med-kit, hoping against hope to save her.

"No. There isn't time," she said, grabbing onto his hand with hers, "They're coming down. I don't have long. You know it's not worth it. You don't have time to waste. With what is left. I will stay behind and *will* myself to buy you what you need."

Ghost didn't want to be alone. He inhaled and exhaled deeply, trying to mask his frustration. He didn't want to cry but couldn't stop a singular tear from rolling down his face. She was the last person he ever wanted to say good-bye too, and now he couldn't even muster the right words. "I understand," was all he managed to say. He turned and sprinted to the set of stairs heading down to the last level.

"Ghost!" she shouted.

She shouldn't be wasting energy talking. "Be quick about it," hearing the echoes of military boots descending from above, he snapped at her. *If only there was more time.*

"What little time we had in this world, I'm glad I got to spend my last moments with you," she said, "I don't know how to say this, so I'll be blunt. I love you."

He nodded, "I love you too."

"Ghost, if by some miracle you make it through this, promise me this: that you will live. And hold no hatred in your heart for the hell we've been through. Promise me that you will find another light. Even a small fading one should suffice. Now go. There isn't time."

Another tear escaped his eye. He could find no words. He nodded to her and turned. *This isn't fair. What did we do to deserve this?* He sprinted down the stairs, down into the next level.

Ghost inhaled the *essence* from the air, and red veins protruded from underneath his skin when he came to a whitely lit room, the metal rods were polished, some were rising with sudden changing in the water levels, there were four large bronze tubes connecting these tubes to more volatile parts of the reactor. His eyes scanned the top of the room to locate the command center, his eyes canned downward again for a doorway, red around the hinges.

He moved around the first bronze tube and strapped the bomb to it. He placed the strap close to the bottom, now, if anyone was looking for it then they would find it, but Ghost was sure they would not be looking for it. They'd be too busy trying to kill him.

Not more than five minutes passed and the room behind him was roaring with gunfire. It would not be long before he was completely, utterly alone, and they would be on him shortly like flies to a pile of shit. He could not be certain if he had enough time to prime the bomb for explosion. And he still didn't know why any of this was happening. He finished priming the bomb, and he inhaled some of the *essence* from the air, and the veins crawled from his skin, moving themselves from him, and encasing the bomb.

One of the silver rods ruptured, and steam filled the room. Ghost felt the radiation, and the tremendous heat filling the air. He felt the heat open up patches of his skin, the light headedness followed, running towards the exit, tripping over his feet. This continued as the radiation seeped into his body at such a high degree, he vomited on the door, swinging it open, he jumped inside and slammed the door shut behind him, panting, and breathing in more *essence*. There was an explosion in the reactor, followed by several rapid strikes against the door from chunks of radioactive debris.

The bomb was unnecessary. I literally came down here in the middle of a meltdown! Are you serious! Well, that was part of the problem anyway, but that didn't mean they can't stop the reactor from blowing. One more thing left.

Glancing up the stairs, he saw the last door leading upwards to the command center. That reactor explosion bought him enough time. He inhaled the *essence* from the air, and the red veins on his skin faded into his body. The veins returned to his body a light cerulean. His strides sent him up the stairs, tackling through the door to an empty command center.

He swiftly looked to the monitors, seeing the soldiers move away from the reactor from where he was going. The soldiers placed iron blockades to the reactor before shifting down other corridors, congregating elsewhere. Ghost shook his head and sighed as he grabbed a chair and logged into the mainframe of the computer, disabling the failsafe procedures.

He locked the console. He took a breath. *Good-bye. Slithers. I love you. And Ticker. And Butcher. And all of you. You're my only friends. I'll see you soon.*

Ghost was fatigued, pushing the chair out from under him, his eyes narrowed towards the door heading out the other end of the corridor, where he assumed the command center evacuated to. He took a deep breath of relief, this last-minute mission was to be a success, but now, he had to pretend to want to make it out, to keep them away from the command center to reset the protocols. *I'll see you soon.*

He breathed in the *essence* from the steel and iron in the room and the blue veins turned grey and opened the door. The corridor was empty but clatter and clamor of heavy boots stamping down the halls. Ghost aimed down his sights as he ran down the hall.

He made a turn down the hall, sprinting down some stairs, and rushed out the door. Bullets immediately shot past his head. He returned fire against soldiers stationed up in the catwalks. His eyes glanced to the side, and his best friend lay there in a pool of her own black blood.

Slithers was pelted with bullet holes filling her body, and all her limbs were pelted and penetrated that they all severed, being scattered across the room. Blood overflowed from her mouth. As if that wasn't enough, for good measure, someone left a kbar knife protruding from her heart, impaled blade deep.

One month ago, Slithers and Ghost were laying down in the fields of Paulding Forest, laying down in the empty space, staring at the break in the trees. The moon and stars shone bright this night. Ghost's hands interwove Slithers fingers together. They were alone, together. They were not off fighting, not with the rest of Task Force Seven, and far away from the U.S. military. They were alone, except for a few crickets singing their songs.

Ghost felt her fingers tightly grip his, and she pulled him to his side, and they locked eyes. Slithers smiled that smile, but bags filled her eyes with exhaustion, the same bags he always wore upon his face. "We'll be free soon," she told him that night.

But she still held that smile, curled upon her lips.

The ground sparked as bullets continued flying towards him. He laid down suppressing fire. He lobbed a smoke grenade on his position and lobbed numerous grenades down the hall and through the catwalks. The halls echoed with gunfire as the smoke obscured his visibility. Taking off his equipment vest he ripped another vest off a corpse. Several more bullets came closer, penetrating him in the limbs and chest. Coughing, he donned on an enemy's vest.

He sprinted through the smoke, firing at soldiers hiding from behind the cover of the other rooms. *Three levels to get to the surface. Just three.* Ghost grimaced, grinding his teeth as the fire from the guns lit up the face around him. His watery eyes glimmered with the bright lights of bullets emitting from their respective rifles. Bullets which struck him in these grey veins sparked around him. He never blinked as he rushed to the stairs.

Clunk! Clunk! Clunk!

A dropped grenade *clinked* against the stairs as it fell, the echo to Ghost was louder to him than the constant gun fire. His attention shifted focused as he was in midstride. The grenade started flashing fire from behind its pineapple-shape, sending shards everywhere. Instinctively, his veins breathed in more *essence,* and he felt refreshed as if water coursed through these veins. He knew this was unnatural. The grey light in these veins over his body thickened.

Find the light. Whichever light flickers. Find it! Ghost thought.

The explosion sent the shards piercing through his body, ripping out through his back, blood sprayed out. He felt cold as the blood dispelled from his body. The explosion propelled him backwards. He landed on the ground, rolling on his side. He immediately stood up and sprinted back to the stairs. He aimed down his iron sights as he reloaded his rifle with his sleight of hand.

He charged up the stairs, screaming as the grey veins persisted on his body, aiming down the iron sights, shooting everyone in his path. His aim was never faulty, despite the lack of spirit he had. His spirit felt like it was a man, hanging from a noose over the Grand Canyon. His heart was empty. He stopped caring as the bullets penetrated these monsters' bodies, letting them plop to the ground like empty husks being prepared for their tombs. He stopped caring about the lives he was taking. He stopped caring about the country he fought tooth and nail to protect, but more importantly, he stopped caring about his life.

He ran, leaving his trail of blood behind him as he made it to the next level, which had little more cover than before. He simply jumped over fallen filing cabinets. Bullets sprayed from above as the roaring continued with heavy-machine gunfire. More of that *essence* filled his body and the veins on his body swelled, *clunk*, emitting more grey light in the room. Bullets hit Ghost but they struck the veins, coming to a halt, the bullet shattered, and fragments deflected off his body. He still felt the impact push vibrations through him.

So much, so much blood. I fought for this? I never would have, if I knew this was going to be the futile result! "Peace, is this your idea of some cruel joke? Because this isn't funny and I'm not laughing!" he cried out loud, his voice screaming into halls, his voice only silenced by the roar of the flames.

He made it through another doorway.

Boom!

A great ball of fire was being hurdled at him from the other side of this level. He swiftly turned, being hit by a burning filing cabinet. He felt the warmth of the flames, and the immediate thrust bruised his arms. His firm grip was nearly ripped away from his rifle. The filing cabinet pinned him against the wall. The fire burned his clothes as he hastily pushed the incendiary filing cabinet off him. He let the orange air burn as he got up, ignoring its caress on his body. It could only be described as an alien sensation: nothing more. Nothing more.

***

At last, Ghost made it to the morning, on top of Area 51. Sighing heavily with a pulsating chest, he breathed in more *essence* from the air, and the grey veins receded into his skin, returning to Cerulean. He carefully eyed soldiers training their sights on him from behind the rubble, no doubt thanks to Ticker, whose body was nowhere to be seen. Standing upon the rubbled plains, he stared, knowing full well, a gun fight with his exhaustion was suicide, Hell, why did he care anymore.

He took a long look at the soldiers surrounding him like an animal in a cage. *After all, that is all any of us ever were. Just an animal who needs to be put down. This had better have been worth it.*

His fingers trembled. Scampering with heightened pace, he raised up his rifle like a club, his cerulean veins crawled from his hand to the rifle. Swinging the rifle down, the rifle, and the veins attached to the rifle shattered as it sliced through the soldier's ballistics helmet, and the soldier's skull. He pulled the pin out of a grenade hanging from the soldier's vest as he kicked the corpse, rolling him into the rest of his platoon. He turned to another soldier, who was running at him, using his own rifle as a club. Ghost ducked and swung his foot into the soldier's windpipe.

The grenade exploded, sending the corpse's limbs flying, and metallic debris into the soldiers nearby. Ghost dashed at the group, loosely pulling out his kbar knife, and slit the throat of another soldier. Soldiers screamed out trying to put down this animal before more pin-less grenades fell from the body of the woman he just killed. Ghost dashed to another group of soldiers: bullets began to impale him again as an explosion sent more debris his way.

Only one platoon left!

Ghost struck the man in the chest with a knife. The soldier, who had some life in him, ripped out a pin of a grenade as he stabbed Ghost in the arm, twisting the blade. Ghost felt the blade twisting in his arm, but pain was just as elusive as ever.

Ghost ripped out the knife from the soldier's hands stabbing his tendon, ripping himself away before the grenade blew. Shards of fragments of the grenade penetrated Ghost, ripping apart flesh. His fingers trembled again. He turned to the side and threw a spinning knife, impaling a soldier between the eyes.

He took a deep breath as he strode on the scorching hot ground with the blue veins, moving faster than before. As his body felt like a soulless husk, his face became still like it was carved in a mountain.

Ghost pulled a grenade from his own pocket. He pulled the pin out and threw it behind him. He pulled out a second grenade. He pulled the pin out of the second grenade, lobbing it behind him. He started slashing at these soldier's necks, with the knife, which dulled.

The grenades behind him blew. The roar of the blast was deafening, and the dying gurgling screams of soldiers behind him continued.

Ghost impaled the last soldier with an iron pipe from a plumbing apparatus. The corpse trembled and leaned on him before collapsing at his feet. He heard groans of soldiers who had not yet passed to the other side. He pulled out his sidearm, and pointed at the nearest one, and pulled the trigger. The man's brains splattered on the ground.

Ghost retracted his sidearm to his holster. Eyes wide, and he didn't want to bring himself to look at the mound of bodies around him, many of which he killed, but he did. The sands were stained in blood, and carcasses were blown away in the wind, and limbs were scattered all over the rubble. His heart sank as he realized again, the sanctity of life, and how easy it was for him to take it away. Violence, it's all he ever knew, and even then, it succeeded, or was he perhaps the epitome of human failure?

Finally having a moment, memories swept over his mind of his comrades, their faces and their smiles, as if compelled to remember them not in pain, but of happiness. A life filled with nothing but constant war, and this was the result. He gritted his teeth as he knew not what to fight for, not anymore. He was the last of Task Force Seven, the only survivor. *Damn it all. Why was this happening? This was supposed to be a training exercise!* He felt like a dull stake was being violently hammered into his chest without ceasing, as the guilt swept over him. *I murdered these people. I murdered. Everyone.*

Bang!

He looked up at the flash in the distance. His heart jumped, and then settled back down as he remembered he didn't care anymore. The caliber round penetrated his chest and blood sprayed out of his back. The blue veins retreated back underneath his skin, and he resembled a normal human again. The numerous bullet holes in Ghost's standing corpse were now flowing out of him, like he was a strainer. *To live and die in obscurity. A corpse is all I ever was, and all I will be.* He coughed as blood sprayed out of his mouth. He still looked onward, at the sniper.

Finish it!

Just as he thought those last words, he heard a loud whistle in the air. His head tilted up as blood drooled from his mouth. Black birds in the morning horizon flew swiftly, their velocity rang in his ears as they came overhead. More whistling came, he looked right above him as the planes swept overhead, and large metallic cylinders dropped out of the tummies of these planes. He smiled, and he let out a chuckle as he grasped onto his elbow with the knife impaled in it. Uncle Sam spared no expense on them. Ghost covered his heart with his hand as he took a deep breath, not making a move. "I pledge allegiance to the flag—"

The bombs struck right beside him, clouding everything in sight. The explosions and flames pushed through him in a torrent of fire. The red air caressed his corpse as sharp debris penetrated him, ripping his flesh apart. Nothing would escape as the fighter jets turned back around and lit the field up with their guns. This continued, until nothing remained.

Area 51 became a crater filled with rubble, limbs and burnt faces, melted dog tags. The smoke was filled with radioactive particles, and the ground became a hazardous wasteland. The buildings were brought to ruin, the remains scattering in the wind. Blood watered the ground. Every. Single. Inch.

Chapter 1

Peace in the Gardens

~Not of my own choice, I became a hero for peace, and I did whatever I was ordered to do. I killed, and I killed, and I killed. I killed without halting. I killed until at last my heart stopped beating. Every life I removed meant I was one step closer to brokering world peace. And then, at last I achieved it. With such an impossible task, you'd think that would make me happy. But that wasn't the reward I acquired 'cause I became unnecessary, and I was framed for treasonous activity not of my own doing, and I was executed. Again, and again, and again!

Samantha and Jennifer sat upon their checkered picnic blanket, their cooler onto the side, they were sitting at the Boston Common across the street from Park Street Church. The church overlooked them, the grand church spanned the entirety of the corner of Park Street and Tremont Street, hovering over the opposite side of the common. The red bricks of the church were dotted with two rows of contrastingly white windows, square on the bottom row and grandly arched on the top. There was a clock on all four sides of the brick church leading up to the belfry, and the belfry above pointed upwards like a castle tower, was white, reflecting off the light of the bright sun.

Samantha and Jennifer took great care in getting the creases out of the blanket. Samantha laid face up, letting the sun beat down on her face, shielded by large sunglasses. She was resting in her t-shirt and gym shorts with her arms resting at her sides. Jennifer was laying right next to her; her face away from the sun as she lay on her belly, her legs bent in the air, shoeless, and buried her face in *Pride and Prejudice*. Samantha heard the birds chirping as they fluttered to the treetops, and the dogs barking at squirrels scampering up the trees. She heard the annoying sound of some pop music being played by some obnoxious college kid with their boom box. *I thought those were out of style. Those shouldn't even be a thing anymore.* She saw at the corner of her eye, Jennifer twirling her brown hair with her finger.

Samantha glanced at her silver-chained watch wrapped around her right wrist. Her ponytails rested to either side of her golden head, "3:27." She read aloud and enclosed her hand to a hard fist. Samantha didn't like being kept waiting, "When are they going to get here? The sandwiches are going to get soggy! They really know how to ruin a good picnic."

"Patience is a virtue," Jennifer snickered, bowing her head deeper into her book before putting a plain bookmark in between the pages before closing the book before turning a playful smile to Samantha, "You know Michael. And Tim is usually only along for the ride. Michael likes to take his time, never a rush to do anything."

"You'd think he'd be able to keep time better," she was being sarcastic, reflecting on the work Michael does: business consultations. "Maybe he's working."

"On a Saturday? Fat chance," Jennifer cackled out loud, turning on her back and covered her face with her arms, "More likely he is just lounging around waiting to come until the last minute, Michael does as Michael does." Jennifer twirled her left wrist in her hair.

"Not like me." Samantha spoke plainly, clicking her tongue. "Consulting and logistics are two completely different things."

"No. But who comes thirty minutes early for everything except you? You are unnecessarily early for everything." Jennifer chuckled, removing her arms from her face, squinting at the afternoon sun. "I swear, you wouldn't be yourself if you didn't get to your own funeral thirty minutes early."

Samantha shot a sharp glare at her. Jennifer wasn't looking, her eyes were closed as her face was pointed to the sky. Samantha closed her eyes again and turned her face towards the sun. She looked up into the clouds and looked at the shapes in the sky. Samantha reflected on this, yes, she was early for everything with anxiety if she wasn't running at least fifteen minutes early but was it really all that necessary? Perhaps she could pray about her anxiety for such a trivial matter.

"I'm not that bad, am I?" Samantha didn't think she was that bad, just punctual. Though, she found more often than not her version of punctual was typically fifteen-minutes early. She was never late.

"Well, yah." Jennifer told her, rather sarcastically. "I invited you over to my house *after* dinner, which was at five. I invited you at 6:00PM. You showed up in the middle of my dinner. You really are funny with time."

"Wait!" Samantha pointed to the sky. "Look right there, it's a cloud. It looks like—"

"What?" Jennifer interrupted, opening her eyes as she shielded them with her hands. "Don't tell me? No. Don't. Sam. Sam. No. Bad. That's bad! Sam! Don't say it!"

"It's a curtain van!" She exclaimed.

"You really need to stop taking work home with you," Jennifer sighed as she looked at the cloud which Samantha pointed at. She saw something different. "I see a cloud, an image of condensed gaseous water. Only you would be excited to see some logistic import solutions in the sky." She looked closely at it and rubbed her chin and smiled. "That might be something, now wouldn't it? A very entertaining idea to have freight stuck in the sky somewhere! No wonder my lab supplies never show up on time."

"I'm not sure if that's what clouds are made from. But it's a curtain van!"

"I'm not a meteorologist. I'm a biologist. Something like that is a little out of my realm of expertise." Jennifer shook her head.

"Cloud gazing?" came a voice above them.

"Late as usual, Michael." Samantha scowled at him; his short light brown hair waved as the wind passed through it.

"Hostility is not appreciated on a Saturday, Samantha." Michael said rather nonchalantly, smiling. "Besides, I brought a Tim with me."

"Cloud gazing," Tim repeated and pushed his glasses closer to his face as he looked to the cooler. "I see you brought the sandwiches. Did you get drinks too?"

"Really," Jennifer put her hand defensively on her chest. "Really? You think we would forget such things? Do I hear a sense of distrust from you, Tim?" She stood up with Samantha as they went over to the cooler to open it, inside the cooler were sandwiches, bottles of water, granola bars, and cans of soda.

"I never knew you to be reliable," Tim directed his joke to Jennifer, wiping some sweat from his forehead.

"Wow!" Samantha exclaimed to Tim. "Rude." She turned her attention to Michael. "So, anyway, why were you so late?"

"Well," Michael sucked his teeth as he scratched his back over his shoulder. "I was with another friend. He needed someone to talk to. Today," he deeply exhaled. "You see, his mother died eight years ago in an accident, I think. Today was the anniversary. She died in Nevada. There was some training accident with the U.S Army that apparently went horribly wrong, killed over two-hundred thousand people. So, he needed a shoulder. Well, that's what he said."

Samantha sucked her teeth in, her eyes stretched open, and her chest puffed to take a breath. "You could have invited him to hang out with us, Jennifer and I wouldn't have cared."

"I did but he declined," His smile faded. "He certainly needed a friend, I was there until he was over it, just to make sure he was going to be okay before I left him."

"Well, let's put these grim talks aside for now." Jennifer said, clapping her hands together. "I'm hungry. We've waited long enough!"

Jennifer pulled out the wrapped sandwiches, tossed one each to Samantha, Michael, and Tim: Then tossed one each to them a bottle of water. They unwrapped their sandwiches and ate.

"What is this?" Tim spat it out. His face cringed as his mouth made obnoxiously loud chewing noises.

"Oh, that's just peanut butter and jelly." Jennifer shot a smile over to him with her eyelid drooped down halfway.

"What! You know this! I am allergic to freaking peanut buttah!" he cried out.

"Well, well, well," she snickered as she covered her smile with her mouth. "I hope you didn't fehget yeh epi pen."

"Tim, shut up and eat. We all know that's a lie. You just hate peanuts." Michael had some of his sandwich hanging out of his mouth.

Samantha said nothing. Samantha was a little distracted thinking of Michael's friend, and those many people who died. *That's a lot of people.*

"Michael?" She asked.

"Hmm?" he took a bite and was chewing on his sandwich.

"That incident you mentioned," she began.

"Not this again," Jennifer shook her head as she took a drink of water.

"Did you ever hear anything about that incident? I can't imagine something like that happening here," Sam asked.

"I have not. But then again, it was eight years ago. We were all likely still in middle school, except maybe Jennifer here." Michael snapped his fingers to point to her. "Where were you eight years ago? Jennifer, you must have heard something. I mean, that's a lot of people. I find it very hard to believe there wouldn't be a lot of media attention. Maybe Uncle Sam covered it up well. After all, a mistake at that kind of scale would only tell our enemies we're weak."

"The only problem with that theory is that there weren't wars we were involved with back then," Tim argued. He rose his chin up. "However, there always was the possibility they were hiding something they didn't want the general public to know, you know about the rumors on Area 51, aliens, spacecrafts, and so on."

Jennifer took a drink of her water. "Not much. I think I was over in Texas with some family. I did hear something about it. But the news came in very briefly and in spurts. Like the news could have been censored, kudos for you Tim." She snickered at him. "News censorship happens, doesn't it? We've had the most recent election to tell us that. Besides, with a wealth of information, any number of them can be falsified facts, and if someone reports on fake facts, they could get their butts sued! For the first few days all I remember was that Nevada was a war zone for over eight weeks. That was the only thing consistent regardless if you watched left-wing or right-wing news. U.S government officials finally came out and said it was a training accident. I didn't believe it; still don't."

"A *training* accident killed twenty percent of a million people?" Michael nearly spat out his water. "I don't know if I believe that."

"Well, I don't think many people believed it. But it did happen around Area 51. So, it is believable it could have been an accident, I guess. I mean they hide things pretty well there, and most people who believe in aliens would believe that. Alien laser just went off!" Jennifer waved both her hands excitedly with the last statement. "Well, it was eight years ago. Most people probably forgot about it by now, well, unfortunately except those who lost someone close to them, and it was in Nevada, so we probably don't know too many people who would have been affected by it. That's not exactly something someone likes sharing. Hey, my parents died in Area 51!" she attempted to sound gleeful. "Nothing. When would that ever come in conversation?"

"Almost never," Samantha commented, she loved Jennifer, but sometimes she can feel cold. She knew Jennifer wasn't a cold person, but with her bubbly and spontaneous personality, the things she says could come off cold. "But they had children who they left behind. It's sad really."

"It is in the past. For some, it is best left there. For others, they will never forget. And the memory will only die when they do," Jennifer replied more calmly.

"Well, it serves no purpose focusing on something like this right now. It is in the past, and apart from Michael, none of us really know anyone directly affected by that, unless they are exceptionally good at hiding it. The only thing we can do is pray for their peace of minds," said Tim. "Hey, I have an idea. Let's throw the pigskin around."

"That's a great idea! I haven't done that since high school!" Samantha jumped up at the suggestion. *I guess it was my fault for keeping up with the subject.* Sam was especially thankful for Tim providing an out of that conversation.

"That wasn't that long ago, it's only been six years," Michael chuckled. "You say that like it's some kind of throwback."

"It is," she replied.

"You were on the football team?" Tim seemed surprised.

"Yes. I was. A little-known fact, I was once a tomboy," she answered.

Samantha proactively packed up the picnic blanket and cooler and brought them to her car, which was parked not too far away. She opened her trunk and put the picnic supplies in, slamming the trunk shut.

A lone man by the crosswalk caught her attention. His hand was in his shorts' pocket and he stared blankly at the trees over by the common. He seemed, happy, with a smile written across his lips, but his eyes told a different story, sunken with lack of sleep and outlined with puffy eyes.

She returned over to her friends, who were already tossing the football. She sprinted in and intercepted a pass intended for Michael.

"Uhm. That's my ball, Sam," Michael turned his palms to the sky.

The first signs of a city at dusk appeared when the streetlights flickered to life, illumining the sidewalks, which were more hushed, and empty. The light over Park Street's MBTA station lit up the faces of people standing in limbo of it. Droves of people briskly walked through the station's steel-frame doors to try to catch the train. Some individuals still lounged by the fountain, sitting on benches and chairs, others relaxed on the grass, laying down and looked up at the empty sky with no sense of time or place to be.

"Michael?" Samantha asked as she threw the ball to him.

"Yeah?" He let the ball strike his chest as he caught it.

"It's getting late. I want to walk through the Garden before the sun completely sets." She pointed at the shining streetlights. "Can we?"

"Honestly, that sounds nice," Jennifer exclaimed, letting out a yawn. "We should all go. Isn't that right, Tim?"

"Tim didn't say no." Samantha answered for him.

"Wait, I didn't—" Tim opened his mouth to protest.

"Then it's decided. Come on, Tim, I know you don't want to but it's not far. It's not a big garden, man," Michael said. "It's literally on the other end of the street."

Tim sighed, "Fine." He put the ball back into his little traveling bag he kept with him everywhere. "Let's go see *this* Boston Public Gahden."

The four of them walked through the other side of the Common, leading them across the street and into the Boston Public Garden through black gates. They were underneath the covering of trees. Some swans were floating down the body of water to the right side, and on the water was a covering of leaves, hiding something underneath.

Samantha found something peaceful about it. It was quiet, soft, like the good Lord's creation. Everything seemed to be in perfect harmony here, nestled away from the city but protected from the loud busy noises of the car horns and alarms, the natural noises of the miscellaneous birds, insects, and squirrels drowned out what little cars drove by. It was a little utopia inside the hustle and bustle of the city, right in the center of Boston! It reminded her of the woods in Vermont, a place she rarely visits anymore now she's left.

Tim and Jennifer were talking amongst each other. Samantha chuckled behind them as the Jennifer, the bubbly biologist had a way of annoying Tim, the introverted events coordinator. One might think that Jennifer should be the events coordinator and Tim the biologist. It was this irony of the personality traits and their respective careers that made Sam chuckle. Of course, one might think they were dating with the way they talked, but Sam knew better.

It was good to just slow down a little. Samantha appreciated that Michael had a similar busyness to their respective work weeks, being able to just simply settle and get drawn back in with the majestic pull of the natural world. They had no time just to sit back and relax.

Samantha suddenly noticed that the air suddenly felt wrong, and thin. Exhaling the frost from her breath, she stopped in her tracks with gaping eyes. She felt the cold air fill up her lungs. Her hair stood on ends. The cold air felt like a cold day of winter to her, she rubbed her shoulders to warm herself up. *It shouldn't be this cold. This is spring!* She turned her head to see the man from earlier. His hand was still in his pocket, his smile was still wide, too wide. Again, just like before, he wasn't looking at anything specific. His stare was just blank: his eyes sunken in, and overbearingly tired. This man was to the world as his smile is to his face: out of place, like he and it doesn't belong here.

She moved her feet again, catching up to Michael before the man would notice her looking at him. There was something off about the man, but she couldn't place her finger on it, the fact remains, the sudden temperature drop was unnatural. Shortly after returning to Michael's side, the warmth returned to the air, or perhaps she just entered an area where the air was warmer. Perhaps she was feeling things that weren't there.

"That's much better." She felt a little at ease returning to a sense of equilibrium, where the air felt natural, rather than the little pocket of superstitious air she walked through. *Did anyone else notice?*

"What?" Michael asked, turning his head to her but kept walking towards the end of the Gardens.

"Didn't you notice the temperature drastically drop?" Samantha's eyes narrowed. "The temperature just dropped back there. I hope I'm not experiencing hot flashes."

"I wouldn't worry about it, I mean, I didn't notice," Michael said. "It's New England. We experience four seasons in less than a week."

"That may be, but it shouldn't have dropped that much!"

"I told you, Sam, I'm not a meteorologist." Jennifer called back to her, turning her head.

"I wasn't asking you!" Samantha snapped.

"Well, that was rude." Tim commented, looking back at them over his shoulder as he kept walking. "What's got you all worked up?"

"I just—I just saw a man."

"This is Boston. There's always someone around." Michael chuckled, likely finding Samantha's little episode humorous.

"Not with a blank stare. Not with a smile as wide as his." She replied, "And the temperature."

Jennifer looked around behind them. "I don't see anyone."

"You could just be imagining things," Michael replied.

She shook her head, clenching her fists at her side, "I know what I saw; I know what I felt." She turned to try to catch a glimpse of the man again, only this time, he wasn't there.

"You didn't have a load to pick up, did you?" Michael asked. "You know, one of those Saturday loads that needs to be picked up, but you have no way to confirm if it did or not until Monday, and by that time it's much too late."

"Gosh no! I took care of that one already," Samantha said as they finally exited the garden.

"Aww. Where did the sun go? I still want to be out," Jennifer yawned. "Kong's is not far off from here."

"Cheap beer," Tim commented.

"Not me," Samantha didn't want to go out anyway, the presence and disappearance of this peculiar man made her want to curl up in bed with a book. She also didn't want to spend more time with Jennifer or Tim, they especially didn't seem to believe her. She was a tough woman, but she couldn't help but feel hurt that none of them, especially Michael, believed her, "It's too late for me right now. I'm still recovering from that nightmare those two drivers put me through yesterday."

"What did they do?" Michael asked. Her trucking nightmares were never boring.

"The driver just dropped their trailer in the doors and unhooked their trucks from their trailer and drove off to get breakfast without telling anyone. Back-to-back. Then my customer got frantic because as far as he was concerned, he lost a truck but inherited two trailers he didn't want anything to do with!" she said, letting out a deep sigh. "Oh well, at least he pays well for every other load he gives me. Alright, I'm tired. I'm going home, going to bed. I'll start fresh in the morning. Tuesday?"

"Yes," Michael said. "As long as I don't get caught in one of those overseas conference calls. Those are a pain."

"I hear you. Michael, are you coming?" Tim asked.

"Nah. Next time," he replied.

"Party pooper," Jennifer frowned.

Chapter 2

Terri Nation

~I've been cursed with isolation, you see.

Bright headlights beaming into bricks and concrete of the sidewalks on Park Street. The trees' branches swayed in the wind, and so did the leaves, like a ballet dancer, droves of people were scampering into the Park Street MBTA station, entering the metal and glass doors, hastily marching down the stairs. The other buildings on Park Street had closed their windows, but some had the lights on, to light the sidewalk for other travelers. And for some, a fancy restaurant on the upper end of Park Street, nearly below the street with no clear way on how to get inside. Samantha wondered where the entrance was.

A car drove by, speeding through the red light, honking its horn. The tires squealed as it turned the corner, and Sam covered her ears as the noise scratched her inner lobes.

"I take it you didn't get an overseas conference call," Samantha knew Michael couldn't make it every Tuesday, because his clients' operated in numerous time zones, and sometimes he was forced to stay late.

"No. I got an email that that's not going to be happening for a while, I think. Tensions are rising quickly overseas, with Poland and Ukraine," Michael covered a yawn with his hand.

"What do you mean?" Tim's head immediately jerked, turning to Michael with alarm. The lights from inside the church flashed out as the receptionist flicked the switch off and on.

"Well," he began, his eyes darted back and forth, making sure no one else was listening. "Look, you didn't hear it from me, and I'm not sure the validity of this, but it has a lot of people overseas concerned. We won't be trading anything overseas for a while, or that's what I heard. And this is just a rumor, but apparently NATO is disbanding."

Sam turned her gaze to the ground, kicking some pebbles to the side. She reflected on what that might mean. *If NATO disbands, will the U.S.A be protecting anyone anymore, and if not, who are the allies? Will this turn into a world where every country is independent, just waiting for a large superpower to come in and swallow them up? What will keep those superpowers in check? What will that do to diesel fuel prices? Ukraine and Poland, what cause do they have to be tense with one another?*

"Wait. What?" Jennifer jerked her head to him. "Why? That's a big development for that to just be a rumor. Michael, you realize it would take fifty liars to even think of spreading a rumor that big!"

"Again. Rumor. That's all I know, and you didn't hear it from me," he replied.

"Dang it. I think I might be fine. I don't know how much my customer takes in imports. I think it's all local though," Samantha said, interlacing her fingers in between her hands. The only thing that would really affect her in the brokerage, would be the gas prices. It makes it difficult to find trucks cheaply to deliver truckloads of groceries.

Michael sucked air through his teeth. "Yeah, and I'll likely take a pay cut as many of my associates are over there. But the effects of that is going to change the market considerably. Sam, I think it's only a matter of time before the effects catch up to you; even if this is a rumor."

"If it's only a rumor, what's the harm?" Tim asked.

"The market changes drastically, constantly. There's no way to accurately predict what it will do. Besides, even these rumors will affect the market eventually, creating a great rift in the economic sphere. These rumors, even if they aren't true, will cause an economic collapse eventually, or just a severe recession," Jennifer explained. The doors opened and the rest of the congregation walked outside. Samantha stared at Jennifer, shocked that she put so many coherent business sentences together in a row. She didn't give Jennifer enough credit, apparently. "I'm not an economist. My brother is in stocks. Options specifically. He told me about all of this. The market is impossible to predict, but we can get close; behavioral finance and all that."

"There's your answer. Even if it's false, it's bad," Michael shook his head and patted his pants with one of his hands.

"Well, there goes my 401K flying right out the window," Tim exclaimed, putting a hand through his hair. "Oh well, I suppose I could opt out of it now, I'll just get taxed heavily on it. Thanks for the heads up."

The noise of the rest of the studiers came out to a dull roar. Brian came up to them, he had a thinly shaved beard and mustache, his eyes were wide awake. He was scrawny for his height, built much like a basketball player, only significantly shorter. "Hey, you guys coming to Terri Nation?" He wrapped his arm around Michael like an old friend and had that overbearingly enthusiastic smile on his face.

Samantha rolled her eyes at the mention of Teri Nation, the local pub right around the corner, where they all went out for some dinner, and drinks to continue fellowshipping together after the study. After all, why waste a perfectly good night to play catch up.

"You know it," Michael shook his hand. "Wouldn't miss it."

"Great! I'm going to head back over here now. I need to recruit some of the newbies," Brian disappeared into the small crowd, talking to a few new faces Samantha didn't recognize.

"Well, I suppose it's time," Michael said. "You all coming? We should start leading the cattle."

"Such a specific metaphor," Samantha said.

"Not really," Michael and Tim started walking backwards up Park street, towards Beacon street, waving their hands towards them, ushering everyone to follow. "Last stop, Teri Nation. Who's coming?"

Michael and Tim started chatting to each other as they briskly walked up the sidewalk towards the City Hall.

Many of the other people around them continued to talk. Others started following in small groups. Jennifer linked arms with Samantha. Erin ran towards them from her group. Her giddiness gave her a child-like aura that was only complemented by the freckles across her cheeks. Samantha braced herself for what she expected to be ten times the amount of Erin's normal bubbliness.

"So, what are you smiling about?" Samantha asked as they walked onwards.

"Well, our office just hired another broker out of nowhere last week. He seems to have already settled in," Erin smiled. "Though he often refers to me as the press."

"The press?" Samantha's eyes stretched open.

"My last name. Gutenberg. The Gutenberg Press," Erin explained.

"Okay, but what does that have to do with you smiling already? Do you like him or something?" Samantha teased.

"Erin's got a crush again," Jennifer chuckled, elbowing Samantha in the side. "Seriously, if it is not one man, then it is an equally terrifying different man, sometimes a stranger."

"I do not!" Erin scolded. Samantha assumed Erin was blushing in the dark. "Jennifer, you always find a way to make something innocent sound so inappropriate. Anyway, he's very smart apparently. He is an excellent resource to go to for help. My job would finally be secure if I went to him for advice."

"How do you know that? He just started the job last week?" Jennifer asked. "No one learns the job that fast."

"He already closed a few hundred-thousand-dollar-deals last week," Erin said. "Either he knows what he's doing or is extremely lucky."

"What?" Samantha couldn't believe it. She herself was working a deal with another customer, but she is not making nearly that much in gross revenue, although it was a different business altogether. "How?"

"I'm going to ask him tomorrow. I'll let you know. Although, I don't know how that will help you. You're in logistics, not in stocks," She snapped her fingers.

"Maybe I'll just invest in a mutual fund," Samantha sneered. She had little interest in stocks to begin with.

"You two go ahead and talk finance if you want. I'm sticking to my germs. Much more interesting," Jennifer said as they turned onto Beacon street.

"So, what's his name?" Samantha leaned into Erin, bumping against her.

"He goes by Ted," Erin answered. "He said he's from Ohio. Not a very social person though, doesn't talk much."

"So, enough about this individual that neither Sam nor I are going to meet. July Fourth. Erin, are you still coming? I need to order the canoes, and I need to have an idea of how many I need to reserve. We plan on meeting at Kendall Square at 6PM."

"Yes, I'll go," Erin exclaimed. "I'd love to go, I might be late, I need to skip lunch to leave work early."

"Don't worry about food, there will be plenty. I'll be packing sandwiches again," Jennifer said. They were approaching Terri Nation which was on the corner heading back down towards Tremont Street. The City Hall was staring down at them with the lights behind the gates, and the Joseph Hooker Statue, riding on a horse.

"That's probably not the best thing. You might want to think of something else. Sandwiches don't taste good out in the open sea," Samantha suggested. "Maybe we can get Michael to cook something with his smoker. Or perhaps just bring some vegetables or something."

"But poor dear Erin will be hungry. She's skipping her lunch after all." Jennifer chuckled as she opened the door into Teri Nation. "I mean to be fair, most of us, except me, will not have time to actually eat something after work. I mean, you get out late enough as it is."

"It'll take a few hours, its fine," Samantha replied.

They walked through the restaurant section of the bar, walking through the wide hallway and took a left of the statue of a little girl flying a kite at the side. Michael and Tim were already sat in the back of the upstairs bar, talking to one another about something, while sipping on their own drink. Michael was always trying the weird concoctions that the bar tender mixed. He was like Scott's guinea pig.

"What's goin' on Sam. What can I get you?" Scott wore a black vest over a white button up shirt and black slacks behind his bar. Everyone on the wait staff wore the same uniform.

"House Cab is fine," she answered pulling out her card. "I'll close out."

Scott took the card and went to pour her a quick glass of red Cabernet wine. He always had a heavy pour.

"Scott, I'll take your specialty. Whatever that is at this moment," Jennifer asked. Like Michael, she was also an adventurous drinker.

"I'll also take a cider. Bottle please," Erin called out; her hand raised as her other hand reached for her pocketbook.

"Together or separate?" Scott called as he reached behind the bar and undid the cap of a frosted bottle of hard cider.

"Together. I'll buy it," Erin said, nudging Jennifer in the side. "The least I can do if I'm trusting you with my food on the Fourth of July."

Erin winked at Jennifer and squeezed her shoulder.

He then made the very odd drink with Bourbon, triple sec, coke, muddle mint and cucumbers. Jennifer frowned curiously as the drink was handed to her. Her eyes skimmed over the physical ingredients, noting this beverage, whatever it might be, should taste refreshing; however, such a taste would likely contrast unwelcomingly with the bourbon. "Well, it is different," she took a sip. And made a puckered face as if filled with something that was too sour. And it did contrast, the way Jennifer expected it to, "Did Michael like this?"

"He liked it," Scott started chuckling. "Do you?"

"It's certainly different, I'll give you ten points for originality," her face cringed. "I haven't decided if I'm going to like this or not yet. Give me a few minutes."

"Gotcha," he chuckled, quickly moving back to address the rest of his guests.

Brian came in with his crowd of nearly fifteen different guests. *Looks like he succeeded in inviting the new people here. Well, this certainly is great for the community. They are all new to Boston, or many of them anyways. This isn't a bad spot to be,* Sam thought. Brian's friendliness and his great charisma was what kept Samantha interested in these little late-night gatherings, and surprisingly, kept her going to Park Street Church instead of some local church.

Samantha knew that Scott was going to have a good night. She sipped her wine as she gazed up at the TV screen. Scott generally kept the news on in the back: unless they requested the sports channel. He was always very friendly, though when she first came here, he did seem like a tired and disgruntled man. He couldn't have been more than thirty. He hid a smile underneath that thick beard of his.

Sam looked over to Brian again, noticing he took out a little pen and piece of paper, engaging enthusiastically in conversation with everyone he invited. He spent more time with the new faces than the old ones, nodding as they spoke, showing his elite listening skills. Sam guessed quite accurately he was offering to buy them a round tonight, by jotting things down on his notepad. Brian leaned over the bar top, and slapped his hand on it, and looked intently in Scott's eyes as they engaged in some unrelated conversation which Sam couldn't hear. Brian read off the slip of paper, and Scott immediately punched some buttons on the electronic touch pad and printed out a receipt, handing it to Brian before hastily disappearing behind the bar. Brian immediately returned to the newcomers, turning their hesitant smiles to enthusiastic ones. Samantha thought, *Brian was better at making anyone feel comfortably at home.*

Then she noticed something familiar. The hair on her head felt like they stood on ends, and the chills came over her, cascading like a powerful wind. Goosebumps rose-up from her arms. She looked around, not trying to alarm anyone, hoping this may have been her imagination. Other people around the bar were putting on their sweatshirts or wrapping themselves with their arms. She chose to ignore it. *Someone probably just turned the thermostat down. But damn it's cold!*

Out of the corner of her eye she noticed someone. He was sitting by himself at the other end of the bar, perhaps ten paces from her, drinking a glass of red wine, like hers. *Merlot? Or Cab?* It was the same man from Saturday, first at the cross walk, then inside the Garden. Now here. And it seems the last time the temperature dropped so much and so quickly was with him around. Who was he?

Scott brought this man a plate of mashed potatoes. This man still seemed to be smiling very widely as he thanked Scott for the plate. Scott asked him if he needed anything else, but he declined, and said, "I have more than I require right now. Thank you." She took a closer look as the man took a fork and put it into the mashed potatoes and started eating it. Sam squinted her eyes at the man to see some lined scars on his face. The words barely made it to her ears with the volume of the bar.

Twice she saw the man in a social setting. Twice she saw the man isolated in the social setting. Perhaps he was new to Boston, and looking for friends, perhaps socially inept. *Well, I'm not Brian. But I'll see what I can do. I at least know something to spin off on,* she thought.

She took a sip from her glass, scanning the bar top for Scott when he got a second. She raised her arm and called him over. Scott walked over, drying a beer glass with a towel. Scott leaned over the bar, both palms rested firmly on the bar top after setting the glass down, "What's up Sam?"

"That man over there," she leaned in over the bar, pointing a finger to the man in the corner, retracting the finger around her wineglass.

Scott turned his head briefly to look, "That's Ted. He's been coming here lately."

"Do you know what he does?" Sam asked.

"No, he's a polite person, but a man of few words."

"Well, thanks for that. That was it. Thank you!"

She started walking quietly towards him. He ate silently. She was standing behind him as he was engrossed in his food, scarfing it down quickly. He took a sip of his wine again, turning the glass and looking into it as if he was lost in thought.

"Well, well, well, so a rat sneaks behind me, eh?" said the man. He never bothered to look from his wine. "To what exactly do I owe for the pleasure of such as this?"

Samantha abruptly halted. Her wineglass trembled in her hand as she looked down at the ripples inside the glass. *Did I make a sound? No. Wait. Could he smell my perfume or was it the wine?*

"The scent of Cabernet was coming closer and closer. I could smell it approaching me, and then suddenly the scent just lingered. You can't be more than twenty-three inches behind me." He turned in his stool and looked up to her, and his smile was still wide. "How may I help you?"

"Startling, well I'm not a rat," she chuckled nervously.

"And yet you came to me as silent as a rat."

Well, he's not socially inept, that is certain. He's eloquent and very formal. She found him to be unnerving, yet intriguing all the same, "Rats can be silent nuisances, but I couldn't help but notice that I've seen you before," she commented.

"Well, this is the Heart of Boston. Odds are there are many faces we see again and again, and maybe we recognize a few reoccurring faces here and there, but we never make a point to meet one of them. I know I certainly don't," he replied. His smile never faded. He stood up and rose his glass to hers. She clinked their glasses together, "Cheers."

Sam found him to be more mysterious, greeting her with a friendly smile, but the words comparing her to a rat was a bit unsettling. He was confident, this was evident, but was there something about her he found to be untrusting? She bit her tongue, fearing she made some kind of social error. *Brian is better suited for this, but I can't back down now.*

"That is something true you have just said. My name is Samantha Harris," she said. She brought her hand out to meet his other hand to shake it.

He reached out his hand to meet hers, shaking it. Samantha could hear the bones in her hand crack: he had a very firm and strong grip. "My name is Ted Anderson."

"It's a pleasure to meet you." She didn't want to make it too obvious she asked about him.

"To be sure, Miss Harris, the pleasure is all mine. Now, I ask again; to what do I owe the pleasure of such an introduction?" There was something different about him though, his brown watery eyes looked right into hers. Ted appeared to her to be in his mid-twenties, but the eyes told a different story, as if they were much older than his body.

"I ran into you twice on Saturday. Right on the corner of Park and Tremont, and then again on the same day at the Garden, towards the end of that night," she admitted, "You seemed to be by yourself, while everyone else was grouped together, or coupled."

"Was that around the time the temperature dropped?" he asked.

Her eyes blinked repeatedly. *So, I'm not crazy.* "Y—you felt that too? I thought I was just imagining things," she stammered as she took another sip from her glass, looking cautiously at Ted. She felt something in her gut, like she should be wary of this man. Numerous people were with her that night, and only she and Ted felt it. And only they acknowledged it. *Why didn't any of them feel anything?*

"Yes, I felt it also," he said, "Well, that's New England for you."

"Yes," she said, lowering her voice a little bit. "Have you been around Boston for very long?"

"A few weeks," He answered.

"What brought you here?" She thought to ask another question, hoping to find something to latch on to. She could hear multiple steps behind her, and the music played from the speakers, and the chatter sounded like white noise.

"Work," he answered.

"Where are you from?" She was dissatisfied with the answer, as simple as it was. Sure, it very well could be true, but there wasn't enough information released from him to pose any meaningful conversation.

"Ohio."

"What part?" *You're like a steel trap.*

"Delaware," he shifted on his stool as he took another bite of his mashed potatoes.

"There's a store I deliver to frequently over there," excitedly, she finally found something.

"Oh, and what is it that you do?" His expression didn't change, but he leaned back against the bar and crossed his hands over his chest.

"I work for a 3PL. I deliver groceries for a major wholesaler. I'm a broker." *Dang it.* She wasn't expecting him to start asking questions, not that she had anything really to hide from him, but she wasn't done trying to figure out who he was.

"As am I. I deal with stocks," he answered. "And options."

It finally hit her. He might work with Erin. "Do you know Erin Gu—"

"The Gutenberg Press? Yes. I work with her," he laughed.

"Yes!" she laughed. "That is exactly what she said you call her. She said something about you today on our way over here."

"Terrible things, I'm sure," he replied, never lessening that smile.

"No, she said you are very good at your job."

"No. I am just very lucky." He got a buzz from his phone. "Excuse me a moment."

He pulled out his phone and opened something up. Samantha assumed it was a work-related email. He read it intently. He shut the screen off from his phone and put it back into his pocket. "Well, on one hand that was terrible. On the other, I'm glad I sold all of those."

"What?"

"Oh, NATO just disbanded, and Russian just declared War on Ukraine," he said nonchalantly. "I just sold most of my foreign assets. Those values are going to drop overnight. I wonder, how will the rest of the European Union fare? Will they follow suit? Will they get involved? Most likely, as they have always done. It's unfortunate that the world came to this."

"How do you know?" she asked. *Well, I guess that confirms the rumor Michael told them, but how exactly are you this calm about it?*

Ukraine is apparently pissing everyone off! Samantha knew that national allegiances were trembling as of late, the news told them that much. To her it seemed most everyone was inches away from everyone's throats at any given time, and Russia and Ukraine were now the only confirmed cases of political collapse. How soon will this uncertainty reach America? Sam couldn't help but wonder.

"Like I said, I'm very lucky. However, some of the higher ups might think I actually know something when I don't," he let out a brief sigh. "Oh well, I'll cross that bridge when it comes to it."

She turned abruptly, "Michael!" she waved at him as he was now talking with Erin. Samantha noticed that Erin frowned at them with her pouty eyes. She noted that Erin seemed to be boy crazy, she didn't expect that kind of behavior from someone going to church weekly. *But we all have our own shortcomings.*

"Ted, this is my boyfriend, Michael," she introduced them.

Michael walked over with a friendly smile on his face and introduced himself. Michael shook Ted's hand, and Samantha could hear the bones in Michael's hand cracking.

"Firm grip. I like it!" Michael released his hand.

"So, Michael, you know that thing you talked about earlier?"

"I said you didn't hear it from me," he said defensively, abruptly turning to her, frowning.

"It's on the news already," she frowned, knowing that since these rumors were true, global collapse might not be far behind, she guessed this would immediately affect Michael's line of work drastically.

"Wait. What?" Michael asked. "Already? I just found out about it, but I thought those were rumors."

"Rumors have an unfortunate way of being steeped in truth. Odds are, if something is completely unbelievable, it is probably true," Ted said. "I knew of the rumor but thought nothing of it until this morning. Thank God I followed my gut. I can sleep peacefully now."

"Well, it is only a matter of time then. Someone's going to punch someone important," Mike replied.

Ted threw his head back in laughter.

"I think that already happened," Samantha said. "Apparently Russia's on a war path again."

The phone vibrated in Ted's pocket again. He pulled it out of his inside pocket and looked at his notification. He read the notification, "That's not the only one on a war path. Well, I guess it was only inevitable that this would happen."

"What now?" Samantha asked. She was considering how this news was going to affect her. It was clearly going to affect her business. Oil prices are going to raise. Rates for truck drivers are going to rise to reflect that change. Her rates are contracted. Renegotiating her contracted rates are likely to be fruitless. Her individual margins are going to decline. Her profitability is going to plummet. *How soon before this all hits home?*

"Trade deals with China aren't going well apparently," Ted explained. "That being said, it's only a matter of time before someone declares war. It is like twenty years ago."

"Those were not good times," Michael said. "Every major nation was at everyone's throats."

"Precisely. The global economy was trash then," Ted rose his hand in the air. He dropped it back down. "And just like my hand, we'll probably be freefalling for a while, well, then it starts to decline that's when we'll be freefalling."

"You seem to know a lot about this," Michael said, taking a sip of his exotic, but potentially terrible tasting drink.

"I was in the Army before I came here, China was never too keen on Americans," he kept his smile, but reluctantly gave that answer. "I know too much already."

Samantha knew this would pique Michael's interest. His brother was in the 75th Ranger Regiment, "What was your—"

"My occupation in the Army is classified, above top secret," he said softly. "I can't disclose any information on what I did. I hope you understand."

"I do," Michael said. "My brother is in the Army. He is much the same way. Doesn't give out much information than what is necessary."

Erin finally walked over, her hand resting across her chest. "Ted, did you just get Adam's email?"

"Yes, Gutenberg's Press. I did. I got both of them. Well, if you have any foreign assets, I'd suggest selling them now. The market is still open. You may find a buyer, but if you don't, I'd advise holding onto it and riding it out, or selling it as soon as possible." This was clearly meant for Erin, and he gave her advice to work on, but

Samantha picked up on something, noting just how volatile the stock markets are: Sell now, unless you can't, then hold onto it until it rises again. Or just sell later. The window of trading that fast was small.

"Did you already sell yours?" she asked. "How did you know this would happen?"

"I didn't. I just guessed. You should listen to those rumors more closely," he chuckled.

"This is going to be a nightmare," Michael said, ruffling his hand through his hair.

Jennifer popped up with her drink in hand. "Michael, you have terrible taste in this stuff. Why do I let you talk me into these things?"

Samantha felt a weight lift off her chest as her attention was immediately turned away from the horrific events happening with the world to something, albeit random, more pleasant. For that, she was exceedingly thankful for Jennifer's interruption.

"First of all, I didn't say anything," he laughed, nudging her shoulder with his.

"I mean seriously, this is disgusting, why would you drink this?" She turned her gaze to Ted. "So, who is this who is hogging up the party?"

"I mean, you can barely call this a party," Samantha said as Erin was back onto her phone, monitoring her emails.

"I have to go. I'll see you next Tuesday!" Erin walked over to her green purse.

Samantha waved as Erin walked out of the bar, relieved as Erin's constant pining after men was growing tiresome.

"This is Ted. You know; that Ted," Sam clicked her tongue as she pointed to Erin on her way out.

"What Ted—oh! That Ted! Well, I'll say little to compromise anything. I'm Jennifer, and welcome to our little dysfunctional family," she joked. "Never mind me. I'm the crazy one."

Samantha chuckled. *She's never boring.*

"Speaking of, Ted," Jennifer seemed to take over the conversation. She would have made a great executive. "We are going to rent a few canoes over the Charles on the Fourth of July. I know it's about a month away. You should totally come with!"

"Fireworks, over a body of water," Ted said. "I appreciate the sentiment, Miss, however, I'm afraid I must decline."

"Oh, well that's too bad. Everyone here is going," she turned her head as if looking for someone. "Now, where is Brian?"

"He drove Tim home," Michael answered. "Tim had an early meeting for an event that's scheduled tomorrow. He couldn't be out too late."

"Such a shame. He really is personable. More fun than I am!" She wrapped her arm around Michael as she smiled.

Samantha and Jennifer's minds were thinking alike. No matter how hesitant one could be, Brian can always get someone to bend.

"I doubt that very much," Ted commented, making eye contact with her. Jennifer's hazel eyes gleamed in the dim light of the bar.

"Oh, well, I guess you can't come under any circumstances, then, huh? Nothing we can do to persuade you?" Jennifer tried to coax some more amiable answer out of him.

"Unfortunately, no," Ted answered. "But I appreciate the offer, all the same."

"Oh, well."

"Well, what about Tuesday next week? Are you doing anything after you get off work?" Samantha pitched in, eager to see more of this mysterious person. She barely struck the surface of who he was, and to her seemed one dimensional. She was eager to get the full picture and get the story of those ragged eyes and enthusiastic smile. The contrast didn't sit well with her.

"Um?" he hesitated. Sam briefly noticed his hand shaking as he hid it in his pocket. "Depends, if I decide to leave work or not. I'm a workaholic, and perhaps that depends completely on the rest of the information I know you are inclined to give me."

"We have a Bible Study that we go to on Tuesdays. It starts at seven at Park Street. This next week is tasty Tuesdays so there are snacks before," Samantha continued, linking arms with Michael.

"I think Sarah is making baclava," Michael said, sipping his who knows-what-it-tastes like drink.

"Oh, yes, that's a splendid idea." Jennifer butted in again, clapping her hands together. "Seriously, Ted, you must come. It's much less of a commitment than going canoeing with us in July. Especially if you're new to Boston. It might be nice to have some kind of community that doesn't include drowning yourself in work."

"I'm not going to lie; I do like working," Ted explained, sipping more of his wine. "But with everything else that is going on in the world, I likely won't be able to find anything worth buying in those oversea markets anymore. What's one day going to hurt? Where is it?"

Samantha began, "It's the church on Tremont and Park street. The door is open on the other side of Park Street where the—"

"Freedom Trail?" he asked.

"Yes, that's the one." She answered.

"7:00 PM?"

"Yes. But its tasty Tuesday so you don't have to show up right at seven. You can show up a little after," Samantha answered, suddenly conscientious about how much she'd been speaking. "It is the best time for it a newcomer. We'd love to see you there, but no pressure."

"I'll be there," he drank the rest of his wine and grabbed his tab. "I'll see you Tuesday."

Samantha smiled as he left, and she felt a weight being lifted off her chest. *I'm still not Brian. Brian could have gotten him to go out for the Fourth for sure.*

"So, how did you meet him?" Michael asked.

"Spill it, Sam, spill it. Details girl!" Jennifer exclaimed. "I need details."

"I saw him twice on Saturday. First at the corner of the church, and then at the garden," she answered.

"Like when you swore the temperature dropped?" Michael inquired. He seemed a little more curious now.

"Yes. He was there when the temperature dropped, and then again when the temperature dropped again in here. Didn't you feel it?"

"Yes," Michael admitted. "But that could have been anything. I wouldn't worry about something so trivial as the temperature dropping, especially here in New England. The temperature and weather changes daily, besides, if it happened here, it was probably just the air conditioning," he glanced at his watch. "And look at the time! It is time to be going."

Chapter 3

Sverdlovsk

~This world would look much better on a mantle, covered in flames.

Major McCurdy sat in her office, a square grey room with a large thick window of bulletproof glass, and an iron door. Her desk was also grey, but with a brown wooden frame.

It was quiet for sure, as it always was at 0400 MSK. She had all the solitude and privacy that could be afforded to her on the remote Sverdlovsk base. Though the location was above top secret, unknown even to Moscow itself, she still felt the need to be up and in her office at 0400 to get an even deeper sense of privacy.

She yawned as she took a sip of her coffee, watched her computer screen, monitored the emails, surveyed vehicles drive by, not suspecting anything at the side of the Ural Mountains. She scanned every single suspicious car. A pang of hurt shot through her each time the framed photo of her uncle caught her eye. She never thought to move it. She only thought of her uncle and what he would have suffered eight years ago. She had to keep his photo up, someone had to be there to remember.

An email popped-up on her screen. It was a report from the CBRN team. The radiation at the top of the mountain spiked up again. This time the levels clocked in at 1.294 Sieverts. These levels were three times higher than the last peak. Scrolling through the report she noticed it was isolated, as usual, but substantially higher up than it normally occurred. She skimmed through the rest of the report explaining the abnormality of the event being instantaneous and without currently detectable residue. And again, through the paragraph suggesting closer investigation to find residue. *Radiation. The ruse we created to have a team of regulars monitoring it. If it were a natural occurrence, yes, there'd be residue.* She sighed, knowing she would have to head up this wild goose chase for residue radiation. *But if I went alone, it would only raise unnecessary suspicion.*

She knew that it was only a matter of time before the higher ups would want a full-scale investigation, to find out why the radiation levels are sporadically spiking, but this wasn't natural radiation: a caster from someone's administrative branch was operating where they shouldn't be. It's about time to send someone up there. *However, the Administration is going to want to hear about this.* She put her hand on her handset, and breathed in. She marked the handset with an insignia, shaped like a vein, the phone gave off a green aura. No one could trace this call; the wires were now heavily insulated with her mana.

"Admin Colton," the strict voice answered.

"Admin Colton, Major McCurdy here. I just received a report about increasing levels of radiation. I'm reading 1.294 Svs. That's not the odd part. The odd part is that it shortly dissipated with no trace. I think some unknown is operating here. Is this cause for concern for the administration? Location: Devil's Pass."

"Yes. That's not radiation," he answered. "I need you to see to it. Whoever it is, and report back. You know what to do. Admin Colton out."

She returned the phone back to the receiver. She removed her mana from the phone. She immediately went to the radio to call in the CBRN team. "This is Major McCurdy. Report in."

"Yes, Ma'am. Sergeant Nguyen reporting," a voice returned.

"Wake your squad up. Report down in the briefing room. Now!" she ordered.

"Yes, Major," his voice clicked out.

"And now I have to get people killed that don't need to be involved. There has to be a better way," she said to herself. *We're devils. We all deserve to die horribly for the things we've done. Damn it all to Hell. I'm always in these shadows, getting these men and women killed. They have nothing do with any of this, but protocol is protocol.* She sighed, breathing heavily as she brushed a hand through her hair. She put on her officer's cap on her head.

She printed the most recent report. She put it in a separate file and walked out of her office. She briskly walked down the stairs, and into the now empty briefing room. She went to the desk, in front of the desk and put her folder down, waiting impatiently for the squad to show up.

Just as she was thinking about calling again, they all came in single file. Specialist Adams, Sergeant Nguyen, Captain Gongora, and Warrant Officer Lee. She smiled as they all came in. "At ease," she said, waiting for them to sit down. The familiar but unwelcome lump filled up her chest with guilt.

All fine men. It is unfortunate, really. They are going to see something they are unallowed to see. Sorry, I'd do this myself if I could, but I can't go alone without raising suspicion. I wish you could say your good-byes, but this is how it must be.

I'm sorry.

Chapter 4

Tasty Tuesday

~It was said that Saul killed his thousands and David his tens of thousands: I'd be fortunate if my numbers were nearly that low.

Ted's blank stare pointed into the sky. He ignored the hustle and bustle of men, women and children scurrying past him like rats running away from a legion of cats. His right hand was in his pocket as the wind pushed past him. The cars were halted at the intersection of Park and Tremont, halted at the light as the cars drove down Park Street took a right turn, avoiding the numerous street signs and jaded traffic cones. He sighed as he looked at the red bricks leading up the stairs into the side of Park Street Church, and the glass doors.

He looked back at his watch. *6:45.* "Well, now is a good as time as ever," he said to himself. "Let's get this over with."

He pulled the first door into the side entrance open. He went to the second opening, scanned the entire room. He noted there was a fire escape to his left, right next to an elevator, but the only other exit was the door he walked through. The receptionist read a newspaper, his feet atop his desk. He seemed disinterested in anything but the paper.

Beyond the threshold of the second glass door was a table, with a banner which read, "Park Street Café". There was a tall man behind it, also very cheery. *I wonder.* There were numerous empty tables behind the other man.

The man smiled at him and waved him in with his large hand. "Welcome to Café," he said, reaching out his hand for a shake. Ted returned in kind, never letting that smile go. "My name is Steve. Is this your first time here? I don't recognize you."

"You could say that," he firmly gripped the man's hand. "Ted."

"You came on the best day for it then! They're still setting up in there, so not everything is ready to get started just yet. They're still setting up the coffee table. How did you hear about Café?"

I'm from Ohio. I'm a stockbroker. Nothing more. You don't need the truth, just the bare essentials. "You could also say a little bird told me. So, tell me, what is the general set up of such a night?" His hand retracted from Steve's, retreating back into his pocket.

"Normally we sing, we pray, then we break up into small groups. There are many small groups here, and there is usually the simple connecting group that works perfect for newcomers. But we do this once a month to foster some sense of community between small groups," Steve answered.

"Trying to make it impossible for someone to be forgotten I see," Ted smiled, making sure to cheerily bare his teeth, hoping this would pass for genuine enthusiasm. *No one needs to know.* "A very good system in place I suppose. I guess that is why I received such a warm welcome."

"I'm glad I was able to warm you up to the place," Steve laughed. "Well, that must be them now. I think they're getting the paper plates out."

"I guess I'll head in. It was a pleasure to meet you, Steve."

"You also," Steve immediately turned to the table. "Oops. I forgot," he took out one of those sticker nametags. He wrote, "Ted" on it before handing it to him. "Just so everyone can know who you are."

"Why thank you so much!" Ted enthusiastically took the nametag and stuck it on the right side of his chest. "Something to identify the body," he chuckled.

Steve stared at him, blinking repeatedly as he jerked his head to the side. "What?"

"Sorry, you'll have to forgive my dry sense of humor," Ted smiled wider. "Oh well, Steve, I'm sure I'll see you again."

Ted turned around and walked into the Fellowship Hall which was brightly lit. The room was a large square, with numerous chairs set up in a circle for everyone to sit down looking at one another, like how friends would sit around at a campfire. Ted pictured a small bonfire in the middle of the room. He noticed the wall in the back, appeared to be a sectional leading to the corner of the main entrance of Park Street Church, likely leading to the sanctuary upstairs.

His hand trembled at his side. He became hyper focused on the menial tasks of making a cup of coffee. His eyes focused on the electric coffee maker at the center of the room with small Styrofoam cups at the side. He walked over to it and pushed the "on" button. He took out a cup and put it underneath the nozzle of the machine and flipped one of the plastic-coffee-filled-cups waiting for the machine to warm up and heated the water to a boil.

The machine clicked. He opened the top and put his plastic-coffee-filled-cup into the machine, softly pushing the lid down. He pushed another button, and a brown-black liquid filled his cup. He waited patiently for the cup to fill. He opened the top back up. He took out the plastic empty cup and threw it in the nearby trash. He clasped both of his hands around the cup and walked over to one of the nearby white pillars. He leaned up against it and sighed. His eyes scanned the room rapidly, watching carefully for anyone who would come in. So far, only the usual blond-haired girl, who was surprisingly tall for an American, came out to put more plates on the table, which included the honey scented baclava.

He looked back down to his cup of coffee, the ripple circling around his cup, waiting to be halted, waiting to stop and reach perfect stillness within these Styrofoam walls. Peace finally reached the cup, and the ripples were stilled, as his trembling hand was now stilled. He at last brought the cup to his lips and sipped on the hot liquid. He let it settle on his tongue and it immediately swallowed the first sip. *It tastes like—*

"Hey, what's up man? It's great to see you!" came a cheerily familiar voice.

He looked up from his cup. He smiled back to Michael, who had a white button up shirt that was buttoned just below his neck, and khakis. "Hi," he spoke softly. "Just drinking a coffee."

"Yeah, I hear you. With all that's happened lately, I bet you're ripping your hair out," Michael said. "Fortunately, I'll be fine, just my conversations are now being recorded over there. I mean, it's not like I actually have anything to hide. I don't have any national secrets."

"Too bad. I wouldn't mind hearing them," Ted laughed. He couldn't scan the room as well if he was distracted by talking to Michael. "Honestly, it's not that bad. It just greatly affects who I can and can't deal with. I can easily move assets around. It's not that hard. After all, they say that if you look at the nations who rose and fell, you can predict the future. I find the same to be true for wars."

"Yeah. I know you mentioned you were in the Army, that must give you a different perspective on what's going on. Maybe you're seeing what I'm not," he went on. "Do you think it's something I should be worried about?"

"Not really," he replied. "However, economically it'll be a disaster. However, it wouldn't take too long to change and get things back on track once the dust is settled. At least, most likely. That is just a guess. I just so happen to be very good at guessing."

"So, I've heard. And you seem to be very lucky," Michael continued to smile that welcoming smile. Michael's hands were at his side, but not in his pockets.

We were never allowed to have our hands in our pockets, but I don't recognize you. Never mind. You were too young, even if you were, I wouldn't have known you. You are inconsequential.

"Some of my old comrades called me the Amazing Doctor, as it appeared, I could tell the future. I was only ever wrong once," he said dryly, his tone dropping. He hoped Michael didn't notice.

"You don't sound too thrilled," Michael frowned.

"Yeah, you could say that." Ted never abandoned his smile, "Sometimes luck ain't all it's cracked out to be. Sometimes luck is just a little more than a curse. For example, I wished I guessed wrong on one deal, because the profit margin would have been exponentially higher than if I guessed correctly," he explained. *Yeah, that's how I'll explain it.* "But money isn't everything. I have enough of it as it is. I really don't need anymore. I just do it now to keep busy. I really don't have a high cost of living."

"Well, then," Michael chuckled.

"Michael, you didn't strike me as the making friends-type." Jennifer snuck up on them, hair was combed, comparatively to last Tuesday and she had it tied with a red scrunchy. She was wearing a green shirt, paired with some gym shorts, "Seriously, how long have you been here?"

Now that Ted had a better look at her, she looked oddly familiar. Seeing her in the bright light of the Fellowship Hall was both a blessing. And a curse. She looked uncannily like his fiancé, before her passing. The appearance was the same, sure, Jennifer was a little taller than her. *Let the dead, stay dead.*

"Not long, maybe five minutes." Michael smiled back at her as he wrapped his arm around her shoulders.

"Well then, Ted, welcome back to our dysfunctional family!" She sipped her cup of coffee while she was juggling a plate with baclava. She looked at Ted and then down to both of his hands, "No baclava?"

"No, I haven't had the chance to grab it," Ted smiled at her as he took another sip of the coffee. *Now, what is it you want?*

"What? Michael, hold my things!"

She shoved her cup of coffee, plate, and plastic fork into Michael's hands. He still didn't have his own cup of coffee, and this flustered Michael before regaining his balance with the new items in his hands. Unfortunately, some of her coffee spilled over the side of the cup and onto his hands.

"Well, as you can quite imagine, she can be a handful," Michael chuckled. "She can be overbearing at times, but we love her all the same."

"I can see that," Ted said. His pupils scanned the room immediately again as more and more people started pouring into the Fellowship Hall.

"You know, you wouldn't think she would be a social butterfly, or even this vibrant as a scientist, but there's always that one who will be unique among them," Michael said, staring at his coffee covered hand.

"Yes. I've come across those myself," Ted said. "There's always exceptions if you know where to look."

Jennifer came back with a plate of baclava and a fork. "Ted, this is for you. This stuff is homemade! You can't come here and *not* have it!" She presented it with a smile.

Ted reluctantly released his hand from his cup and grabbed hold of the plate, watching carefully of the people in the room, memorizing every face, every verbal exchange he could see, and he studied each facial expression and their changes. He could tell when they were sad, and when they were happy. The faces had stretched smiles, and the light twinkled in their eyes, the dimples in their cheeks shone brightly, and their smiles didn't seem to have much effort behind them, like these smiles were genuine. Ted wondered, why weren't they miserable? How happy could they actually be?

"Come on. Take a bite!" Jennifer smiled enthusiastically to him, and she looked at him, "You must tell me how it is?"

"Why are you focused entirely on the baclava? You didn't even make it," Michael said. "Come on, let the guy eat it at his pleasure. Sheesh. You'd think you're some raving chef shoving food they're allergic to down their throats, like Tim."

"Excuuusse me!" Jennifer raised her voice to Michael. "Well, I was clearly talking to Ted. Now, perhaps I wouldn't have to be over the top if you weren't romanticizing your own bromance."

"What?" Michael's jaw dropped and his pupils moved side to side inside his head as they gaped open. Ted guessed Michael was not expecting that comment from Jennifer.

"You've been hogging his attention for five minutes! I want a turn to pry into that little cage trap of a brain he's got."

Ted's heartbeat raced inside his chest. He felt his palm accumulate sweat.

"I'll let you two have your privacy. I'm sure you'll want to be alone," Michael gave Jennifer her coffee and baclava plate back.

"Thank you," she handed them with care, taking a sip of her coffee.

"Why would I want that?" Ted protested, never losing that tremendous smile of his. He mustn't appear nervous, as nervous as she was making him. *Is she going to trigger me?* He fought his hand's sudden urge to tremble.

"Ah, I'm sure I'll see you around. Come hang out with our group, like Jennifer said, it's a little dysfunctional," he laughed, using this excuse to get away from Jennifer.

"So, I hear you're a scientist?" Ted asked.

"Now, now, eat your baclava first. And tell me how it is. Then we can talk."

He snickered, "You put into a lot of effort in me trying to give baclava a chance."

"You know it," she smiled and waved a finger at him. "Now eat up, mister."

He took a small bite of the baclava. The sticky honey dripped on his tongue, a taste he was certain was supposed to be sweet, but alas, it tasted like nothing. He could also feel the enthusiastic piercing stare coming right in front of him, "So, tell me how it is!"

"It's delicious," he lied to her. "I thoroughly enjoyed it. Thank you," he moved his focus to his coffee.

She looked up to the ceiling. "Well, I suppose you *could* call me a scientist, but I am more of a researcher than anything."

He sipped his coffee, "And what's your area of expertise."

"Biology. I study organisms, virus', bacterium. An old man once said, 'The more germs I get, the happier I am'! I suppose that sums me up pretty nicely, now that I think about it. Oh well, one can't exactly marry a germ, but they keep me plenty of company."

"I can't tell if you're eccentric, or objectively insane," he joked.

"Well, excuuuse me good sir," she said, pressing her forefinger to his lips. "Are you accusing me of being socially ambiguous?"

He retracted his head from her fingers, shaking his head. He paused a moment and smiled back at her. "Absolutely," he retorted, unsure if this little interaction of her touching his mouth was appropriate. He couldn't be certain.

"Well, good," she chuckled, taking a bite out of her own baclava. "That's what I was going for!"

"Alright," came a loud booming voice. Ted immediately turned his head to the nearby speaker. He saw man in his thirties, who also looked to be a little tired, not nearly as tired as he was though. He was holding a microphone and speaking into it. "Alright, welcome to Café, my name is. . ."

Ted tuned out the speaker. He had little patience for long monologues. His eyes started scanning the room again: some people like him were not paying attention to the speaker, like they didn't need to: as if they'd heard the same thing a million times. Over and over and over again. He looked closely at the exit.

He noticed Samantha chatting with someone else over by the exit towards the main lobby closer to the background. She had a cup of coffee, but not the baclava. *Perhaps she's dieting. Or came in too late to make her way to the food. Doesn't matter.* She was leaning against the doorway.

Ted tuned back in.

"If this is your first time, we'd like to welcome you. Of course, you are most welcome to join any of the open small groups here, but if this is your first time, I recommend joining our connecting group, led by our leader there, Jack. . ."

"Is your *family* part of that group?" he asked.

"Oh, yes," she had a playful smile, as if she remembered the punch line of some unrelated joke, then she giggled, "Shall we, mister Ted?"

"Absolutely," he replied. He walked with her, by her side, eyeing carefully for the trash can, drowned out by the large number of people.

So, people still believe in the faith, despite all the lack of faith in it. I wonder why? Is there something here than can quiet my mind? He was nearly pushed to the side, and missed the last trash can, which was merely on the side of the door. He threw his cup and plate with the rest of the baclava.

Eating is such a chore.

Nearly lost again in the crowd, Jennifer quickly grabbed his hand. He fought the urge to pull it away. Instead, he just let her have it, but he didn't hold her, his hand was limp in her grasp. They walked through the initial doorway back into the main hall, shifting just right past the elevators. He noticed a few people going into the elevators and entered the doorway to the left up some stairs. He followed Jennifer into the back of this part of the church where there were three additional rooms. They moved to the left, although he never took his mind off each individual face that walked into those separate rooms.

The door to the room he entered was the only exit. The tables were arranged to form a boxy circle, creating the similar feeling of the hall having a bonfire in the middle of it. This was a place for friends. *I don't belong here. Why am I here?*

The ceiling stretched for what Ted could reasonably guess without a ruler was approximately fifteen feet high with a second floor. That floor was set up like an internal balcony, looking down on him were rails and bookshelves that layered the room.

Jennifer led Ted to the right corner, closer to the door, and close to Jack. Samantha came in shortly, with another girl, who Ted didn't know. Michael came in, and he waved, trading a smile as he sat down next to Tim and immediately went into a side conversation.

The man leading the discussion looked at the clock in hanging above the white board at the back of the room, and the woman, presumably his wife or other equivalent, wrote something on the board, "Meaningless." Both of them were casually dressed.

Well, I knew that already.

"Alright, so I see some new faces here," the man began, greeting new people as they came in. "So, let's get started while we have some stragglers coming in."

"Icebreaker anyone?" the woman suggested. She looked up to the ceiling, her chin resting on her hand with her index finger resting above her nose.

"Well, I'll start. What's your name? Where are you from? What brings you to Boston? And uh, what do you wish you could see more of?" the man started, addressing the group sitting around the tables. "As you know, my name is Jack. I'm from Houston Texas. I was brought to Boston through work. I work as a nuclear physicist at your local plant. No, it's not all that local," he chuckled to himself. "So, if there was one thing, I wish I could see more of? Good question, if I do say so myself. I suppose I could stand a little more rain."

Ted listened intently to everyone as they went across the room. They all went across the room, telling their name, their wish, where they were from, and their occupation. With a little more digging he could find out exactly where and what time they worked. This is dangerous information being given so carelessly. They came from numerous states, and numerous countries. He counted that there was at least one from every time zone in America, and every ethnic group.

They for one reason or another, didn't want to see any more from the world, but they desired to see less of something. They wanted less racism, less strife, less hunger, less death, and less conflict. Without adding anything, by just omitting these things could they obtain more peace, a perfect peace. *A peace like ten years ago. That bloody peace. If you take one conflict away, you are only enforcing another. It is all meaningless.*

"New guy. Hello? It's your turn. It's not time for bed yet!" He heard Jack's whimsical cry, as he clapped his hands repeatedly.

"My apologies," Ted replied, returning that smile back to his face. *How long was I in that trance? This whatever it is, was taking control again in my mindlessness. I need to be better with it.* "My name is Ted. I'm from Ohio. I came to Boston for a different change in pace. If I could see more of something—" his voice trailed off, "I can't think of anything."

"Nothing at all?" the woman asked.

Ted felt Samantha staring at him, and pointed his pupils towards her, seeing her frown as she studied him like he was some kind of rat in a maze. Jennifer nudged him with her elbow. A smile returned to her face. Ted blinked quickly with the sudden pressure assaulting his arm, and he felt the nerves in his fingers want to tremble.

"Come on Ted," Jennifer pulled on his arm. "I know you want to see more. Everyone wants to see more of *something* in the world. What is it?"

"Now, now," he turned to her with his wide child-like smile. "I've seen plenty of the world already. If I saw any more of it, that would be downright selfish of me. I can't take in anymore of the world while the sights can be enjoyed by someone else."

"Well, I suppose that's one way to look at the world," Jack chuckled.

"Well, if Ted doesn't want to say anything, he doesn't have to," the woman replied. "We are an open book, but we don't expect that of anyone here. Now, Ecclesiastes."

"Yes, one of my favorites," Tim commented.

"You would say that," Michael joked.

They studied the first chapter, and all Ted gleaned from this, was that everything is meaningless in life. Every dollar one made, every friend he made, relationship maintained, career goals, life goals, and everything in between, whatever they were was all meaningless. All these things were meaningless. *I already know that.*

Yes, Ted had money, he had a house. It was all pointless, and he knew it. He knew the feeling all too well. And he didn't care for any of it. He doesn't work for money after all, just for something to do, something to keep him busy from his own thoughts. It was all pointless.

His hand started to tremble. *No. Not now! Damnit! You stay still.* He put his trembling hand in his pocket.

"Well, now we don't like to popcorn it up here. We'll split up into smaller groups of three or four and offer prayer requests," Jack explained.

The chairs started moving rapidly into numerous smaller circles. Ted felt uneasy as his hand wouldn't stop trembling, however, he kept the trembling to a bare minimum. Even a sniper couldn't tell how slow his hand trembled, even though to himself, it felt like a speeding bullet.

Ted was in a circle with Jennifer, and Erin. He looked at them with his bright smile. He was careful, he always was when dealing with circles like this. His ears would be his eyes, and he could sense the room, every movement, every noise, no sound, no matter how little would escape his ears, just like nothing and no one can escape the defense of his mind's eye. He is as he's always been, ever watchful, but no longer by his own choice. He became conditioned to it so much that it just turns on. This is the exact reason he's failed at his one goal, that same goal he gave up on, he keeps failing. Again, and again, and again!

"Well, now this is the part where we wear our emotions on our sleeves," Jennifer explained. "Forgive me if I sound like a tour guide." She turned her head to Erin. "Prayer request?"

Erin frowned, "I—I do." Her voice was solemn, her head was bowed down low. Her eyes were wide open, staring blankly at the floor, as if what she was looking for was buried below the bowels of the church. Her thighs were closed shut, and her elbows met her stomach and one hand wrapped around her other fist, keeping them close to her, as if holding in some secret desire she longed to keep hidden. Her right heel rose from the ground, and then rested back down. Again, and again, and again. "My mother was di—diagnosed with stage four liver cancer." Tears streamed down her face; she began coughing up tears.

Ted tried to look concerned. He noticed something else. He would have thought there would have been others around who would have rushed to console her weeping. But at last, he found that she was not the only one weeping in the room. There was at least one other person in the additional small groups weeping, likely due to some cruel hand fate had given them. *Like the hand I was dealt.* It was also the first time he ever noticed Jennifer not enthused. She wrapped her arm around Erin and pulled her close. She said nothing. She just let Erin cry over her shoulder. That was a prayer in and of itself. Words needed not say more.

Should I really be caring about this right now? No.

Ted did his best to show his concern, however, he retained that smile. He moved his chair a little closer and put his hand on Erin's back.

"Ted," Jennifer began, shedding her own tear. "Before I begin, do you have something to pray for?"

"Nothing that cannot wait. This is more important I think," he answered. *But is she?*

"Okay, then please, but don't feel pressured, bow your head."

Erin's head was already bowed down low, and tears dripped down from those closed eyelids. Jennifer's tears were more controlled, but she bowed her head and was much more composed. Ted bowed down, but he didn't close his eyes. He kept his eyes focused, his pupils continued scanning the room. The rest, as if they all received the order from the same commanding officer had their eyes closed, and heads bowed. Most were holding hands.

He immediately wiped a tear from his face. *Was this genuine? No. It can't be.*

"Amen," Jennifer finished her prayer. Ted tuned out the entire prayer as he was focused on his own individual thoughts, and the behavior of everyone in the room. One by one these prayerful people rose their heads up, opening their eyes. Many of them were happy, as if a burden was lifted from their miserable chests. *How?*

The room was filled with chatter again. *Thank God.* The silence irritated him. He could find that he could no longer keep tuning everything out, not in the silence, not like this. Silence was much better when lives were on the line. He looked around the room again, some people were getting up, and putting their chairs right back towards the tables and were leaving. Some of them left in pairs, and others left by themselves after departing amiably with someone they engaged in a good conversation with.

He sought to do the same. He got up before his hand was grabbed by Jennifer. "Hey," she wiped her face clean from tears with her free sleeve. "I told you we wear our feelings on our sleeves here. I hope we didn't scare you off."

"Miss Jennifer, I'm afraid it will take a lot more than that to scare me off," he lied, turning to Erin with a solemn face as she was still weeping and wiping tears from her face with her palms. "I am sorry. Truly I am."

"Ih—it's not your fault," she looked to him, "You don't have to be sorry. Buh—but I appreciate it."

"Now," he turned without skipping a beat and returning that smile to his face. "I must really be going."

"You're not coming out with us tonight?" Jennifer frowned.

"Not tonight. Maybe next time," he said. He tried to pull away, but Jennifer wouldn't let go.

"Wait. Let me get your phone number," she said.

"As you wish, milady," he spoke dryly.

"My, my, aren't you the romantic," she pulled out a pen and piece of paper from her purse and handed it to him. He immediately wrote down a phone number on the piece of paper and handed it back to her. "At least you're honest about it. Unlike some men." She took out a piece of paper and wrote her own phone number on it. "Here, take mine."

"It's a pleasure," he took the phone number and placed it in his wallet.

"Now, now, Tedward," she smiled at him. "I think you know the pleasure is all mine."

"Of course, it is," he smiled back. *You have no idea how true that is.* "Maybe I'll see you next week or around. But I must be going."

"Good night, Ted," Jennifer said.

Samantha transitioned from her seat, pushing it in, briskly walking towards them, trying to catch up to Ted. How good of a host could she be, if she didn't at least make the effort to make sure he was comfortable. After all, it was her who invited Ted to the study; however, he made a beeline for the door, at a brisk pace she knew she couldn't keep up with. She glanced over to Jennifer, who turned to Erin. For a moment, Samantha thought that perhaps, Jennifer came on too strongly for Ted's comfort, prompting an exit, or perhaps something else was going on with Ted, something unseen.

"Are you coming out tonight? If you are, I believe it's my turn to buy you one," Jennifer's hand wrapped around Erin's shoulder.

"I think I need a break," Erin said. "I need some rest actually. Maybe next week. I just—I just need to get some sleep. Start fresh in the morning."

"What's wrong?" Samantha turned her gaze towards Erin, noticing wiped tears and reddened eyes. She placed her hand on Erin's back, rubbing it.

"My mother has stage four cancer," Erin said abruptly.

Samantha felt a sudden weight fill up from inside her chest as she covered her mouth with her hand. "I'm so sorry. I'll pray for that, and healing for her."

"Some rest will do you good. I understand Erin," Jennifer said, "I'll put your chair away. Don't worry about it. If you need someone to talk to, you can always text or call me."

"Thanks," Erin stood to leave.

Michael followed and put her chair away. He smiled at Jennifer. "So, how did it go?" he asked.

"My dear, Michael, whatever do you mean?" she snickered as she pushed her chair back in.

"You got him alone," Samantha shuddered as Michael mansplained himself to reiterate the obvious. This was one of her pet peeves. *I'll work on that.*

"Well, I certainly couldn't let you hog him. Besides, I don't think he'd care to listen to more of your business monologue," she gave him a slightly annoyed glare. "I suppose we can finish this up at Teri Nation. Let's be off. I have very important business at Teri's Empire."

"Only you can make it sound so much better than it actually is," Tim chuckled, shaking his head.

Samantha, along with Jennifer, Michael, and Tim followed the crowd out of the room and back towards the lobby where there seemed to be an abundance of people, talking with each other like old friends. Samantha always found it interesting that these people seemed so close to catch up weekly, even if they were only apart for a single week, to her, every Tuesday seemed like a reunion. They briskly exited the church, and recruited a few people to go out, not that they needed to do that, Brian would take care of that, as he always did. But it was good to show interest to the newcomers.

Samantha and her immediate friends walked to Teri Nation and walked towards the back end of the bar. It was much less crowded than last week. Perhaps there was some foul thing in the air. Samantha did notice four unique individuals by the bar, towards the end of it where she met Ted from last week. Two men, and two women having strong gin. They were talking to one another in a variety of accents, *that* is what got her attention. Samantha picked one up as Irish, and the other English, and one she could only guess as Russian. The fourth wasn't quite Russian, but it had a similar sound to that of the eastern European countries. It would seem odd since Russia declared war on neighboring countries as of late, and as if these individuals were speaking to each other as if there was no animosity between their nations. She found this most peculiar.

Scott made their drinks, Samantha was drinking a dark beer this time, and Tim was held off with a white wine sangria. And of course, Michael and Jennifer got whatever the special was. This one he served in bola glasses.

"So, Scott, what have we the pleasure," Michael began.

"Or displeasure," Jennifer added.

"Of drinking today?" Michael finished. They drank well together. Tim and Samantha were smiling as it was rare that they could get this close together with the two of them. They paired well together, like a fluffernutter sandwich. Their banter bounced off one another like they had been friends for years, but truth be told, they've only known one another for a year, and they all met here, at this bar through Café.

"It was some recipe I found on some website," Scott answered as he printed out separate slips. Jennifer already took a sip. Samantha guessed she enjoyed it with the way Jennifer rubbed her buttocks against the stool, "I don't know much about it, but last time it was made a lot of people died." There was silence. Scott turned around. "I'm kidding. Its vodka, chocolate, and seltzer. Nothing too fancy. I may have put some basil in there."

"Oh my God! I am allehgic to freaking basil!" Jennifer joked. Scott's eyes lit up in surprise, like he was looking at a dead person.

"Isn't that my line?" Tim laughed as he brought up his glass to sip his sangria.

Jennifer placed two fingers on her lips as she looked Scott in the eye mischievously. "Two can play at that game."

"Okay, cool," Scott laughed it off and went to his other guests as he walked backwards with two thumbs up.

"Alright, you've kept me in enough suspense. Now that you've had him all to yourself, what was he like?" Michael asked.

"Yes. I am dying to know. Spill the beans, Jennifer!" Samantha pushed.

"Whoa, whoa, whoa," Tim put his hands up defensively. "You leave my beans out of this. It wasn't my fault."

"No, Tim, it wasn't your fault. And we're certainly not talking about your beans," Michael jeered. "Besides, that was actually some good chili. Jennifer, spill it!"

"Fine," she took another sip, "Really nothing more than what he shared from the rest of the group, during that very questionably boring icebreaker."

Samantha pondered with the fresh liquor to her nose, and then she remembered something which she neglected to mention previously, but perhaps a sensitive question, "Jennifer, did you make note of the scars on his face?"

"I did notice those scars, like lines or streaks across his cheeks. I didn't say anything. That isn't something you want to ask someone who hardly knows you," Jennifer said, trading that playful smile of hers with those half-dropped eyelids. "Your brain is working, what is on that mind."

"I haven't formulated a complete thought. I'll have to get back to you," Sam's gaze shot back to the other end of the bar.

"Did he have something to do? He seemed in a hurry to leave," Tim's smile faded.

"Yeah, I wondered about that too," Samantha commented, turning back to Jennifer.

"Well, he didn't say. I was able to snag his number before his prompt getaway."

"Getaway. Yes, that's the appropriate word for it," Michael poked fun at Jennifer again. "It's hard to escape your clutches."

"I wonder if it had anything to do with the study," Samantha wondered if that was the most appropriate study for someone in a field fueled by money.

"Could be, honestly it isn't the best first book for someone. After all, a wise man once said, 'Meaningless, meaningless, it's all meaningless'!" Jennifer rose her hands in the air as she sat back down on her stool and cross her fingers.

"Well," Samantha said. "Tell us how you really feel."

They all looked at Jennifer, waiting for her whimsical response.

"My thoughts on the matter are all entirely 'meaningless'." Jennifer smiled.

Michael, Tim, Jennifer, and Samantha all laughed at the joke. It was ironic, and certainly the lesson could be very depressing if taken out of context. After all, not everything was meaningless.

Samantha could feel her hair standing on ends. Her hands remained in place as the ripples in her cup of beer moved towards the end of the glass. She looked closely, and Tim, and Michael didn't seem to notice. Jennifer put on her sweatshirt in response to the chill. *Where is this coming from?*

She looked at the strangers in the bar. She noticed one of them, the taller man, the one with the Irish accent appeared to be flicking his fingers back and forth, violently tapping against a piece of paper on the bar top. She looked back down to her cup and drank some more. She fixed her eyes back on the man and the piece of paper was gone. *I'm not that drunk, am I? I hope not. I barely had a drink.* Was she imagining it? The paper was gone, and the man didn't appear to be tapping anything anymore. This man wore a black suit to match his lengthy black hair tied behind his back.

"You okay there, Sam?" Jennifer glanced at her, and she tossed her head back.

"No, yes," she corrected herself. "I just thought I saw something. It's nothing."

"Soooo," Jennifer began.

"Are you okay or not?" Michael asked, putting his hand on his hip disapprovingly. "I'm beginning to worry about you."

Samantha moved her gaze back over to the strangers. "I thought I saw one of them violently tapping a piece of paper. The tall one," she whispered.

Michael shifted his attention towards them, hiding his body and face behind Samantha just enough to avoid looking suspicious. "Are you sure it isn't the air conditioning going down again? You've mentioned this numerous times now. I really don't believe a person could be the cause of it. Besides, tapping a piece of paper isn't exactly unusual."

"I—I'm not sure," she replied.

"Well, only one way to find out for sure," Michael said.

He took her hand. "Michael! Wait! What are you doing?"

He ignored her as he pulled her to the strangers. One of the women there looked at them and smiled; she had a very youthful face with red eyes. Samantha found her eyes to be especially peculiar, unless; was she high? The tall man looked surprised and turned to them, there was an unpleasant scowl on his face.

"Well, well, well, what sort of beast have we ensnared?" he said in his Irish accent.

"Well, we're here every single Tuesday night, and haven't seen you here before. Me and my friend here would like to say hi and introduce ourselves. My name is Michael, this is Samantha, Sam for short." Michael introduced himself and her charmingly.

"Hii!" Samantha introduced herself awkwardly. No matter how hard she tried, she didn't do well in friendly social situations, she was great on the phone though.

"Okay," the man said. "And to what do we owe the unfortunate circumstance for such a forced introduction?"

"Culain, I do not want another repeat from last week's escapade," said the girl with black hair. She was the one with the Russian accent. "Please, it was a mess. We don't need another one."

"As you wish, Ilya," he replied and returned a sneering smile towards them. "Now, I don't know what it is you think you saw, but you didn't see anything. I don't know what you think you felt, but it was nothing. You don't know anything. Now kindly piss off!"

"Wow!" Michael replied nonchalantly. "I was just being friendly. There was no reason to be rude. And what we—"

"What you think you saw was nothing. Now, before I lose my temper, kindly piss off," the man called Culain said. "The less you know, the better."

"Michael, let's go," Samantha pulled on his arm and shrunk back behind him. She didn't trust them, nor did they seem like people, or at least the man called, *Culain,* she wanted to be friends with. Culain seemed like a man that would sooner hurt you, and then make you apologize for inconveniencing those around you. Michael nodded to her and turned around, pulling her back to their quartet.

He seemed unnecessarily rude and unprovoked. There was so much anger in his voice, despite that smile. There was a raw emotion to his tone, as if they were less than he was. *It is wrong for me to judge the man. I don't know who he is or where he comes from, or what he's going through.*

"There once was a couple in a bar; in life they hoped to get far, thought they were destined, their ankles nailed in, I needed their love to be marred." Culain mocked them as they retreated.

Chapter 5

Dyatlov's Pass

~I'm honestly not enjoying this.

Major McCurdy led her small nuclear specialist platoon up the pass. Rather, she followed behind them, directing them where to walk. Even though it was summer, the weather couldn't be trusted to remain warm. They each had a large bag which had their hazmat gear, the suit with its oxygen tanks and tubes. As they were going into a potentially dangerously radiation infested environment, and every precaution had to be made. McCurdy knew it wasn't natural radiation up here, but even mana was poisonous to the normie.

McCurdy looked down the mountain pass, glancing at the dirt and gravel, crumbs of the mountain rolling down the hill until inevitably coming to a halt when the kinetic energy lost all movement. Just like the radioactive readings this team picked up in the facility. She let out a deep sigh as her ears trained on the four of those with her, listening in on them while they took a break, discussing the fabled incidents of the Dyatlov's pass, infamously called, "Devil's Pass". *Such a fitting name for such a dismal place.*

She wished she could have come here by herself: it would save her from the guilt, save her from the grief of killing these men, or getting them killed. But an officer just simply going off base while on duty was suspect, and she needed a believable ruse, and these men fit the bill perfectly. Just how many more people, close to her, would she have to kill before she became utterly numb to the grief and guilt? How soon until her heart became one large callous?

McCurdy walked over to them as they finished their conversation. Looking down at them from a ledge, she said, "Lee, get the MicroR Meter and start measuring. Breaks over."

"Yes, Ma'am," he got into his pack and pulled out a brown box with knobs and a little white screen with readings and a moving needle, he measured the radioactive activity with the device on the terrain.

"Not too far to go now," she said to them. "We're to the final destination."

"Is there some kind of bunker up here?" Gongora asked.

"No," McCurdy turned her gaze to him. *Idiot.*

"Major, the readings are picking up again," Lee said. "It's very minimal, 0.83 svs."

"Not terrible," Nguyen said. "However, we still need to be cautious. Let's hope it stays that low."

"Put on your Hazmat," McCurdy ordered.

They slipped in through the yellow material, some were clumsy, but McCurdy put these on thousands of times, and so did Lee, by the looks of it. He was already helping Gongora put on the clumsy black gloves. The face shield fogged up their vision with the breath inside, and nowhere to exhale from, except through the air filter. They put these suits on in the matter of ten minutes, including the oxygen tank. McCurdy noticed immediately that Adams was fumbling his oxygen tank, and getting the tank attached to the hose. She shook her head as she breathed heavily, walking over to him. Her face's visor fogged up with each breath as she slowly made her way over to him, and grasped the hose, attaching it to the oxygen tank for him.

"I never liked these things anyway. They're stupid, and unnecessarily complex," she commented. *Of course, I would think that, unlike you, I don't need it.* Her vision was fogged by her breath. "Everyone ready?"

"Yes, Ma'am," Lee commented, pulling up his now empty pack to the side of his pocket, his breath began to fog up the inside of his visor. His rifle was at his side. "The svs read higher up."

"Lead on."

Lee led them onward, climbing and following the radiation levels as the svs grew higher on the meter. They climbed up, taking steady breaths along the way. Lee climbed up another ledge which looked like it could be the top of Dyatlov's pass, but the pass sunk back down into a basin.

Around the edges of the basin was a rock labyrinth, leading to a wheel-locked door. It was steel and embedded into the mountain, like a trap door. Lee looked down at his meter, and the radiation stopped reading. He hit the meter a few times. The meter still didn't read any radiation.

McCurdy observed the specialist, Lee, taking his meter to the side. She couldn't make out his facial expression with his fogged visor, but she knew his file, no one knew these old meters better than he did, not in any of her other units, certainly, he knew what he was doing. Lee flipped the microR meter upside down, and unscrewed the back, and took out the battery, and replaced it with a new one, screwing it back together for an updated reading. This is when she knew something was wrong with the machine, those meters can only handle so much.

"What happened?" McCurdy asked, wondering why he stopped. Her eyes scanned the basin, looking for runes scraped on the sides, or mana circles from previous casters, or mana residues, anything to clue her in on the possibility of an enemy here, but so far, found nothing.

"Radiation killed the battery," he replied. He turned the meter back on. "Much better. Only 0.043 svs. Its less than before. Gongora, I think I found your bunker." He turned to McCurdy. "Is this place showing up anywhere on the map? Or even in something classified?"

"No," McCurdy answered. "There is nothing to indicate there was something like this here. Be careful, that radiation can spike back up any minute."

"Do we know why this is happening?" Adams asked.

"That is precisely why we are here," Nguyen said.

"We need to climb down. Keep your eyes peeled. Odds are, I don't think we're alone," McCurdy stated. "Check your fire. I needn't remind you Ukraine Officials could be up here."

"Then why don't we call for backup then? We're not infantry!" Adams exclaimed.

"Don't you get it," Gongora said. "We aren't even supposed to be here. This was a last-minute mission, likely didn't get approved by the higher ups. We're here now, and that's that."

"What do you mean higher ups? She's right here! We're not going to find out bickering," Lee started climbing down and the rest of them followed.

She shook her head in her suit. *You got too comfortable for insubordination.* She kept her thoughts to herself, not wanting to clue them in on the real reason they were there. She didn't need them to know she was sending them to their graves, but she was most of all disappointed. This Army wasn't the Army she once knew, filled with discipline and respect. The unit underneath her was undisciplined, unchecked, and disrespectful. Such men do not belong in the military. *Perhaps this is for the best.*

McCurdy looked to the rocks to her left, and she squinted her eyes as she noticed a glowing circle embedded in the rocks, numerous shapes and designs lay within it. She recognized the ancient language, the ancient runes; runes only a caster would know. To these soldiers, should they see it, would only serve their superstitions. *Another Caster is here. Who are you?*

They continued to climb down, carefully to get into the basin of the pass, a rip or tear in their hazmat suit meant inevitable death, and they all knew it. McCurdy was the least disturbed by that fact. They observed the basin, carefully monitoring for extra radioactive activity, around the basin. McCurdy observed with her hands crossed behind her back, subtly pulling mana out from the rock into her mana veins, hiding inside her hazmat suit.

"Your orders, Major?" Adams said. "Radioactive activity has depleted."

"Affirmative," Lee replied. He turned to the door to the unmarked bunker. "Do we need to go in there?"

"Yes. Lee, I want you up front. Gongora, and Nguyen behind him. Adams, you're with me," she said, "Lee, get that door open."

"Yes ma'am," he stated, walking over to the iron cast door and placed his meter softly on the ground. With his hazmat covered hands, he turned the wheel, unlocking the rusty mechanisms behind the door. He slowly pulled the creaking door on its hinges. Dust came out and clouded his face shield. He wiped the dust from his suit.

He picked his meter up as everyone turned on their flashlights.

The entrance into the bunker was dark and musty, and felt desolate as if it had been abandoned for decades. They entered in, observing the radiation levels, which appeared to have settled down, the clicks of the meters only activated every few seconds, flipping the needle back and forth. They looked to either side of them to see various tables and other rooms with doors that were forced open, dented and twisted beyond repair.

"What happened here?" Gongora asked, shaking his head as he looked at the carnage. The rooms were completely in disarray. There was coagulated blood on the ground, the gel shimmering crimson on the walls with their flashlights. Some of the blood was smeared like the entrails of a man with his torso ripped open and dragged off further into the dark.

"Silence," McCurdy sternly called. *This is just an illusion. I can tell, damn caster, whoever you are. This was recent.* "Shut up and keep moving. Someone is still here."

They followed the entrails, even though, Gongora silently protested. It was heard among comrades, sharing the same hellish living conditions. Nguyen was laser focused, his almond-shaped eyes narrowed as he peered into the darkness as they walked forth, scanning the room with every step they took.

This reminded McCurdy of a horror movie, entrails dragging themselves down the hall, the iron doors rusting, and each step she took creaked. She felt unnerved as her fingers in her suit began to tremble, feeling this unnatural place, void of all life, but she knew something more, sieverts did not just start and dissipate naturally. There was a caster here, or perhaps a threcket. She hissed silently at the thought, not keen on fighting one of those down here in close quarters, whatever form the threcket chose to take. She knew this was a false sense of security.

The meters didn't pick up anything new and stopped making their gurgling sounds altogether. The darkness became cold and oppressive, the deeper they adventured into these godforsaken halls, until they came to an end of it all.

They came to a room, no, an altar. Blood smeared all over the place, and many shapes and circles were carved with human blood over the walls. There was no reactor, no working generator, nor was there any viable source of uranium or plutonium anywhere: no radioactive materials.

Lee grimaced as he looked on the altar. He put his meter on the cold metal floor. He turned to McCurdy, and he wasn't smiling. "Major, you have some explaining to do. Do you know something we don't?"

"No," she lied; her heart started to race. *I can't kill a threcket in the middle of a mutiny. Damn it, Lee!* "And don't question me." She stared him down with cold eyes from behind her visor. Her heart started to race, the stakes rising.

"No, I think this is a valid reason for questioning. We've all been here. The radioactive activity died as soon as we came here, and there is no evidence that there was any radioactive activity here minus the readings. Do you know something, we don't?" He pointed a finger directly at her.

"Watch your mindless speculations, Warrant Officer, I don't have time for this," McCurdy snapped at him. "And no, I don't."

McCurdy could tell Lee was scowling behind that fogged mask, rising with a sense of distrust for her, and the distrust will soon spread to the rest of them. *You are right to distrust me. I would.*

"Major, we are soldiers, not exorcists," Adams interjected. "We need a priest for this, or back up. We don't know what is down here. Something is unnatural about this place, and we don't know what we're getting ourselves into. These readings are sporadic enough as it is without us being here!"

"That is precisely why we are here, Specialist," she said, "We don't know, and we need to know."

"You all came to the worst place," said a voice in the corner.

All five of them swiftly turned around to see a man, holding a pile of red shlop in his hand: pumping like a heart, but this was no heart, at least, not any heart that McCurdy had seen. He bore a sinister smile upon his face, a man filled with bloodlust that would never be satisfied. The man held himself in high esteem, as if looking down on all of them, McCurdy could feel the condescension. His pants were ripped in parts, and he had many cuts over them, as if he himself just fought off a threcket. The man was bare chested, with rippling muscles, and blood dripped down several cuts on his face and chest.

"Onhlidan!" he chanted. "Onhlidan! Onhlidan! Onhlidan!"

A red light emitted from the shlop. The soldiers panicked, drawing their side arms and pointed it at the man. They all aimed down their sights, ready to fire. The light lit up the room, and they found themselves in a room filled with nothing but bones beneath their feet.

They glanced below. Bones, human bones, flesh and blood covered their feet.

"What the hell is this shit!" Lee cried out. He stamped his feet on the ground, crushing bones beneath him.

"Who are you?" McCurdy asked. "What are you doing here?"

"I think that not be the question you should be asking, Major." The man said, throwing the beating shlop of mass directly at her. She moved to the side swiftly, letting the mass strike the wall behind her.

"And what question might that be?" She asked.

"Orders! Orders!" Nguyen cried out, his pistol trembling in his hand. "Major! What are your damn orders?!"

"Orders, Major, what are they, Major." The man mimicked Nguyen. He sighed as he moved his bloody hand's palm to the side. "I guess it matters not. Secrets. That is all they are: secrets."

"What are you talking about?" she ignored Nguyen's cries for an order. Orders were order, but right now was not the time for her to wear her military hat, but as a caster of the administration. "Why are you here?"

"I was looking for the Grail. It appears, it is not here. And I don't think it holy. After all, wasn't it the key to pandora's box?"

"I didn't think anyone would tell anyone where the Grail is," she inquired. "And don't speak of the Grail. That is on a need-to-know basis, and no one here, yourself included, needs to know."

"Major! What is he talking about?" Gongora interjected.

"That is need to know. You don't need to know," she snapped.

"You, casters of the administration aren't very smart, are you?" The man asked. "It doesn't matter. You are out of time."

McCurdy heard a frightened gasp from Lee. She glanced over to see his fogged mask; she imagined his eyes were stretched as wide open as his skull would allow, assuming, with such a worrisome response from a Warrant Officer only meant one thing: the radiation maxed out the microR meter.

"Five-thousand!" Adams exclaimed. "That is—"

"Not an accurate reading!" Lee shouted. "Our meters only go up that high. It's much higher than that. We need to get the hell out of here or we'll be fried to a crisp or on our deathbeds with cancer next week!"

"No," said McCurdy. "It's fine."

"Have you lost your damn mind!" Gongora exclaimed. "This is not what we signed up for. We are not getting fried because of whatever the real reason is why we're here! We aren't infantry! We aren't trained to handle something like this!"

"Look," she pointed.

A gate of fire and ice opened behind the man. He passed through it, and both the gate and he was gone. McCurdy could feel, even with her suit, the temperature dropping in the air, and the hairs stood on ends on her back, as she was certain everyone with her felt the same. Only she knew their hearts were much closer to beating out of their chests. She was certain they were left unaware of these ancient arcane elements kept hidden to them for the last fifteen-hundred years. Just here, they were made aware of everything, magic, casters, portals, illusions, and least of all the Grail, whatever this person was truly after. These were all things that, according to the Caster's Code, must not enter the minds of normies, lest the threads of creation come undone. That is what she was told, anyway.

The microR meters measured back down to zero immediately.

None of them needed to be here for this. I hate this code. She let out a sigh.

McCurdy's eyes narrowed behind her mask, the mana still being pulled through the oxygen in the air and through her suit. She backed away from the group of her specialists, who still trembled as they pointed their guns at the precise location from where the portal vanished. She could hear their sporadic breathing over the coms. They were terrified, and why shouldn't they be? No matter how disciplined they were, which they weren't, everything they thought they understood about the world came undone, just like their sanity, as it became unraveled.

They could hear the rapid bubbling from behind them. McCurdy's eyes angled, *it's one of those threckets.* She now knew what the beating shlop was, just a little vessel for the threcket to form from this world. *Whose heart did you take?* "Shit," she swore under her breath. They all turned around to see a large bubbling red mass forming from the wall. It slowly began to take shape. McCurdy had a better idea of what she was looking at, but even to her, the bull's head protruding from the clicking segments of a centipedal body made her ill. The disgusting creature stood tall on strong horse legs; many arms baring stingers were already flailing towards them.

She let out a sigh of relief. *Well, I don't have to kill them now.*

"What the actual hell is that!" Lee raised his rifle, aiming down the sights to the threcket, pulling the trigger. "To hell with your orders. Damn it!"

Gongora and Nguyen marched to the side, their rifles firing. The bullets sparked as they struck the threcket. No surprise there, those hides were damn near impenetrable, and needed specific things to pierce it. Weapons of the modern era were completely useless.

The beast roared and smashed into Lee, digging its stingers into him. He cried out in agony as the stingers began to inject him with poison, blood and poison immediately saturated his body. Gongora and Nguyen immediately opened fire. The bullets penetrated the threcket, and the holes in the creature produced purple puss that filled the air. McCurdy walked backwards, leaning against the back wall, waiting patiently for the creature to kill them. After all, she felt that if she personally killed them, it would shatter her spirit. *I'm sorry.*

The creature immediately flung itself into the direction of the gunfire. Nguyen dove to the ground shooting at it from below. Juices oozed out of the threcket's wounds, raining on him from above, eating through his suit like acid. The beast impaled Gongora with its venomous stingers and ripped him in several pieces, his limbs twirling in the air spraying his blood in all directions, splattering on McCurdy's visor. She imagined the kind of pain Nguyen should be feeling right now, but he didn't show it, never made it known even in a yelp. He started running out of the hallway only to be impaled from behind the deadly stingers, and likewise ripped apart. He didn't even have time to let out a final cry for help.

"Well, now that that's over with," McCurdy said. "It is time to send you back."

She pulled the mana from the air into her Mana Veins. She pulled out her knife. Her blue mana veins crawled from her glove and onto the knife. The beast sprinted at her. Immediately, she swiftly cut into the air, shapes of circular runes into a circle, leaving her mana's residue there, cutting into the Threads of Creation like flesh.

"Deoful Spreot!" She chanted. "Deoful Spreot!"

She pulled the mana from the air. Wind picked up the dirt in the room, striking her suit. She felt the air cooling around her and heard the miscellaneous debris of office supplies strike her visor. The mana swirled around her, crafting a red flame, and red spears, fashioned from the mana in the air. The creature finally barreled into her, but she did not move as her blue veins turned grey, forcing her in place like an irremovable statue. The red spear penetrated the beast, pouring its blood on the floor. It screeched in agony as it crumpled on the ground. The mana she pulled in the air protected her feet from being burned from the acidic blood.

"Deorfald," she chanted again as she drew another shape in the air, this shape was more square and less elegant than the shape before. Black chains grew up from the ground. They encapsulated the beast, pinning it to the stony floor. The beast writhed against the chains. In a puff of ash, it disappeared. All that appeared left were the chains that collapsed noiselessly to the ground. She breathed in the mana from the dead that rested here: Nguyen, Lee, Gongora, their husks bubbling and burning away, until nothing was left except the iron ground. There was no evidence that they were here. *They just simply vanished.*

She shook her head, swearing underneath her breath as she hastily took off the Hazmat Suit. Her veins turned blue again as she bolted out of the room with her flashlight, and the mana spear in her hands. She sprinted through the corridors and exited the bunker. Adams was sat on a rock outside, his helmet rested next to him. Clearly, he was no longer disturbed by the radiation—or to call it what it was: concentrated mana. Something invisible, that caused a slow, albeit painful, death must have paled in comparison to what he'd seen in the cave. To what McCurdy wished killed him.

Adams looked up to her and jolted up, backing away from her. "Major, what the hell was that?"

"You have no right to question me when you left us to die like that," she said, holding the spear in her hand.

His eyes were fixed upon the spear, something he didn't see McCurdy come up with, "Nothing about today made any sense. A bunker with high radioactivity, with no source to cause said activity, a portal or some shit, and a—a I don't know what to call that, some bubbling goo, and not to mention this illusion or what—"

Adams breathed heavily, his eyes glancing past McCurdy, presumably towards the hatch into the mountain. He lost sight of the spear until he found it in his chest, the blade cut through his chest easily. She ripped it right back of him, spraying blood over the basin of the pass. He coughed blood and placed his hand on his chest while he stepped backwards, tripping over the rock behind him, "Major! What are you doing?"

"I'm sorry kid," she stuttered as a tear dripped from her eye. *Shit. I missed the heart.* "You see, normies like you. No, accidents like you aren't supposed to see caster nonsense! It would destroy the very fabric of your beliefs. Trust me, ultimately it is for the best. I didn't plan on you being a little chickenshit and running away. Now, *I* have to kill you, something *I* was trying to avoid!"

Adams' eyes stretched open as he reached for his side arm. McCurdy swiftly swung the spear. The force of the elongated red blade slicing through his wrist threw the disembodied hand with his side arm through the air. He cried as he turned around and sprinted; his heart racing, beating through his chest like a heavy metal drum solo. He made it to the path where they came from, and tried to climb it, but his stub of a hand was beyond useless.

She walked around to him and pushed him away from the path. As he tripped on the ground, and crawled away from her, McCurdy stared at him with teary eyes, "Honestly, I'm not enjoying this either, for the record. Honestly, this is the part about my existence I hate the most," She felt her heart sinking, and the spear trembled in her hand. *You are all family to me, brothers and sisters in arms.* She firmly grasped the spear in her hand, returning her resolve to do what must be done, despite the singular accepted fact, she didn't want to kill him, but she had no choice. She thrust the spear into his chest, not missing his heart this time. She twisted the spear, tearing his flesh and heart apart.

She looked into his eyes as the life left them, sighing, she took a step back; dropped the spear to the ground. When it hit the ground, it dematerialized in the air, creating little red lights as it faded into nothingness, floating in the air like reverse snowfall.

She leaned against the wall leading upwards. Her mana veins thickened on her skin, pulling the refreshing mana from the air, the clunky mana from the stone, and the thick mana from the blood. Adam's corpse boiled, fading away all parts of him as McCurdy converted his body to mana entirely, drinking it through her veins. His body faded into nothing.

She cried into the sky as the guilt constricted her heart as if a sadistic snake slithered its way through her ribs, and wrapped around her heart and lungs, suffocating the air and blood out of it. She didn't want to kill him, or get them all killed, but that was the nature of this *cursed administration.*

There has to be a better way, but everything's already been tried. The administration is so cruel. Why does it have to be this way? Why can't these normies know? We would have to kill so much less, she thought.

She remembered something, something important. Her job here was not done, even though the site was now confirmed secure. She had to radio in the Administrator. She pulled out her phone, and planted her veins into the phone, preventing any unwanted listeners.

"Admin Colton," the voice said on the other line.

"Major McCurdy."

"Status report."

"There was another caster involved. It wasn't anything nuclear on the pass. Someone was using it for experimentation and summoned a threcket here. The caster was looking for the Holy Grail," she replied. "The man seemed to know much. He is skilled enough to open a portal from Pandora, and enough about necromancy and demonic magic to bring threckets into this world."

"Appearance?"

"White. Accent was southern United States. Maybe Georgia. Dark hair. Five-eleven. One-hundred-eighty pounds. Muscular. Estimated. No name was given. But he spoke as if he was not a caster himself, and held disdain for the administration, and he seemed to know I was a caster before I did anything."

"Go dark. You are being transferred to London immediately," he said, "Don't worry, you'll have more information on your email in a few hours. Get on the next plane to London. Don't worry about your replacement."

"What's my mission?"

"We can't trust the head administration anymore. Odds are, whoever that is, was a rogue, and a mole sent to spy on us. That is the only logical conclusion, and he may have had a goal in mind that wasn't the Grail, and that was just an excuse to throw you off. You are going to retrieve the Grail from them, diplomatically, covert, choice is yours. We can't leave it in their hands anymore, not when they're so corrupt as it is."

"I understand. If it is the will of U.S.A branch of the Administration, I will see it done."

"See that you don't disappoint. Colton out."

Chapter 6

Crests

~I had a dream once. It was the only thing I was born with. There was compassion in my heart and a drive to strive for peace, to help others. Was that so wrong of me? I helped others and found it to be meaningless. At the end, it was all meaningless, because saving others, means killing someone else.

Ilya looked down from the penthouse on Wednesday night. Her arms crossed over her chest as red veins colored her eyes. Her eyes squinted as she studied the now barren streets of Boston. Struggling to keep her eyes open, she rapidly shook her head. These veins allowed her to see traces of elusive mana threads crawling across the streets, pulling apart the creation of the world, and linking Earth to the cursed land of Pandora, a place their kind go when they die, most of them anyway. Some of them might be lucky, and just end up in a hole in the ground. She steadily drank the mana from the air, and the salty perspiration of Culain and Alexander. It was refreshing, and she needed this after her third straight night of no sleep. She twirled her black hair with her finger.

She remembered the previous night, at Teri Nation, their own little hang out spot to make futile attempts to wind down, and of course the girl and boy who approached them out of, presumably curiosity, whereas then greeted with hostility from Culain. Such a shame, really. A part of the world she could never have, some silence, some peace, and a mind of harmless curiosity. They were curious. That's all. *All I want is a friend, someone to talk to and not have to worry about these damn Threckets! Is that too much to ask! Why was I born this way? And born into an endless war.*

Culain and Alexander held out a map of the state of Massachusetts with multiple red markings on it, filled with stars. All in all, there were over two-hundred stars on that map. Culain and Alexander were talking amongst themselves. Alexander had dark moppy hair, and was much broader built than Culain, but Culain was not a small man. Blanka was eating a granola bar in the corner, seemingly exhausted, they all were. Ilya knew that, it isn't like she was the only one living in misery. Her thoughts lingered again on the hostility Culain displayed towards the normie couple.

"Culain, must you be an unbearable ass to everyone we meet?" Ilya rebuked him, glaring at him. Her youthful face grimaced underneath her hateful glare. "They were only being polite, something you could stand to do sometimes."

"People are polite to get close. You know this better than anyone. Besides, Caster's rules. If they saw anything, you know what has to be done. Even a risk is too much," Culain replied, never taking his eyes off the map, his eyes narrowed at the map, he tapped on the table repeatedly with his index finger, "I did what I did to avoid having to enforce that rule. After all, you know how much I just love killing unnecessary normies," he said sarcastically. "I fucking hate it!"

"You and I know you hate it," the white-haired Blanka said, her red eyes looked compassionately to him, and then they narrowed towards him, "You act a tough game, but you're just like them."

"We're not like them, and you know it. They don't know half of what goes on in the world, and they sure as hell don't know half of what's going on within their own hearts," Culain replied. "Blanka, you know as well as I, we are forced to play a game in a façade, wearing our masks, but we can't remove them. They, however, can remove the masks whenever they fucking want. They can take that damn mask off, we can't. Because we have a dark job to do. If they get too close, and they see something they're not supposed to see, you know we have to kill them. And let me tell you, that's a lot harder to do when you have a relationship with them."

Alexander spoke up as usual to defend Culain, "Lay off him. You know full well he's experienced killing more than any of us. Those orphans in China."

Culain was visibly uncomfortable. Ilya wished for his sake that Alexander would just shut up. She knew he wouldn't.

"God, if they'd just all died in that fire. He'd had shared drinks with some of the survivors. You know that. Still had to kill them," Alexander continued.

Ilya wished he'd get off his damn high horse long enough to know he wasn't helping. She knew Culain well enough to know when he tried to hide something. His usual hard stare softened, tears glimmering in his eyes. His right hand started to tremble, and he retracted it into his pocket.

"It's a dark job," Culain growled and returned a glare to Blanka.

"What happened?" Ilya asked.

"Some jackass thought it would be funny to take some mana from the Grail and feed it to a normie. Yeah." Culain was normally reserved about recounting this type of event.

"Jesus, doesn't that cause a chasmic rift between dimensions?" Ilya had known that the incident had been large. She hadn't been part of the team thirteen years ago and had never been brave enough to ask.

"Yup. Bloated the man up. Chasmic rift. Damn threckets from the other side the size of Germany. The whole show."

Alexander chimed in, "The dude flew up into the sky. His body was like a giant freakin' rock. A second moon. Then he just popped. Cursed essence everywhere."

Ilya knew to shut up. Blanka did not, "Did anyone survive?"

"The mana did most the job. And the creatures. But, yeah, there were some survivors. I wasn't proficient enough to kill all the witnesses. Too much ground to cover. But hey, who would believe them anyway? They'd just be escorted to some asylum before the administration found out. Bye-bye witnesses."

"Yeah, enough of the past. We can talk about that later," Alex turned his gaze to Ilya, pointing his index firmly on the map, "Look,

Ilya, are all those portal crests in place? And sufficiently fueled with mana?"

"Yes," she replied, the source of mana was efficient, but in certain places will kill people that don't need to be killed. "I don't like the way I had to do it."

"Will it last?" he asked.

"Yes, there are plenty of them to disperse the energy at any given point; however, the source of mana isn't exactly going to be reliable in such a large area." She walked over to the table with the map and put her finger on a singular location. "I could only afford to make a single seal there. It will act as a gate towards our one teleportation circle in Gosnold. However, with a population that small the seal will not hold for long. If the seal breaks, the mana used in it will deplete. So, if we need to teleport there, the teleportation will exhaust the mana reservoirs in Gosnold, effectually killing the entire population."

"In other words, God in Heaven Forbid anything happens there, everyone dies, and there is hardly enough mana left to make it back to the mainland. There are a few towns like that in Massachusetts," Blanka simplified the explanation.

Culain smiled to Blanka, "And this is why I'm not an arcane wielder. Because that is way too complex for me to handle. Not to mention I don't think I would even be able to pull something like that off. This is a good thing though, it means you don't have to use your own mana for that, and you can focus your energy on other things."

Ilya brushed her hair behind her ears, tilting her head. "Yes, but I still don't adore the idea of having things being done at the expense of humans who know nothing of us. They know nothing of the conflict, and they know nothing of the Hell we've seen. The Hell, the demons and devils are just underneath the ground, and are not far off from wreaking havoc across all the Earth. This—"

"These humans who cannot even channel mana are merely expendable assets. They are nobodies. They choose to wear a mask that we are oppressively forced to wear. So, what if they die in the process, if a small amount must be sacrificed along the way to achieve the higher good, that is acceptable. That is the code of a caster," Culain's tone became harsh. "This world is cruel that it would submit us to this fate, but that is not our choice to make. All our decisions were made before we were born, and there is nothing we can do about that. We have a hand, and we need to play that hand as best we can, and hope the other player has a crap hand, or is a shitty card player."

Ilya was silent, sitting on the windowsill, resting her elbow on her knee, and her hand covered her mouth. These normies were nothing but cattle to them, a stark and unfortunate truth, and she hated it. The code they are forced to go by calls for the killing of normies who see mana being used, and other restricted activities. It was there way of coping. It was far easier to kill someone once you've stripped away their humanity.

"It is necessary, Ilya," Blanka sided with Culain. "I don't love the idea any more than you do, but what choice do we have? Culain is right. They are tools and resources that we can use to do our job. You know the risk, we all do, and you know we have to keep it on the hush hush."

"Which would you prefer: another World War, or the necessary sacrifice of one small meaningless town?" Alexander asked. "I vote for normie extermination personally. Are you finished?"

There was silence. Culain waited to speak more.

"Alright, now that that's over with. Ilya, are any seals loosening?" he asked.

"Half a moment," she said as she closed her eyes and folded her hands into fists while resting her chin upon them. She reached out with her spirit, pulling in the mana from the air. Her flesh was crawling with emerald veins, which began to change color from a green, to sea blue, and finally flesh red. She opened her eyes, and the flesh veins entered the whites of her eyes and her pupils turned golden.

She could see darkness, with streams of light cascading over her vision. The many shapes tossed and turned into her sight as the seals remained locked. Her gaze shifted over towards Springfield, and the seals remained in place, and none of the Threckets attempted to unlock the seal, nor tried to attack the barriers from the other side of Pandora.

The veins disappeared from her eyes and body immediately and her pupils returned to their normal color. She took a deep breath as she focused on the door behind them, making sure that no one was listening on the other side. "The Hell remains silent in Massachusetts. They are not moving against seals or the gates."

"Good," Culain sighed. "I can't believe we almost didn't succeed here."

"Yeah, the loss was bad though. I'm certain the Caster's Administrator will call us back to London shortly," Alex said.

"Not likely," Blanka said. "They'll want us monitoring activity here for a while before they declare this project safe and finished. They'll want to make sure the seals and transportation circles are working before sending us back for vacation."

"Vacation sounds nice," Ilya let out a sigh of relief. *A little rest is in order.* "Hopefully, we can make it."

"Yeah," Culain agreed.

Chapter 7

The Empty House

~After all my years of living, I have only one regret: not strangling myself with my own umbilical cord, now I can't even die right.

Ted forced a smile, his eyelids getting heavy as he sat with his bag resting on his lap on the subway. At 9:00 PM, the redline was fairly crowded riding towards Alewife. Listening intently, he rested his head back as he sat, watching everyone on this subway, hoping not to see any familiar faces. He noted the diverse population on the subway, white, black, Hispanic, Asian, male, female. There was a significant diversity in the socio economics of the people on the train; some seemed to be struggling families with old purses with the color fading, and others seemed to be well off, dressed professionally with pressed clothes, and the women wore makeup. Some of these people were singular, just monitoring something of no value on their phone as it was glued to their faces. Some were coupled up, talking to one another, and some kids had their faces lit up by phones given to them by parents who, sitting behind their respective children, leaned their heads back hoping to get a moments rest. He saw many isolated single persons curving their lips to a smile. Some of these people wore their smiles genuinely, while the smiles of others were blank, there was no life behind those eyes.

He kept his trembling hand in his right pocket. *Just a—just a few more hours, then Hell can presume.* He smiled as he inconspicuously watched everyone. Many people here had no quarrel with one another; however, many buried their wretched faces into their terribly cursed hands. They had no problem with showing their emotions to such strangers. Perhaps they knew they would never see anyone on this train ever again. The sense of anonymity was appealing, but something Ted dared not risk.

The next stop came. Many people walked off at Harvard Station. Fewer people walked on. These were students and professors. The professors immediately opened their briefcases as they sat down and worked on grading or additional source material for another class they were teaching, pushing their glasses closer to their faces. The students were busy talking, and he noticed one in particular; a girl who looked like she should still be in high school. She put in her headphones and sat at the end, pulling her knees up to her chest and wrapped her arms around them to keep them close. She stared down the train with an empty expression on her face.

He felt like he was looking at someone familiar. The face, the hair, the stance, and that damn blank stare. There was nothing inside her. No happiness, no sadness, no hope. It's like she was tired of sharing her smile, jaded from putting up with the damn façade called life, nor was she particularly open about showing her despair to others, she might not want to inconvenience anyone from her erasing herself from this world. The emptiness, he knew it all too well. The emptiness was hungry, and it ate happiness and hope like a pig. Why bother as hope is only a façade: all it is, is a postponed disappointment. It only ends one way, with despair.

He looked away from her and turned to look out the window in front of him. The subway started moving again. His forced smile met that of another tired woman, probably in her thirties. Over a decade older than him, he presumed. She also looked tired, brushing away her ragged blond hair out of her face, her eyes like his were sunken in, but she made an effort to smile back at him.

He tried to navigate his gaze away from her and to an inanimate object. He found a convenient advertisement on the pole. It was an ad to a show on broad way. The show looked like people would be entertained, a group of ethnically diverse characters wearing a variety of clothing. Their faces were brightly lit, and smiles painted across their lips, and they even had a twinkle in their eyes, or he imagined they were twinkling at the time of the picture was taken for the advertisement. He only found a handful of people that shared that same twinkle, just a little spark of light in their souls, and yet, with everything moving, he felt trapped in this train. He envied the people in the picture, not their clothes, not their smile, but that little twinkle of light, that happiness or joy, or whatever it is, that was what he was after. He saw the same twinkle in Sam's eye, in Jennifer's and in Michael's, but he can't be around them.

He waited patiently as the subway came to Davis Square. The doors opened and he scanned the train again. Everyone was laughing as they were walking off, from their jerseys and back packs, some satchels and purses, he assumed these were college kids going to some party or a nearby bar. He followed them out. He walked through the dimly lit, concrete corridors to the escalators to the fresh breeze of Davis square. Cars were honking their horns and buses were dropping people off in droves. He walked through the Square onto College Avenue.

He looked up at the sky. Like the girl on the train, it was empty of clouds and stars. Feeling the oppressive moon mocking him, he walked on the sidewalks. His trembling hand remained in his pocket, and he kept his smile bright and wide, as he blankly stared at the sidewalk on which he walked. His heart raced inside his chest and sweat dripped from his palms.

He walked down five kilometers, coming to a blue house with white trims on the door and windows. Walking up the stairs and inserting the key into the keyhole. The door creaked open into the black dark mouth way into the house. Stepping inside, he closed the door, locking the knob lock. He turned and locked the mechanism for the bolt. It clicked shut before he turned, lifting the chain to lock the door with its final lock.

Leaning against the door, he dropped his bag to the floor. It knocked on the wooden floor, sounding like a rock.

His smile began to fade as his lips curved downwards. He grinded his teeth as he stifled a noise from his mouth. His face cringed as tears streamed down the side of it. He felt his knees tremble; his feet slid from underneath him. His body struck the ground, and both of his hands were in front of him, trembling uncontrollably. He clamped his eyes shut as he cried out. He took one hand over his chest where his heart would be, clenching his shirt.

He took heavy breaths and choked on his sobbing. His weak knees struggled to pull himself back up; however, it is unlike someone from Task Force Seven to allow such an inconvenience to bring him to a halt. He *willed* his knees to be fixated and forced himself to stand up.

He *willed* the first step. He couldn't stop sobbing, his tears dripping from his face to the empty hardwood floor. He felt nerves snapping throughout his body, physically telling his body he was in pain, but he never felt the pain itself. He took regulated interval breaths as the tears came down.

He *willed* his second step, and he pulled out his arm to the wall, leaning against it.

He scanned the room hastily, looking for something to use to walk around. He couldn't do it himself with the constant trembling inside his body like earth tremors. He was in his living room. The floor was empty with no trash on it. There were no bookcases, no tv, no radio, no coffee table, nor other miscellaneous furniture on the ground. There were no pictures on the wall, there were only two things, a display case and a noose on the floor, at least, cut up in pieces as it was worthless to him; he couldn't use it effectively. Inside the display case was where he kept certain items of internal value, half of which would be absolutely useless to everyone else. Otherwise, the room looked like he just moved in today without the moving boxes.

Inside the display case was a spear. The spear he could use. It was the same spear Metal used, quite often was useful. He remembered Metal reaching out for hard-to-reach places with his scrawny little arms when he was just a kid. The red handle of the spear was wood, had some written markings upon it, but since faded, the spearhead was rusted, and Ted couldn't find a way to restore it safely, not without being caught. He was actually surprised to find the spear shortly after the Nuclear meltdown in Area 51 eight years ago.

He *willed* his third step. He cried out as his knees gave out again, as the oppressive mockery of the damned moon light entered his house, beating down on him with its great mocks. The burden of this was too heavy for his knees to bear, even his iron will was not enough to *will* himself back up as he tumbled forward, hitting his head on the ground.

"Why?" he sobbed. He reached out his right hand and pulled himself towards the display case. "Why? Damnit!" He reached out with his left hand and pulled himself closer across the empty living room. "I did everything you told me to!" He reached out his right hand and pulled himself closer, the tears came down so hard, they were missing his face and merely dripping on the floor. His shirt became wet with his tears as he dragged himself across it. "Damnit! I hate you!" his voice was like that of a child, disappointed in their father and mother for bringing him into this cruel world. "Was that not enough? I didn't have much to take anyway. Why did you take them from me?" He continued to grit his teeth together as he pulled himself closer and closer to the display case.

He finally reached the display case. He pulled himself up, his tears dripping onto the glass. He leaned against the wall and pulled out another key from his pocket. His hand trembled as he tried to get it into the keyhole. The key trembled in his fingers and fell to the ground. It struck the ground with a force; the noise was so heavy he could feel it slipping away from his grasp. He took a heavy breath, and slowly let it out. "Fuck it," he took his free hand and made a fist. He slammed his hand into the display case, cracking the glass. Shards went everywhere and cut his arm. His arm was bleeding, and his knuckles became raw with the impact.

His hand reached for the spear, and his hand froze in place as his hand hovered over it. His tears still streamed down, and his eyes stretched open when he came to the sudden realization, reacting to the shards of glass imbedded in his flesh. He could feel the red, warm blood cascading down his arm. "I—I still can't feel it," he said silently to himself. "Iah—I can't feel anything. I can't feel anything anymore." He grabbed his spear, and it trembled in his hands. He pulled it out of the display case and put the haft of it against the hardwood floor, and rusty spearhead raised up to the ceiling.

The unwanted emotions flooded him again as if there was nothing in between them. He struggled as his knees became weak again, as he made his way to the kitchen. He took staggered deep breaths with every step.

He found the wastebasket by the doorway into the kitchen. The wastebasket was filled with empty plastic cups and plastic silverware, and paper plates. He avoided the basket and made it into the kitchen.

The kitchen was almost as bare as the living room. The cupboards were disheveled, there was no kitchen table nor chairs. The counters were empty apart from a roll of paper towels and napkins. There was nothing like a toaster, toaster oven, or even a coffee maker on his counter. It was bare. The sink was the only thing that had anything else in it. There were dirty pans.

He managed to get himself to the sink. He reluctantly took his hand off his spear and leaned it into one of the empty cupboards. He took out the sponge and put soap on it and ran the hot water. He scrubbed the dirty pans clean, slowly putting everything into it, doing whatever he could to distract him from his thoughts. *Anything!*

Dismayed he was that nothing would empty his mind. He cried even louder, his tears fell into the sink, splashed on the pans. He cleaned the last frying pan and threw it into the wall. It made a loud noise as it stuck into the wall, it just hanged there.

He gasped as he suddenly remembered the noose that he made for himself in the living room. He hanged there last night, but as if some fluke of nature, he phased through the noose.

Ted firmly tied the noose, hanging it from his ceiling, giving it a strong tug to ensure it would hold him. The rope was thick and sturdy enough, but one can never be too careful to make sure it's done right. After all, this was going to be the last attempt, either a success, or he would just give up trying. Satisfied, he grabbed one of his kitchen chairs, and planted it underneath the noose. Stepping on the chair, he slipped his head through the noose. He used his hands to tighten it around his neck. Exhaling, he kicked the chair out from under him.

He fell, the rope held onto him. He felt the air to his lungs restrict, and he felt that unwelcome refreshment of the essence, yet again fill his body. His arms jerked at his sides as the grey veins protruded over his skin. Air was completely exiled out of his body, and he felt his consciousness wane: if only it was that simple. Another type of essence entered his body, and the veins darkened from gray to black as he phased through the noose. Another failed attempt, and as promised, the last one.

That was the last straw. *I can't even die right!* He stared at the frying pan, stuck into the wall like a knife. He sighed as he turned and leaned against the sink. His head was raised up as the streams never stopped coming down. He was a slave to his own thoughts, and his master was relentless!

His trembling hands went back into his pockets. He took out his wallet and opened it. He found a picture and took it out. He opened up the folded photo. His hand trembled as he looked on sixteen faces in military uniforms. All of them were of the same height, half of them male, and the other half female. One of the women was wrapping her arms around the waist of someone else. That other someone was himself; his own face was scratched out of the picture.

He sucked in some air, clamping his teeth down. The tears rolled down a little faster onto the photo. *This fate is cruel.* He allowed his feet to slowly slip from under him. He looked closely at the photo. Their uniforms all had their number "Seven" on the patch, right above where the charging American flag would be, that is, if they weren't forbidden from wearing it. He glared up at the ceiling. *You mock me.*

He trembled, pulling himself from the ground. He leaned towards the sink again, glancing at the frying pan stuck in the wall. He took his spear and used it to walk, however shakily, towards the other room. This room was dark. He turned on the light.

This room was large, and square, and just like every other room in this house, this was next to empty. This had only two things in it, a sleeping bag, with no pillow, and a safe. That's it. Even the paint on the walls was bland and passionless.

He walked over to the safe and laid the spear to the side of his sleeping bag. He turned the knob of the safe to open it. There was no money, and nothing that anyone would find of value to steal. He pulled out a notebook and turned to a blank page. He brought a black inked pen to the page and his pen hand froze in place again as his hands trembled. He gritted his teeth once more, and his face twisted from abstract tormented sadness to nothing short of an ungodlike rage.

At last, he put the quivering pen to the page:

My name. My name. My name. Your name? What were they? Were they as generic as Michael or Samantha? Or were the names on your birth certificate more genuine, and more unique? I never knew your names. I don't even know what was written on mine.

What were we? For years we spent together, and we never even got a proper serial number. We were insignificant. Too insignificant and too much of a burden for the common man to even come up with a name, or even a number. They didn't even care enough about us to assign us a number.

What were we to them? Nothing more than a tool? A valuable all-purpose tool? A tool that only has one use, to strive for that sense of purpose. We obtained that purpose, for even a short while, now it's being ripped apart! Were we too expensive to keep around? Why even bother with us then?

I had but one wish, that this Hell could be undone. But what good of a world is that without conflict? We had no purpose without conflict. And we got rid of the conflict. We shot ourselves in the foot and watched it bleed!

Eight years it's been. Eight long damn years. I loved you. All of you. And I will never be able to tell that to your faces. I will never be presented with that gift, and now I am cursed to live in Hell. Yes, that is fitting for a wretch like me.

Funny, isn't it. I've killed more people than I care to count. It's funny, how someone like me, can take life so easily. The first one was someone close to me. The first. That was the only one that truly mattered. Every single one after that became nothing but a statistic. Why then? Why? Why do I still see their faces at night? Every single one of them? Can I not rip out my eyes? Then would I stop seeing them? No. I have no hope in that. Because now each face is seared into my brain.

I have no hope in life. I have no hope now in my living death. And I can't kill myself. I've tried too many times to count. Just the sadness of my heart, my heart, if I could rip it out to show the world, it would be filled with scars and bullet holes, but the wretched thing still keeps pumping! It still keeps beating as if it itself is too stubborn to die. Why can't I be like normal people? If they are sick and tired of it, they hang themselves and die. Why must I be cursed with a living death, and cursed to fail every single attempt? Damn it! I can't die right!

This gift I have, I know not how I got it, or why. I don't even know if you had this gift, but I imagine you don't. Not when I saw you being shot to shreds. Why can I fade through reality when you remain solid? I valued this gift enough when you were around because I needed to be alive to protect you, all of you. Now that you're gone, and I failed, why won't this just shut off and let me die?

What were your names? What was mine? We didn't have any. We didn't have any serial numbers. We weren't given any dog tags. We truly were given no identity, only to assume a fake one for the duration of your short lives, and for the rest of my cursed one. How fortunate you are, to be dead right now. You can't feel anything. You have no heart, and I myself am nothing short of a monster filled with ancient regrets. No.

That's not true at all.

After all my years of living, I have only one regret: not strangling myself with my own umbilical cord, now I can't even die right.

He closed the notebook. He placed it in the safe and locked it up. This notebook was the only thing keeping him grounded in the world. It was the only thing that allowed him to function every day. These little reminders helped remind him of his own suffering. He got into his sleeping bag and leaned his phone against the safe. He put it on, so the clock was facing him.

There was no need to set an alarm for himself. There never was. Not anymore. His eyes were drifting to sleep, and the clock read: 10:23 PM. *Here we go. Again. And again. And again!* His eyes closed as he drifted to sleep.

Chapter 8

Reassignment

~It was all a mistake, you see. I adopted a dream that wasn't mine, forced upon me with a promise, the reward for that promise was so great, I didn't care about the risk, however high that might be. That dream was to attain a world without war, and for a time, I succeeded. I suppose they kept their promise to me, that I wouldn't have to do any of it again. I was such an idealistic fool to believe them!

Sarah McCurdy sat on the plane as it soared through the air. The flight departed early in the morning, the vast majority of the passengers on the plane slept with night masks hanging over their face, or with their caps tipped down over their eyes. The flight attendants were disinterested in the passengers, hanging out in their little cubby area, some of them were on their phones when they thought no one was watching them. She leaned back in her chair, with her hands over her chest, looking out at the black sky, the darkness, she knew it all too well. She knew the night welcomed the threckets, and when darkness came, so did they. For whatever reason, nothing significant ever happened during the day, as if darkness can't survive in the light, but then again, can light survive in the dark?

Feeling her phone vibrate in her pocket, she opened it, seeing a notification of an email coming directly from Administrator Colton. She closed the screen and returned the phone back into her pocket, and pulled out her laptop from her carry-on, turning on the laptop to access her email. The email sent to her had multiple attachments, and this was a special email address, exclusive to the Caster Administration. This email read:

Major Sarah McCurdy,

As per our discussion, you are to perform a certain task in London. These attachments are to be forwarded to Administrator Sander for reassignment. You start immediately. There is only one reason, and only one goal. Do not fail the American Administration. Failure will mean further influence from the outside, and we cannot allow that for obvious reasons. Also, if you can manage to track down whoever it was at Dyatlov's pass and find out what their real goal was. Like I said, odds are, they are working against the Administration, but they must be affiliated with an administrative branch, and not the American one. However, even if he was affiliated with ours, we don't get too many casters from Georgia, like you suggested.

Regards,

Admin. Colton.

She hesitated in opening the attachments, "'Forwarded to Administrator Sander for reassignment,'" she whispered to herself. Releasing a deep sigh, she rested her chin upon her palm. *Colton, what exactly are we doing here? If the UK administration branch finds out— when they find out it was an American who stole the Grail, they will hunt you relentlessly. Just what exactly are you planning? I don't exactly trust the UK branch to do the right thing, don't make me regret this, Colton.*

Finally, she opened the attachments. Just her name, and complete file with the American Branch of the Administration. She immediately forwarded the attachments to the email provided and shut the laptop off, putting it back into her bag.

Adams' face came into her mind. His blood seeping out of his mouth as his life left his eyes. Her hand trembled in her seat. She felt like there was an anaconda in her chest. Wrapping its way around her lungs. Forcing her air out. She hid her trembling hand in her pocket. Her free hand clutched her chest. She breathed heavily. *Adams, why didn't you stay there to help. I didn't want to have to murder you.* She opened her trembling hand and closed it onto a fist. She repeated this several times until the trembling stopped and looked out the window. *That damned code. Don't they understand, a little part of us dies when we enforce that code. Silence, it's called. Absolute silence, and then erase the bodies as if they were never there. It's sickening! They're people, not just some mere pawns in a game of chess. It's sick!*

***

She kept her bags with her inside the taxi as she departed. She noticed the people seemingly cheery, as they always are, ignorant of the Hell that roams the streets at night. The rain was light with greying clouds above, emptying the heavens with dismal tears of the lives lost, especially Adams: Heaven wept for even someone like him, someone so insignificant.

The taxi dropped her off on Newman street.

The building before her was large, and had numerous windows, with bright chandeliers that could be seen from the outside. She walked up the large marble steps and opened the door. She carefully stepped inside, wiping off her shoes before she entered, walking on the beautiful green carpet, which looked much like a bed of majestic grass. There were many men and women about, talking with one another with pleasant tones, and seemed much more relaxed than they ever were in the American Branch. Many of them wore some semblance of a cloak, while others more casual attire.

She walked up to the receptionist, carefully placing her bags on the floor. She leaned over the desk, as the receptionist hung up the phone politely.

"Name?"

"Sarah McCurdy. American Branch. I'm being reassigned to the U.K. division," she answered.

The receptionist giggled, "Okay,"

The man behind her laughed at her. "The U.K. division? The U.K. doesn't have a division. Nope. Nope. Nope! This is Camelot little lady. The Heart of it all. I'd think you yanks ought to have known that by now."

Well, that was humiliating. She clenched her fist at her side, not appreciating the casual haze at her expense.

"One American transitioning to Camelot!" The receptionist said with a jeer. Her name tag read: Lois. "ID?"

"Sure," she pulled out her purple Caster ID. To the eye of a normie, the card was just as mundane as any business card. To another caster, the spell that bewitched it revealed everything about her: her ID number, address, name, aliases. The card afforded no privacy, "Here to see Administrator Sander for reassignment."

"One moment," she dialed an eight-digit extension. "Sander, I have a Sarah McCurdy from the American Branch who is transferring to Camelot. Okay. Right away sir." She turned back to Sarah. Follow those halls," she said pointing down a long corridor where the carpet turned from green to blue. The corridor was wide and had several paintings of historic figures hanging on the walls. "You are going to take a right at the end of the corridor and then a left. The door is locked, so you're going to have to knock."

"Understood," she said coldly.

She picked up the bags and about faced, marched through the room to get to the corridor. She could hear the snickering of laughing Brits from behind her. She ignored them as she entered the corridor and admired the paintings of the historic figures. She loved some of the old histories of the legends, which were greatly exaggerated to hide the actual truth behind those myths.

She made it to the end of the hall, where a giant portrait of the founder of the Caster Administration was. It was he who founded this administration, and it was he who put the oppressive codes in place. King Arthur, raiser of Camelot, Founder of the Caster Administration. For many, he was deemed to be a hero, fusing the box of Pandora to the Holy Grail, forever limited the chasmic rifts connecting Hell and Earth. But to others, like to Sarah, a symbol for oppression in a caster's world she had no stake in.

In this portrait, she gazed upon the scenery, wrought with war and corpses, slain by King Arthur himself, and in his left hand was a depiction of the Holy Grail with divine light emitting from its entrance, filled with crystalline water, and behind him, filled with all its curses, was the Box of Pandora, and it had been opened, never closed.

She passed on, continuing to follow the directions of the receptionist until she eventually came to that door. The door was wood, and plain. Upon the front of the door were numerous engravings, that, no doubt imbued the door for it to last. These engravings were outdated, written in Anglo Saxon, and this was the creed penned by King Arthur. Translated into modern English, it read: "I solemnly swear, as a Caster of the Administration, to uphold absolute secrecy, for the secrets of the world is not ready for the common person. This I swear, as a knight of this round table, to slay all demons who come crawling out from Hell. This I swear for life, and at the cost of it."

She knocked on the door with a heavy hand. She waited, still holding both of her bags at her side. The door swung open inward. There was a handsome man behind a desk, tall, and physically large, much like a marine, his hair was neatly combed, and it shined through the light. She looked at him as he was penning some paperwork. Right behind him was a woman, standing smugly behind him, leaning against the back wall, her arms disrespectfully crossing her chest.

"Come in," he said. She walked through the threshold. He tilted his head up with a smile, "Make sure to close the door."

McCurdy closed the door. She heard the locks and gears turning inside the door from unwanted ears and eyes from the outside. She didn't prompt the door to lock. She walked over to the chair, sitting down as directed.

"Welcome to Camelot," Sander said. "Well, we are much different from you people down at the American Branch. As you can probably tell, we can be relaxed but don't let that fool you, we can hold our own just fine here, especially at the epicenter of Pandora. So, tell me about this previous incident up in Dyatlov's Pass. It seems highly unusual, but that is usual for us."

"Yes, Sander," she began.

"Here, we don't use last names. I understand you are accustomed to that. Not here. Too formal. Here, I am Adam. If you want to be formal, just call me Administrator. This is Bridgette. You are Sarah," said Adam.

"Adam," Sarah started again before recounting all the data she had regarding Devil's Pass.

"Two possibilities. Either he's not one of us, or he is. If he's one of us, he must have gone rogue, and is just saying that to throw you off on the real reason he was there. We all know where the Grail is, so there would be no excuse for him to go *looking* for it there. Trying to get his hands on it is another matter entirely. If he is not one of us, he is probably the husk of some unfortunate soul who now must be put down because he was possessed by a threcket from Pandora. He could be an idiot too. That's also a possibility. Anything else?" Bridgette said.

"He did talk to me as if he wasn't one of us," she admitted. "I may have left that out."

"Yes, well, then he's probably possessed. Sucks for him now, doesn't it?" Bridgette said.

"Yes, well, Sarah, it isn't like you had a full team at your disposal to actually get enough information on the subject, and yet, we have nothing. We just simply have to wait for him to appear again, whenever and wherever that might be," said Sanders.

"But if he appears again, it could be—" Sarah objected.

"Catastrophic. I know. But we don't have enough information. So, if he ends up leveling an entire city with these creatures, that should be big enough to gather enough information," Sander replied. "Besides, there isn't enough information to go hunting on."

"So, you will sacrifice an entire city of people for him to show up again? You can't be serious!" *You heartless bastards!*

"Sarah," the look Bridgette gave was uncannily similar to that which a mother gives her small child when they draw all over the kitchen table, "You really have no one to blame but yourself for this. You have nothing for us to go on. You've given a location. That's it. He isn't going to be returning there, that's a fool's move. You really gave us no choice but to wait. So, if you have a problem with it, you can blame yourself for what is to come. It's as simple as that. I couldn't have stopped him alone, most likely. However, I could have at least gathered enough information for us to look into it. We have nothing. If you want to place blame on the Administration for allowing an entire city to die, well, blame yourself for not gathering enough intel for us to start a global manhunt."

"The blame isn't entirely on you. The American Branch should have sent someone out there last minute before they decided to send you up there. I don't know what they were thinking." He scratched his forehead. McCurdy was beside herself, not knowing how to engage in the irony of the power dynamic between Bridgette and Sander. Sander was the lead administrator of all the branches, and Bridgette, not sure what her status was, was undoubtedly lower, yet she carried with her the confidence of an administrator, "Bridgette, why don't you show her around. She must be tired. After all, it is going to be a long night."

"Understood, Administrator," Bridgette's tone turned cheery, "Well, let us be off then. I need to get my tea."

Sarah was put off by Bridgette's code switching. She couldn't trust someone who could cool down from a sharp attack to be a cheery guide with a few short exchanges.

The locking mechanisms released, and the door slowly swung open. Sarah grabbed her bags immediately as she stood up, walking right behind Bridgette. She understood her as a respectfully harsh woman, but one that didn't have a bad figure from behind. Much too tempting, and equally dangerous.

"So, when did you find out about your reassignment?" Bridgette asked her.

"Immediately after Dyatlov," she answered. "It was unexpected, but my administrator was quick to find a replacement."

"Ah, Americans, quick to act when it doesn't matter, but when any *important* decision is to be made, it seems like the entire world is filled with naught but red tape. Seriously, it is easier getting a corpse to move around."

McCurdy remembered something, that some researching caster, she couldn't remember his name, was trying to do some research into Necromancy. She was curious about the research that went into it, and she knew, just like elemental magic, it was a forbidden craft. Well, that isn't exactly the best explanation, more like a caster was insane if they so much as entertained the idea. A necromancy experiment had a failure rate of over ninety-nine percent. A failed attempt would mean either the death of the one casting the ritual, and destruction and contamination of existing materials for the ritual, or opening a portal into Pandora, allowing the caster in a weakened state to be possessed by a threcket coming out of Pandora; however, with the rumor of someone wanting to do research on the matter, she was curious.

"Bridgette, did anything ever happen with the research into Necromancy?" McCurdy asked.

Bridgette gave her a curious stare, "Oh, we never funded that research, nor are we going to. What on earth would we use it for? Besides, the person who was going to do research into it was given an ultimatum, he could do the research, but he wouldn't be with his unit anymore, because of numerous conflicts involved with it. Trust me, it is for the best no one messes around with it," Bridgette sighed. "Besides, only King Arthur ever succeeded in doing that. Same reason why no one researches elemental magic, while being able to use the elements as tools would push us leagues above those nasty little threckets, it's risky because it's almost impossible to control. Honestly, if someone wanted to do research into making that kind of magic usable, those resources would be better spent."

Well, that answers that. But she knew Bridgette was right, the risk far outweighed the reward, and shouldn't be entertained. *Except in the need to rattle someone.*

Bridgette walked her into the main lobby, with a tea kettle. She filled the kettle with water, flicking it on to a boil. She poured some milk in, hanging the teabag on the inside of the cup. The kettle beeped, and the light turned off on the side. She poured the boiling water into the mug, stirring some sugar in before discarding the teabag in the trashcan. Taking a sip, she inhaled the sweet fragrant aroma. Turning to McCurdy, "You want some?"

"I wouldn't mind."

"Help yourself," Bridgette said, reluctantly turning away from the boiling kettle. "By the way, there are no biscuits."

Sarah made herself a cup of tea in the same fashion.

"Okay, onto the tour, if you really want to call it that is all. You're not goin' to want to carry those all day. Let us get you to your quarters."

Sarah followed her with her bags at her right, and the teacup in her left hand, sipping the tea. It was okay, and something about it soothed her. *Maybe I should stop drinking coffee.* She followed her to the back of the main building, and through some large doors.

Bridgette was a talker, and she never stopped walking. Sarah half assumed Bridgette would have kept talking through the sips of her tea had it not been delicious. On the way, she noticed some elevators, some went up, but there were those elevators that *only* went down. These elevators were closer to the Archives, which seemed impressive on the outside. *A likely hiding place for the Grail, and other artifacts.*

Brigette took her through a large room, and pulled out her ID card, swiping it on the solid black console on the side. Sarah was amazed as she walked through the threshold of the room, at the pristine condition of the floors, cleaner than glass. The standard of cleanliness was much higher than any other barracks she has ever been in. The room was filled with numerous beds, some unoccupied, others had some sleeping or studying casters here.

"Let's get you a bed, now. Wouldn't want your precious belongings being stolen, now would we?"

"I'm staying here?" Sarah wasn't quite sure what to expect, but she figured there might be a little more privacy, not much, but not in an open space with numerous triple bunks.

"Yes. I don't care if it's not satisfactory or not. Yes. You sleep here. You live here. You eat here. You make friends or whatever it is you Americans do. We all do, well, most of us. Even I stay here." She escorted her to a triple-bunk. The desk beside it was equally tall and had support on all sides. "You get the top. I'm at the bottom."

"If you say so," she griped, handing Bridgette her tea. She climbed at the top of the bunk and lay her bags there.

"Well, get down now. We have more to see. Come on. I don't have all day you wanker."

"That was rude," Sarah rapidly blinked her eyes as she attempted to stare Bridgette down. *There is something wrong with this woman.*

"Who hucking cares! Just get down here."

Sarah climbed back down with haste.

"You know we're all casters here, right? You could have just jumped down. No one would say anything."

Bridgett was right. Sarah knew it, just, her casting abilities were under lock down, subconsciously trying to repress it, constantly denying who she was in front of her peers. Her brothers and sisters in arms were never really her own, isolated by her own birth, from her own inheritance.

"I'm sorry."

"Don't be sorry. Just lighten up. Sheesh. Come on! Off to my favorite place. The Archives. Oh, and by the way, you will get your own ID badge at the end of the day. Unfortunately, you're stuck with me until then. We can't just have you go off all willy nilly and just roam around freely, you'll get stuck somewhere."

"Yes, Ma'am."

Bridgette led her out of the room and the door shut behind them. She led her back towards the elevators and opened the door into the archives. The archives were filled with numerous filing cabinets, and shelves filled with innumerable books and tomes.

They went through the vast dusted off shelves in the archives, looking at the many impressive monoliths, portraits, paintings, scrolls, tomes, and of course even the carpet was decorated with many archaic, albeit, beautiful designs. Whoever funded these archives spared no expense, a price high enough for even a treasury.

Sarah saw stairs over to the side.

"Bridgette," she said as she drank the last of her tea.

"Hmm?"

"Those stairs. Where do they lead?"

"Well, I'm not supposed to acknowledge questions about it, but it should be common knowledge to casters at this point. We keep the

Grail there. It is under protection at all costs, those go down to the vaults where we keep some sacred artifacts, besides the Grail there. It is under lock down, impossible to get down to the lower levels without a key or capsizing the entire building."

Now, just an opportunity. I can frame her, if need be.

Chapter 9

Area 51

~We were supposed to get married on Saturday, but for her, Saturday never came.

Ghost was watching downwind in the arid heat. The day was still young, however, these past eight weeks felt like four decades! The heat was dehydrating them, and he was without sleep. He couldn't afford sleep, and neither could anyone else, not with the overwhelming rattling of gunfire, nor the roaring of engines, and the tremors from the earth underneath the massive weight of the tanks.

This was supposed to be a training exercise, but this was something more than just that. This was no exercise: this was a massacre. His ACR rifle was beginning to jam up. And he was running low on ammunition. He wasn't around any useless bodies he could easily loot for more. And only God knows how many more there were out there.

Ghost, Ticker, Butcher, and Slithers were hiding in a crater out in the desert. This was no natural crater, but a crater built by artillery strikes aimed directly at them. The sand was scorching hot, much like what Ghost imagined death would be. His hands held his rifle tight as the noise began to die down.

He could feel the sand pouring down his back from the sides of the crater as numerous trucks were driving by. The trucks were mounted with MGs, and bright flashing lights. He caught the sight of a car, splattered with blood like someone poured a bucket of red paint on it. The windows were smeared in it, and even the wipers were coated in the flesh of someone who blew up nearby, most likely another useless grunt caught in friendly fire. For now, they were safe, and out of sight in the crater, for how much longer, he could only guess.

"Ghost," Butcher whispered. She kept her hand on her rifle while pointed at him with three fingers. "What is going on?"

"For once, I don't know," he answered. His mind was rattled, still completely in the dark since the first shot, "And keep it down."

"Is everyone dead?" Slithers asked, her hands were burying her face. Her face was smeared with blood, but it wasn't hers.

"Ghost," Butcher's voice trembled. "What did you do?" She pointed her rifle at him. "What did you do?" Keeping low to the ground, he edged towards her training his rifle on her in response. He was already on high alert, even the smallest form of hostility forced him to react immediately.

Ticker sighed and dropped his rifle to his side. "Look, right now, that doesn't matter," he interrupted their little squabble. "Look, we need to find a way to get away from this all. We were fools."

"What do you know, Ticker?" Butcher demanded, she turned abruptly, face cringing as she spat on the ground.

"Don't you see? I pay attention. What are we? Soldiers. All we are, is an expendable asset, and nothing more. We are only tools to be used and then discarded. We should have seen this coming!" he answered. "There haven't been any wars lately! Hell, we haven't been deployed in two years!"

Butcher drew her knife and was prepared to throw it.

"No," Ghost replied, his finger hovered over the trigger, careful never to touch it until he intended to fire. "Butcher, that is enough. He's right. We should have—no. I should have seen this coming. I'm sorry."

"Captain," Ticker began. "Think of something, get us out of here."

Suddenly, the radio coughed. *"Captain? Are you out there?"* The voice of Venom said. Her sweet innocent voice spoke volume and trembled through the radio. *"Captain? Captain?"*

Venom was with one of four separate units of Task Force Seven split up into four for this training exercise.

"Answer that!" Butcher hissed.

"No," Ghost responded, he stood up as he scanned the blackened red horizon. "We can't, if we are going to get out of here."

"Everyone else is dead, damnit!" Butcher snapped again, her hand pointing a trembling finger at him. "How can you leave them to die like this!"

"They are soldiers, just like we are," Ghost told her. "We have to trust that they'll make it out. Besides, they're listening at least. If we make it known someone else other than she is still alive, we're only asking for more trouble than we already have."

The radio coughed, *"Captain? Is anyone out there? Is anyone there?"*

"Then do you have a plan?" Ticker asked.

Ghost put his hand over his mouth as he bowed his head down to the ground, scanning each independent grain of sand like each individual grain represented an idea. These ideas were innumerous and all bad. He sighed, "Well, we are going to need a distraction."

"God, no," Slithers looked up to him with wide teary eyes. Her hand clenched his tightly. "You can't possibly be considering killing her?"

"What? No. I would never even think about killing her, or any of you for that matter. Something that our dear leader would consider without a second thought. No. We need to get to Area 51. We'll blow up the pillars holding it in place, which will greatly affect the reactor below it."

"There are civilians nearby. Ghost, you are proposing desecrating the nearby cities. If we do this, we would be no worse than they. We would be murderers." Ticker looked at him with stretched eyes. Ghost could tell that despite of it all, he was not keen on getting innocent civilians killed, especially recreating Chernobyl.

"Look around you Ticker, like it or not we are murderers. We are the orphan makers!" Ghost snapped at him. "I don't like it, but that is our one chance out of here. All other chances are gone and will lead to one-hundred percent failure. This has a chance of success, no matter how small."

"Yeah, and what is the success ratio?" Ticker asked.

"Half of a percent," Ghost said. "They have us right where they want us. We are out of food and water; we'll be dead before the day is out. Whether by being shot or by natural means. We don't have the luxury of waiting for the perfect moment to strike. That is our only chance, and we need to take it, even if the odds are infinitely worse."

"A lot more people are going to die tonight," Ticker said, bowing his head with a graven face. "Is this what we've become?"

"The monsters and demons aren't hiding in our closets or under our beds. We'd be fortunate if they were that far away. How do you run from them when they're hiding in our heads?" Slithers asked. "We weren't born for this world. We were born with the sole purpose to live and fight for peace, and we've obtained it. Now there's no need for NATO anymore. There's no need for the military or hostile occupations. We've taken that need away. And now, we're meaningless. We were born with the sole purpose to live and die in obscurity," she wept softly. "Even if we did make it out, what would we even do? We have our lives ahead of us, and—and—and then what? We have no identity to stand on. We have no hope. We have no families, they're all gone. It will be impossible for us to integrate into society. We don't even know how they behave! Maybe it will be better if we all just lied down and died."

"Don't say that!" Butcher snarled, but even her harsh tone couldn't keep out the tears from her voice. "Don't you say that again!"

"No," Ticker wept, wiping the tears with his sleeve. "She's right. Can't you see it now? We were damned from the start. We have no friends. We have no family. We have no name and no identity. We lived and trained together for fifteen years, and this is our end. This is a tragedy if ever there was one. Can't you see it, how much better off the world would have been without us in it?"

Ghost caught a glimpse of Slithers as she bowed her head and folded her hands together, touching her forehead as saying one final prayer. She said something so inaudible, he had to pull in the air towards his ears to hear. The soundwaves from her soft voice traveled swiftly into his ears. "Mommy, I never knew you, and the only contact I've ever had was coming out. I never got to hear your voice. I never got to see your face. I never got to see your smiles and laughter and never got to experience the good times with you. I'm sure you're a good person, a much better person than I ever came out to be. I—I'm sure you wouldn't want to see me. Not like this. Not a murderer."

Ghost knew Slithers was talking to her own genetic parents, not the parental units they each were assigned far before they could remember. He was dreadfully assigned the Nakamura's. None of them knew where they came from; what state they were born in. Any identifying records were lost. Ghost knew, he actually looked. There was nothing, as if just a blank slate.

Slithers sniffed her tears and snot back into her nose and she turned to Ghost and smiled. A smile, how cruel of a mask. It could have been like a bandage, a useless tourniquet. It covered up the wound, but the pain still remained. All the emotional baggage was hidden away behind the façade. Her smile was like the whitest bandage, pure, and utterly pointless. It's only a matter of time before nothing will remain of that bandage, except when it's dripping with crimson blood. "Let's go. Let's go and make what's left of our lives count. We'll make it count for something, but for what, I don't know yet."

"To Area 51 it is then," Ghost repeated himself, stone-faced. "If we die tonight, we'll make sure they won't soon forget us. If we die, we'll drag that base and everyone in it down into the depths of the blazing hot sand with us."

"We'll be walking into Hell," Butcher stated, resting her arms at her side. She scanned the opposite side of the crater.

"You still don't see? We were born in it, destined to never leave," Ghost replied. His gaze narrowed.

The squad climbed up the blazing hot crater, slowly. Ghost ensured that the radios would be silent. There was no longer a need to use them. The rest of Task Force Seven was dead, dying, or as good as dead.

Helicopters hovered over the air, their blades spinning and dusting the sand, creating a smog. Soldiers in the helicopters aimed their rifles down towards the ground, as the choppers' searchlights from the helicopters moved on the sand. The bright light was blinding in the middle of the artificial sandstorms caused by the helicopter's blades.

The lights shined on Humvees and blown-up trucks, there was plenty of metallic debris stained with flesh and blood. A small unit of Humvees drove through the sand, windows open, and rifles pointing out of them from behind a masked face.

Ghost signaled them on the ground. The heat was still getting to them, but they knew how to survive in worse conditions. They were completely buried underneath the sand, crawling through the sand like worms in the dirt. They proceeded to crawl due south, towards Area 51.

The humming of the trucks grew louder as they scratched their ears. The vibration of the earth pounded against their bodies. They managed to crawl over six kilometers.

Ghost inhaled *essence* around the air, hearing a radio cough in the distance. *"Task Force Seven spotted at sector 8."* Immediately the vehicles revved up again and many soldiers started whistling. The helicopters shifted direction, flying west. The vehicles started driving faster than before in the same direction.

Ghost waited patiently. The pressure was lifted from their bodies, and all noises became distant. He immediately stood up from the sand, scanning the area with his rifle pointed down towards them. Butcher, Slithers, and Ticker did the same.

"Well, that is lucky," Ticker said.

"That, or insanely misfortunate," Slithers said.

"We need to start running," Ghost replied. "Our luck will eventually run out."

Ghost turned his radio on so he could listen in on the conversation between soldiers. He refused to say anything. They sprinted swiftly. He knew, he saw nightmares over and over again. No one makes it out without any scars, seen or unseen. Their lives were all fated to be a tragedy, one with no moral, no hope, and fraught with disaster and a never-ending pain. Truly, the world would have been a better place had they never been born. Two years from that day, contracts and agreements between all the nations were signed. Everyone agreed to it, Ghost was there. Two years since Task Force Seven was deployed. No one dared even to entertain the idea of bombing their neighbor again, not while they were in the picture. He did it. He achieved what most thought impossible: World Peace. And all it cost was their lives, their futures, and an enormous amount of murder.

How many families did I destroy for this?

The radio coughed, "*They moved onto sector six. We need to move now, and corner them there. They can't have much fight in them left.*"

"*How many do you count?*" Another voice came out. Ghost recognized it as General Snells.

"*Four, sir.*"

"*How many bodies are accounted for?*"

"*Eight, sir.*"

"*Ghost?*"

"*Negative.*"

"*His squad is still alive somewhere. Watch your six.*"

"*Roger.*"

That tells me what I need to know, he sighed.

"Ghost!" Butcher exclaimed. "Sector six is on the way."

"I know," Ghost replied. "They're going to be in the way."

"You have to be considering stepp—" Butcher began.

"I reconsidered it. Not worth it," he interrupted. "We need to focus on our own task. Even if there were four more, I have no idea what the numbers on the other side are. Even I can't predict that. Besides, we're all exhausted as they are. Even with four more, we won't last the night."

"But—" Slithers protested.

"No buts. This is final. Look, we need to hide back in the sand. They will be coming here shortly," Ghost snapped.

The four of them buried themselves back under the scorching sand. They waited. Their hearts beat through their chest as the vehicles rolled back over the sand. The helicopters were churning their blades in the air, pushing the sand away as they hovered over Sector six. The soldiers were making their way down the crater towards a large-abandoned building, and hid behind some scattered debris, some were large helicopter doors which were scorching hot with the flames.

Another officer called out on a megaphone.

"Task force Seven. I know you're in there. You are surrounded, and we know you can't continue for much longer. Come out, and this won't have to get violent. Just stand trial for your crimes, and no harm will come to you until after the trial."

What crime?

"What crimes did we commit?" said another voice. It was Viper. "What did we do? Tell us that and then we'll consider coming out! Otherwise, you'll just have to blow us up in here."

A feisty one she was. Ghost remembered her well, she was hard on the outside, but had a little soft spot for Ticker.

Ghost got out from the scorching hot sand. He scanned the area before hiding behind mounded rocks. Ticker, Slithers, and Butcher followed silently, but close behind him. They were concealed from the rest of the U.S soldiers and they could get a better glimpse. The sand was stained red. The soldiers were still numerous, and too many for Ghost to guess how many there were.

He peered over the rock, down a large basin with a square building. The building was abundantly surrounded, and the soldiers placed claymores around the exits. MGs were stationed around every blockade and protected with a three-inch steel plate. In front of the building were four iron poles, freshly erected for the occasion. *How respectful. They really put a lot of thought into this.*

The silence was deafening. Ghost examined the scene, calculating all possible next moves, knowing the wrong one would be the end of it, and they wouldn't complete their mission. Task Force Seven needed to make a move, because the good old brothers of arms were willing to wait. After all, they had all the time in the world. Task Force Seven was the one running out of time.

Venom, they can wait. You must do something. You and Viper.

Nothing happened. The soldiers began stretching, still cautiously watching the building. What appeared to be an eternity passed. And then it happened. Glass was broken from the windows. Guns, unprimed grenades, and knives were just tossed out of the window. The front door was kicked down. The soldiers immediately focused their attention on the door with their rifles aimed down, their fingers just above their triggers.

Ghost clutched his chest. *They had given up and had enough.* He let out deep measured, but silent breaths.

Venom walked out with her hands up. She was weeping tears of anguish, and her face grimaced, shining bright with the flames. "Don't shoot. I'll come out. I just want a fair trial."

Viper hesitantly walked out, her hands behind her back. She glared at all the soldiers, baring her teeth at them. She let out a sigh before looking up at the sky. Tears streamed down her face as she grimaced. Her hands made angry fists behind her back.

Wraith came out, his hands atop of his head. He glared at everyone, not letting anyone out of his sight. Ghost knew something, this wasn't going to be peaceful at all. They were utterly alone down there. Wraith stood behind Viper, never looking to the ground, never to the sky, and he didn't let tears swell his eyes, as if he held some small fragment of hope that there was the faintest chance he could survive, but it was clear that even he was jaded.

Finally, Metal came out. He was a little taller than the rest of them, but he was the youngest of them all. His hands were folded in front of him as he reluctantly walked forward. His steps were small, and his knees trembled beneath him. His head was bowed down low as he came out, grinding his teeth.

"We're out. You damn bastards! What was our crime?" Wraith demanded. "I want answers, and I want them now!"

"You will be tried. Cuff them," came the officer's voice. He was smoking a cigar and kept his left hand in his pocket.

"Not until we get our answers!"

"You will be cuffed, or I will light you up right here!" General Snells scolded. "With what you did, you're lucky you're getting that much. You've already been tried, traitor!"

This stifled Wraith.

Sixteen soldiers sprinted up to them. They kicked the back of their knees. They cried out in pain as they hit the ground. They were cuffing their ankles and wrists. Knees were pressed into their backs, and they were crying, all except Wraith. He was scanning the basin for a way out.

Viper cried the loudest. Her screams were heard from miles like a dying banshee, waiting to be released from this Hell. She, Venom, and Metal were waiting for the sweet release of death, as Death had always been their one true friend.

Ghost couldn't look away, no matter how hard he tried to force his head down. It was as if his body refused to move, like he was stuck in a single time frame while the rest of the world continued to move.

Venom, Viper, Metal, and Wraith were struck in the back of the knees with batons, crying out as they collapsed forward. These batons swung wildly. They tried to move away, but these soldiers swiftly tied them with zip-ties. The soldiers beat them relentlessly, until blood spilled on the ground. These four from Task Force Seven just wept, unable to move. Satisfied, apparently, the soldiers dragged them through the sand, hoisted them up on these erected pillars, and tied them firmly with rope, chains and duct tape. Ghost assumed these soldiers believed them to be monsters, and needed to be as secure as possible, and in order to kill one of them, they needed to be brutalized beyond repair.

General Snells paced back and forth. Their faces resembled that of mere dogs trapped in a cage by a master who's beaten them so many times they anticipated the strike. The man was terrifying, and even more terrifying for a dog who was on its last legs.

"You want to know your crimes," he said. "Treason."

"What did we do?" Venom sobbed, her face cringing. "We didn't do anything! What did we do to deserve this? We fought for you so that you could hide behind us! Your Medal of Honor is a disgrace! That belongs to us!"

Truth is the only mistake they ever made was being born. Now they know not to make that mistake again. The more he looked on, the more he saw the events unfold, Ghost felt unnecessary, and his whole life was a lie. One thing he slightly understood now, having Snells confirmed it, the reason this was all happening was because of something Task Force Seven did, and it was labeled as *Treason*. But what was it? His eyes narrowed as Snells flicked the cigar out of his mouth.

Snells glared at them as he took multiple steps back, "Light them up."

"What?!" Wraith protested. "You said—"

His voice was abruptly drowned out by the road of rapid gunfire. The four of them screamed as their eyes widened at the onslaught, the flashing lights of the guns coming for them. Their bodies were penetrated with bullets, ripping apart their uniforms and flesh. They cried out, but their screams were voiceless.

But one voice reached above the gunfire, only one voice. The voice of Viper, "MAMA!" she cried. Her left arm was completely severed, and blood came out of her mouth. She looked to her left, Venom was already dead, her head dropped down as her waist fell from her torso. Her cries became screeches as she was pelted with more burning bullets into her torso. She turned the other way, and saw Wraith, he was already dead, numerous bullets made it through his skull. Her other arm was finally severed. And then onto Metal, who had it worse of all, his head had finally been sliced from his neck, and his chest was already opened up, his heart and intestines falling out of his torso like a drooling mouth.

"MAMA!" she cried, louder than before. Her eyes were stretched open as her chest started to open with the gun fire. "MAMA!" She could feel her waist coming apart, "MAMA!"

Ted woke up, springing himself up from his sleeping bag. Crossing his arms over his chest, as if trying to hold on to something. A violent scream expelled from his mouth as tears streamed down his face again. He coughed, sucked in his teeth, his eyes wide open, grimacing with his own torment.

He sees this in his sleep, again, and again, and again!

He slowly turned to his phone to look at the time. It read: 10:53 PM.

Chapter 10

Evasion

~The world is a funny place. You can sacrifice your life and soul for the world, and it will never return your kindness. The world is such a cruel mistress.

Samantha was running later than usual. Her heart was pumping in her chest heavily, feeling the sense of anxiety swelling over her like a plague. She sat in the shuttle, anxiously tapping her finger on the cold window as she watched the pedestrians. With every stop, ever moment the shuttle stayed still, she felt like she was going to be late to Park Street. She nervously chuckled, such a silly thing to be concerned about, being late of all things. *Sam, you need to stop bringing work home with you.*

The shuttle dropped her right off at South Station. She walked up the stairs and stepped into the busyness of Downtown Boston. The cars drove by, blasting their music with their windows down. Buses made their stops right next to her, letting numerous people off, she smiled at the people as they came off, either distracted with their phones in their hands, nodding off into some world. Others seemed jaded, as if they were repeating the same routine, again, and again, and again.

She walked west on Summer street. She paid close attention to the cars, and the streetlights. Surrounded by tall skyscrapers, she felt insignificant, in a city filled with so many skyscrapers representing decades of hardworking individuals. She wanted that success.

She crossed the street onto the side of a convenient store. There were several men there, some lively, smoking cigarettes or joints, with no care in the world.

Samantha had always been a people watcher, but not often did people stick out to her as much as the man sitting across the road, on a side street. He was perhaps in his forties with an ungroomed beard with white streaks in it. His eyes looked exhausted, much like Ted's, and in his mouth was a cigarette, and in his left trembling hand was a paper bag, held in such away where she could tell plainly, there was a bottle in there. Whisky, gin, bourbon, or some other cheap but strong liquor as his breath reeked of it. Hanging around his neck was a pair of dog tags. His coat was tattered, with an American flag on the shoulder, also fading in color.

She sighed as she looked around the area for a bank. *No. That won't help him.* She walked into the convenient store. She looked around, speeding her way into the refrigerated section and pulled out two bottles of water. *I might as well, while I'm here.* She turned and looked around for something suitable, and nutritious to eat, one where she didn't risk killing him because she didn't know if he was allergic to anything. She found a salad with chicken in it. *Better than nothing.*

She didn't bother with any plastic silverware, there likely was none to be found.

She walked out of the convenient store with her purchases and walked down the side street: Arch Street. The man's eyes were fading out into sleep. She went up to him and placed one of the bottles of water next to him and left the salad next to that.

She left him to drift off in his sleep. Images and video clips flashed across her mind of soldiers, laying on the street with nowhere to go, no one to call, and were just left, abandoned on the street. *I wish I could do more; you all deserve so much more than this.* Sam assumed this man was one of the tens of thousands of veterans who were left abandoned by the country they sacrificed so much for. She had enough money to live off, that was true, but she had little in the way of spare change. She didn't have her big-refrigerated freight customer for very long, and she was waiting for her first commission check, which would allow her more freedom to help more strangers she walked into, like this one. *But there is only so much one person can do.*

She walked up Summer street. She was in no hurry to get to the study on time, as the topic was indeed depressing, and she was already late, and she already decided this was a silly thing to be anxious about. Despite her rise in anxiety, she intended to walk ever so patiently. She walked through the streets, watching the lights flicker on, and some of the summer performers playing around in the trafficless square that separated coffee shops, clothing stores, and Downtown Crossing over towards Washington Street.

The moon peered out from behind a veil of clouds from on high. She looked up as the blue mystic light shone down on her. She took a deep breath as she kept walking further on the street. Summer turned into Winter real fast. The moonlight was hidden by skyscrapers, but at the end of this street was Tremont. The corner of Tremont and Winter was decorated with the state flower of traffic cones, parked behind was a police cruiser, with the office leaning against his car, looking at the traffic. His eyes seemed emotionless as she passed by.

She waited with a score of people of diverse origins, waiting at the wide cross walk to cross Tremont Street, the wide street that always had construction here for some reason or another. *It's been the same for years. What are they doing?* She wondered.

The traffic lights turned from green to yellow, and at last red. The cars came to a halt, except the one who was speeding through the yellow light and just missed it. Massachusetts drivers, you can't trust them. They're insane. The cross lights permitted her to cross the street. She ran across diagonally to Park Street because the window for authorized walking was limited. On the front steps of the church were people sitting on the marble steps, many with a joint hanging from their lips. Their clothes were tattered and not well kept. There were flies buzzing around, and she wasn't surprised, one of them smelled like they soiled themselves, the rank reaching her nostrils. She assumed they were homeless, and this was the one place they could socialize, seemingly without the police arresting them for loitering.

Not wanting to be rude, she briskly walked up Park Street to the glassy entrance of Café.

Her phone buzzed in her pocket. It was buzzing a lot these days, between high alert news, to grocers and reefer trucks going out of business, which was good for her, but terrible for the competition. She felt bad for them, and that was the one part of her job she hated. She had to beat those rates down with the drivers, even if they were desperate to get out of Maryland or California, they'd take any rate. Today, the truck driver was beat down so low, she was certain the driver took a $200.00 dollar loss taking the load.

She pulled out her phone and opened the email.

Samantha Harris,

Driver picked up PO 3840172 at Shed Baltimore, MD. 1834 PM. CI 1534 PM CO 1834 PM. Groceries. 30 pallets sideways. Outbound to Cincinnati OH.

Regards,

After Call.

She let out a sigh of relief. It was a close one, the load never got picked up. But something was in Ohio, enough where the driver was willing to take a steep loss on it. He'll make up for it. She smiled as she walked up the street. Her phone buzzed again.

She looked at it again before turning to the glass doors, reading *breaking news! China enters in trade war with U.S.A.* Staring at it, her hand trembled with the phone. She sat down on the stairs for while she read the article.

News was filled with nothing but horror stories these days. Europe seemed to be in flames, and Asia was not far behind it what with all the declarations of war and last-minute alliances that occurred with the dissolvement of NATO. *What were they thinking?* U.S.A seemed to be out of it for the most part. For that at least she was relieved. She didn't want to think about what a war with U.S.A would be like. As it stood, the U.S.A seemed to be out of everyone's conflict since about ten years ago.

According to White House officials, negotiations with important nations which disbanded from NATO are falling through. The world is in shambles right now and the only thing that is certain is uncertainty. U.S.A is trying to maintain relations with nations formerly within NATO after what they call it, "A colossal mistake!" Eastern and Western European countries are at war with another, and many nations in Africa have followed suit. Fortunately, the instability hasn't quite made it to the Americas, but White House Officials state it is only a matter of time.

The world is filled with uncertainty. White House officials announced that it has entered a trade war with China, they implied that negotiations went nowhere, and that China was not amiable with them. When asked further about the future with China, White House officials stated that the future is uncertain, and updates will follow. However, they are anticipating a declaration of war from China.

Opinion: it seems rather unclear why the U.S would enter a trade war with China. It is even much unclear as to why they're anticipating war, unless nations are like dominos, next to one another, once one falls, another falls, tumbling after the one next to it. There is little information being revealed to us, and our nation's leaders are hiding something from us.

"Well, there's a surprise," she said sarcastically to herself. She looked up to the sky, now empty. She grimaced as she put her phone in her lap. She bowed her head down as she began to pray silently to herself.

After her silent prayer, she looked at her watch. It was 7:27 PM. Large group was over or ending. She stood up and went inside and went to the welcome table. The receptionist was still very much disinterested as he was paying attention to something on his computer screen. She pulled out a name tag, wrote her name on it, and placed it on her suit. She then took out a cup and put it underneath the cheap coffee machine, placing a coffee cup in the machine and clamped it back down, waiting for the coffee to drip.

As her coffee finished pouring out, the rest of the members of Café were walking out of the fellowship hall and into their various small groups. Samantha followed as Jennifer came out.

"Hiii!" Jennifer called out, running to Sam's side. "Isn't it a little late for coffee?"

"Too late and coffee should never be in the same sentence," Sam answered, smiling back at her. Jennifer and Sam walked side by side like two best friends in middle school.

"Hey, you didn't by chance see Ted out there, did you? On your way in?" Jennifer asked. She still had that giddy smile on her lips.

"No. I can't say I have," Sam answered, confirming her suspicion that Jennifer might have a thing for Ted. "Did he not show up?"

"No. Maybe it's nothing. Maybe he'll be here shortly. He did say he was coming back," Jennifer said.

"You seemed to get along with him well last Tuesday," Samantha responded.

"Yes, I did. He seems pleasant enough, oddly romantic." Jennifer snickered as they turned the corner into the granary room, getting into their corner of the table, waiting for others to start trickling in.

"Well, you did say once you prefer a man in a candlelight setting. Like a romantic emphasis from a Jane Austen Novel. Which one did you want? Was it Knightly or Darcy? Is he a keeper?"

"If only I could get those Knightly qualities in someone like Darcy," she laughed. "Hard combination to come by. Ted could be Knightly," she joked.

"I get that," Sam replied.

"No Ted tonight?" Tim asked as he sat down next to them.

"Regrettably, no," Jennifer replied, looking at him in the eye. "I was really looking forward to seeing him again."

"Don't you have his number?" Sam asked. "Text him."

"I'm not going to pressure him just yet," Jennifer smiled suspiciously. "You can't just push him to come if he doesn't want to. Look, if he doesn't show up, I'll text him and tell him he's missed."

"Fair enough," Samantha said. *She's totally into him.* And she was amazed at Jennifer's self-control, not texting Ted right away, or so she said. Samantha turned to Tim, "Where's Michael?"

"He was with me a short while ago, but he said he had to go back to the office to check on emails. He got some breaking news or some bother that he thinks is going to affect him," he replied. "He said he'll meet us at Teri's."

"Did he say what it was about?" Samantha asked.

"Something to do with China," Tim answered.

"I see. He probably has to work another hour to read the room." Sam suggested, assuming it would take that long for Michael to get a grasp on what was likely to happen to his account with work.

Jack interrupted everyone, "Welcome to Café, welcome to connecting group. I see we still have a few stragglers and new faces. So, that we can all get a sense of one another, I'll start. Say your name, where are you from, what brings you to Boston? And the icebreaker, hmm." He said as he scratched his neck as he looked up to the ceiling. "If you could meet any person, living or dead, real or fictitious, who would it be? My name is Jack, I am from Houston Texas, and I work as a nuclear physicist at a nearby nuclear power plant. I came to Boston for work. If there is someone I would like to meet? Julius Robert Oppenheimer, I'm really interested in his thought process in the Atom Bomb."

They all went down the line, introducing themselves with elation, giving them their background information, and locality. It was routine for everyone, but the differing perspectives always kept things interesting. Even though Sam had known Michael, Tim, and Jennifer the most closely, she couldn't say she knew everything about them.

The line finally made it to Tim, "My name's Tim. I am from Colorado, Denver specifically. I came to Boston for college, and I settled here over in Dorchester. If I could meet anyone, living or dead, I'd have to say Jesus."

"No! No! No!" Jennifer exclaimed, pointing at him. "No. Bad. Tim. Bad. No cop outs! We all want to meet Jesus. No! I *demand* a do-over!"

The room settled with laughter.

"But I really want to—"

"Tim. Bad. Bad Tim. No! No! No!" she exclaimed. "Give us something juicier than that!"

"Fine," Tim chuckled. "Hmm. Come back to me."

"Cheater," she elbowed him. "My name is Jennifer, I am originally from upstate New York, and I moved to Boston for a change in scenery. New York is terrible. I am a biological researcher right around the corner. If there was anyone I wanted to meet, dead or living? Real or fiction? Well, King Arthur. I've always loved his tales as heavily fabricated as they are. He was such the romantic."

"Not Mr. Darcy?" Sam joked.

"Oh, please, Darcy and Arthur, there just isn't any comparison!" she said.

The room was filled with laughter. It was clear that Jennifer was the life of the group, or the class clown. Sam wondered how she behaved at work. She let her own laughter subside.

"Well, my turn! My name is Samantha, I also moved here for work after college. I am moving back. I was from Peabody, went to school down in Virginia, and am relocating back up here when I took a job as an account executive for a Logistics brokerage," she began. "If there is anyone that I want to meet living or dead, and not Jesus since that's off the table," there was another chuckle across the room. "Well, let's go historical shall we, I've always wanted to meet Joan of Arc. Her story sits a special way with me."

"As you can see, we are a very diverse group of people," Jack said. "So, if any of you are new here, and I think there are a few of you, we just started Ecclesiastes. We are going into the second chapter, so without further ado. . ."

***

Samantha joined everyone at the back end of the bar of Teri Nation, it was a slow night. There was no one except the food runner, and Scott, who seemed very happy with bright shining eyes and a smile past that thick black beard. Samantha, Erin, and Jennifer sat together at the bar as Tim and Brian were chatting away behind them, not ready to get a drink.

"What are we having today, and no Michael?" Scott asked.

"Nay—" Jennifer began. "Well, the eccentric drinker should be coming in rather shortly, or so he said."

"He did, but Tim said that. And you know how spontaneous Michael can be. He might just not show up," Sam replied.

"Who did Tim say wasn't coming?" Came a loud obnoxious voice behind them. Sam, Erin, and Jennifer looked behind to see Michael smiling down on them, his hands resting on Erin and Jennifer's shoulders.

"You," Jennifer said. "Dang it. And here I thought I was going to have a normal drink for once, like some brandy, a glass of wine, a beer or even some rum and coke. Oh well, I guess my dream died early tonight."

"No one's stopping you," Michael laughed, turning to Scott. "Bar Tender's special! Whatever that is!"

"You're stopping me," Jennifer smirked. "Make that two, and for God's sake, don't spit in it like you did three weeks ago."

"That was sweat!" Scott laughed.

"I was joking," Jennifer replied.

"So was I," Scott sneered as he cleaned the bar top and ducked down to get some glasses.

"Just the dark Crellic," Erin asked.

"Cab, for me, please," Sam asked.

"Make that together," Jennifer said. She slipped her card over to Scott. "Close it out if you would."

Scott hastily went over to pour the wine and simple beer for Erin and Sam. He sliced some cucumbers, mixing in muddled mint and blueberries, poured in some vodka and soda water, and what Sam guessed was simple syrup, and he started shaking them all together.

"I don't see Ted. I take it he elected to go home earlier today?" Michael asked.

"No, he didn't show up," Samantha said.

"Erin. You work with him, right?" Michael asked. "How is he?"

"I don't know. He made another big deal again. This was one of those one-offs and not likely something he's going to repeat." She said as she sipped her beer. "I don't know how he does it, he must be really lucky or have some insider information, but even if he did, there is no way he can accurately predict when something will just plummet. Even with inside information, he can't make those calls at precisely the right time. Yet, he is making those calls at precisely the right time. He seemed fine though, but when he made the deal, he seemed disappointed."

"How much was the deal worth?" Michael said, his eyes widened in curiosity.

"Our manager clocked it in at $350K," she said. "I don't care who you are, no one can predict the market the way he does. He is consistently beating it, even with all of the uncertainty in the world. It's like he can see the future."

"But why was he disappointed," Sam asked. "Shouldn't he be happy with that?"

"I don't know. I know I'd love a deal like that! But I am nowhere near to his expertise actually," Erin explained. "He also has the nasty habit of leaving late and arriving early. However, he left earlier today, in the middle of a meeting."

Scott came back with the drinks. They were identical and had a foggy color to them. He slid the drinks on the table to Michael and Jennifer. Jennifer took a sip. "Wow, so this is what it's like to be on cloud nine. Tell me, you didn't spit in it did you?"

Michael took a sip of his.

"Just his," Scott answered, laughing because he wasn't serious. Michael coughed and spat it out.

"Now, now, Michael, I'm sure he's joshing you," Jennifer sneered.

"Who even says that anymore?" Michael chuckled, and his smile lit up.

"I said what I said!" she took another sip. She licked her lips. "Not bad, this one."

"Hey, Scott?" Sam asked.

He was about to turn to another guest before he turned back to her. "Yeah, Sam?"

"That man, that we met two weeks ago, over in the corner. Has he been coming here often?" she asked.

"Yes. He usually just gets a glass of wine and some potatoes," he answered. "He is always pleasant. He didn't show up last week though."

Sam knew that to be true. *Wait a minute.* "Last week? Do you mean he was here earlier?"

"Yes. He left fifteen minutes before you arrived," he answered, turning away to address the rest of his guests around the bar.

"That's not good," Erin said. "I'll try to talk to him tomorrow if I can. I have plenty of reasons to."

"I can't say I'm surprised," Michael commented, sipping his drink, whatever it was. "After all, the discussion we had was depressing."

"And to continue it today would have been worse," Sam admitted.

"It is depressing if you don't finish the context," Jennifer commented. "The moral of Ecclesiastes was and always will be, is that if this world is all there is, and God doesn't exist, anything we do is pointless. Our friends are pointless, our family is pointless. Our accomplishments don't mean anything and even our marks on history are pointless as they won't stand forever," she sighed. "But that doesn't mean that we should stop trying to live our lives," she pulled out her phone and scrolled through her contacts. She texted a message, "I just texted him. Hopefully, he'll say something."

"I'm sure it's nothing," Michael said. "Besides, the world is crazy right now. I wouldn't be surprised if he's just exhausted all of the time and needs a break. I haven't done stocks, but I imagine its exhausting work."

"Yeah, it is!" Erin said, taking a gulp from her beer. "You have to pay attention to everything that's going on in the world. Literally anything could affect the market from good news, bad news, global news, a shipping company goes out of business, or even the materials of certain commodities skyrocket into the air. The more information one has the better, the problem is there is so much information to digest, and not every single thing is going to affect the market. Like, Michael did you read about that Trade War thing?"

"Yeah, that's why I wasn't at Café today," he answered.

"I read the same thing too," said Sam.

"Yeah, well, it's like this. Something like that is undoubtedly going to affect the market, it's probably going to crash, my assumption of course," Erin replied, tilting her arm as if to illustrate a graph, "Now, let's say that Trade War was with China and Russia instead of the U.S. There is a high likelihood that it will affect the market with increased commodity prices since we get a lot of business from China. There is no guarantee that *that* Trade War will directly affect our Market. Its effect on the Market would be indirect to us over here in the U.S. but it will likely affect it, if not immediately. But there is no promise that it will send the market down. Many people will assume that it will, and then sell their assets, hoping to buy them all back when it goes below, this is called shorting a stock, but the way the market works, that kind of behavior may drive the value of the assets up instead of down, causing a lot of people to lose out on money. But since it's us, I'm sure the market is going to crash, it's just a matter of when."

Samantha was annoyed. There were way too many variables with finance, stocks specifically to care about it. Honestly, she never got into finance for that very reason, and she didn't care to have it repeatedly explained to her.

"Well, that is going to make my head hurt. I'll stick to my 401K thank you very much," Jennifer said. "So, what's everyone doing Saturday?"

"I'm free," Michael said without skipping a beat.

Erin and Sam both nodded.

"Excellent. It's decided then. I'll see all of you Saturday, and Tim. Hopefully I can get Ted to come," Jennifer said, clapping her hands.

"What are we doing and where are we going?" Michael asked.

"Why, my house silly," she smiled at him with her bright smile. "Game night of course. I have a little game we play there. It's a great way to get to know your friends."

"Okay. Time?"

"Noon is fine," Jennifer said. "I've got the refreshments already arranged!

Chapter 11

Game night

~It was all a mistake.

J ennifer woke up Saturday morning bright and early. She stretched out as the sun beamed down on her face. She yawned and stepped outside of bed and moved over to her nightstand. She picked up her phone to check for her text messages, checking to see if Ted responded. Her texts looked lonely on the screen: *Ted, we're meeting at my house for some games, Samantha, Michael, Tim, and Erin. I did invite a few more that I'm not sure you met or not. Text me later.* The text message was alone, like it didn't want a response. She stared down at it, contemplating what to do with it. She put the phone on the nightstand again and crossed her arms around her chest, violently tapping her arm with an intense index finger. "Tedward!" She finally decided to pick up the phone again and hit the phone icon.

The phone rang, dialing the number that Ted gave her. *I really hope he didn't give me a fake number. If he did, there's nothing I can do.* The phone rang a second time. *Come on Tedward. Wakey Wakey!* It rang a third time before forwarding to his voicemail.

"You've reached Ted. I'm sorry I can't get to the phone right now. Please leave your name, phone number, and brief reason for your call and I'll get back to you as soon as possible."

Beep.

"Ted, this is Jennifer, I hope you're not ignoring me. Please get back to me, you're invited to my place for some games and dinner today—"

"Hello?" the voice on the other end of the phone picked up.

Jennifer was surprised, not thinking that cell phones would allow someone to answer mid voicemail. Her smile lit up her room, even though only she was in it, "Heeeey, there buddy! This is Jennifer."

"I know," he chuckled. *"I memorized your number. How may I help you?"*

"So, the reason I'm calling is because I'm hosting a small group of friends, I'm not expecting more than ten of us, for games, drinks and food at my place today. We're starting around noon today, and I want to invite you here for that also," she brought down the excitement in her voice, speaking softly into the phone. "By the way, we missed you this week!"

"I see," he said, his voice went soft over the phone. *"This is kind of sudden, to be frank."*

"I texted you Tuesday about it. You never answered," she said back to him. "Come on, what better way to get closer to your friends over games and fellowship."

"Uhm. I don't know."

"What? Do you have plans already?" Jennifer asked him.

"*No.*"

"Then come on. Look, if it means that much to you, you can take me shopping next week," she joked.

"*I don't recall making an active effort to take you shopping,*" he replied.

"Well, at least I got a full sentence out of you. Can you do me a favor?" she asked.

He chuckled on the other end of the phone. "*What?*"

"Do you have a pen and some paper," she asked.

"I do."

"Take my address down. You're coming. I won't take no for an answer."

"*What am I, your servant?*" he asked.

There was some silence on the phone. Jennifer turned her head and then back to the phone as if she was consulting an imaginary friend. *He might find this funny,* "Yes."

He burst out laughing on the other end of the phone, "*As you wish, milady.*"

"There's the romantic Tedward I know," she laughed and gave him her address, certain that he was actually writing it down. "Ted, it starts at 12:00 PM. You can come early or come later. Or on time. That's cool too. Up to you. But you are coming! Or I'll track you down to the end of the earth and feed you my amazing, boxed macaroni and ketchup."

"*Ketchup?*" he sounded confused.

"There may or may not be cheese involved in some way shape or form. I don't know. Maybe you don't have to find out, huh? Just come," she joked.

"*Do you need me to bring anything?*"

"Just yourself," she answered.

"*I see,*" he gave his reserved few-word answer.

"I speak for myself and everyone coming that you should also bring clothes. Yeah, that's a good idea. Don't come naked. That would make for a rude awakening, although a very comical story a year down the road."

He chuckled again, "*Okay, I'll see you there. Is there anything else?*"

"No. Just give me a time when you'll be here."

"*I'll probably make my own lunch, so I'll probably be there around one.*"

"Okay, we'll see you then!" She exclaimed before hanging up the phone. She immediately started a group chat with Michael, Tim, Erin, and Samantha. *He's coming. He'll be here around 1:00PM today.*

She hastily went over to her kitchen and poured herself a bowl of cereal and milk. She started cataloguing the games she wanted to have available for them, as well as making the plans to order the pizza. She swiftly ate her cereal before arranging things around the living room, making plenty of space available for the "Acting Game". She didn't have the cards for the physical game, but it was a close substitute.

Hours passed. Jennifer had gotten everything ready, the drinks were in her cooler, and of course the pizza was on its way. She ordered four pies to be safe: pepperoni, chicken and broccoli, cheese, margherita pizza. That would satisfy everyone with their dietary restrictions. She didn't think any of them were vegans, God forbid, at least it wasn't clear; however, she did in fact know Tim was a vegetarian.

There was a knock on the door. She quickly glanced at her watch, which read 12:03 PM. She immediately went to the door to answer it. Samantha smiled as the door was opened. She entered the apartment. "Sorry I'm late. There was some problem on the redline today."

"What happened? Did it derail or something? I hate that line," Jennifer asked.

Michael was behind her. He lived in the same neighborhood over by Davis Square, the place he calls, "Heaven on Earth".

Michael laughed, "When was the last time you heard someone say they liked the red line? It's like asking if a morbidly obese man likes the tape worm inside his own belly."

"Now that's a specific analogy if ever I heard one," Jennifer said, her face twisted in disgust. "I'm not touching any of the chicken now. By the way, the pizza should be here in about a half hour."

"Great, I'm famished," Michael smirked.

"It's barely noon," Jennifer mocked him. "I swear, where do you put it all?"

"Fast metabolism," he chuckled.

"Wow. I wish I had the ability to eat the things you do and not gain weight," she was about to shut the door.

"Waaiit!" came a familiar cry. Jennifer looked out of the hallway of her apartment to see Tim sprinting down the corridor. "I'm here. Don't start without me."

"Tim!" she smiled at him, and placed her hand defensively on her chest, "I would never!"

"Oh, yes you would!" he shot back as he came bolting down the corridor and stopped the ajar door. He panted.

"You're right," she laughed, tossing her hair back. "I'm a monster."

Sam and Michael already took a seat on one of the sofas. Michael's arm was around her shoulder. "Jennifer, did Brian say he was coming?"

"Yes, he did. And you know he'll bring you know who," Jennifer said. She looked at the watch. 12:10 PM. "But you know him, he probably went to bed seven hours ago, so he'll probably just be waking up, if he's even up already. He probably won't be here 'til closer to three. That's a man that knows how to show up fashionably late," she turned to Tim who was still panting. "Tim, I have some bottled water in the cooler, go get some."

"No, thank you," he panted, while making his way to his seat. "You know—"

"Yes, yes, I know. Environmentally friendly and all that," Jennifer sneered. "Well, I have some plastic cups you can get tap—"

"Don't you have real cups?" Tim stared at her blankly.

"Tim! Do I look like some girl who wants to wash her dishes all the time?" She snapped at him. "Of course, I do," she walked over to her cupboard, grabbed a cup and filled it with water to give to Tim.

"So, I want to know," Samantha said to Jennifer. "How did you get Ted to agree to come?"

"Well, I called him this morning. He finally picked up the phone as I was leaving a salty voicemail," she put her fingers to her lips, but her smile never faded. "I talked him into going. He tried to push back but I wouldn't let him get out of his corner."

"Well, that must be—" Michael began.

Ring.

Jennifer took out her phone and looked at the caller ID. *Erin.* She answered the phone. "You've reached the city morgue, you kill 'em, we chill 'em."

Tim spat out the water from his mouth.

"Hey, Tim! Tim! Tim! You clean that up!" Jennifer scolded him.

Erin was chuckling on the other line, "Which door do I enter?"

"It's apartment number 658. I'm on the sixth floor, when you come out of the elevator, take a left. See you soon! Bye-bye now," she hung up the phone. "Tim, who gave you permission to spit water all over my floor?"

"You must have been the class clown," Michael replied.

"Oh, dear, dear sweet little carpet," she said. "That wasn't me. That was some guy named David, a terribly dreadful little creature."

"You read Jane Austen last night again, didn't you!" Sam accused, shaking her head.

"You know it! Jane Austen a day keeps depression away," she laughed. "Or was it something to do with apples? I don't know. I'm not a doctor. I'm just a researcher."

There was a knock on the door, "Erin, or Pizza?"

"Erin," Michael answered.

Jennifer went to open the door, and Michael was correct. "Welcome in, excuse the spit, Tim did it. Tim, are you done cleaning?"

"Yes, I am," he was cleaning it with a washcloth. He hated paper towels.

"Good grief. I give you my glorious tap water, and this is how you repay me. Some friend!" The room was filled with laughter as Erin walked in. Jennifer was confident around her friends, but it did take some people some time to get used to her. She knew that. After all, she came come off as an unlikeable jerk, but that's her love language. *And that's the way I like it.*

She looked at her watch again; 12:20 PM.

"Pizza running late?" Michael asked.

"Not yet," Jennifer said.

Jennifer lounged next to Tim on the couch, Michael had his arm wrapped around Samantha's shoulders, and Erin was poking about Jennifer's bookshelves, looking at the impressive Jane Austen collection, in a variety of different editions. Jennifer smiled as Erin pet the spines so casually, especially the leatherbound editions reprinted in '08. "I recommend *Sense and Sensibility,* that's my personal favorite."

"Jennifer," Erin gazed back at her. "How many times have you re-read this collection? And why do you have so many?"

"I re-read the collection yearly. You might call me the hopeless romantic."

"Ted bug?" Erin sneered.

Taken aback, Jennifer turned her head to the side, and her cheeks blushed red, "Maybe."

A half hour passed and there was another knock on the door. "That must be it." She opened the door, paid the pizza man and brought the pizza to the island. There were numerous paper plates that came with it. Of course, Tim scoffed at them.

Michael went over to get a slice, "Get your frail hands away from that!" she slapped his hand away from the paper plate. "Now, now, my sweet little carpet, we are waiting for Ted. I can reheat the pizza in the oven if I need to. Twenty minutes isn't going to kill you."

***

An hour passed. It was 1:50 PM in the afternoon. There was not another knock at the door. Jennifer felt discouraged, she was a little concerned for Ted not showing up yet, and there was no communication from him indicating he was going to be late. *I hope he didn't get into an accident.* She sighed, "Well, I guess you all can eat now."

Why did I feel it necessary to make them wait?

Tim, Erin, and Michael immediately went over to get some pizza. Jennifer was tired of listening to Michael complain anyway. She felt Samantha's hand on her shoulder, "It'll be fine. I'm sure he got caught on something."

"I suppose," Jennifer took out her phone and sent another message to Ted: *where are you?* She put the phone back in her pocket and slouched her shoulders as she walked to get a slice of pizza, and on that dreaded paper plate.

"Hey, Erin, did you ever follow up with Ted the other day?" Michael asked as he took a bite of his pepperoni pizza. He should really have his taste buds checked.

"Yeah, I did. He only gave me few-word answers," she replied, taking a bite of her chicken and broccoli. "He said, he was fine."

"Well, you know when someone answers that way, they're insecure," Sam said. "That's what my boss tells me when I say I'm fine."

"I'm sure it's nothing," Michael said. "As he mentioned before, he works in world markets, I wouldn't be surprised if he was still working and had some remote meeting he forgot to mention."

"Seriously, Michael, how much does he have to be working if he's doing that!" Jennifer exclaimed, gritting her teeth. "Erin, didn't you say he was one of those come in early leave late kind-of-guys?"

Tim frowned.

"Yeah," she replied.

"That isn't unusual for someone in a high-pressure job," Samantha explained. "I do that frequently too."

"So, do I," Michael said, he scratched his chin as he was chewing on his crust. "But if I had to guess, he was probably working close to sixty-hours per week."

"That isn't unusual," Jennifer admitted, "And if he works on the weekends, wouldn't he be closer to seventy-hours?"

"Perhaps, and that's a little extreme," Michael admitted. "I would never choose to work that much, unless maybe he has a reason."

"Maybe he just really likes money," Tim said. "I mean, if he's in stocks, that's usually the reason."

"No, that's not it. He admitted that he only does it for something to keep him busy, like he enjoys doing it. He said he has more than enough for him to live off," Michael replied.

"Honestly, that's impressive. He doesn't seem to be older than any of us," Tim said.

Another hour passed. Jennifer received no confirmation from Ted that he was coming or that he was running late. It was two hours later than when he said he would show up. Did he lie to her, just to get her off the phone? She couldn't discount that possibility. She felt like her heart was heavy. *Did I push him too hard?*

There was a knock on the door. Her smile lit back up again. She rushed over to answer it. She opened the door with a smile on her face and when she saw who was on the other side, her emotions fell heavily upon her heart, like she was chained to the ground by large boulders, and she couldn't move, or risk having the weight crush her. Being the polite host she was, she exclaimed enthusiastically, "It's Brian!"

"Yeah! It's Brian!" he repeated in the third person, nodding his head enthusiastically. "Sorry I'm late."

"Don't fret, my sweet little fox, come on in. The pizza is here. I was just about to pull out the wine," she said, ushering Brian, and Steven, and his little friend, Rosa in. Brian was the oldest of them all, nearing his mid-thirties.

"Oh, excellent, plenty of time for drinking. I brought my own wine actually, it's from the Valley up over in Westford."

"Wait. Really?" Samantha asked. "I love their wine, it's something about their grapes. Their wine is of the best quality."

"Yeah!" he walked over to the island in the kitchen and placed two bottles of wine on it. He put the corkscrew in one of them and immediately opened it to allow it to breathe. Brian, Steven, and Rosa went over to the others and started talking about their week. No one brought anything depressing into the conversation.

Jennifer was happy they're able to have such a good time in such a small apartment. The games hadn't started just yet. But she was beginning to lose hope that Ted would be showing up tonight. *You could have at least told me you just didn't want to come. But maybe I shouldn't have put you in that position, forcing you to either lie or hurt my feelings.*

She pulled out all her wines out onto the island and started pouring cups of wine into wine glasses and delivered them to her guests, smiling as she handed each one off. She saved Brian's wine for last. He usually bought the expensive wine anyway.

"Hey, whatever happened to that newbie?" Brian asked. "I don't think I ever succeeded in getting him out. I haven't seen him in a while."

"Are you referring to Ted?" Michael's head tilted in response. "The one from two weeks ago?"

"Yeah, that one," Brian took a sip of his Cabernet. "What happened to him? Did someone scare him off?"

"I don't think so. Actually, he was supposed to be coming tonight, but he hasn't shown up yet," Sam replied, the curve on her lips faded.

"Well, it's probably nothing to worry about," Brian said. "A pity, I wanted to meet him. I never got a chance to say hi to the new guy."

"Maybe you'll get that chance still tonight, or—"

A heavy knock at the door interrupted Samantha.

Who was that? Jennifer thought. *It's way too late for it to be Ted.* Of course, at this point she assumed he was no longer coming, "I've got it," she walked over to the door, her hand gripped the handle and turned it. She opened the door wide with a smile as she looked to greet whoever stood behind it.

Jennifer breathed heavily as she looked at him in the doorway. She felt her smile drop to a frown as her heart raced, and she couldn't quite make out the emotions her heart was trying to feel. Was she angry? Upset? Excited? She couldn't tell, but her hands trembled at her side. She grimaced at the man, as his presence suddenly made her angry.

"You know, Tedward, when you tell me you're going to be here around one, I expect you to be here around one, maybe fifteen minutes late or so, but around one. It is four o'clock! I already told everyone you would be here at one. Would you make a liar out of me?" she said with an uplifted tone.

The room filled with laughter went silent. The silence was deafening, and Jennifer scratched the back of her neck.

He gave her a polite bow. "My apologies, milady. For you see, I just couldn't bring it upon myself to come to some kind of party without bring something of value to my beloved host," he spoke very smoothly, and he was not at all flirtatious, he seemed very sincere. He took out a large bottle of wine, a red wine, and of a fine glass, a fine bottle with the price tag ripped off.

Jennifer's eyes lit up as she immediately grabbed the bottle from his hand and read the label. "This is Colossus' Rome Red Ca'habielli!"

"What?" Brian called over. "Ca'habielli? Jenn put my wine back in the cooler. You can't get much better than that!"

"Ted, that's a $1,200 bottle of wine. Where did you get this? More importantly, why would you give it to me?" She knew the value of such a brand of wine was only reserved for the finest of occasions, and not something easily obtainable in the United States. This was strictly imported from the wineries of Rome.

"Eh, I'm not going to keep it around my house," he replied. "It's much better shared among *friends*."

An expensive vintage such as the Ca'habielli, imported from Rome, an expensive wine, meant to be enjoyed slowly. Yet, such a gift should not be squandered, and then again, Jennifer found herself wondering why in God's name he would think to bring such an expensive wine as a gift. That bottle of wine costs more than some pay for rent individually. She was not going to squander the gift, lest he feel offended, despite the social insult of providing such an expensive gift. She also took special notice of his sudden tonal change in the word, "Friends," and she couldn't ignore that. What exactly did he mean?

"Come on in!" she invited him in, immediately changing her tone from ire to a sense of joy. "There is pizza, I know you said you ate already, but it's here if you want it."

"I appreciate the sentiment," he answered as he walked through the apartment, scanning the room, as if to read the reaction of each person.

Samantha walked up to him, "I'm glad you came."

"I'm glad I made it," he smiled to her; the bags under his eyes were puffy.

Jennifer put one of Brian's unopened bottles of wine in her cooler, pouring out opened bottles into several wine glasses. She uncorked the bottle of Ca'habielli. She placed it on the counter where she would let it breathe for an hour. This was such a gracious, and unnecessary gift. *Ted, why?* Feeling self-conscious, she delivered the poured glasses to every one of her friends in the room, and yes, she considered Ted a friend among them, despite not knowing him for very long. *Ted, why did you hesitate?*

The party drank all of Brian's wine, and allowed the entirety of the hour to pass by, speaking until the Ca'habielli had completely breathed.

The party grabbed their now empty wine glasses and got into a line. Jennifer poured Ted's glass first, he smiled that impeccable smile; there was something soothing about it. Like the genuine smile of someone who knew no pain, who knew only the kindness of the world, and was sheltered from the many horrible, physical, psychological traumas from the world. He was always in a safe place.

Jennifer poured the wine into the empty glasses, filling them halfway so she could distribute it equally to everyone in the party. The party stood around in a circle, and Michael raised his glass up.

"A toast, to friends all under one roof, some we have been with since high school, and others are newer than some," he smiled, specifically looking at Ted. "And let us not forget to thank Jennifer for hosting us this evening! For we wouldn't be here without her, and I doubt Ted would have made it without her, cheers."

"Cheers!" the rest of the party repeated in unison.

They all took a sip for the Ca'habielli. Jennifer let the wine sift through her lips before tasting the sweet and bitter arrays of the beverage. It was without a doubt the finest wine she has ever laid her lips upon. She has spent her years drinking a number of wines, but all paled in comparison to this legendary bottle shipped all the way from Rome. *No wonder this wine is so pristine.*

Chapter 12

Raw Brutality

~Prepare yourselves. You've have picked a terrible person to jump. Don't give me that look when I know you don't have the stomach to sit through Raw Brutality.

Hours passed, and after the last of the bottles of wine were consumed, and after the final game was played, Ted moved around to one of the windows, staring out at the window, looking down at the city lights, illumining the empty city streets. He could hear some background talking as Tim, and Brian were leaving Jennifer's Seaport District apartment. Jennifer was engrossed in a conversation with Michael, and they seemed to be getting a long quite famously.

Samantha walked over to him with her glass still half full. He turned to her, thinking he mustn't let his guard down around her, after all, she was the one who got him involved in them, initially. She could pry out of him secrets he wanted to remain hidden. He didn't want to know them himself. She joined him, sitting on the wide windowsill. She returned his smile back to him, and he thought the smile was genuine, with authentic happiness and sincerity. She said, "Ted, I have a question, and I hope I don't come off as offish, I hope you don't mind."

"I don't mind at all. The moon is out, the wine is delicious, and any matter of question is allowable," he smiled, and yet he felt exhausted, "But because a question is allowed, it doesn't necessarily mean I'll answer."

"Okay," she replied. He could tell she was put off by his answer. *Perfect.* "We didn't do anything to offend you two weeks ago, did we? We were concerned that something might have happened to you when we didn't see you. And we were especially concerned when Jennifer told us you would be here at one, and still no response when you were late," she let out a nervous laugh. "I think Jennifer thought you might have died on the way here."

"Well, as you can see, I am here now, and not dead," he replied. "I don't mean to cause concern, as I did not come to think me to be part of this, how does she put it, part of this 'dysfunctional family'. As such, I didn't think my absence would play a major part in your day's concern as you and I only met three weeks ago."

"Okay," she nodded. "Then, do you consider yourself part of us, then?" She looked at him seriously. "Answer me honestly. You have a hiddenness about you, I'm having a hard time reading you."

He smiled, "I don't intend to keep anything from you, but I will speak on such matters required for our *relationship*, and nothing more. I am difficult to read, so you say, and this is the first time I'm hearing of it."

"Because there is some sense of mystery about you. All I really know is what you do and where you are from. I don't know what your likes and dislikes are. Does anyone?" she answered again, pushing for some non-ambiguous answer.

"I suppose I like working. I guess that is one thing—"

"About that," she interrupted him. "How many hours do you work? From what I hear, you are something of a workaholic."

"I suppose one could say that," he chuckled. He looked up at the ceiling. "I work about as much as one-hundred and sixteen hours a week."

"What?" She repeatedly blinked: she couldn't believe her ears. "Can you repeat that?"

"One-hundred and sixteen hours a week," he answered. He was careful to retain that smile.

"I thought that's what you said. How can you possibly maintain that!" she exclaimed. "Do you even sleep?"

"I sleep enough," he replied.

She realized something, underneath his eyes were the jaded expression of a man who knew little sleep. "Ted, how much do you sleep?"

"I sleep enough," he replied.

No wonder he can just go out and buy a $1,200 bottle of wine. "Why do you work so much? Do you even have something you would consider fun?"

"I find work fun, and it keeps me occupied," he answered.

"You're avoiding the question," she accused.

"No, I'm answering the question. The truth can be so hairy. Like I said before, I will answer your questions and reveal some of myself as necessary for our relationship," he kept his smile, but his tone lowered an octave.

"That—that's not the same thing!" she exclaimed. "It's not the same thing. You are avoiding the—"

"Miss Harris, I believe you might have had a little much to drink," he suggested. "Might it be time to retire for the night?"

"Perhaps you're right," Sam looked down at her glass, which was now half empty. "I'm sorry, Ted, I shouldn't have said anything. Can you find it in yourself to forgive me?"

"I'm afraid I cannot. There is nothing to forgive. There is no reason to be sorry. Humans are humans," he smiled at her.

"I will leave you to your view then. Will we see you Tuesday?" Sam asked.

"Time, I suppose will tell, assuming I don't have any fires in the market to put out," he answered.

"But look, I know that we just met you, and us going out of our way to make you part of our little group may seem off putting, and for that I apologize. I hope you will see that we mean you no discomfort," She stopped speaking for a moment to allow him a moment for a response. Seeing that there was no response, she said, "That will have to do for now," she took her wine glass and went over to Michael, who wrapped his arm around her shoulder again.

Ted took to the window again and looked at the black, empty sky. The darkness was familiar to him. It was like the murky waters of the Dead Sea, filled with nothing but hopeless light. His eyes were beginning to droop, and his attention shifted to his hand. His hand was not twitching as was common this time of night.

It is all meaningless, as you say, then why don't we all just lie down and die?

Why are you not trembling? What is different?

The door closed behind him. He turned to see only Jennifer in the room. She smiled to him as she took her glass with her to sit with him and stare emptily out of the window, down to the city lights. She let out a sigh of relief.

"Well, that was fun. Did you enjoy yourself, Tedward?" she asked him.

"Well, it certainly wasn't dull, and I'm sure I have you to thank for that," he smiled back at her. The moon light was oppressively pushing down his spirits.

"So, tell me, Tedward, what is one thing I don't know about you?" she asked him. "Answer, and I will reveal something about myself."

He hesitated.

"So, there is something human about you after all," she laughed, her eyelids dropped down halfway, leaving her smile. He could have sworn there was something sinister behind her watchful gaze.

"Well, I suppose it's been a while since I've played twenty questions, but I can't help but think that's not how it works," he chuckled. "I suppose you'll have to ask me something specific, isn't that how it works?"

"Okay," Jennifer smirked. "So that's how it is, you sly little fox."

"I think I am much closer to a wolf," he joked.

"Perhaps a wolf raised by foxes," she let that sink in. "Well, my dear—"

"So, I'm a deer now?"

"You are whatever your sweet self wants to be. You be a deer, a fox, a wolf, something else of some other cute little characteristic attributed to all animals. So, here's my question, and forgive me if I already asked, but I cannot recall; have you any siblings?"

"There are those that I would have called brother and sister," he answered.

"Well, were they half siblings, full siblings, adopted?"

"I suppose you could say they were adopted siblings," he answered coldly, but he retained his smile.

She smiled, satisfied with the answer. "Now, Tedward, I believe it is your turn to now ask me a question. As reserved as you are, surely you have a question."

"I have many questions," he replied. "Sadly, very few, if any at all involve people."

"Then I beg you to make a question for me. What would pique your interest about me?" She leaned closer to him.

What are you doing, Jennifer?

"I suppose this one I can ask, what do you find peace in?" he asked, revealing nothing else, he merely retained that smile as he asked it.

"I suppose I haven't given it much thought. I suppose if I found anything that gave me peace, is that I can be of some help to someone along the way with this very short life I've been given. Like many, I will not live for very long, humans do not live very long lives, as they used to say, what was it, before they all started digesting liquid detergent, 'YOLO', you only live life once," Her face went dark. "I guess I find the opposite to be true, you live and die just as many times as the other, and they equally plague us. Like both are a disease that must be vaccinated. But life's vaccination is death, and death's vaccination is life."

"How very, Tao of you," he said.

Her smile returned as she laughed sheepishly. "Then it is my turn then. What do you find peace in?"

"I'm not sure if I like that question," he snickered. "And was it not the same question I asked you?"

"Yes, it is. Is this question a little too revealing, Tedward?" she laughed like a little cat tugging on its yarn of string.

I asked you that to find an answer for myself.

"You could say that, but I also know you will not like the answer," he replied.

Her face went graven again. "Look, Ted, I will decide if I like the answer or not. If I like it, then you would be pleased you were wrong. If I don't like it, I suppose you'll be satisfied knowing you were right all along. But I will accept whatever answer you give me, as it was my question that I asked. The point of this, was to get to know some facet of you that is hidden underneath that shell. They say darkness loves company, but it hates what's on the surface, as the surface is where truth lies."

"Well, they say darkness can't live in the light," he said.

She smiled again. "That is something true you just said," she paused. "Now, might I have my answer?"

"Well, I suppose it doesn't matter if you would like the answer or not, so I don't have a reason to deceive you," his voice dropped.

"Tedward," her voice dropped, and she tilted her neck. "I know you may not think that we know you, and you're right, we don't know you as well as we would like, and I suppose you don't have a reason to trust me, but I trust you. I might not reveal all my little secrets just yet, but I trust you."

He let out a sigh, but he kept on smiling. "I suppose I don't find much of anything peaceful. I work a lot, and don't leave myself time for such luxuries," his voice dropped as he broke eye contact with her.

"Ted?"

"Do you know why I chose life as a stockbroker?" he asked. He didn't let her answer. "It is the one job in the world that I can think of that will let me work around the clock. I barely sleep. Maybe, I am lucky if I sleep more than thirty minutes at a time," he paused, looking back into her eyes, trying to analyze her reaction. She patiently waited for him to finish, looking him in the eyes, nodding, "I have no peace within myself, so I drown myself in work hoping to keep my mind occupied."

"Does it work?" she asked.

"Yes," he replied.

"Is it worth it?"

"I don't know," he replied. "I think I've spoken enough of myself for one night. I think it is time for me to go back."

"Home?" she asked.

"That is such a funny word," he said, standing up and leaving his wineglass on the nearby coffee table. "I've been in many countries and moved countless times. I don't think I've ever been to a place I would call home."

Frowning, her eyes glazed over. "Ted, that is so sad," she went to grab his hand. He pulled it away. "Look, before you go, and I know you must be eager to leave. Perhaps it was wrong for me to push you to come tonight. Perhaps, it is my fault, and this was wrong of me. I didn't know that bringing you here would bring back so many memories, painful, and reminders of what you once had, or never had, and may never get the chance to feel again," she sucked in her teeth as she looked him carefully in the eye. He took a step back. "Iah—I know that I can't imagine what it is you missed, because I don't know you and I'm not going to pretend I do. I will say that I want to know you. Now, I am sorry for pushing you to come, and Iah—I hope you can forgive me. I want to know you more, and I hope that I've made it clear that I want to be your friend, and I'm not going to push you anymore to tell me what you don't want me to know."

"I thank you, Jennifer," he answered. "I must be going."

He turned around and walked to the door.

"Ted, will we see you on Tuesday?" she asked, just as the door was still slightly ajar.

"Time will tell," he answered truthfully.

As the door shut behind him, Jennifer's hands trembled as she walked over to the door to lock it. She started picking up the paper plates and threw them in the trash, with the now empty pizza boxes. She placed all her cups in the dishwasher before making it to her room.

The room was large, and her bed looked like it was freshly made, and patted down with the utmost care to avoid any wrinkles. She crawled into her bed and lifted her knees to her chest as she stared blankly at her bedroom door. Tears started to stream down her face, because she remembered something, the look in his face was all too familiar. She remembered the same look on her uncle's face, the same over tired look, the baggy and swollen eyes. The one-word answers, and a fake smile while all the same, giving a genuine laugh, laughing at his own misery.

She remembered her uncle being elusive with the truth, not exactly lying, but he wasn't telling the truth either. The man was a hardened veteran, seen his fair share of battle, and the fatigue showed with the lack of interest in anything. The last night she saw him whole, well, he was hanging from a ceiling, his torso stretching. No one knew, or no one made known how long he was hanging there, but if he was stretching, Jennifer knew it was quite some time before anyone made the effort to check in on him. It was long enough anyway, that no one seemed to miss his sudden absence.

Even if just for a moment, she saw the ragged look on her uncle's face to match perfectly Ted's face, and then she knew that Ted was hiding something that he wanted to keep hidden. Some mischief, regret, trauma, but the Ted she knows, is not Ted as he truly is. He wore a fake smile, the social bandage to put on a show, to show everyone he's fine, but it was nothing more than a mask, and underneath that façade was a festering wound, and it hurts. *Damnit. It hurts.* She felt a part of her heart in agonizing pain, and she knew there wasn't anything she could do, but she wanted to do something. But what?

***

Ted inhaled deeply, gritting his teeth as he leaned against the back of the elevator all the way down. He started breathing heavily as the elevator lights blinked from floor to floor. He glared at the lights as if they mocked him. His fist clenched until he reached the bottom. The elevator bell shot through his head. He took a deep breath and again, hid his misery. The double doors slid open, and he crossed the threshold.

He went down the stairs and opened the last door to enter the empty street of Seaport Blvd. The streetlights were blinking. The cars were empty, and the street was void of all humans. Just the little pieces of trash that flew out of the public trashcans. He parked all the way towards Government Center. He walked west, following the many empty buildings, burger joints, coffee shops, ice cream parlors, and fisheries.

The moon beat down on him, and not a star was in sight. He held that same defeated smile as he walked down the boulevard. He took deep breaths through his nose until he passed the bridge across from the Boston Tea Party Museum. He smelled something foul in the air. He looked behind him, and he could smell the stench of something that was all too familiar to him: blood.

They say that blood doesn't smell like anything. But he's been around too much of it to know better. Someone without a strong sense of smell can't smell it, that's for certain, and those with a good sense of smell might miss it with the other smells in the air. But he can pick it out, because it smells like raw hatred. He turned around in the middle of the bridge and he could see cascading purple, pink, green and blue lights flaring up from the end of Seaport, getting much closer to Black Falcon Avenue. They looked like short-fused fireworks without the noise.

He turned around and walked away from the lights. Whatever it was, he wanted no part of it. If someone was getting murdered in an impressive array of fireworks, he didn't care. Besides, even if he did get involved, he'd only end up killing someone, and get caught in an endless loop of violence and murder. That was the last thing he wanted. He continued on in the moonlight, the lights behind him ceasing. He crossed the bridge over the water, walking underneath some trees as he arrived at an intersection, and waited for the crosswalk. There was a large skyscraper in front of him, and a hotel, the dark side of the hotel with the only windows of the tenants. The entrance was on the other side. There were no lights here. The lights in the skyscraper were shut off as there was no one working on it this evening.

He heard the breath coming from some bush, someone with foul intentions. He sighed and turned to the bush. A man came out of the shadows. He could sense six other men coming out. The one in front of him with the bush pointed a pistol at him, it was a 9mm. The other six had makeshift melee weapons. One of them a bat, the other a two-by-four. The others carried miscellaneous metal apparatuses such as a crowbar, a pipe, the other two had machetes. *I wonder where they got those from.*

"Empty your pockets!" The man with the pistol said.

Ted raised his eyebrows at him.

"Do you think this is a game! I'm not playin'! Empty your pockets! Or I will shoot you dead!" The man's hand was shaking. Ted knew the man had never held a gun before in his life, especially holding it like that, he knew the pressure of the gun would never make the intended target. He said nothing, "Do you think I'm playin'?"

"You're not going to shoot me like that," Ted smiled at him. "Did you really intend on robbing me with such a shaky trigger finger?

You're not fooling me, so if you would kindly let me be on my way—
"

"Hit him!" the man with the gun said.

He could hear the scurrying footsteps coming from behind him. He laughed as the crowbar struck Ted in the leg. He never reacted to it. He turned to the man who hit him and smiled at him, mocking the man, just as the moonlight mocks him.

"You see, I don't want to kill you. Don't turn me into that monster," Ted said.

"Again!" The man with the gun ordered, his voice shaking as if this was his first time trying to rob someone, or perhaps this man had robbed many people before—just not with a gun—and this was his first time encountering someone who didn't bother to budge to his demands, and even mocked him.

The man with the bat struck Ted in the side, it sounded like some ribs were cracked. Ted shrugged it off and stepped forward. It was not his ribs, but the barrel was splintered. The man with the gun got his grip and pointed it at Ted, looking at him with hatred in his eyes.

"Oh, don't even bother looking at me like that." Ted's smile changed, finally showing his teeth and mania and blood lust in his eyes. "I know you don't have the stomach to handle raw brutality!"

Ted sprinted towards the man with the gun. The man opened fired with a silenced pistol. Ted's eyes scanned the trajectory of the bullets, seeing each 9mm round leaving its chamber, hearing the clicks from the gun, precisely knowing the moment each round would leave the barrel. Just as he predicted, the man didn't know how to shoot the gun. Ted followed his bullet lines to avoid being hit, and with a gunman as inexperienced as this, there was no need to try to catch any of them. He heard the footsteps of the two running behind him, trying to stop him from getting their ringleader.

The gunman's face contorted, clearly surprised. The clicking trigger of an empty gun being repeatedly pressed was like a count down. The ejection port was pushed back, and the inside of it was smoking. He dropped the gun and stepped back; his face turned to that of a scared old man.

"I'm sorry. I was jo—"

"Fat chance, and you're too late!" Ted was right in front of him.

The warmth left the air, and everyone could feel it. His left fist and up to his arm revealed blue veins, glowing in the dark as they came to swing a haymaker, and with his right leg, he kicked around to the side. The gunman was spinning in a cartwheel in the air before hitting his head on the sidewalk. With his same leg, the blue veins appeared as he brought it down to the skull of the gunman, crushing it instantly, blood, and bone smeared on his shoe and the sidewalk.

He swiftly jerked to the side, turning around, missing a swing from the crowbar. The man with the bat swung at Ted again. He caught the splintered end with his now glowing hand. He kicked the man's elbow with his right foot. *Crack!* The man's forearm broke, letting go of the bat. Ted swiftly moved the bat into his hands, turned it around and stabbed the man in the shin with it.

The crowbar came swinging again. Ted moved to the side to avoid it, and kicked the man hard with his left foot, sending him into the street.

The two men with machetes were close, swinging them in unison to either side of him, to cut him off from dodging to the side. Ted looked closely at them. He moved off into the side, grabbing the machete from one of their hands, stabbing the other with it, pulling it down until his guts spilled onto the ground. He took his bloodied hands and pulled them around the other man's head and twisted it backwards.

He missed the other man with the crowbar, running up at him from the street. "You bastard! You killed them!"

He swung the crowbar in many directions, furiously. Ted sighed as the man came in grabbing distance, he heard the disturbance in the air, of the crowbar parting it in front of him. Ted thought for, if only a moment, this could kill him, but then why should it? When everything else failed. His heart pumped blood to his head. He snarled at that man. He sidestepped, deflecting the crowbar. He heard the rev of an engine. His eyes scanned the street, seeing a parked car turn its light on. He ignored the car and returned a hateful glare at the man. *Death surrounds everything I touch.*

His left arm lit up with his grey veins. The crowbar swung downward, and Ted blocked it with his arm, and the man's arm was jerked back as the crowbar was vibrating violently in his hand until he dropped it. His eyes were bulging out of his skull as Ted's hand seized him by the throat, lifting him up. The grey veins turned their color back to blue. The man could feel the strength of his fingers digging into his throat. He clawed at his hands to get free, but Ted's strength was beyond human.

The car's tired screeched. The man's life was fading. Ted's eyes shifted towards the car speeding its way to him. He snickered as the man's arms dropped down, lifelessly. He smiled, sneering at the car. "If you intend to run me over with that, you better be wearing your seatbelt!"

Ted's blue veins glowed from his hands, crawling rapidly into the corpse of the man he now held. This man was like an extension of his arm.

The car sped towards him, the wheels moving round and round as it screeched, staining the pavement with its black rubber tires. He smiled as he thrust the corpse into the front of the car, crunching the hood, blood spattering everywhere. The car came to a screeching halt as the front of the car dented into the axel, sending both front tires spinning off. The crunching metal filled the air as innumerous shards of glass started falling in the air like sweet, bloody snowflakes as the driver ejected through the windshield.

Ted picked the flying driver out of the air by her neck as he let the other man fall from his grasp. The car flipped over him, and crashed into the highway, slowly scraping and sparking down the pavement, followed by a trail of streaming gasoline.

The woman was still conscious, still in shock she tried to grab hold of his hands to release herself. There was nothing she could do. The veins entered his right hand again, pushing itself into her neck. He squeezed her neck tighter, she tried to cry out, but her windpipes were crushed, and she could feel the man's grip touch her spine. Her eyes started gawking extensively as her mouth desperately tried to scream.

There was one man left, too scared to scream, too horrified to run. He squinted as he tried to pull out the splintered bat from his leg. He grunted. Ted briefly turned, and to him, it seemed this other man wanted to help his driver. Ted curled his lips, seeing the despair fill his eyes, because there was no fighting against something or someone who even Hell rejected.

Crack. Buckle.

Her arms and legs fell lifelessly. He squeezed her neck tighter until her eyes were pushed out of her sockets, hanging on by its retina. He threw her to the side. She rolled over like a ragdoll. He started laughing, with blood on his hands and feet, he was laughing. Whoever they were, they picked the wrong man to try to rob.

"That was oddly therapeutic," Ted said, smiling up to the empty sky. "I should probably be doing this more often," he turned to look at the petrified survivor. "Whenever you find a man filled with murder in his heart, you stand aside."

Ted's shoes lit up with his veins and he sprinted through Seaport Blvd at an inhuman pace.

Chapter 13

Rogue

~Even a corpse is a witness.

Ilya sighed in the darkness, hiding behind a shipping container over on Black Falcon Pier. Her hand was on her chest, puffing in and out, inhaling heavily. Her face was cut by the threckets claws when she got too close. She turned her head right around the corner of the black container, looking at the threcket, which was the size of a house. Its mouth was like that of a boar, and the twisted snout of a deer, its antlers protruding out of its forehead. The four legs were thin, just like a deer's and had hooves. The arms were the most diverse out of them all, one pair of arms were the paws and claws of a raging dire wolf; another the size and width of a troll, another set of arms had bear arms, and the final set of arms were covered in scales, and the claw was what one might imagine a dragon would have if they existed, but they don't. This threcket also had a tail, long and flexible like a snake, and when it whipped through the air, it summoned lightning.

Ilya looked at one of the other shipping containers, Alexander stood upon it, his bow in hand. His many green arrows pierced the threcket's hide. The green arrows began to fade, turning into small green ashes as they fell into the sky. Her gaze turned to Culain, who wiped blood from his lip, keeping his black spear impaled through its chest. Blanka's mana veins covered her chains as they held down the threcket, keeping the creature still. It was dead, they were only able to react as quickly to this due to Ilya's teleportation circles. A personal victory, but it would wake people up with the sudden chills to their bodies at night.

"Ilya," said Culain.

These threckets had a nasty habit of not staying dead.

"Right," she nodded as she came out from behind the container. Taking her knife from her side; the knife glowed a mystic purple. She cut runes into the air, cutting the flesh of reality itself to create the runes, which hovered in the air until she was finished. Her body was slowly covered in purple veins, she pushed her mana into the runes, gliding towards the beast.

The bright purple runes covered the beast. The bright lights emitting from the runes forced Alexander, Blanka, and Culain to shield their eyes. "Cu'er na vorgen. Cha. Lathuka prath'haken!" Ilya chanted, closing her eyes as the purple veins entered her pupils. The mana streams from the creature looked like massive multicolored rays of sunlight, the air around her turned crimson. Her mana started streaming out like tentacles, reaching for the mana source for the creature, weaving themselves around the different arrays of light. Her mana streamed into the runes imbedded into the creature. Culain could see the massive concentration of mana being attached to her from the beast.

Ilya was pulling all the life force of this beast into her and harmonized it with her own. The runes, she felt, pushed themselves into the corpse of the hybrid of animals, and the first layer of skin ripped off, and was pulled into the sky, burning away as the source of mana was stripped away from it.

The corpse was being violently stripped away of its mana, the muscles themselves being burned into the air as the mana that held it together was yanked into Ilya. Her eyes glowed as she jerked the mana from the organs and the blood started boiling down to nothing as the mana stream turned crimson. The marrow of the bones was being pulled apart, and the bones cracked like splinters, fading into the ground as the last of its white mana yanked into Ilya.

There was now no evidence the creature was here.

Ilya's mana veins faded into her flesh; her vision returned to normal. The chains, spear, arrows and bow dematerialized into fading blue lights.

"Ilya," Culain began. "Did you catch its mana location?"

"No. It faded during all of that. There's no indication of where it came from," she answered, weeping in the moonlight. She took a heavy breath as the mana she absorbed was heavy in her chest, like she was heavily saturated. Absorbing a creation of the dark's mana was never a good idea unless a caster could expel the mana. She knew it was like poison to her, "Cutha krevorthen era," the air around her turned black, obscuring her. The black cursed mana faded into the air.

Her mana veins bubbled up to the surface. She let out a deep sigh and continued to breathe heavily.

Culain ran to her. Ilya felt his grip on her shoulders, pushing her up. She wrapped her arm around his shoulders. The cursed mana of the beast was poison, and it was heavy, and thick, like molasses.

"The—there has to be a better way," she coughed up blood into her hand.

"I wish there was," he said. "But this is it."

Alexander fixed his eyes upon something in the distance.

"What is it?" Blanka asked. She gazed in the same direction.

"Someone's getting robbed," Alexander answered.

"Not our business, not our problem. Let the poor fool die or get mugged. He shouldn't have been out this late anyway," Culain said coldly.

"Wait," Ilya said. Her mana veins turned red, and her vision expanded. Images of Downtown Boston entered her mind. Her vision looked like it was blurring everything as her mind's eye past through the streets. She saw a car crash, and now seven dead people. But she could also see red and blue mana streams, just floating into footsteps all over that area, over by the intersection, "I see a mana pool."

Alexander's eyebrow raised. "Culain, is there anyone else out of the Boston's Administration supposed to be out tonight?"

"No," Culain admitted. "Let's get over there. Find out what happened. If a caster is involved, he should have cleaned up the mess. Now we have to do it."

Ilya's entire body trembled, still feeling the residue of the cursed mana fill her veins. *Well, at least I can harvest pure mana instead of that diseased shit.*

Ilya inhaled through her mana veins, now showing on her skin, covering her from head to toe. The mana source from the air, rushed through her body immediately, turning the mana bright blue, and it glimmered in the moonlight. This mana was in its purest form, from the air, without any artificial tampering. Mana from the air strengthened the muscles in her body, allowing her to push off the ground, and sprint off at speeds like a speeding car. Weaving past cars and street signs, her vision blurred. With each step on the street, the impact sounded like a clap of thunder in this silence, but she knew her senses were heightened, and to a normie, they would hear nothing.

They relaxed their mana veins, fading back into their skin as they ran over the bridge. Slowed down to a brisk walk, they looked at the carnage before them. Culain was the first one running at a normal pace, getting to the intersection. Ilya was right behind him, and she saw the totaled car, blood streaming on the streets, guts littering the nearby tree, and bone fragments scattered all over the place. *This is brutal. Unnecessarily so.* The rest of her team was not far behind them.

Ilya looked around, and they saw one of the bodies, with a bat still protruding into his leg. The leg was bent out of shape, as if damaged by something else other than the bat. His leg appeared to have three joints, instead of one: one at the knee, the other where the bat impaled his shin, and halfway up his thigh. His body was shaking, and his hands were dropped down. His eyes were opened wide as if he saw a ghost. Ilya went over to him, waving her small hands in front of him to see if his pupils will follow.

He remained silent.

Culain squatted right in front of him and pulled out a badge, BPD, (Boston Police Department). "My name is officer Culain. This is the part where you tell me exactly what you saw. Speak quickly."

The man was quiet.

"What's your name, kid?" Culain said. He turned to Ilya, "Give him some space."

Ilya moved away. Alexander surveyed the carnage. Blanka drew circles filled with triangles in the pavement with a *mana* pen. Ilya knew what Blanka was doing, after all, there was going to be a lot of screaming soon. Once Blanka finished with one shape, she moved to another location to draw another circle. And another. And another. This was going to silence everything around them, as if the air and time itself remained still.

"Ja—Jamal," he stammered.

"Jamal," Culain spoke softly. "What happened here?"

"We were desperate, we were going to rob someone," he began. "I'm sorry. I know it's wrong but, but the man we tried to rob; he was a devil! His eyes glowed like that of some evil faerie! His arms were strong, and he was fast. He was faster than any man I've ever seen. Even—even when he was run over by a car, he left unscathed, like he was a boulder. He killed everyone. Everyone."

"What did he look like?"

"He was white, maybe just five-and-a-half feet tall, average build, scars on his face, and moppy brown hair I think," he replied. "He was always smiling."

"I see," Culain said, "Ilya, help me take this bat out of him."

She nodded. She held Jamal's hand as Culain ripped the bat out. The man grinded his teeth together, sucking the air through his teeth as he tried to stifle a cry, failing miserably. Culain pulled the bat out. And dropped it to his side. He stood up and leaned against a tree which had blood smeared on it. He peered up at the sky with his stern look as if condemning the moon for its very existence.

"Blanka—" he began.

"Already done. No one can hear us," she said, her silver hair shimmered behind her as she looked towards Jamal. Her blue eyes glazed over.

Culain could see the mana magenta lights creating a box around them, something only a caster would see.

Jamal was still in a mode of shock, arms trembling at his side, and he blankly stared at the ground with wide eyes. *Cruel. A world like this, with people like that, wrapped up by people like us.* Ilya thought.

"Ilya?" he asked. He never looked to her.

"Yes, Culain?" she replied.

"I need you to find out what our mysterious person looks like. You don't have to kill the kid. I will. I don't want your hands stained more than mine." This he whispered in her ear.

"I understand," she walked to Jamal and smiled to him. "Take my hand."

Jamal, being emotionally rattled by it all, he didn't hear Culain. After all, they've done nothing but help him at this point, take the bat out, help him to his feet. He took her hand.

Jamal felt her warm hands wrapping right over his. She had a beautiful smile, but her eyes were swollen, and watery. She closed her eyes, and with a forced smile, he could tell, she didn't want to do this. But what was *this?* His eyes stretched open as the air around him turned ice cold, hair on his arms standing on ends, and goosebumps covered his arms. This woman had veins over her body, black and purple lights flared on his hands. He wanted nothing but to be free of her, but with his leg, he wouldn't get far, and the air around him seemed frozen in place. He physically couldn't move. The veins on her hand crawled on his and crawled their way up his arm to his shoulders. These veins to him, felt like worms crawling, burying themselves in his skin.

The veins burrowed, connecting their nerves to Jamal's circulatory veins, sending messages throughout his body. The veins carried those messages to the brain, connecting Ilya's veins to Jamal's amygdala, feeding Ilya his most recent memories, specifically what caused him to be so frightened. That is where this memory would be.

Jamal felt violated, and insecure. His pupils rattled inside the whites of his eyes, pinning back and forth, feeling the worm-like veins crawl over his entire body, and invaded his internal systems. He felt the veins wiggling through his body and felt sharp pains throughout his body where the veins were: Spine, heart, chest, the bones, neck, and finally his brain, producing a severe migraine. Finally, he was able to scream, and from the look on the woman's face, it seemed the scream was sharply unexpected, and scratched her ears.

Her veins retracted from him, and receded back to her own body, and within a few moments of her heavy breathing, the veins completely faded back into her skin and the warmth returned to the air. Jamal's body trembled, leaning heavily against the tree, coughing. Jamal covered his mouth as he felt something coming up from his stomach. Coughing, blood spurted out of the hand he covered his mouth with.

"Do you know what he looks like?" Culain asked.

"Yes," Ilya answered. She looked with a concerned face to Jamal. *It won't be long before mana sickness kicks in. You have one week, and the mana will kill you.*

"Good," Culain sighed.

There was a wind that moved through the air as Culain looked Jamal in the face. Then Ilya looked away from Jamal and towards Culain, whose hand was outstretched to his side as if he was holding something, and in his hand materialized his black spear with the elongated red spearhead. Alexander lit a match and dropped it on the ground, streams of flame lit up the gasoline river streaming towards the car in the middle of the street.

"Sorry kid. No witnesses, besides, you don't want to die by radiation sickness," Culain glared at Jamal. "Caster's rules. You aren't permitted to see our shenanigans. Honestly, I wish there was another way."

"Wh—why?" Jamal whimpered, stumbling backwards over the curb. He quickly stood back up, carefully watching Culain, and he looked like a cornered rat without a hole to scurry off in, "Please don't kill me! I'm sorry! Since when was robbing someone an executable offense?"

"You are nothing, but lambs sent to be slaughtered!" Culain's face cringed as his mouth opened. The spear came at Jamal faster than a speeding train, piercing his heart, and protruding out of his back. Culain retracted the spear back out, tearing through more flesh, blood sprayed everywhere. "Besides, you don't want to be alive when Ilya absorbs your life force. Trust me, that is worse than what you've just been through. Nothing is louder than having the world erase you from existence!"

Ilya looked down to Jamal, tears swelled up her eyes. She felt his eyes must be growing heavy, flickering like a candle, and his eye lids drooped down as he clutched his chest. Blood poured out from his wound. Before Jamal died, he looked up one last time, squinted at Ilya. While he said nothing, Ilya felt like he was asking to be spared, but she wasn't going to disobey that commandment.

She contorted her face as she pulled out her knife. She drew the purple runes in the air again. Her body was covered yet again in mana veins. "Cu'er na vorgen. Cha. Lathuka prath'haken," she pushed her mana streams out as the normal mana streams of human flesh, organs, blood, and bone was slowly burned away by her own mana. These bodies soon faded away into nothing as their mana entered Ilya's mana reserves.

She let out a sigh of relief and let out a smile. She felt like she drank a nice cold glass of water, feeling refreshed. *I'm sorry. But I needed it.* She smiled as she clasped her own chest. Blanka removed the shapes she drew around them, and the purple barrier vanished. Time and space returned to normal, and there was not one trace of mana left, no evidence there was a crime, for the oil and gasoline were burned away. Ilya converted the wreckage and glass into mana, which she then drank through her mana veins again.

"They say that dead men tell no tales. That's a boldfaced lie," Culain said to himself. "The reality is this, there is no witness more reliable than a corpse."

Chapter 14

The Holy Grail

~Why do you want my friendship? There isn't a point in a life like
mine.

Sarah patrolled the empty streets of London with Bridgette. It was early in the morning, where the only people they would see at night, would be the police officers patrolling the streets or driving around in their ugly cars, or the occasional disgusting mistress of the night, or conman dealing with illegal deals. *Such worthless creatures. They aren't worth saving.*

Bridgette was quiet tonight, a nice change of pace as Sarah was getting rather annoyed with her constant talking and yappering. In many ways, she reminded Sarah of the new girl playing in the little sandbox, trying to make friends with everyone, and everyone returned the felicity; however, they all secretly hated her. In this case, she knew why people hated Bridgette, she was an ass to everyone she encountered. Well, there was no helping it, she was stuck with her until her task was done. She was here for a while and she knew that it was only a matter of time before someone might catch hold of their ruse, but she couldn't leave without completing the task of stealing the Grail, damn Brits. But she needed an opportunity to get down to the

Archive's basement, and it wasn't like an opportunity would just reveal itself. She had to make one, but how? She turned her attention back to Bridgette, who snarled, baring her teeth as she walked.

"You seem quiet tonight. Why? Do you feel uneasy?" Sarah asked, trying to seem sympathetic, but she didn't honestly care.

Bridgette let out a sigh as she peered at the bare moon, with the few stars to accompany the black sky, filled. The perpetual black stain of the world caused by someone's careless opening of Pandora's Box perpetuated the foul stench of humanity, and demonology. Nothing sits right in the world. "I'm jaded, I suppose. I am exhausted, much like everyone else, and much like you. I feel like a blanket with too few stitches, there are holes in it, and it easily comes apart. Every caster you see feels the same way, and those that strive to get from with it, by breaking through the code are immediately put down. We put them down, you see, for the fabric of the world would come undone if all this information we held made it to the rest of the world. There was one time where it all came close."

"Hitler," she knew the history of it too well.

She knew the story, the books in her elementary school called him a devil, and without further context, sure, he's the devil. But the truth of the matter was, some Jewish people discovered the Holy Grail as it was in the middle of being transported from Scotland to London. They found out about it and started circulating some rumors across Europe. Now, no one knew where the rumors started, but it got out of control. The High Council decided that to fix the problem, a World War would need to be started, and someone had to volunteer. That volunteer was Hitler. They had the scapegoat; they had the means. He would forever be known as the Devil of Humanity, and the Caster Administration put him up to it.

"Yeah, and like Hitler, none of us want any part of it," Bridgette said. "And I'm jaded, we all are. Eventually we'll all be nothing more than soulless husks."

"Is it worth it?" Sarah found herself wondering. The world she knew was abundantly different than the one her classmates from elementary school knew. She began to wonder if unraveling the fabrics of creation would ultimately be a better solution than continue on a living death; in doing so, God's heart would truly be broken.

"I don't know if I think it's worth it or not. I think so, or maybe that's just the lie I keep telling myself. Makes it easier," Bridgette replied. "But I'd be lying. I don't think it is, but I keep doing it. I keep obeying these orders for the hopes of preserving creation, sometimes I think it's better just to let it burn, hell, maybe we should light the match ourselves." Sarah opened her eyes. She didn't think anyone would openly say that, but even she believed it. "Ah, that's just me talking. Pay it no mind."

"We were never told any of this at the American Branch," she lied.

"Because you are all fools," Bridgette replied, looking back into the distance. "Americans don't spend time learning everything that is important, where you come from. You are all hypocrites."

"I'd say that's hardly fair, and misguided." *That's it. Just make her think we're all arrogant asses.*

"Maybe I'm wrong, or perhaps you're wrong. Be that as it may, we can never accept—"

Sarah felt the wind abruptly change direction. She felt chills as the temperature around her dropped, her hair standing on ends. She felt the mana in the air being pulled on a singular focal point in front of them. The wind churned again from another direction, spiraling up with heavy winds; Sarah felt like she was in the eye of the storm. Sarah turned around swiftly, jumped off to sidewalk, away from the spinning vortex. Bridgette stood by, glaring at the center of it, the wind whistled in the air that the moisture turned into razor sharp ice blades.

Bridgette gazed dispassionately as her hand reached out. Her blue mana veins glowed throughout her body, channeling the mana from the air into her hand, materializing a broadsword. The blue veins crawled from her arm, encapsulating the blade she held in the air.

A flash of lightning ripped through the ground, and then a clap of thunder roared. In the ground was now an opened chasm with freezing wind pushing up from it, pulling Sarah's hair away from her face. She pulled her hat down as she gazed into the abyss. She took a deep breath and pulled all the cold mana from the air into her mana veins. Her body was glowing blue, like Bridgette's, and she held her hand to the left of her, and her spear manifested into her hand.

A second flash of lightning struck the ground they stood upon, followed by another clap of thunder. This lightning was blacker than the hole that seemed to completely empty inside, and with no end in sight. The rocks of the crust of the earth swirled around in the large vortex, making the hole larger with every passing moment.

Sarah investigated the hole, and then turned back to Bridgette. A third strike of lightning rained down on them, emitting from the hole. The chasm produced numerous streams of lightning.

She took a deep breath as there was a loud hissing noise coming in from the hole. She looked down, and she saw a vast mass of shimmering scaley light at the end of the tunnel. She looked closely and it was a large mass of snakes, curled up in a large sphere, rolling up from the chasm. The hissing continued.

"Get away from the hole!" Bridgette called out.

The sphere picked up momentum, vibrating inside the hole, releasing various rocks and debris from the crust of the earth. Sarah jumped away from the hole, pointing her spear at the epicenter. Bridgette was muttering something underneath her breath. Sarah pulled in the mana into her eyes, observing the mana streams Bridgette was casting. The streams of mana, brown, grey, silver, blue, green wove together like a basket, marking many runes into the air.

The sphere of snakes crossed the threshold of the portal into Pandora, hissing. Sarah pushed her fear behind her, as it came rolling towards her. She firmly planted her spear in the ground, her mana veins turning silver as they started wrapping around her spear. The sphere rolled onto the spear, and she thrust upwards as her mana veins turned silver, pulling the mana from the poor quality of the essence from the minerals in the earth. It wasn't ideal to be using concrete for that, but it was something.

The hissing was like that of a burst pipe, and numerous streams of yellow mana from Bridgette's mana source shot out like a beam into the sphere, ripping apart several snakes, casting them aside as they withered like dying plants.

"Don't look into their eyes! That is a Medusa! Don't look into their eyes. The Greeks got that myth right, although only partially. Their gaze will turn you into dust!" Bridgette pointed her sword at her.

Sarah saw another creature climbing out of the hole, the black silhouette had the body of a giant with a horse's head attached. The beast, whatever this one was called was the size of a small house, and certainly very agile. Bridgette struck its arm, and it *clinked.* Her blue mana veins penetrated her sword and struck through the arm, slicing it off, and the beast squealed as its blood sprayed.

Another source of black lightning struck the earth over into the next block. Sarah pushed off from the sphere, ducking behind a street sign. Medusa, completely manifested from slithering serpents, threw a small serpent at Sarah, who stabbed it with her spear. She noticed at the corner of her eye, another creature coming out of the hole. She couldn't tell what this one looked like.

"Sarah! Get back to the administration and wake everyone up. We have a Portal Storm on our hands!"

"What about y—"

"I'll be fine, but this is beyond anything you and I can handle by ourselves!" Bridgette asserted. "I can hold the three of them for a time, I can't handle any more than that. I don't know how useful you are yet, but two casters can't handle a Portal Storm! I'd call, but bloody hell, too much mana interferes with electronic communication."

Sarah nodded before slicing at the Medusa with her spear, ripping through its flesh, spraying its green blood on the ground. She inhaled the mana from the air through her mana veins, and her entire body was covered in them. With a jump, she landed onto the roof of a building, and started running across the rooftops, thinking to herself, *this is strangely convenient. Colton, did and how did you plan this? What is your game?*

***

Bridgette looked at the blue streams of light moving across the sky. She dropped a stone on the ground and jumped away from the horse beast: the humanoid creature with flesh decayed, and the side of its mouth was exposed. She saw a large hand with a claw, ripping up the concrete, making obnoxiously loud noises as the various rocks and stones struck nearby buildings.

Why such a heavily populated area, and why here of all places! There is no way they can keep this hidden. We're going to have to kill a lot of people tonight.

This other creature flew above her. She penetrated the sword with her blue mana veins as she jumped up, cleaving its left wing. Red blood sprayed as the wing came off, the creature crashed into the building behind her, collapsing the roof, and killed the people inside. Her heart filled with dismay as Medusa came over to her and especially since she started to see lights get turned on. *A lot of people are going to die tonight.*

Medusa tossed a snake at her. She closed her eyes, moving away, and she felt a pinch in her arm. . .

***

Sarah pushed the door open into the Administration building. There were few people inside the initial threshold into the office, minus the receptionist. There were some others enjoying a cup of tea who immediately turned their heads with alarm as the door swung opened violently, nearly pulled off its hinges. The receptionist immediately stood up and glared at her.

"Portal Storm. We have a Portal Storm!" She pointed her spear outside.

The receptionist's eyes opened wide and immediately picked up the phone. She pressed a button and dialed a number. As her phone rang, she opened her drawer. "Administrator," she said. "We have a Portal Storm. Yes. Understood."

The people in the office immediately gulped down their tea, leaving the cups on the tables in the lounge area of the vestibule, and turned, walking to Sarah. "American. Where?" the man asked. He was stern, tall, and menacing, well, to anyone else, but not Sarah. He had scars on his face.

"Corner of Sanford and Edward street," she immediately answered. "Bridgette was there."

Click!

The lights in the room turned red, and a machine in the corner started emitting silent waves of mana, completely undetectable to the normal human.

The man took the others in the room and ran out the door, sprinting in the direction of Sanford and Edward Street.

She could hear the rattling coming from behind the corridors of the administration building. Administrator Sander came running out, with about fifteen other casters behind him, their mana veins already breathing the air, blue lights flashed as they sprinted down the halls. Sander stopped to look into her eyes as a man who had seen far too many battles. His shoulders were broad, and his eyes angled down his nose as he looked into her. "Yes, did you report this in?"

"Yes, Administrator," she replied, looking intently into his eyes. "It's at the corner of Sanford and Edward Street."

"Well, one of the portals anyhow. With me. We need to get down to it," he immediately turned to the receptionist. "Melissa, call in help from Cambridge. We need to put a stifle on this immediately. Operation Black Light."

"Lead the way Caster!" shouted one of the women irritably in the back, wiping sleep from her eyes.

McCurdy nodded her head and sprinted out the door. The Administrator and the casters followed behind her, blue mana veins lit up the streets as they sprinted through them, over buildings and across alleys, keeping eye on the blue shining lights and the lightning Portal Storm looming not far ahead of them. McCurdy thought to herself, *a lot of innocent people are going to die tonight, by accident or threcket food, however, more people are going to be killed by the Administration itself for witnessing such a thing while the rest of the casters halt time to clean up the mess.* She grimaced at the thought as she led them closer to the Portal Storm. *It is sickening. There must be a better way than to kill those we are made to protect. There must be a better way. But be that as it may, the Casters Administration building is now empty, guarded only by a mere receptionist. Casters from Cambridge are sure to come by and trying to clean up the mess is going to be damn near impossible to do over night. This is far too convenient to my liking. Colton, did you plan this?*

Bridgette was nowhere to be found amidst all the shining lights of blue, green, red and blinding white. There were a handful of casters about, and an innumerous amount of these creatures, pouring through the cracks of the earth. All the lights were on in all the buildings, and some sirens poured out with ambulances, police, and fire trucks, which didn't last long without being torn to shreds.

Flames roared, buildings collapsed, bodies crushed and bled out into the sewers.

Children and babies cried as their parents ran with them in their arms, without a moment to think about what they saw. Their flight response moved them away from collapsing buildings, and exploding cars, and flying debris.

To her horror, but not to her surprise, there was an archer, his blond hair was filled with dirt, and his eyes were focused. One might think he was a trained killer, had it not been the tears and hesitation in his eyes. He followed protocol, as only he could, the one archer on the field, taking his mana infused arrows, shooting through running men, women, and their children. He sprinted off the buildings he used for his vantage point. One after another, he killed these innocent people. The arrows pierced his targets every time, never missing his shot, and the corpses of the dead bubbled as their life force faded into burning ash. But she noticed it wasn't just this archer killing normies. There were a few more archers patrolling the streets of London, with the sole purpose of killing normies while Sander and the rest of the casters were dealing with these portals and house-sized threckets.

Their life force was then imbibed by surrounding casters approaching the scene, using the mana to slay these threckets, and creatures coming up from these portals from the *other side*.

The casters Sarah was with went on without her. Jumping from the streets to the buildings, summoning their weapons: chains, spears, lances, swords, and axes to their hands as they moved down on the portals. Another class of caster came out, the *True Casters* which were few and far between, and exceptionally dangerous. They took their mana infused knives and drew runes at the sides of the portals, screaming incantations.

They left her by herself. *This is too convenient. Or the UK branch is very stupid.*

She drank the mana from the air, and the bright blue veins crawled up her legs as she sprinted back towards the administration building. She looked behind her, saw flares of red, white, green, blue, and black lights. The threckets roared, buildings and cars exploded, and more people died. Merely unlucky people just to be seen by that cursed archer. And there he was again, erasing all proof of their miserable existence. All those casters were far too occupied to be dealing with her, and she knew it, and she was skeptical. Because this was all *too* convenient.

She arrived at the building. She sprinted through the doors. The receptionist gave her a surprised look. The receptionist reached for a button underneath the counter. Sarah's eyes narrowed as she threw her spear into the receptionist's head. She fell silent, dead, her body going as still as a limp fish as she was impaled against the wall behind her.

Sarah yanked the spear from the wall, she pulled in mana from the air, weaving it with mana from the wood in the table, and the glass from the mugs, and her veins protruded from her flesh, crawling onto her spear as it faded away. She ran down the hall towards the library of archives. She broke right in with ease and ran down the stairs. She ran down several flights until she came to a large square room, filled with various artifacts, but she came here for one thing only. And she found herself looking at it, the Holy Grail, fused with the purple welding to the Box of Pandora. The Grail, it was this beautiful object, golden, with silver lettering in old Anglo-Saxon language, a language that was dead, but there was just something so beautiful about it. The silver writing appeared to glow, carved by the Holy Hand of King Arthur Pendragon himself, or that is how the old stories were told. King Arthur, how shamed would he be if he saw the state of the world today, or even the wretched treachery of his Beloved Caster Administration. But the Box, Pandora's Box, the cursed wretched thing was so infused to the Holy Grail that it was beyond separation. She cautiously walked over to the Grail, to touch it. Her hand stretched over to the threshold of the Grail, and before she could touch it, a searing pain filled her wrist as a sharp red light flashed from the ceiling to her.

She sucked the air through her teeth, retracting her hand as she moved to the side, observing the runes implanted in the ceiling above the Holy Grail. *Should've known.* She placed her hand out at the ceiling, her fingertips were spread as she imbibed the mana from the air. She then took another drink of mana, pulling it from the steel and concrete of the floors and foundations. Her arm was covered in concentrated mana of red, violet, and magenta colors swirling around her arms. Colored runes swirled around her body, pulling mana from the room from various sources into her body. Her eyes glowed red, fueled with complete passion, complete hatred as the mana veins penetrated her pupils, "Geinseglian Liesing!"

The light emitting from the ceiling faded, and the contents of the Holy Grail was revealed. The liquid inside, should have at one point been golden, but as it was infused with the Box of Pandora, the content was filled with purple smoke, filled with nothing but curses. The same force that created this cruel world and all its malformities. She grabbed the Holy Grail, and the Box of Pandora and sprinted upstairs.

She ran through the archives and out the main hallway. To her surprise, pleasantly, no one was here. *They should have sent someone back here by now to ensure the archives integrity.* She scoffed as she sprinted to her quarters. She grabbed her bag and put the Grail inside it. She strapped it to herself before facing the wall. She drank the mana from the air, the bars, the floor and the foundation as the mana veins flowed through her body again. She approached the back wall and placed her hands on it. The veins glowed black this time as her entire body was covered in black mana, and she phased through the wall.

***

What felt like hours passed, Bridgette was leaning against a building, her sword dematerialized now that all of the threckets were slain, and portals were closed. She breathed heavily, covering her left eye with her hands. The rest of the administration was searching the now abandoned buildings for surviving normies. If anyone was found, and might be savable, they were killed immediately. All part of the damn dreaded code.

"Still alive?" She heard a voice from above her. He jumped down from the rooftop.

"Unfortunately," she answered. "Did anything happen to Sarah?"

"I did a brief roll call, and everyone is accounted for, except her," he said. "I went back to the office, and I'm just coming back now. Melissa is dead, and it turns out, someone went into the archives, and the Holy Grail is missing."

"You think she did it, don't you?" Bridgette asked.

"Everyone else is accounted for. The threckets wouldn't dare look for it there," he replied.

Bridgette stared at him like that was the dumbest thing she's heard. "What would she even want with it?"

"What would who want with it would be the better question," Sander replied. "This was all too convenient. Someone was behind the portal storms, and that someone in all likelihood knew what Sarah was here—"

Bridgette heard coughing from underneath the rubble and turned to it. Some rocks moved and a little hand stretched out, attached to a little boy. The boy cried, "Help me. Momma! Momma! Papa!" he kept weeping. Bridgette knew the boy's legs were crushed underneath the weight of all that rock, and a weight filled her chest, because this was all too familiar. She knew what needed to happen next.

Sander placed his hand over the boy's head; magenta mana veins covered his hand as the boy now laid dead, a quiet death, and a simple one. Bridgette looked at the boy, a mop covered head, dirty face, and a face that the worst of mothers would love. She knew he was dead and knew that the way Sander killed him was painless, and that was a mercy. *But why is this even necessary?*

She started weeping, sliding down to the ground, burying her face in her hands, "Sander, there has to be another way."

"Do you think all I do is send you all out to fight these threckets and erase evidence? No. I'm researching for a better way. The problem is, I have a theory, and am ultimately disappointed. I end up in dead ends of things that have already been tried," he sat down next to her. "I've ran out of ideas. Everything's been tried already."

Chapter 15

Façade

~As everything fades, the music, the laughter; the smile, the bandage; the makeup and the masks, once it is all removed, we find out for ourselves that we were never okay.

Two weeks later, since Sam saw Ted, she was back at Park Street on a Tuesday night, walking upwards of Park Street, taking a right on Beacon street. They all had umbrellas, some were small, and others were wide, colorful, or plain black.

The air was cooler when the breeze passed through their clothes, caressing their bare, exposed skin. The rain was falling down ever so lightly, as if the heavens were undecided if it wanted to rain, the *drip drop* landed into puddles in the sidewalks and streets as cars were driving by, their wheels spinning out water, drenched unsuspecting pedestrians too careless to bring an umbrella.

As Samantha was leading the study this night, she couldn't help but think she might find Ted at Teri Nation. He wasn't there last week, according to Scott, and seemed to avoid them the week before that. She also noticed that Jennifer seemed a little down today, not her usual self. Samantha hasn't seen Jennifer at all since the game night she hosted two weeks ago. Samantha looked down to the ground at her feet, her shoes splashed in the small shallow puddles in the sidewalk.

Did something happen between him and Jennifer after we left? She thought.

She hurried up and hooked Jennifer's elbow, who seemed startled. Samantha saw something in Jennifer's eyes that she hadn't seen before, and it filled the air like a stench of regret. She should have known something was off, Jennifer wasn't her usual joking self, not these last two weeks, and the last time she saw Jennifer as herself was at the party, before she left her and Ted alone in the apartment. *He didn't try to hurt her, would he?*

"Hiii!" Jennifer exclaimed. Her face lit up with her bright smile again. "What brings you to my side on such a rainy night?"

Sam needed only to speak to her, and they were far away out of earshot from everyone else following them that night. Their conversation would be kept private.

"Well, I was thinking. I haven't seen Ted in a while. Have you heard of anything?" she asked.

Jennifer sighed through the rain, and sucked the air through her teeth, hissing. "I can't say I've heard from him," she answered, turning her head away from Sam. "I haven't heard from him since that night."

"Have you tried calling him again? Or texting?" Sam was suspicious and couldn't help but fight this feeling that Jennifer was hiding something.

"Yes," she answered. "I started getting abrupt responses again."

"What did he say?" The curve in Samantha's lips became less prominent.

"The last thing he told me, was that he wasn't someone I wanted to get close with. Whatever that means," she exhaled deeply, "Oh, well, nothing we can do about it, right?"

Jennifer's smile returned to her face, and the rain grew heavier, pounding her umbrella with such a tremendous force, as if handing its burden onto them. *Ted.* Samantha followed Jennifer through the bar, waving at Scott as they entered.

Jennifer sat at the bar and took out her purse. Sam sat next to her. They were alone for the most part, the rest had yet to catch up to them. They did manage to see the four foreigners drinking to themselves in the corner again. She was not going to bother them tonight.

Scott asked Jennifer, "Having the special?"

"Not today, Scott," she answered, smiling at him. "I'm afraid I'm not in the mood for an adventure tonight. The house bourbon on the rocks is fine by me. Just for tonight."

"Who are you?" Sam asked, joking with her. "I'll take a merlot."

"Big spender today, aren't we?" Jennifer joked with a half-enthused smile.

"You could say that," Sam turned to Scott and slid her card across the table. "I'm buying today," Scott's eyebrows raised as he disappeared behind the bar top. Samantha turned back to Jennifer with a smile. "I got my commission check last week. And you always buy my drinks, it's time I returned the favor."

"Why thank you so much!" Jennifer exclaimed.

Scott came by with the drinks in hand, including the receipt. Samantha took the receipt and wrote in a generous tip. Scott eyes popped. "Thanks, Sam." He sped off to check on the foreigners.

"What's wrong," Sam asked.

Just then, a wave of people came in, flooding the bar. The noise came in like a rushing wave. Out of the corner of her eye, she could see the foreigners getting uncomfortable with the noise. The hostile man she met two weeks ago sneered from across the room. *Or was it last week?*

"Iah—" Jennifer began.

"Hey!" Michael's arm reached over Sam's shoulder. He waved down Scott. "I'll take the special."

Scott smiled back at him, "Whatever that is."

Michael looked down, smiling at everyone, until he noticed that Jennifer was *not* drinking a strange concoction, "Not feeling adventurous today?"

"Can't say that I'm up for an adventure," Jennifer smiled back at him as she took a sip from her rocks glass. "Maybe you can use this as an excuse to finally coerce Brian into drinking some of Scott's lovely aromas."

"But I like my drinking buddy," he jested. "Oh well, maybe next week. I need to catch up with him anyways."

"Ta ta for now!" Jennifer laughed. But it was slightly lower than usual, as if somewhere between a reluctant laugh, or a forced one. Sam couldn't quite tell as Michael scurried off into the unusually larger than normal Tuesday night crowd. *Brian was real busy today.*

"So, Jennifer. What's wrong? I can tell when you're not yourself."

Jennifer smiled at her as she took another sip, "Why, nothing out of the ordinary."

"Jennifer. You're laughs are half genuine. I can't tell if you're actually happy right now," she said, placing one of her hands atop hers on the bar top and looked her in the eyes. "You can pretend to borrow Ted's smile, as wide as it is, but they can't hide your laughs. You have unique laughs. I love your laughs. So, out with it, please. What's wrong?"

Jennifer let out a sigh and placed her drink on the counter of the bar. "It's Ted," she said. Her smile began to fade, and her eyes watered. "He showed me a part of him, a part that he kept hidden. He is not what he seems."

"Did he hurt you?" she exclaimed softly. "Don't—"

"What, no!" Jennifer corrected herself, turning abruptly to her, "Don't even mention the idea. He is not like that! He may not be what he seems, but he is far from a monster that would hurt someone in her own apartment!"

"What did he show you?" Sam brought her voice down low.

Sam looked into Jennifer's eyes, those cold, trembling eyes, glimmering in the bar as golden light reflected upon them, like the emission of little flames. "I saw nothing but agonizing pain. Just that. Pain, and nothing else. He is restless and suffers from what I can only imagine the most extreme form of insomnia I have ever heard of. He sleeps not more than thirty minutes a night. It's like he's hiding pain that just wants to get screamed out, but when he tries, he can't."

Sam remembered asking him a question that may have touched upon his insomnia. She recalled he would only give her vague few-worded answers that never really answered the question. *The man is mysterious, and a tough nut to crack.*

"We talked a little about peace, in our little conversation there. In there, I found that he does not hold any peace in his heart. He has never known a home. Or so he said. He has some siblings, but he talked as if they were just part of his past, and nothing of their relationship remained," she took another sip of her cup as it trembled in her hand. "A man like that, can truly exist. But the mere act of living brings nothing but pain to him."

"Do you think he's suicidal? Because if so, we need to get him help!" Her smile was gone.

"Someone once told me, 'The brightest smiles bring us the greatest of joys. The loudest laughter is like a grand orchestra, and the most beautiful faces are covered in makeup, because we are okay, and everything is fine. The brightest smile is like a bandage, it looks okay, but inside the wound still festers, asking to be cut off. They say laughter is the best medicine. And the mask is our way of making ourselves look more beautiful, to reduce our flaws and hide our scars. When the smiles fade away and the bandage is ripped off; when the laughter is silenced and the music stops, when the makeup is washed away, and our mask fades, we find that we were never truly okay.'" She ignored the question.

"Oh my god!" Sam covered her mouth with her hand. In the most obscure way, Jennifer answered the question with an anecdote to depression. She understood the imagery loud and clear, but Jennifer never actually said she believed Ted to be in danger of suicide.

"Iah—I just wished I thought of it sooner," Jennifer said, her face went blank, as if staring at something that wasn't there.

"When was the last time you got a response from Ted?" Sam asked.

"Last Friday," she answered. She put the glass down. She buried her face in her hands. "Sam, if you would, leave me alone for a minute. I just can't. I can't." She choked on the last, "I can't".

Sam patted her shoulder. "If ever you need to talk," she found herself choking on her words. "You know I am here, and you know how to get in touch with me. You know this."

Samantha went into the crowd, searching for Erin. If anyone's had contact with Ted, it would be her, although Erin didn't seem to have any kind of relationship with Ted at all, Jennifer seemed to be the only one. *And she wasn't even the first of us to speak to him.*

Samantha caught sight of Erin and walked up beside her, elbowing her. Erin looked at her, sipping from her cider. "Well," Erin said to her. "You made me spill by drink."

"I'm sorry," Sam hesitated. "I needed to ask you something. Has Ted been showing up at work at all?"

"Yes. Still the workaholic. What is it with you and Ted? Aren't you and Michael dating? And I thought Jennifer had the hots for him." She turned in her stool and took another sip of her cider.

"What?" Sam stepped back. "No, I'm not dating Ted, but that's not the point. Look, it's just that, it's just that he is new. I'm not romantically invested in him at all. Here he is in Boston, by himself, and doesn't seem to have any network of friends of family here. He comes off as a loner," Samantha replied. "Did *he* seem off to you?"

"No, he seems like the same old Ted," Erin answered. "I mean, he comes around like clockwork. He moves around the clock always. His behavior doesn't really change."

"What about after Jennifer's apartment the week before?" she asked.

"No," Erin scratched her chin.

Sam felt defeated, she was trying to piece together who Ted was, and knowing now that Jennifer was emotionally invested in him, she felt a wave of concern fall upon her heart. Ted was like an already drawn on canvas, vibrant in colors, but the artist is unknown, and his strokes of the brush was unknown, hidden upon layers and layers of paint, layers of layers of different personalities, all competing for dominance on one painting.

"Wait," Erin said, her voice dropped a bit. "Actually, I suppose this was a little unusual. On that Monday, he seemed very energetic, more so than usual. It would have been like he got a good night sleep or something, or accidently inhaled some speed. That would have been cause for concern, but he immediately went to his typical self the next day."

"I see."

"Did he disappear again?"

"I suppose you could say that."

"Look, Sam, a man like that sells himself to his work. For him, it's like nothing else matters or exists outside of it. Trust me when I say this, you may see him again, you may not. He may readily move across the country tomorrow if he thought to. He isn't the type of man to keep friends. At least, that's the vibe I get from him."

"That's a sad life to live," Sam's voice dropped.

"He seems satisfied with it, all the same," Erin sighed. "As much as I would love to have his level of success, I mean, that is a ton of money, I wouldn't trade my friends and family for it."

"Satisfied does not mean fulfilled," Sam reasoned, *but what if he didn't want to be fulfilled?*

"I don't think he wants a fulfilled life," Erin gave her rebuttal. "Look, people get into stocks to make money, and to make a lot of it. Ted, as far as I can tell, has never lost anything so far, his portfolio, and the portfolio of his clients grows exponentially. He doesn't seem happy with it, like he goes through the motions," she let out a deep sigh. "It's like, whatever he is going through, that he's just stopped caring. He doesn't seem to care about the money at all, and he's raking it in every single hour. My suggestion, if you don't see him again, is to just let it go. Just let him go."

"I see," Sam didn't feel like talking about this anymore. She was concerned, as if something was pulling at her heart. "Thank you for that."

"Look, Sam, I'm sorry," Erin looked her closely in the eyes and put her free hand on her shoulder. "For what good it is worth, I completely agree with you, and I don't think it's a healthy path that he's walking on. And I don't know if this is going to help you get anywhere with him, but I asked him about that last big deal he brokered out, and why he didn't seem satisfied with it. It was because he knew the answer. It's like he wants to be wrong, as if there is one mistake in his life that led him to believe was inevitable, like being wrong would undo that mistake."

"Thank you for that, Erin. You gave me more than I could have hoped for," she smiled, but she couldn't say she felt happy about the answers she received tonight.

Samantha left Erin to continue whatever conversation she was having with Brian. She understood that Erin spoke from a place of matter of fact, and with little empathy. Of course, she meant well, and certainly no malice was ever intended, it didn't always come across that way, especially with this. She certainly was upfront about things, and blunter than Michael. Sam works with truck drivers; she should know how to deal with this by now.

She walked back over to the bar where Jennifer was. Her glass was empty, but her umbrella was still there, leaning just underneath the bar.

Jennifer's coat was gone. *Maybe she got a call from Ted. That is highly unlikely at this point,* she sighed.

"So, did you finally make your rounds?" said a very smiling Michael.

"I did," Sam looked up to him. She finished her glass of wine. "I'm worried."

Michael's phone buzzed in his pocket. "Why are you worried?" He asked as he picked up his phone to read something he found enticing on the web.

"Ted. I feel like we made some headway with him, but—"

"You get the feeling he never showed us who he was and are now concerned that something might have happened to him. You are concerned because you feel like he was growing on us to the point where he would consider himself to be one of us?"

"Well, yeah," she said indignantly.

"I wish I could think like that," he laughed, and his face immediately went dark as he read the headline of a news article. "The reality is that we often don't know ourselves well enough to read into others, and we think we can read into others so easily. There are those who protect themselves with an unbreakable wall," he sighed. "Do you remember that philosophical question, 'what happens when an unstoppable lance meets an immovable shield'?"

"I remember the question. I don't remember the outcome," she admitted.

"The shield won. The lance shattered and its rider came tumbling down," he replied. "Look, some shields just can't be broken, and some walls won't come down, no matter how hard you smash against them. There is only one way through, and that is around that shield," he pointed his finger in the air with a half-raised hand and moved it in a circular motion, "hoping there is some kind of crack in there. You can only make it through the crack."

"So, in other words, pain," she came to the sudden realization, that only pain would make it through. She can only talk to Ted through pain, and that is the only thing he truly understood. Or so she thought. She focused on Michael's phone, "So, what has your eyes so captivated when I'm right here?"

"The suicide rate just spiked up," he answered. "We are beating Japan."

"Great," Sam sighed, *and Ted might become a victim of that.* "As if the world didn't have enough problems. That is not something we need to be beating Japan in."

"I guess, in part it is our fault," Michael said.

"How do you mean?" She looked into his eyes with concern.

"How busy are we? We constantly move and move and move, never slowing down for a second, never checking in on our own mental health. It is inevitable that we will follow the same road, down our own broken-down insanity. How many times do we see the same thing on the streets? How often do we turn our eyes against those who are struggling with their own strife, never lending out a hand?" He locked his phone and put it back in his pocket. "How many times have we seen someone, and not offered to help them? I'm guilty Sam. Every single day. I wish, there was more than we could do in the world, you know, something that's more than giving someone a meal, more than giving them our spare change that we know we'll never use. Our spare change, is it really giving it to them? Or are we merely just discarding that which we think is already garbage? Our scraps, we have many, but to those who have nothing, to those born with nothing, those scraps are like mounds of gold, piled up. We, as Christians, need to be doing more than whatever it is we've been doing. Our inactivity is what is killing us inside. It's like every single one of us is living off borrowed time and we don't know it."

"Michael," Sam immediately thought of Ted again. "Do you think Ted is—is at risk?"

"I'm afraid I don't know him well enough to answer," he replied, shaking his head. "I feel the only one who may have some inkling of an idea of how he feels, is Jennifer. I don't have an answer."

"I'm going to go," she said, her face turned graven at the bar. She put the rest of her wine on the counter and left it.

"Do you need me to walk you to the T?"

"No," she answered. "I'll be fine. I just need to clear my head."

He smiled at her as she turned away, walking out of the back of the bar. She made it down the stairs and walked over the red carpet, being made aware of everyone around her, waitresses with artificial smiles walking with empty glasses on their trays. The people in the pub were laughing with their smiles, without a care in the world.

Were they hurting somewhere, deep inside, Sam wondered, were they all patched up with those bandages, and were their laughs singing? Did they remember to wear their masks and put their makeup on?

She turned to ignore them. She was relieved to find that it stopped raining outside. There were puddles in the ground and Jennifer sat on the side of the curb, her knees up to her chest and her head was buried in her hands, just like she left her. Just like how she'd been inside the bar.

She sat down next to her; the puddle soaked her bottom as she wrapped her left arm around Jennifer. She said nothing. Jennifer raised her head, looking up at the top of the building in front of her. Her eyes were swollen as tears continued to stream down her face. She leaned into Samantha's shoulder. She tried to stifle her own sobs by intermittently sucking in the air through her teeth.

"Iah—I wish there was more I could do. I can't. I can't do it anymore!" she cried.

Sam's heart was forlorn as she leaned her head against Jennifer's. She found herself weeping with her. Jennifer sniffed the snot back into her nose. She offered no words; she knew her friend didn't need words, only an ear to listen to, a lost art in the world. Most people were quick to console their wounded friends with words, with the best of intent, they only pour salt on the wounds. Not Samantha. She listened, and offered no words of encouragement, for that would be undeniably worse than rubbing salt into a festered wound begging to be cut off.

"Why can't I be better?" Jennifer sobbed. "I know I'm not perfect, but I could stand to be a little better. A better person, perhaps if I was more like you, Sam, then perhaps Ted would still find it in his heart to come back to us. I saw—I saw pain, undeniable, unspeakable pain in his eyes. Eyes are like the door into the human heart, his human heart! That isn't something you can easily hide, at least—at least not for very long. Why must I talk so much, without much listening. Why couldn't I have been more like you, Sam?"

Sam rubbed her tears from her own face with her right palms, twisting the tears out. "Because then you wouldn't be you. My gift is listening, but you have something I don't have. Together, we are a complete person, our friendship is something that few can claim. You are a great observer, and you can see pain, where I can't. I just can't," she sobbed with her. "I can listen, but even I can't hear pain. Listening is only good when someone talks to you. But no one can hide from the eyes, no matter how hard they try."

"But if only I—"

"Jennifer. It is possible Ted only spoke to you because he knew you were a talker, and that I am a silent listener. He may not speak to me or open up to me. A man like that doesn't miss anything, not even the smallest detail will slip past him," she sighed. "I must be going, now, Jennifer," she stared at the empty puddles. "Look, God will make a way, even when the gates are completely closed. If God wants him, He will make a path for him to follow, to alleviate his pain."

"And if He doesn't?"

"Then I'm afraid we've done all we can, and all we can ask for," Sam took her hand and pulled Jennifer's head to hers, kissing her forehead. "Good night, Jennifer. We can offer prayer, that's all we can do now. It is out of our hands. Come, let's get you home."

Home.

Samantha took her hand and pulled her up from the sidewalk. They walked the streets towards Park Street Station. Samantha consoled her as they got on opposite sides of the red line, Samantha taking it towards Alewife, and Jennifer taking her train to Ashmont.

Samantha looked overhead at the announcements of the next train towards Ashmont, while not ignoring Jennifer who was sitting on a bench on the other side. Samantha kept thinking to herself as she waited, and she heard a loud screeching noise coming from the subway, bound for Ashmont. She covered her ears with her hands as she watched Jennifer disappear behind the subway. The subway started off again, and she could see a large number of people exiting the station, and Jennifer was no longer there.

Her thoughts drifted off into emptiness, and couldn't shake Ted's face, and his happy smile that seemed so genuine, but now she wasn't so sure; in fact, she was certain the opposite was true. And another thought plagued her mind, at this moment, he was a man of mystery, of which she knew so little, and yet felt compelled to bring him into their own friendship. Especially when there didn't seem to be any rational reason for it. *He needs help.*

She said a silent prayer to herself.

There were bright lights in the tunnel. She looked down the tunnel for the train that was coming this way. The T was never presentable, at least not this late at night: cans and bottles rolled on the floor, used napkins glided across it, and crumbs littered the seats. The train screeched as it came to a halt, and the doors slid open. No one came out, but there was a full train. She stepped on it, grabbing hold of one of the rubber straps secured to the metal bars at the top.

She stood over a woman, maybe in her forties, her right palm planted firmly on her forehead, her face turning red with the passion of some unknown negative emotion. Sam might not be able to see all pain, but this woman was in dire need of a friend, someone to assure her that everything was going to be all right, just a little more encouragement in the deafening roar of everyday city life in Boston.

If only Jennifer was here. She could be that friend. You were always the talkative one, and the reassuring one. Why can't I be like you too? Perhaps, would things have been much different if yours and my personalities were switched? Would we be asking the same questions?

After each stop on the red line, more and more people got off, and fewer and fewer people boarded to replace them. Eventually, after Harvard Square, she found herself utterly alone on that car. She stared out at the blackened tunnel, with the empty glass and irrelevant ads pasted inside the subway car in various places.

To her, he was as much a mystery as many unknown things in the world, like the hostile man, the tall man with a strange name she didn't remember. Ted seemed happy, but she knew now that he was not at all what he seemed. He was more than a happy person, excited about all things, but she knew something deeper than his skin, some layer he revealed to her when no one else was worthy in his eyes.

The light to Davis Square lit up. She stepped off the subway car and walked up the gray-stone stairs. Samantha stepped underneath the roof of the station, gazing out in front of her, the square filled with bars, and now empty restaurants. The rain picked up again. She was about to step outside when she noticed the luminescent light coming from above; looking upwards, she could see the moon gazing down with its light, shining on the streets, glimmering in the puddles. She sighed, taking a step forward, pulling out her umbrella to shield herself from the torrential rain and oppressive moonlight.

The air, it's different tonight. The moonlight, it is different also, alien.

It was like there was some toxic gas in the air with nearby leaking oil drums, just ready to be lit on fire and spurting its gasoline all over the place, setting fire to everything around it.

The stop at Davis did not release too many passengers, and she started to feel like the only one. She was alone in the dark street, like a lamb, or sheep drawing in a pack of wolves to devour it.

She walked on the side street, heading up on College Ave, towards her apartment. The rain kept coming down, harder and harder, splashing bigger puddles in the streets. A late-night car was driving down the road. Its wheels turned, splashing Sam with a large wave of dirty water.

The tears of the heavens were strong. Whatever it had cause for weeping, it kept it in too long, bottled it deep down, never talking to anyone about its problems. The Heavens were silent, keeping and holding all the pain in until finally its flood gates broke open, revealing the insides of its turmoil.

She walked up to the path to her apartment. Her door looked blue in the peeking moonlight. Out of the corner of her eye, three houses down, she saw a man fumbling through his keys to open a door. She looked down as she creaked her door open. Taking a better look at the man, she recognized him, and that bright smile. *Ted. You were this close to me all this time?*

The man opened his door. Sam closed and locked hers. She walked over to the sidewalk and made her way to his house. He entered his house; he shut it firmly behind him. She made it to his door and heard the locks.

First, she could hear the tumbler being locked with the knob. The second lock, she could hear was the deadbolt. And finally, the third and final lock, was a chain. She knew she needed to be secure in her own apartment, here in Somerville, but three locks seemed too much.

The door shook in front of her. She stifled a gasp, covering her mouth. She placed her hand ever so lightly on the door. The door was stilled, and she heard him cry. His cries started as stifled, and intermittent sobs. Then, as just a little time went by the cries went louder. The cries to her, was like that of a child, higher pitched.

Did he have a childhood of grief? Was he exploited or abused? Was he the victim of relational rape? Did he lose his family? Or perhaps was he a child who was born with nothing and wanted nothing more than the experience of children who had even the minimalistic comfort? Was he once a child without innocence, or was that innocence stripped away from him? If so, why did he enlist in the Army, where such things would only break him to the surface, never leaving him. *What is in that brain of yours?*

Samantha took a small, bated breath, and turned away from his stairs. Tears filled her eyes. *Jennifer, if only it was you instead of me. Then, then perhaps it would be different, and maybe there would be a little less pain in the world, and a little more peace. Maybe things would be different.*

She returned to her stoop, bringing her keys back to the door. Her roommate was sleeping peacefully naked on the couch.

Her roommate she did not share in the same standards of living. She wouldn't say she was particularly fond of her roommate either, as she tended to leave things messy. Especially when she knew Sam wouldn't be home until well into the night.

Samantha walked into her roommate's bedroom, yanked the blanket off the bed to tuck her in on the couch her naked body was laying in. Walking into the kitchen, she pulled out some light cleaning gloves before walking back into the living room to clean up the bowl of half-eaten chips, and collect bottles of beer, which were scattered throughout the room. Now, she wasn't afraid of the beer, but she dared not touch the discarded semen-filled condom on the ground with her bare hands. Picking it up, she discarded it into the trash.

She pulled her gloves off, discarding them in the trash and went to the sink, and washed her hands. She walked into her room and changed into blue pajamas. Her tears became swollen as she stared up into the ceiling. Her thoughts drifted into an old story, that she now felt she had to contemplate, this was one she'd read numerous times before, and was a case for inspiration for her, especially when things got difficult. The story of *David and Goliath of Gath*. She re-read the story to herself in her head, told within the first book of *Samuel*. She went over the entire tale, thinking to herself, *why is this coming to me now? And at a time like this? I need action. Not some story about some hope when I live in a world without any.*

And then, it finally came to her. In that story, it was not with man who held victory that day, David was nothing more than a tool. The battle was already won, as was constantly drilled into her brain at Sunday School. But though God never required the assistance of man, He wanted it. God is like a father who asks his six-year-old son to help change the tire of the car on his day off. Of course, He didn't need the help, and with the help of a little boy it would only make the task more difficult, but it was an excuse to spend time with His child, because after all, that tire never needed to be changed. And so sometimes, action was required by humans.

So, Lord, that is what you ask of me.

She pulled out her phone off her bedside table. She opened up her calendar and went to this coming Saturday.

10:00 AM Saturday, Brunch with Ted.

Just hang in there, Ted. Just a little while longer. Please, just a little while longer.

Chapter 16

Steel Trap

~When Hell's Gates were opened, the friendliest faces are demons and monsters. When Hell's gates were opened, what was left of humanity became nothing more than soulless husks.

I t's just brunch, Samantha tried to calm herself. Besides, she had to think about any additional questions Ted might ask, like, how did she know where he lived? Perhaps the truth wasn't as creepy as she thought it might be, after all, it was incidental.

She walked down the stairs. She opened the door, and her phone rang. She took it out. It was Tim. She picked up the call. "Hey Tim, it's Sam."

"I know," he laughed. *"I called."*

"Yes. Yes, you did," Samantha wasn't exactly amused. She sucked the air through her teeth, "What's up?"

"Michael, Erin, Jennifer and I are going out for brunch in thirty. Wanna come with?"

"I can't. I'm actually in the middle of something," she replied.

"What? Already on a date?"

"No. Michael is with you, that should be obvious it isn't a date," she scolded him, and she shook her head. "Look, I don't have time as

I'm in the middle of doing what it *is,* I'm doing. I'll talk to you all about it later. I just can't do it right now."

"Have you considered not doing that and coming with us instead," Tim pushed her. She knew he wasn't serious this time. *"I'm curious though, excuse me while I'm putting my shorts on. This seems important to you. What is it? If you don't mind me asking?"*

"Ted," she answered. "Turns out, he doesn't live far from me."

"Sam, I know you and Jennifer obsess over him. Give him his space. He'll come around," said Tim.

"Shut up, Tim," Samantha scolded.

"Fine, but be careful," Tim's tone dropped. *"Remember, if something happens, text us."*

"Don't worry, I'm not going to get into trouble of any sort," she snapped. *At least I hope not.*

"Just be careful."

"You know I will. Okay. I gotta go. B—" she interrupted herself. "Please tell Jennifer, I'm doing this for her."

"I'll pass it along. Bye-bye." Click.

Jennifer, I'm doing this for you. You weren't yourself that night, I can tell, and I have my suspicion it's because of Ted, not because of anything he's done, but what he revealed to you that he showed no one else. He's a man that needs help but is afraid to ask for it.

Sam put the phone back into her pocket, opened the door and crossed the threshold into the warmth of daylight. She took a deep breath as she closed the door behind her and locked it. She walked down her stoop, and to the sidewalk. Her heart pounded with every step, filled with anxiety. She stood straight with every walking step, making sure to at least look like she was confident, when the reality was not that, as her heart trembled inside her chest.

She walked three houses down, and up the steps to his door. She took a deep breath. *This is it. Please, let this be the right thing to do.* She knocked three times on the door. She kept silent, listening for any footsteps or movement. She searched the windows to see if anyone would open, or if curtains would move out of the way for whoever lived here, ideally Ted, peeked out to see who knocked on the door. She heard nothing and saw nothing; her smile faded as she feared the worst. *Don't tell me, Ted. You didn't do it. You didn't do it! Please be alive.* She knocked three more times. She waited again. Just like before, she heard and saw nothing change. She waited again, nervously as her gaze trembled on the door. She bowed her head down, letting out a long sigh. She knocked on the door one last time and waited.

At last, she heard the chains from behind the door moving. She returned the smile to her face and stood up straight. The dead bolt came undone. She let out a sigh of relief. Finally, the tumblers inside the knob's lock became undone. She stared right at the edge of the door where it would open as the knob slowly turned.

Ted opened the door with that bright smile of his, looking at her, and seemed not at all surprised to see her. He was wearing the same cargo shorts she first saw him, and fatigues, "Good to see you, Sam," He said to her in his smooth tone.

She looked at his brown eyes, to see if she could see the same thing Jennifer could see. All she could determine was that he appeared tired, with bags underneath his eyes, as usual. "Yes, it is good to see you also, Ted. It seems that you've become somewhat of a stranger of late. We missed you."

"And I suppose you tracked me down to find out if I would come back?" His eyebrow raised.

"Not exactly. Well, I didn't exactly track you down, I just simply noticed on Tuesday night that you lived here. I live a few doors down. And I thought, since I only live a few houses down, I thought I might invite you out for breakfast," she replied. "I think it might be nice to share a meal with you."

Share a meal? Really? Sam! You're better than this!

"No thanks," he replied, passing through the threshold, closing the door behind him. "I already ate."

"What did you eat?" Sam asked. She managed to peek at the floor behind the closing door, finding it to be bare. *Clearly, he knows I'm not leaving without him, but he's still hesitant. Perhaps this is the closest to asking for help he's going to give. Otherwise, he'd slam the door in front of me.*

"Food," he answered.

Abrupt replies again. "Okay, how about a cup of coffee then. I'll eat breakfast."

"I have coffee, there's literally no reason for me to come out of my house for that," he chuckled.

Why are you like this!

"Ted," she said. "I'm going to be blunt. You need friends! You can't be isolating yourself like this! We appreciated that gift of wine that night, really, we did. We appreciated not because it was expensive or of the highest quality, we don't care about things like that. We cared about it because it came from a friend. *You* are that friend, Ted. I know you can't see it, but we want you to be our friend, and we want to understand what's going on in that thick noggin of yours!

"I know you don't exactly wear your emotions on your sleeves, I get that." She peered into his eyes: those cursed baggy eyes, and there was a shimmer of light in them, like a candle refusing to burn out. "Why would you tell us when you've only known us for a short while? You wouldn't, but it's your fault for not getting to know us either. It's like you don't want to get close or risk having your heart shred to a thousand pieces."

She clenched her fists at her side, sighing. "You can't hide your pain from me." She felt tears swelling in her eyes. "I came to this door, and I heard everything. Jennifer is hurt because of whatever it is you said to her, and she was emotionally distraught. Are you afraid of us hurting you, or of you hurting us?"

Ted never once changed his facial expression. He continued to smile that dastardly fake smile. *Damn this man!*

"Look, I can tell I'm not getting through that steel trap of yours. You know I'm not great at talking. Jennifer is excellent when it comes to talking. I'm good at listening, but, so help me God, I am not taking no for an answer." *Damn you! I came here to listen not talk. Ted! Why are you making me force a monologue!* "I don't care if I need to come into your house to drink a cup of coffee with you, I will. But you and I are having coffee! I said no to brunch to Michael, and Tim *and* Jennifer for the purpose of talking with you today, and I'm hungry!"

"Well, sorry to disappoint but I don't have any food in my house," he opened his palm to his side. "I have coffee, but if you're hungry, I'm afraid I have nothing to offer but an ear."

"And I don't want your ear, I want your words. I'm offering my ear!" She stamped her foot. "Ted!" She hissed. "Alright, that's it. Give me your hand! I'm taking you to Joe's Bagel Bin. It's a mile this way. At the rotary, you know, where College Ave turns into Broadway!"

Ted shook his head, "Fine, I guess I'll begrudgingly grant your request. After you."

"Chivalrous as ever," she scoffed. "Give me your hand!"

"No," he sternly spoke. "I will walk with you to get your breakfast. You may not hold my hand."

"Ted! Why must you be so difficult? Seriously, how am I supposed to know you're not going to just run off when we get to the rotary?"

"You don't," he replied. "Now, Samantha, let's go. The sooner we get there, the sooner I can leave. Upon my *honor*, I will not leave you until I've heard everything you have to say."

"I came here with the sole purpose of listening," she shook her head. "Come!"

She led him along the sidewalk and to the rotary passing underneath many trees from the warmth but overwhelmingly bright rays of sunlight. Neither of them spoke. She just led him with the unrelenting force of someone fueled with anger and indignation.

They crossed the cross walk into the rotary and turned around the bend into the coffee shop that looked like a fancy place for breakfast, apart from the large bagel that loomed over the sidewalk, shielding the pedestrians from the oppressive astral rays, whether they be the sun, moon, or even the stars.

Ted sat across from her in the diner. She crossed her hands over the table, and her ankles were also crossed over each other, feeling proud she got him this far, but insecure not knowing how the rest of this conversation was going to go. She noticed Ted observing everything in the room, his eyes scanned every moving person, and spectacle. He seemed to be looking for an exit through all windows and all ways in and out.

"Are you done?" Sam asked, irritated.

"My apologies," he said as he turned his head to look at her, never losing that smile, nor did it seem to curve even a little less on his face, like he really was just a portrait.

"Ted, seriously, sometimes you just need to calm down. You're scanning the room as if there is someone out to get you. All the time. I noticed it at the party when you first came in," she admitted.

"Welcome to Joe's Bagel Bin. How may I help you?" the waitress spoke to them. The waitress had dirty blond hair tied behind her, she was skinny, and had the cheerful smile, probably fake. She held the same fake smile across her face when she waited tables to pay for college.

"Two coffees," she pointed at Ted. "You're not skipping out on this! I'll have two eggs, scrambled, and side of home fries. Ted, what do you want?"

"I'm not hungry. I told you I ate already," he admitted.

"I've never met a man who didn't think with his stomach," she said.

"Surprise me."

The waitress left and returned promptly with two hot mugs of coffee. The steam poured out of the cups as they were placed in front of the drinkers. Sam took a sip, and returned her gaze to Ted, softening up her irritation. Ted still had that stupid smile on his face.

"Where was I?" she asked.

"I believe you were berating me," he chuckled as he took a sip.

That stupid laughter. It became a part of him, genuine but he did it way too much for it to be.

"Yes, now I remember. Do you hate us? Be honest. It will be easier for you, and me, and everyone involved if you spoke the truth. I don't want your riddles, or deflection. I am directly asking you! And I will ask another direct question until I get an answer."

He placed the coffee down and gazed into her eyes, maintaining that smile. "Someone once asked me a question, her smile seemed innocent at first. She was a lovely person, or so I thought. She asked me this, 'Tell me some things that you like, some things that you hate'. Well, looking back on it, my answer was very childish when an answer escaped my lips back then, and I guess it's similar to the question you asked. My answer was this, back then, 'I like my friends, but I hate violence'. Such an odd concept, and a childish answer for someone like me, someone who joined the Army, and did things contrary to my nature. If you were to ask me the same question today, I suppose I would answer it like this: there are many things that I hate, and I'd be hard pressed to find anything that I didn't hate. And I don't particularly like anything," he paused and let her think about what he said. "Is that enough to satisfy your curiosity?"

"So, you only hate us because you hate everything," she repeated. "Even though we've done nothing to you."

"Those icebreakers, as Jack calls them, are dangerous things. They reveal personal information, information that one can hold on to, and use, and twist to their own cruel designs. When you give out that information, you're just asking people to stab you in the back."

"You're a man who has no trust in anyone, or anything," she commented. The food arrived in front of her. Ted's plate came by with a heaping portion of scrambled eggs. "What about your family, or friends?"

"I had people that once held my confidence," he answered.

"And?"

"They're all dead," his tone dropped, but he retained the façade.

Sam's eyes stretched open, and her fork trembled in between her fingers; she felt there was a great silence at the table, as if the two of them were in soundless bubble where even screams can't escape one's lips. Her expression went from irritation to sorrow, her eyes watered as she took a bite of some of her home fries, "And your siblings?"

"We aren't on a talking basis," his tone dropped.

"I see," she replied. "You said most of the people you held your confidence in were dead. What about the rest of them?"

"None of them can be trusted. I was foolish to trust them. But did thank them, for everything they've done for me. It is through them that I knew I only ever had fifteen friends. No more than that. Now I have none." His voice dropped even lower, and his smiled faded. His eyes dropped down as if they themselves were exhausted. "Funny thing, really, a soldier, a sailor, a marine, a guardsman, coast or national, they all join the service to sacrifice for the greater good, to fight for honor, to fight for peace, and our freedom. They would like to say that they would lay down their lives for peace, freedom, and honor, but I know the truth. Not one of them will question an order if it comes from the top. Every single one of them will commit genocide and not bat an eye, just because it's an order, they'll do it." He sighed, while she continued to listen as she ate. "I'll tell you what I told Jennifer, and now I realize it was mistake on my part giving her my number, and exchanging it, I am not someone you want to be close with. I'm not someone anyone *should* be friends with. With everything that I've done, my name will appear in the history books, but not next to Martin Luther King JR, not George Washington. Not even President Lincoln. No, you'll find me in the history books, but not compared to them. The only people you could compare me to, is Hitler and Stalin."

Ted, why would you compare yourself to them? The worse people who ever lived. Surely it isn't that bad. What did you do that made you feel this way?

He continued, "You asked me the other week, why I felt I needed to work so much. Honestly, I want to be working more than I already am. I don't need the money. I don't want it," he waved his hand. "What am I going to spend all that money on? I *need* to work. I need to drown myself in it. It's the o—" he covered his mouth, tightly gripping his jaw. The light in his eyes faded. "It's the only thing that's drowning out all of their screams. It is the only thing that is masking all of those faces," he gritted his teeth. "They said that Saul killed his thousands and David his tens of thousands. I on the other hand would be lucky if my numbers were nearly that low. I'm nothing but a cold murderer."

She put her fork down to the side of her plate. She looked down at her half empty plate, trying to determine the meaning behind his words, or if he was lying to her. No man, no matter how cruel or sinister, would willingly admit they were a monster. A man who would call himself as such, would be a dangerous man. But could there have been something else behind those words? A hidden meaning perhaps? Was this true? Was any of it true? Or was it, just like a mask, a façade to hide the truth? *No. Ted, why are you lying to me, or perhaps do I not completely grasp the situation?*

"Ted," she looked back at him. *Why are you like this?* "It would be better if you didn't lie to me. I can't imagine what it is that you're going through, or how it tugs on the strings of the heart. I can't imagine a man would compare himself to Hitler, and yet you've done that. I don't doubt you have done things you regret doing, but that is something we all have done. That is what makes us human. Yes, we lie sometimes. Yes, we betray our friends trust, that is who we are," she sighed, and leaned back in her chair, relaxing with her arms crossing her chest. *God, please put in my mouth the words to speak. I'm lost.*

She continued, "I have no doubt that you have killed in the service, that is to be expected. I don't believe you killed more than tens of thousands of people. I believe you may feel the rotten stench of regret for the things you've done. I know you must see the nightmares. When I found out where you lived, Ted, I walked up to your door and almost knocked after hearing you lock all your locks. And I heard a man, removing his bandages, removing his laughter, and removing his mask. I'm sure you suffer from guilt and trauma, but you cannot do this alone, no matter how hard you try," she sucked in air through her teeth as she tried to stifle a cry, but she already felt those tears streaming down her face. Her spirit felt jaded with melancholy. *Is this how you feel, am I making it worse?* "You can't do this alone, Ted. You need friends, and we are offering it to you. There are no conditions attached. All we want is you. That's all we want, that's all Jennifer wants. We don't want your excuses, we don't want your lies, we don't want your laughter or your jokes, or even that smile that you and I both know isn't real. All we want is you and your friendship.

"Maybe, it isn't even fair of me to ask this, but what happened that turned you into this?" She's seen enough war movies to recognize the symptoms of PTSD, and it was clear he suffered from it, but that wasn't all he suffered from. There was more, much more he was hiding underneath the surface. This steel trap was far more complex than she realized, and she couldn't crack it alone. She was the spear, and he was the shield. The shield might crack, but she is at risk of falling off the horse.

"Well, it appears that you have found a way to tug on something that I forgot was there once," he answered. "But I can't tell you what happened. Everything that happened is classified above top secret. I will hold this in, bottle it in forever, and never talk about it to anyone at any time. Because I can't. You don't understand, I want to talk, but I can't. And I can't even tell why I can't talk about it."

"But if you keep doing that, this bottle is going to explode!" she whispered.

He deeply sighed, "I'm afraid that bottle has already exploded. And it was pieced back together, much to my dismay. That bottle won't stay broken, as much as I want it to."

"What are you talking about?" she didn't understand his analogy, leaning forward on the table, her elbows propping her head up.

"In all my years of living, twenty-three regrettable years, I have but one regret: that was not strangling myself with my own umbilical cord, and now I can't even die right."

Sam shifted uncomfortably in her chair. He was obviously trying to redirect the conversation away from how he was truly feeling. She knew he must feel this way, but she hadn't expected him to come out and say it. Or for it to be so unsettling. *He is suicidal,* "Ted, what did you try to do?"

"Everything I can think of," he answered grimly. "And nothing works!"

"If nothing works and you are a living husk, why not try to bring life back into it? Why not try to make friends with what you have? If nothing works, something is trying to keep you alive, or you're not quite ready to go," she waved the waitress down. Ted merely smiled at her, mocking her as if she did fall off her horse, and that shield remains uncracked, and unbroken.

The waitress came by. "I'll take a box for his eggs and the check. I'll pay for it."

The waitress nodded and left for the box and to print out her check.

"You barely touched your eggs," she commented.

"I can't taste anything. I haven't tasted anything in over eight years," he replied. "Eating for me is like putting fuel in the car, it's tasteless. It's nothing more than a careless chore. There," he smiled again, the façade which he knew wasn't fooling anyone anymore. The smile seemed sarcastic. "Now, you know a lot about me. You can believe my tale or not, but that is me. A bitter man filled with nothing but hate and regret. Tell me, then, Sam, would you really want a man like me as a friend, when taking life seemed second nature to me? Or am I just a tool to you, a project for you to work on to make yourself feel better?"

Sam pointed a stern finger at him. The box came with the check. She gave the waitress her card. "Ted, I'm going to ignore that, and forgive you for this. Why? Because I know you don't mean it. I think you revealed to me much more than you intended, or you are the best poker player alive. You are making yourself look like the Devil, like I'm sharing breakfast with Satan to make me feel better for breaking a friendship with you or any kind of bond, and that I would be free to do so easily. That doesn't work on me, for the Lord taught me better than that. My friendship, as well as Michael's, Erin's, Tim's, and Jennifer's are still on the table. We want you to be part of us. Now, will you come with us for the Fourth of July Canoe trip?"

"I'll dec—"

"You will accept this invitation."

"I will think about it."

"You will come."

"I said I'll—"

"And I said I'm not taking no for an answer, Ted," she replied. "Unlike before, I now know where you live. I'll drag you on the canoe if I have to."

"Fine. You've got me. Heaven knows even I can't relocate fast enough for that," he snickered.

"You better not even think about that!" she said. "Are you taking your eggs?"

"No."

She packed up his eggs into the box. "Well, I'm not about to let this go to waste. Are you coming on Tuesday?"

"I'll think about it," he replied.

"So, no," she said. She knew what his maybe's or think about its meant. They were the polite way to decline an offer. "I'll see you Saturday. We meet at Kendall Square at 4:30 PM. You will be there then, no. I expect you there at 4 PM. If you are not there at 4 PM. I am assuming you're trying to escape, and I will drive to you and pick you up myself!"

"I see you don't trust me," he said, returning that forsaken smile upon his lips.

"I trust you, but I also trust that you will try to avoid it, using any means necessary," she said. "I know you don't trust us, and I'm not going to pry any further," she picked up her purse and stood up. "I will trust that you will be there at 4:00 PM. If you are not there, I'm dragging you here myself."

"I understand."

Chapter 17

Ducks

~The unstoppable spear might not be able to penetrate the immovable shield, but it can still make a crack, and a weapon with more force than the spear can break it open.

Ted took a short walk, crossing the street and walked into the Nathan Tufts Park. He walked upon the shaded path to the tower. He took a brief look at it, making it look like he was even marginally interested in it. He investigated the blank, empty gate that went into the tower. It was locked. He walked down the path to find an unoccupied bench. Looking around, he made sure that no one else was here, so he could relax a moment. Satisfied, he sat himself down on the bench.

He looked out on towards the empty street. The sun gazed down through the clouds and through the tree line. He leaned back into his seat, crossing his legs and his arms relaxed behind the back of the bench. He deeply sighed before retreating to his thoughts.

"Why? How cruel can you be? You will not let me part from this world, and that is the only thing I want. I don't want friends, and don't want or need a family. I entered in this world with very little, and what little I had was violently ripped from me and left me to ponder the cruelty You left me in, and God, here You are, mocking me, trying to give me hope when I can't see passed the tunnel." He whispered softly to himself, barely audible past his lips, even he hardly heard those words, mildly distracted by the chirping birds up in the sky, and the ribbits of the frogs nearby. "You have shown me the light in the tunnel, but as with all good things, I can't trust it. You know I can't trust it. You know I can't trust You. How cruel can You be?"

A warm summer breeze brushed past him. He caught the sweet aroma of wildflowers in its wake. The scent of pine was pungent, and assaulted his nostrils, but he didn't care. It was one of his favorite smells. Funny, he lost his sense of taste, but not his smell.

"By some fluke chance, I missed something. I let my guard down once, for just one minute out of a desperation to get in my door, and now *she* knows where I live. Was that—" he stammered. "Was that Your doing? Lord, are You trying to tell me something? Are You really trying to tell me I should be giving this cursed life one last chance before cancelling out a subscription I never signed up for? This was something I didn't want. I never asked for any of it, and yet You forced me to pay a price higher than any have paid."

Ted was not a praying man, nor was he a spiritual one. He was never given the opportunity to tell his friends how he felt, to process his grief, nor could he trust a therapist. Yet, here he was, praying to nothing, just talking to himself in a public park.

"By some fluke, You want my heart when it is garbage. It is filled with scars. You stabbed it. You shot it full of bullet holes. You cast it into the furnace. You crushed it with buildings. My heart is beyond repair, and it is dead, and yet, because You stubbornly say so, it keeps beating and powering up this soulless husk. I feel just like Frankenstein. I didn't ask for the life my Creator gave me, yet I'm cursed with this cruel existence.

"Even for the very purpose I was thrust in that life. Ten years ago, the wars stopped. Ten years ago, there was no further need for me to kill anyone anymore. You knew that. And yet, forced me to kill nearly two-hundred-thousand men in the blink of an eye, and every single one of them I would have called my brother, or my sister. Now, I know better. What do You want from me? Why won't You just let me go and let me die? Your forgiveness can't reach me, and I am cursed to go to Hell, and with a monster like me, there is no better place for me. Just let me go and let me—"

His train of thought severed when a little flock of ducklings, led by their mother walked in front of him. He counted the flock, and the flock was large for ducklings. There totaled fifteen ducklings, and the mother. There was a duckling in the back that caught his eye. The little duckling had a few black spots on its feathers, and it waddled with a little limp. The little duckling squeaked.

Ted watched its little webbed foot, and it appeared that something was not quite connected right, as if the poor little creature was born wrong. Would it be a mercy killing to put the duckling out of his misery?

He leaned over and placed his hand on the ground, his palm faced the sky. The little duckling turned its little head to him. As if everything stopped, and as if the little duckling knew something, he waddled over to Ted's hand, and climbed on top of it. Ted rose the little duckling to his face and pet the little duck. He smiled as the cute little feet stepped onto his hand like a marching band. Ted investigated the black, empty orbs in its skull.

The mother duck stopped waddling and looked at Ted, as he pet her little duckling. She quacked, flapping her wings erratically, waddling towards Ted who simply traded a gaze, lying even to her. He placed the duckling down, no longer considering killing it. The little duckling returned to its flock and went back in line as the mother duck led the way into whatever paradise awaited them, a paradise *he* was banished from.

"I'm glad you haven't lost your soft spot yet," he heard a familiar voice right next to him. The voice was so nostalgic, that he lost his sense of location. The voice of so many memories, the good ones, swept over him. He turned to the left to see a little girl, aged if he remembered right was fifteen. She was the youngest of them all, and she was the closest one to him. She wore torn black Cargo pants, a black long-sleeved shirt with her vest draped over it. Her black hair was down, and one blue eye was hiding behind her hair, while the other one had blood smeared over it. Just below her abdomen was bleeding black blood. She smiled at him, that same playful smile he fell in love with. It was full of energy and hope, and the love to match it.

He frowned.

"Suh—Slithers," he gasped. He didn't mean to. She looked real to him, as if he was looking at an actual person, and not the ghost his mind conjured up.

"Ghost," she answered, smiling as blood dripped down her head. "I miss you. We all do."

"Iah—iah I love you," he choked on his sobs. He knew he was overdue for this, but he didn't expect it to hit him out in the open, exposed.

"Ghost, I love you too. We all do," she smiled back at him. "Tell me, have you lost your tender heart already? I don't think you have."

"Every morning, *every* morning it breaks a little more each passing day. Every single day. I dream these nightmares as they cascade over my insomnia, oppressing me far more than *they* ever could. I am stuck in the past, and I want to leave it behind, but I don't want to leave it behind," he sobbed, tears streamed down his face, and his smile faded, and his face was cringing. "I know when I wake up, I'll never see any of you again. I'll never see any of you again."

"The life we lived was cruel," said Slithers. "We were all tormented inside, especially with everything that we had to do. We were darkness. We were bitterness. We were hatred. But you taught us all something, before the end. Do you remember what you said to me?"

"I can't remember," he sobbed. "I can't remember."

"That the odds were against us. But if there was a chance, a slither of a chance that we could succeed in doing something good, in leaving some kind of legacy for humanity to follow, just one chance, it was worth it. Whatever it was, even if that chance was infinitely worse, it would be worth it for a chance to get this Hell undone," she answered. "Ghost, we were darkness, and when the darkness was too oppressive, you were our light. You were our Captain, our moral compass. It was through you that we never killed anyone innocent. It was because of you no civies were ever killed on our watch. That was something, wasn't it? Was it worth it for even just that?"

"And everything we fought for is being undone now as we speak," he sobbed. "Our sacrifices were all meaningless."

"Was it, Ghost? Was any of it meaningless?" her hand touched his. He felt the warmth blood touch his hand. She grabbed it and brought it to her cheek, and his hand felt her flesh, as it was, before the last fires raged eight years ago. The flesh was so real in his hands. She took her free hand and pulled out a ring, a scrappy ring at that. The ring was nothing more than a few nails welded together, and embedded in the ring were fragments of bullets, welded together.

He recognized that ring. He looked, but never found it. The ring he made for her over eight years ago. The ring that he made for her was akin to that of a marriage, something he picked up from listening and watching his parental figures, Major and Lieutenant Nakamura, and whatever it was they had together, was what he wanted with Slithers, and he nearly had it.

"Was this meaningless?" she said to him.

"No," he sucked in the air through his teeth, gasping as he tried to stifle more sobs. But this was not normal for him, for the tears never stopped like a river dammed up with a cracking dam. The wall was finally chipped. "I—it was worth everything. Everything was planned. You and I were to be together that Saturday, but for you, and for them, you never got to see that Saturday."

"I know," she said. "I know. I know our parents wouldn't have wanted to see us like that. But that wasn't for them to decide. No, we were born with a purpose, and our tale ended. But yours still goes on. Ghost, if there is a slither of a chance to undo this Hell, if there is a slither of a chance, and if that chance is infinitely worse than it was back then, it is still worth it. Our time is over. Your time is still moving forward. Time stopped for me, and it kept going for you," she leaned to him and looked at his now sobbing and swelling eyes. "We all lived with a cruel existence, but you gave us light. Who else can you bless with your light?"

"How can I when I see only darkness. The mask faded and it's not all okay. It's not okay anymore," he knew she referred to her biological parents, the one she never met. Ted didn't know who his parents were either, only the dreaded Nakamuras.

Her forehead touched his. He closed his eyes. "You say you're not okay. You say that all you see is darkness around you. That's okay. Because that was once my reality. You broke the darkness, and the light forced its way in. The light is there, Ghost. It is right there! You know it is. You must let it in. Just let it in! We can't stand seeing you like this. Just let it in."

He opened his eyes, and he saw Slithers with her hair pulled back in a ponytail. She smiled at him, shading his face with her white sunhat that wasn't there before. Her blood-stained uniform faded to a blue sundress. "Just let it in. You need to let the past stay in the past, Ghost. I know you don't want to forget us, but this pain isn't doing anything good."

"Maybe—"

"Maybe, Ghost, the reason you can't seem to really kill yourself, is because you know that doing that will kill all memory of us." She said, this cut through his heart, and he could feel it bleeding inside his chest. "You gave us hope when there was none. Now, it is time for someone to share that hope with you. I love you. We all do."

She kissed him gently on the lips before her body changed into a wind of flowers, flying like petals as they burned away from his hallucination. His hands trembled uncontrollably and the light reflecting upon his eyes shimmered. His body felt weak as he leaned forward.

He curled himself up on the bench, holding his knees tightly to his chest as the tears swelled into his eyes, streaming onto the bench, making a waterfall drip onto the pavement of the path. He felt like a soaked sponge, being twisted and rung dry and then cast carelessly to the side of the sink.

"Juh—Jennifer," he stammered. "Why do you look like her?"

He couldn't deny the similarities between Slithers and Jennifer. Granted, Jennifer was older than Ted, by perhaps five years, assuming his estimation of his own age was accurate. They had the same build, the same-colored hair, the same colorful and playful smile and laugh. Even the smell seemed the same, the smell of patience and care. It was something that he didn't smell much of in the world. No matter how bad things got, or hopeless, Slithers always smelled like there was an abundance of patience and care.

Maybe, just maybe it was time to let it go.

Chapter 18

Fireworks

~To fight for peace, that kind of courage requires a specific type of person. You are not that person: I am that person. And I hate it. Let me tell you something, if you want to truly fight for peace, and if you want to be that kind of person, I'll tell you how: you have to kill yourself, again, and again, and again, until what's left of your humanity is dead and you become nothing more than a murderer. You'll bear the burden of all the hate and discourse of the world, but you'll save the world from itself. Can you bear that burden? I thought I could. No one can.

Samantha previously arranged for everyone to be at Kendall Square at 4:00 PM sharp, and a little earlier. That would give her enough time to track Ted down in case he bailed, *again!* She looked carefully at her watch as Michael, Tim, Erin, and Jennifer were sitting down on some of the benches. Jennifer peered diligently down the stairs of the subway station.

There were droves of people coming up, and going down the red signs reading, "Kendall Square". Samantha and her friends were shaded by numerous trees and banners hanging on the side of the shops and restaurants. These were brick buildings.

Jennifer's fingers interlaced with one another on both hands; one hand squeezed the other tightly, while the other fingers rested over each other. She had a white visor which covered her face in shadows, mixed with a khaki-shorts and a black shirt. Samantha walked over to her as she was alone, isolated by herself, clearly bored of all the finance talk. Obviously, Michael led most of that conversation, with his confident demeaner, owning that salmon-colored shirt that less secure men would not wear.

"So, what are you feeling right now?" Sam asked Jennifer, sitting down next to her, wrapping her arm around her shoulder.

"Well, I suppose I'm feeling overjoyed, that I might see him again. Thank you, Sam," she said cheerfully. Sam felt relieved Jennifer returned to her usual upbeat self, "And I'll be relieved if he doesn't show up. I am satisfied either way. Of course, I'd like to see him again, but I will no longer force his friendship with ours. It is—"

"Sometimes, we need a friend to be an enemy," Sam said, looking up at the sky, looking for an answer, and something genuine to say, "Only a true friend will insult us to our face. Only a true friend will call us out on all our shit."

"Sam!" Tim called out. "Language."

"Sorry, Tim!" Sam called back, she was grateful for him holding her accountable, "Look, I can't say what I heard on that night when I forced him to come," she glanced down at her watch; 3:57PM. "But I know what he needs. He doesn't need that soft and passive friend. He needs a stern but active friend. I didn't know that was something I could be, but I think we all need to be part of that. We all need to be active, or else we'll all lose him."

"There are times when we need a stern hand. There are times where we need a motherly caring hand, and the occasional whip up the butt with a wooden spoon," Jennifer chuckled. She took enough beatings with that wooden spoon before. "I read something before, once, many years ago at my undergrad, that a man who grew up in a violent household responds best to order and direction. Such a man is responsive to those who lead them, for fear of being punished. Such a man doesn't respond well to a passive friend because they can't offer that guidance."

"You have no idea how right you are," Sam commented, looking back at her watch. 4:02 PM. "Can you call Ted. Ask him where he is please. Else, I'm driving to pick him up."

Jennifer took out her phone. She hesitated before forcing her thumb violently down on the touch screen. She brought the phone to her ear, listening to the dial tone.

"Why don't you put that on speaker?" Sam asked, eager to hear the tone of his voice.

Jennifer nodded, and placed her phone on speaker, and held it away from her ear. Her free elbow propped her head up by the thigh, tilting her head, and her hair dropped to the side. The phone rang three times.

"Hello?" came that familiar smooth voice.

"Tedward!" She cried out; her face lit up with excitement. "It's me, Jennifer."

"Oh, I know," he chuckled softly into the phone. *"I have your number in my phone, remember?"*

"It's good to hear from you again. Are you coming? Where are you?"

"Oh, you know, around," he joked. It was a very corny joke.

"You've certainly got that Bostonian sarcasm," she jested.

"Oh, please. Bostonians do it better."

"Don't threaten me with a good time."

"Jennifer! I would never!"

"So, where are you?"

"I told you, I'm not threatening you with a good time."

"Tedward!"

"Open your eyes."

Jennifer was looking at an empty subway station. She blinked repeatedly and took one hand to wipe away any sleep from her eyes.

"What am I supposed to be looking at?"

"An empty subway station."

"What?" she turned her head around and found Ted standing on the other side of the street, right in front of the Merlien Building on One Broadway. He waved and bore that smile. "Tedward! What are you doing? Get over here!" Jennifer found herself yelling at him from across the street, but it was apparent her voice carried over his phone as he pushed his phone away from his face.

"Well, that's a relief," Sam said, and took a deep breath as she turned her head towards him. He was wearing his fatigues, wrinkled, and khakis. His hair was still a scruffy mess. "Now I don't have to go chasing him down," She felt a major burden being lifted from her chest. She smiled as Jennifer met Ted at the crosswalk. *Thank you.*

She went over to Erin, and pushed her to the side of her bench, and wrapped her hand around her waist, "So, what do you think?"

"I didn't think you to be much of a matchmaker. I mean, how long did it take for Michael to give you the slip?" she chuckled, elbowing her in the side.

Sam looked at her awkwardly.

"Jennifer would have said it better," Michael laughed.

"Sh! Sh! Sh!" Tim put his finger to his lips. "You don't want her hearing that. Last time someone made that assumption—" he shuddered. "So many accidents."

"That was completely unrelated! The pipe in the room burst!" Samantha teased, chuckling.

"Yeah, it didn't help we were on the top floor," Michael scratched his chin as he tilted his gaze skywards. "Oh well, not like she caused it."

"So, where's this canoe place?" Erin asked. "Oh, and I suppose I know him a little better, but even I have my hesitations. They seem a good match. Way to be an *Emma*."

"Oh, please, I get enough of that from Jennifer. I don't need that from you, Erin," Samantha scowled at her. "I'm not a fan of Jane Austen, personally."

"Before you go off some unnecessary tangent that is likely to make us late—" Michael began.

"You're one to talk," Sam replied sarcastically.

"For the record, I came early today." Michael shook his head as he pointed an index finger at her chest. "It's about a fifteen-minute walk."

"Michael, I'm sure we'll be fine. We originally planned to be here at 6:00 PM in case something happened. Then Ted happened. And he was on time, contrary to popular belief, it was either on time or not at all. We have plenty of time. Fireworks don't start until later. Which reminds me, food," Sam rebutted.

"I'll go grab something. Anything in particular we want?" He asked.

"Didn't we plan this—forget it. Go to the store, get some snacks, soda, and anything else you can think of. Fortunately, some of us had a late lunch," Sam pointed at herself.

"Come on Tim," Michael grabbed Tim as they went along the opposite side of the street to a nearby convenient store.

***

"So, you finally came on time, or even at all," Jennifer said, smiling up to Ted. Jennifer relaxed to the lovely melody of walking and chattering noises. The background noise was like music to her ears, reminding of her violin playing days. She felt the warm array beat on her skin. She saw cars driving by, merging onto different lanes on this busy street, and some honking, because some inconsiderate tourist cut off a driver. She shook her head, whoever that tourist was, clearly ignored the *no turn on red* sign, "What changed? I didn't think I'd see you today, or at all ever again."

"I hope my sudden surprise was welcome," he smiled, but this smile wasn't as wide as all the other smiles he gave her. There was *something* different about it, but Jennifer couldn't quite place it.

"It most certainly is," she smirked, her eye lids dropping a bit like she was planning something. "Honestly though, I was going to be content in whatever happened. Although I would say I wouldn't have liked to have not seen you again, I don't think my sensitive little eyes could take any more of that, and don't dodge my question, you sly fox, you."

"I wasn't planning on it," he let out a small laugh that came out more like a cough. "I know something's changed: I haven't quite determined what yet."

"So, are you going to tell me something pleasant about you? Unlike that dreary excuse of an explanation the last time I saw you," she asked.

"I—I think I will save that for tonight. I have to think of something that you don't know about me, that is pleasant," he answered. Jennifer could tell his smile lessened about a few centimeters. She found herself relieved that to her, he couldn't maintain that façade, or perhaps was willing to trust her of all people with something precious, "It is—hard for me to find something pleasant."

"Then, think on it. But don't filter yourself, Tedward. If you must, give me something precious, and I'll give you something precious," she poked him.

He paused, rubbing his chin. "I don't think any of that came from a Jane Austen Novel."

"Nope!" she cackled, pulling her head back and let her hair fall, "I came up with that cheesy line myself, or if it was pulled from some fake crap romantic novel with unrealistic expectations, this was purely coincidental."

"I see. It seemed a little dry for Jane Austen."

"I'm not Jane Austen," she defended herself.

***

Ted went with all of them to the rental, renting three canoes. Of course, they didn't originally plan on filling all the canoes with passengers, this was something Ted picked up on. One of the canoes was meant to be for storage for food, and snacks while they were out at sea.

"I still think a whole canoe is too much space for this," Erin said as they tied the canoes together with bungee cords. "I think two was enough."

"Well," Samantha said, putting some bags of snacks into the canoe she and Michael shared. "We did think Brian was coming, he flaked last minute."

"Typical Brian, he's probably with you know who," Jennifer quipped, loading the canoe she and Ted would share. "Let us be off! Very important business!"

Ted watched Jennifer as she stumbled into the canoe. Ted and Michael pushed the canoe out from the shore, and hopped in. Tim and Erin helped balance the sudden weight in the additional canoes to prevent them from tipping. All of them rowed out and waited for the sun to set.

The skies were clear, and the sun was finally setting over the western horizon of Boston, and the darkness was swooping in over the east. The lights were still very much widely used, taking away any lights from the stars from above. All of them were wading in the canoe, and Jennifer and Ted shared one.

"10:28," Samantha said. "The Pop concert should be ending soon."

"Why did we come out here so early?" Tim complained. "I have to pee."

"Bro," Michael laughed. "You have a whole ocean."

"That's not sanitary, what about the fish? I don't think they'd like that," Tim replied.

"You do realize they pee in the same water they swim in, right?" Michael said. He reached out to grab an empty coffee can. He tossed it over to Tim. "Use this if you're concerned. My Uncle Jack used to road trip with these things. He'd never stop even to use the bathroom. He just kept driving."

"Uncle Jack," Tim said. "How fitting."

Tim swiftly turned around, using the can as his toilet. Ted noted how careful Tim seemed to be with it, trying to hide his private parts from the rest of them.

"You better dump that out, Tim!" Erin exclaimed. "If I'm sharing a canoe with you, I don't want to have to smell it the entire time."

"But—" he started to protest.

"Dang it. Just give it to me!" She smiled and took the bucket and dumped the urine into the water. She rinsed the bucket out with the same water.

There was a loud whistling in the air. They all jerked their heads and pointed at the white shaking stream following the rocket in the air. Sam, Erin and Jennifer leaned back in the canoe and pointed at it. The numerous lights lit up the skies and shimmered in the ripples of the water.

These three seemed to Ted, to be the most like children, if that is, how he would expect children to behave.

The first boom of distant tank fire echoed in his ears, the cannon blowing up, overwhelmed by the enormous pressure of the exploding powder, sending flares and flashes of white. The noise it sent ripples between the canoes. Ted could feel the weight being shifted in the canoes. Again, and again, and again, the lights would flash, blue, red, green, and white lights, sending debris into the ocean.

His fists clenched at the sides of the canoe. His eyes flared as the beautiful exploding lights lit up the blackened sky. The loud bangs concussed his skull. He took numerous soft, measured breaths as his hands dug into the side of the canoe.

He grinded his teeth as unwanted memories began to assault his mind:

Afghanistan, August 13th, 2012.

The air was dry, the moisture was gone, and the sand scorched.

Ghost sprinted in the sand with Viper behind him. Ticker was to his left, and Butcher to his left, her katana drawn. Her current height made the katana look like a five-foot Odachi!

Their legs sprinted through the sand, through the whistling howls of the tank fire aimed directly at him. Ghost saw, he jumped to the side, and Viper jumped in the other direction, just missing impact. The sand went everywhere, pelting his body like bullets.

More shells of tank fire followed, the whistling never stopped, as if the tanks themselves were the form of their hated oppression. Ghost took a good look at the line in front of them, the tanks kept firing, and the buzzing of bullet fire came, obscuring their vision.

"Ticker! One hundred-thirty-six meters!" Ghost yelled as two bullets grazed his cheeks. He ignored it. Pain was all too familiar for him to bother with it anymore. "One O'clock!"

"Ten-four," Ticker replied.

He could hear the rapid sprinting of Ticker, the little soldier sprinting faster and harder. Not more than fifteen seconds later did he hear cries, and a loud explosion.

The sound cleared.

Ghost saw the right most tank was nearly toppled, but completely ripped to shreds; Afghan soldiers were dying near the tank, with gunfire, explosive debris, or even the flames themselves.

Ghost, Butcher, and Viper picked up into a full sprint, leaving clouds of sand in their wake. They jumped behind the sandbags. Ticker swiftly blew up another tank. The Afghan soldiers were in complete disarray. It was like they were surprised they stood over a foot and a half above their enemy.

Ghost let his rifle fire; he constantly pulled the single shot trigger numerous times as he aimed down the iron sights. His gun ripped through the second-rate bullet-proof vests the Afghan soldiers were wearing. One of the other men threw his rifle at him. Ghost was briefly distracted as he sidestepped from the man's swing with the scimitar. A second swing was made. Ghost pulled out his knife. He grabbed the man's hand and twisted him down to his height. He thrust his knife into the man's chest, twisting the knife and ripped apart the man's heart.

Ghost watched as the man's corpse collapsed to the ground and watered the sand with its blood.

More fireworks started firing and whistling in the air. Ted realized he dazed off in an experiential nightmare and attempted to return his smile to his face. He released his grip on the canoe. He stared out at the open sea, and the lights of the city, there were many canoes and other boats with people smiling happily at the bright exploding lights.

His breaths were still short and measured. He needed to control himself, or something worse will happen than these sudden flashbacks. He bowed his head down. *They can't see this.*

He gasped. His eyes were wide open as he felt something warm touch his hand. His hands started trembling but was much too afraid to do anything. His gaze suddenly shifted to his hand and found a warm matter of flesh covering his trembling hand. He looked up at the arm from which the warm, gentle hand was attached. He found himself looking into the concerned eyes of Jennifer, who held his hand firmly.

"Ted," she whispered. "You don't have to go at it alone. That's what friends are for. That's what we're here for. You don't have to live life alone."

She crawled to him from inside the canoe, still holding his hand over the side. His smile faded and his eyes trembled in the exploding lights. He leaned back, breathing heavier.

No! Stuh—stay away!

She came closer to him. He leaned into the back of the canoe.

No! Stuh—stay away! You don't know what I've done.

As if reading his thoughts, "No, you don't have to go at it alone. That's what friends are for."

Jennifer, stay away. Please. You don't want any part of this—of this monster. No. I am not a monster. I am something—something so much worse.

She lunged her body softly into his chest and embraced her arms around him, her chin rested on his shoulders. "Ted," she whispered. Her trembling voice spoke volumes as he felt this alien embrace him.

He felt darkness all around him. Her voice, that *damn* trembling voice, it can't be trusted, no matter how much comfort it brought to him. The smiling face of Slithers entered his mind. She smiled at him in the darkness, it was as if Slithers lived on in Jennifer. He closed his eyes as he stifled sobs from within. He took a deep breath with her body leaned so close into his. *How cruel. How cruel can you be, forcing me to look back into memories that I know I can never relive. What would I give to have that again, even just one last time?*

"I can't begin to understand what you're going through, but Ted, I want to understand it. I know you're in pain, and this life, or whatever it is, it can be Hell. But it is like that for everyone," her tears streamed down on his shoulder. "I know you want to bear this alone, we all do, but we can't. We just can't. No matter how hard we try; we can't do it alone. Share the load!"

He felt a weight on his chest, as if his heart was in his stomach, crawling its way up through his throat, restricting the air he could let in and out. "I—I can't. Because what's on my heart," he began to whisper. "I can't tell anyone. Jennifer, the less you know, the better."

"Then tell me what little you can. Tell me how you feel? If you can't trust any of us, trust me or trust Sam. But you can't grow unless you open up more, or at the least, come out more often. Ted, we consider you a friend. Even if that feeling isn't mutual. I don't know what must have happened to you when you can't trust anyone."

"What I went through, is classified," he stammered. "I am not allowed to talk about it, and this would be information that would only place you in harm's way, even if you believed it."

"Then tell me something about you. Something I don't already know. Something precious," she requested. She leaned back from him and looked him in him watery eyes. "Anything. Tell me what makes you happy. If you can't manage that, tell me what makes you hurt: just give me something."

"There used to be a girl. Her hair was black, and her smile lit up the sky, even when there was no sun to illumine the darkness. She was always happy. You could say, given our circumstances, we were class sweethearts. We were even—what's the word for it: engaged. It was going to be held on Saturday. We were going to invite our little, small group of friends."

"What happened?" She asked, gazing deeper into his eyes. He sensed while they were worlds apart, she understood that, but she was trying to understand him in whatever way was possible, pushing and applying pressure when needed, and releasing him just at the right moment.

"For her, Saturday never came. For them, they never got to see that Saturday either," he answered.

"I'm so sorry."

She placed her hand on his shoulder and grasped it firmly to console him as the whistling of the fireworks continued. They continued firing at a much rapid rate, the grand finale filled with innumerable explosions, filling the air with multiple different colors of exploding lights.

"But what bothers me the most about it, is I can't talk about what happened, and that—and that you look so much like her, it's uncanny. It's disturbing," he said feeling he needed to desperately push her away. This was all too familiar, and it only went one place: pain. Either for himself or hers, if he let her into his life, no matter how small of a part she could play to him, he would hurt her, and she would hurt him. It was only inevitable, but he also knew that if there was going to be any shot at providing peace to the turmoil in his heart, it would be through her.

"Well, I hope I can bring back some of her memories if that is what will keep you grounded," she said, leaning back. "Now, it is my turn, but I'll show you."

She leaned back from him and pulled up the sleeve from her left arm. She showed her wrist to him. In the faint light, he could see something all too familiar: scars. There were faint flesh-white scars slitted in x's across her wrist. She smiled at him as tears escaped those slitted lids, well meaning, sincere, he was sure of that.

What is she thinking? She's just handing me this! Jennifer are you stupid! I could—I could use this to harm you. You know this! But you have no reason to believe I would use this against you. Why? You know how cruel people are, why are you trusting me, a stranger with the scars of your heart?

"Why are you showing me this?" He asked. "This is frail info—"

"Because my dear Tedward," she smiled, and looked into his glimmering eyes. "I know you don't trust me, but something tells me that you will never do anything to hurt me."

He let out a sigh, "Perhaps you're wrong. Perhaps you're right."

The fireworks were over. Sam whistled as she saw Jennifer and Ted cozying up over in the other canoe. They immediately moved into where they were, hoping no one saw anything. But Sam saw. She saw the whole thing and left with a smile.

***

The six of them returned the canoes. They all made it to the Kendal MIT train stop, outbound to Alewife. The subway was crowded, and they all huddled around in the corner of the back end of the large subway car. There was a lot of talking and commotion in the subway car from rolling bottles and cans: it filled the ears of all the listeners.

Michael started engaging in a serious conversation with Ted, asking him about markets. Ted answered those questions in depth, keeping his mind busy from the demons flying around inside his head. Sam said little until they all got off on Davis square. Jennifer and Erin lived closer to Boston, but they were spending the night with Sam, and Tim was planning on crashing at Michael's house, which was not far off from College Ave.

Ted held onto his smile, looking up at the near empty sky, filled with little stars, and that old oppressive moon, beating down on him. The weight of the light was heavy as they walked up towards College Ave. Michael and Tim waved their farewell as they took a right on Morrison Ave. It was now, just Ted, Erin, Jennifer and Sam. Of course, seeing as Ted's house was only three houses further down the road, they might as well have been going to the same place.

Ted's fists clenched at his side, and his right hand trembled underneath the pressure he put them under. He tried to maintain that fake smile, but now, he knew it became less of a mask now, as there were now two people who could see through it. And they knew it, and he knew it. He felt naked before them.

And yet, the damned majestic moon beat his spirit down as they walked down the sidewalk. *Just a little further, and I can close the door behind me.* He thought to himself. He kept his pace as his heart felt like it was beating through his chest. The breaths became more rapid, he resorted to breathing through his nose to limit his noise as they walked. Erin, Jennifer, and Sam were caught up in some conversation that Ted tuned out. He didn't want to be bothered by anything useless. *What good is it? Everything is pointless.*

At last, he could see his beautiful, peaceful, and empty house. He was close. The three women moved up the stoop to the apartment building. Ted waved good-bye briefly before picking up his pace.

"Tedward!" Jennifer called.

Damn it! "Yes?" he turned his head towards her and greeted her with his smile.

"I'm sure I'll see you Tuesday?" She brushed her brown hair out of her face.

"I haven't given it much thought," he answered vaguely.

"Will you come?" Her smile faded into a stare much more sincere.

"Time will tell. It always does," he answered.

"Yes, or no?" she asked again. "No more dodging the question."

"I don't know if I'll come or not. I'll think about it," he replied, lowering his voice as his hand began to tremble.

"Don't make me text you in the dead of night again."

"I wouldn't dream of it. Good night."

He turned around. He started walking back down the sidewalk at a brisk pace. He could feel visions flashing before his face, the nightmares were not far behind. They never were. He could hear the opening of the apartment building behind him, and Sam, Erin, and Jennifer started walking inside.

Suddenly, he couldn't move another step. It was not as if his legs were heavy, or that he suddenly lost all energy to move, it was like his body lost the will to move. He grunted as he tried to move something, but his body did nothing. Even the will power of Task Force Seven was not enough to move anything. He could feel his knees getting weak again. *Not here. Damnit! Not here! No! No! NO!* His knees buckled and he tumbled forward, catching himself from hitting his face on the concrete.

He could feel the darkness coming in around him. The oppression from the moonlight pushed him further into the darkness and deeper into the prison inside his own mind. His whole body trembled.

He gasped, breathing heavily. His eyes closed as he started choking by the pressure inside his own chest. Grief took over him again. And he couldn't hold it anymore. He shrieked; his mouth opened wide as tears streamed down steadily at the side of his face. His sobs turned into agonizing screaming.

Feeling the chills come over her, Jennifer's hair stood on ends, and the goose bumps were raised from her arms. She turned from the door before closing it, running outside. She ran towards Ted, and she gasped, seeing him on all fours like a beast, sobbing, and choking on the tears of his sadness. She sprinted over to him and tried to place her hand on his back. She tripped forward. Her hand passed through him like a ghost. She turned around immediately, catching herself. She looked Ted in the face, his eyes open, but swollen with tears. He looked straight at her, but not to her. Like he was in a corner, staring at a wall. His sobs, she recognized them. These were not the sobs of a man, but that of a child.

I—I passed through him? No. I must be imagining it. She walked back over to him while he continued to sob. He didn't move at all. She went to place her hand on his back, and it passed through him again, touching the ground. She retracted her hand. Her hand trembled she felt her heart growing heavy, and she found it hard to breathe as the air chilled her throat. She looked at her hand, and it was solid, and there wasn't anything wrong with her, but—*I didn't—I didn't imagine it. What is going on? Is he real?* She heard Erin and Sam's footsteps behind her, both wide eyed. Tears entered her eyes as fear sunk her heart and she clutched it, "Ted?"

There was no answer.

"Ted," he continued to sob, moving from his tones to that of a child, to something even younger.

"Ted!" Sam exclaimed. "What is going on? Answer me!"

"Tedward!" Jennifer cried.

The wind started howling around them. Jennifer looked beyond Ted, looking down the rest of College Ave, seeing nothing out of the ordinary except that the road didn't end. It kept going, and going, and going, as if she found herself in some figment of another reality: a reality of endless despair.

Ted continued to sob. There was a pool of tears below his face.

Walking up briskly to Ted, Samantha placed her hand on him, only it passed through him, as if he was an empty hologram. She felt the darkness coming in, swirling around her. Her vision saw nothing but blackness, and the temperature dropped drastically, forcing her hairs on ends. She placed her hand in front of her face, and saw all five of her fingers, bright as day, but everything else was dark. She found herself utterly alone in a black pit.

"Ted! Jennifer! Sam! Get up!" Erin cried out.

She was not about to touch Ted. She reluctantly stepped forward, in the attempt to shake Jennifer and Sam up. But she couldn't touch

Ted. *Was he some kind of wizard? Why are they like this?* Her heart thumped inside her chest, and she was flooded with a ton of thoughts that wanted to be turned into questions, for she didn't fully understand what was going on, why Ted, Sam, and Jennifer seemed to freeze up, Ted first, and as Sam and Jennifer touched him, they seemed to pass through him, but merely found themselves frozen still, and in place as if time itself was frozen still around them. She didn't understand it, and this mysticism cut something in her faith in God, for a world with magic does *not* exist. Erin touched Sam on the shoulder. She shook Sam out of her trance, and she was weeping.

"What was that?" Erin looked down at Ted, in his shocked state, as she pulled Jennifer away from him. Jennifer was not weeping when she woke from the trance.

"I don't—I don't know. It was like—" Sam began.

Ted gasped and his weeping stopped. His arms stopped shaking as his head focused on the end of College Ave.

"Ted! What is going on?" Jennifer went back to him, despite the protests from Erin. "Answer me!"

"Jennifer, I don't think—" Sam objected.

The temperature dropped again. "Jennifer get back!" Sam pulled her away from him. The three of them took large steps back, keeping their eyes, fixed upon Ted, kneeling on the ground. His hands grabbed the sidewalk, and they could see blue veins rose up over his skin, the blue veins crawled over his shoes and clothes, emitting a black light from them.

Ted? Jennifer thought to herself.

Ted pushed himself off the ground in a sprint, and within a singular stride, he landed nearly two-hundred feet away. He sprinted off another stride, and another until they couldn't see him anymore. There was silence in the air, and the summer heat returned.

Sam and Erin started walking back into her apartment. Jennifer could hear them speaking in flustered tones, discussing specifically what it was that they saw, and the sensation of absolute darkness and the sudden chills. Jennifer couldn't hear anymore of what they were saying, but she imagined their reaction would be as much the same as hers: confusion. Veins on the skin were not prominent, and she was unaware of any new scientific discoveries about an additional circulatory system. Those were veins, she recognized them, but they're not supposed to be black, or changing color, nor should they even be able to climb and crawl on the skin. She sighed heavily, and clenched her fists at her side, feeling the tears stream down her face.

Tedward, my Tedward, what did they do to you? Is this the source of all your pain? If it is, I don't even think I could forgive it. This is inexcusable. I'll let you go for now, but I will find you again.

Chapter 19

Ghost

~I was destined to live and die in obscurity.

Culain sat down in the hotel room. He sat on the bed waiting for a call, his mobile phone rested on the glass coffee table. He sent Ilya off to London to report to their Headquarters. Blanka and Alexander were sent to scout this late at night. The moon was full, and he knew full well, that when the moon was full, the likelihood of a gate being opened was higher. Any number of those threckets could show up in someone's house or on a rooftop.

But there was another problem here, something that needed his attention. Another caster, unknown or operating underneath someone's radar. He knew full well that whoever did this wasn't supposed to be operating seaport that night, least of all, killing normies. *Whoever it was didn't even finish the job.* He was waiting on a call from headquarters about any additional information on the man. They had his face through the mana veins of Ilya, who absorbed all the final memories of Jamal, who Culain then executed before Ilya converted his essence into mana that she could use. Whoever this was, he was going to be a problem.

His laptop was sitting on the coffee table.

Ring.

He picked up his phone with urgency, fumbling the phone in his hands as he carried it to his ear, "Culain."

"Culain, this is Administrator Sander."

"Yes. I take it you got the information you needed?" Culain asked.

"Yes. Ilya is being sent back to you now. She'll be arriving tomorrow. Did you check your email?"

"Not yet," Culain logged into his computer and pulled up his email account, opening a secured email. It had a few attachments from the administrator. He opened it to look at the face of the man in question, of course, Culain never saw him, but this person looked very young, perhaps in his teen years. There was a long document attached as well. He opened it and it was a single one-paged-report. "I have it open."

"That is all of the information that we have on the face that we've been able to come up with."

Culain scanned the page. Atop the page read: *Ghost 199437029401 24.* He blinked perplexed. He scanned through it again. The report wasn't very long. It only gave specific locations in countries, no report on what was done there. No date of birth. No Social. No physical name. "Sander, I don't mean to be rude, but did you forget to leave out his name?"

"No," he answered. *"That is all of the information we were able to locate on this man's face. Granted, it doesn't exactly match the face of the image Ilya provided. Probably due to an old photo."*

"That is what I thought," Culain commented. "How did you come by this information?"

"I had to pull some favors from the American Administration. Unfortunately, even our inside operatives only know so much. That is all they were able find out. American military erased everything."

Culain laughed out loud. "Of fucking course, they did. Damnit. When the fucking American yanks want to keep something a secret, they're almost as good as we are."

"Yes," Sander said. *"Which begs the question: why?"*

Culain shook his head and scratched his chin. "They want to keep something hidden. So, either this person knows something he shouldn't, or he is that something that they wanted hidden. But then, why would they just let him roam free?"

"No idea."

"How old is this photo I'm looking at?"

"Eight years."

"So, the most recent documentation anyone has on this person is from eight years ago," Culain scoffed. "Well, can you have someone look into anything useful that might have involved the U.S. military eight years ago? I'll keep an eye out for this kid. I can't just have him messing around whenever the hell he wants. Besides, I want to keep unnecessary deaths down to a minimum over here. You know how hard that is."

"Yeah, I'll keep you in the loop."

Culain hung up the phone. He looked closely at the features of the man, but it wasn't a man he was looking at, and this looked like, to Culain, a teenager. The kid had broad soldiers, standing at a mere 5'3. Culain was certain the kid would have grown taller at least, but it wasn't far off from the description of height he received from Jamal.

What were you doing there? And why that night? The thoughts rolled around his head when his laptop *pinged.* He opened another email. It was bcc'd:

Attention all agents,

At approximately 2130 GMT, the Holy Grail and Pandora's Box, was stolen. The only known lead we have is Former Major Sarah McCurdy, from the American Administration. All agents are to treat Sarah McCurdy as extremely dangerous. Teams will be sent in to track and locate McCurdy at all costs. Any information you have on McCurdy's whereabouts are to be communicated to Administrator Sander immediately.

It is unknown what she intends to do with the Grail. Keep the general population out of this. I don't think I need to remind you what failure to comply will mean. This is of the utmost importance.

~Administrator Sander

He marked the email as unread. He shook his head. "Of fucking course, she did. The dumb white American bitch. For Americans, you especially are intolerable."

He took out his phone. He dialed Alexander's number. Alexander picked up the phone after the first *ring, "Alexander."*

"You, and Blanka, get back here now. There is a code red emergency." *Click.*

Culain started swearing underneath his breath. He made a cup of coffee, probably a bad idea but he needed to stay alert. He knew the history very well, and whenever someone *else* had the Grail, bad things tend to escalate. Culain drank his coffee black as he waited for Blanka and Alexander to get back to the hotel.

The door opened. Blanka and Alexander walked in briskly. Culain couldn't have been waiting for more than thirty minutes.

"What's the emergency?" Blanka asked, wide eyed.

"An American stole the Grail," Culain answered, he guessed Blanka's surprise, and concern because it was rare that these emergencies popped up.

Alexander's eyebrow raised, "What?"

"You heard me right. An American stole the fucking Grail," he snarled.

"Why would they do that?" Blanka shook her head and rose both of her hands up with open palms.

"I don't fucking know!" Culain snapped. "Obviously, we can't exactly do anything about it now. All we know, is that Major Sarah McCurdy from the U.S American Army, and the American Administration has the Grail; why, I don't know. She succeeded in stealing the Grail not that long ago actually. So, it stands to reason it's on its way here. Or somewhere here. Probably DC. We don't have to worry about that now. But everyone needs to know.

"Secondly, we have new orders."

"About?" Alexander kept his fists trembling at his sides.

Culain guessed the trembling was caused by a sudden sense of anxiety. They all had it, hell, even he had it. There wasn't any person immune to it, and the best anyone could do was hide it in a pocket.

"What do you mean we don't have to worry about that now? Last time someone else stole the Grail, we had to start World War Two to cover that mess up!" Blanka pointed a stern finger at Culain.

"Not so loud!" Culain pointed back with gritting teeth. "Walls are thin. Right now, that is going to be another office's problem."

"What if—what if it's a conspiracy? And the American branch is behind it," she asked.

"We'll have to cross the bridge when we get to it," Culain explained. "No need to worry about it now. If that is the case, we're the poster board definition of being irrevocably screwed. Someone else will deal with it, and Sander is good at getting a team together for that purpose."

"World War Two was a messy situation to get into," Alexander admitted. "But our new orders."

"Yes, our current order still stands, but we need to be keeping an eye on any unregistered caster activity," he answered. "That kid, whatever, from seaport that night, there is limited information available on this guy, and we need to track him down."

"We tried that night, but his trace disappeared," Alexander said.

"Ilya may have mistakenly absorbed the mana reservoir of what he left behind for us to track him efficiently," Culain explained. "She should be back tomorrow, and we can get some kind of plan in place when she does."

"What do we know about him?" Blanka asked.

"A code name, and he's American. That's it," he answered.

Blanka and Alexander exchanged confused looks with each other. "What?" Blanka broke the silence.

"I said the same thing. His code name is Ghost, and we don't know who he is, identity or otherwise. We need to keep an eye out for him. Besides, if McCurdy is working remotely, she's probably getting help with someone off the grid, and he seems like he's off the grid."

"I find it hard to believe that's all we know," Alexander said. "That is too little information on anyone."

"That's what I said. Sander is looking deeper into it, but this is the only reliable information we have on him, that, and he lives somewhere in the Greater Boston Area."

Chapter 20

Hedgehog

~Humans don't take their own lives because they want to die. Every day, every day they wake up in this nightmare. Every single day, I wake up to see the lives of those whom I killed. I see them every waking moment, and in my sleep. I can't escape from them. We take our lives because all we want is for the pain to stop. Is that so much to ask? Is that really so terrible?

Four weeks later, Sam and Jennifer lost hope for Ted. He never answered the door. He stopped answering phone calls, and text messages. The mail in his apartment never left the mailbox, just sat there, as if no one ever bothered to take any of it out. Even Erin, didn't see him at work anymore. When she inquired, Ted, simply left. He was no longer part of that brokerage. His porch grew dust, floating and clouding every time a small gust of wind would blow into the house. He was gone. She assumed he packed everything up, and he just left.

Samantha knew Jennifer had high hopes for him. He seemed to have come a long way that night, July Fourth, but was it too far? Was he pushed to the brink where the only option for him was total isolation? Did he live in that house anymore? Sam couldn't be sure.

But every single Saturday and Sunday morning, she would knock on his door. There was never an answer. *Did we treat him like a project, and not a man? Is that where we made a mistake?*

She still didn't understand what she saw that night. Ted showed veins, glowing in the dark in numerous colors, she couldn't even tell how many shades of green she thought she saw on his body *and* his clothes, and not to mention that he made an inhuman stride. She, Erin, and Jennifer all saw the veins and agreed amongst themselves that they should never mention what they experienced to anyone else, for fear of being labeled as insane.

It was a whole month ago. Perhaps she was just imagining things, but that was the first time he showed his pain openly to them. It was not something to take for granted. *Ted, we tried. We failed. I'm sorry.* She placed her hand on his door, one last time. *I just hope—I just hope you're alive. If you can't find help from us, find help from somewhere. Please.*

This was the last Sunday she would choose to knock on this door. Perhaps constant badgering him with texts and phone calls did seem rather stalkerish. She should have known, if a man at her office started doing it, she would feel the same way: isolated. A man as alone as he intended to be, perhaps their attempts at friendship finally drove him off, leading him to leave everything behind. *Should we had brought him there? Perhaps the fireworks was the worst thing we could have done.* Forcing a military vet to fireworks should set them off. *I'm sorry.*

She removed her hand from the door that Saturday, never to knock on that door again.

***

Tuesday came around. It was the last Tasty Tuesday, and Sam's load was picked up early and without delay. She was enjoying her commission checks but made sure to put plenty of it aside. She walked up to the church and grabbed a cup of coffee in the fellowship hall, nice and early. Granted, the coffee from the coffee machine maker with the pitiful excuse of coffee capsules was disgusting. Still, it was better than nothing.

There were volunteers coming in and out from the side kitchen, bringing in plates of cheese and crackers; some were even gluten-free. She leaned against the pillar, watching as people came by, talking with one another, often with a full mouth or in between bites. She sighed as she bowed her head down, drowned in her own thoughts of isolation.

She felt an arm wrap around her shoulders. "What's got you in a slump?" Michael frowned.

She came to and looked to him, "It's Ted."

"I don't think Jennifer or Erin's heard from him either," he took a bite of some sliced cheddar. "I suppose it's time to let go."

"I know, I—I just—I don't even know anymore. I just, from what little he let us in on, I just know he isn't going to get help. Michael, I don't even—I don't even know if he's alive," she started tearing up a little, bringing her hand to her mouth. "Can a man really live with all of that darkness?"

"You and Jennifer knew him better than I did. All I could really talk to about him was work. I did my best, but his walls were up around me also," he answered. "But I think that we've done all that we can do. I don't think there's any more we could have done."

"But there must have been something more, something else," she explained. "All it takes, is one more good act. All it takes is to know someone is there. You said it yourself, we as Christians need to do better, but how can we if we can't even do this?"

He let out a sigh, "You're right. *We* can't. We can't do anything. Only God can, and perhaps this is exactly what needed to happen." He let out another deep sigh as he swallowed a cracker, "Have you ever heard of the hedgehog dilemma?"

"No."

"These little creatures that shoot quills outside of their hide as a defense mechanism. Whenever they are cold, they try to huddle with each other for warmth, but fail to do so because whenever they get too close, they hurt each other with their quills, making it painful and dangerous. Effectually, they don't want to get too close for fear of hurting themselves or others. So, none of us know what happened to him because he won't tell us. He seems withdrawn to us, because he's afraid of being hurt. He feels that the closer someone is to his heart, the harder it is going to hurt."

"That makes sense, I think I understand now. He hides behind his mask, the smiles, the laughter because he doesn't want us to know how he actually feels, because he'll be giving a part of himself over to us, or other people. It is easier for him to live in a life of solitude than it is for him to trust others."

"I think, someone, or many, probably many people stepped on his toes and betrayed his trust numerous times where he has no faith in any person. He doesn't trust anyone."

"But Michael, he needs someone to help him carry the load. He needs help."

"He won't accept it. It is a cruel reality. I can't help but wonder exactly what he went through in the military. Maybe, just maybe, inviting him to the fireworks was a bad idea."

"Maybe," she admitted. "But we would never know unless we try."

"You truly are trying to be a new kind of hero aren't you," Michael smiled.

***

Park Street Church emptied into the street on a dark and dreary night. Fog rolled in filling the air with an aura of decaying mud and sadness. Sam felt its oppressive weight fill her lungs. She let Michael lead her up Park Street towards Teri Nation. The group followed behind them, following behind the heavily concentrated fog.

Sam could find in herself, beyond the miscellaneous chatter of everyone around her, she found it difficult to breathe in the fog. Her heart weighed heavily with every passing step. She was missing something. But what was it? What was the one thing she could do, one thing she could have done differently? Or was this opportunity gone? And was Ted lost forever? She remembered the veteran she bought some food for a few months ago, sitting careless on the sidewalk, unable to function in civilian life led to one of destitution. No one to care for them. No one to love them or take them off the street. Would Ted end up like him? *I'm so sorry.*

She knew she had to let it go, but something kept telling her to try, just one more time. She took a deep breath as her thoughts filled her heart again. *If I must knock on that door all day Saturday, Ted, I will. So, help me, God. I will until you answer the door, or my knuckles bleed.*

Samantha held Michael's hand, being led through the threshold of Teri Nation. As they walked, Samantha paid special attention to the faces around her, the smiling faces. Not one face held the grimace of despair. These genuine smiles told her there wasn't a care in the world if there was one less person, especially if they didn't know that person. So cruel, she reflected within herself as she frowned. In a world filled with smiles hiding the fact that the world around her was filled with smiling devils, and kind hearts damned to be broken. Anyone with a kind heart was damned to die here, and the cruel smiling little devils would bury them all.

They turned the corner into the back of the bar. Sam found her eyes scanning the bar, looking for Ted in the faintest hope he might be there, and be like the hedgehog in the anecdote Michael shared with her, that he might make an attempt to connect with them, not that she knew if he felt he had a reason to. All of this, assuming he was still alive, and somehow didn't kill himself. She thought of Jennifer and her relationship with Ted, how it seemed oddly romantic, yet, even one-sided. Jennifer would take it the hardest, if she didn't accept it already. Ted was gone. But something else caught her attention, a half-drunk glass of red wine with the beverage nap resting on it. There was no one sitting right in front of it.

Sam let Michael walk her to the bar. Jennifer and Tim were not far behind, still talking between themselves. Even Jennifer still seemed depressed, and mildly angry. Her face frowned and her eyes angled emptily at the bar top. Honestly, she knew Jennifer drew the conclusion that Ted may have offed himself, but Sam was unsure.

As Jennifer walked behind them, she swayed side to side, looking downward at her feet. She wasn't mad at Ted, how could she when she didn't know the whole story. She wanted, out of her own morbid curiosity to know the whole story, tucked away in a steel trap, but she now knew that she would never get an answer, and would never see Ted again; however, whatever the story was, whoever or whatever did it to him, was so horrible, it led him to his perpetually hollow existence.

Scott took their order and brought their drinks over, a glass of wine, a cider, and two mystery drinks, one for Jennifer and Michael. They stood in silence as they looked into their drinks, waiting for the bar and ruckus to start as. Sam didn't pay attention in the least about what was in the mystery drinks. She twirled her cup dispassionately, staring down at the endless ripples inside her cup.

"Well now, let us not let the drear and gloom get our spirits down, shall we?" Jennifer forced a cheerful smile. "Our life is frail and fleeting. Let us not remain in the bitter pit of despair, and then let us remember what we were able to do for those not us, while we are here," she raised her glass, her hand trembling with tears streaming down her face. "To my dear sweet Tedward. May you find some hope in this fragile world."

"To Ted," Tim raised his glass.

Tim looked compassionately to Jennifer closely before bringing the bottle to his lips. Samantha hovered her lips over her glass as she studied Tim, shifting uncomfortably in his stool. Of course, why wouldn't he be uncomfortable, Jennifer forced a eulogy in the middle of a bar!

"To Ted," Michael raised his glass, he frowned as his glass was raised.

Samantha felt it surreal to be raising a glass to someone they didn't know if they were going to see again. She felt like she was saying good-bye as she raised her glass in the air, "To Ted." *Good-bye Ted. Until next time, if there is a next time.*

They all took a sip of their dismal toast, inside a bar, which was filled with many happy faces, without a care in the world.

Sam leaned into Jennifer. She knew that out of all of them, Jennifer would take it the hardest. Ted seemed to have Jennifer under some spell, intentional or not, she couldn't tell. She wrapped her arm around her shoulder and swayed with her back and forth as they drank. They offered little words. They only drank, in the middle of this period of mourning for their friend's departure, however long ago it was.

Sam looked through the bar again. Seeing friendly faces, those not aware of the pain around them. They don't care. They don't care about anything or anyone. Those smiles, those faces, were mere simple contracts of agreement of respect, giving the impression they truly cared, and everyone was always in violation of said contract. Only through this, and only through Ted, did she understand this sudden truth. Even if Ted was no longer here, she would find him teaching them all something about the frailty of the human mind, and of mortality. *Who could actually be trusted?*

"Scott, I'll take another," came a loud voice from across the other end of the bar.

It seemed familiar somehow. Sam looked in the direction from which it came. She excused herself, walking in the direction of the crowd. She passed through the clumps of people. She followed Scott as he brought another glass of red wine to the other end of the bar. She followed him until he made his delivery at the end. She made it to the end of the bar.

"Ted! You're here!" she exclaimed as the man took the cup of wine and looked down at her.

"You again! What the fuck do you want? Get out of my face! No one wants you here," he said.

"I'm sorry. I thought you were someone else," she said, bowing her head as she turned around. *Culain, yes, that was his name.* She remembered, "My mistake."

"Yeah, keep better control of your friends, Bitch. I don't want to talk to you again," Culain snapped at her.

Culain, the name didn't exactly roll off the tongue. She frowned at him before turning around, letting the man enjoy, or attempt to enjoy a lonely glass of wine. She realized something, that man carried himself much like Ted, and while he was ostensibly happy, the rude demeanor, and those blank eyes told her a different story. Did he also go through a life fraught with misery or despair? Could he perhaps relate to Ted where she could not? It was wrong for her to judge, taking another step away, perhaps like Ted, he was a veteran with a harsh demeanor, and he pushed people away because he was aware of the negative stigma people would have on him. Maybe that's why he pushed them away and told them some poorly constructed limerick about killing her and Michael, or that's what she thought it was about.

Finally, out of earshot of Culain, she came across a less crowded part of the bar. Her eyes found a man, leaning against the large wooden wall which attached itself to the seat he sat on. His face was behind a menu, and he had a smile, all too familiar, and in front of him, a plate with some mashed potatoes, with only a singular bite out of it. There was a glass of water resting on the wooden polished round table.

"Ted?" she asked.

"Hmm?" he looked up to her and smiled, he hadn't decided to be relieved or disappointed yet. Emotionally, he was exhausted. *I came here for one thing, and one thing only, and it wasn't the potatoes.* He did want a friend, but with everything he's done, he would only bring pain to them. Or he would somehow end up with another knife protruding out of his back. "Oh, it's you. How have you been?"

"That is a painful question, and not one that I need to answer right now. Where have you been? We thought you were dead! Your mail, it's still sitting there!" she exclaimed, taking a seat next to him. She pointed a finger at him to emphasis the rage she had in her facial grimace, "Are you okay?"

"I'm about as okay as I'll ever be," he answered. "I'll not get any better. I'll only get worse."

"How much worse can you get?" she said. "Look, I'm still not sure what I saw, and I'm not going to make you tell me. I'm not. If you want to talk, I'll listen. But damnit Ted, you need help."

"I know I need help," he continued with that accursed fake smile.

"You know!" she was angrily sarcastic. "If you know, why don't you get help?"

"I don't trust therapists, and there is no one living I can trust. Sure, some people experience emotional pain," he let his smile fade, growing weary of the mask he was forced to wear. "Some deal with grief, or depression, some deal with loss, and others deal with lack of trust, others feel guilty. But it is rare that they must put up with more than two or three of those at a time, and not near to the extent that I feel." He frowned, and finally she saw tears watering his eyes. "My heart is always heavy, it's broken and it's nothing more than a ball to be played with, filled with scars and bullet holes. This heart is broken, and the body hasn't caught up yet. Besides, I'd hate to be an inconvenience."

"The only way for someone to understand is for you to talk about it. You don't let anyone try to understand. You keep pushing us away by your little disappearing acts," her tone became soft. "Look, Erin isn't here. Michael, Tim, Jennifer and I just did a little eulogy because we thought you were dead, or at the very least none of us will see you again."

"I've told you before," his voice dropped down to the whisper, his eyes angled to her eyes. "I'm a murderer. I see the faces of the dead around me when I'm awake. The faces come back full throttle in my dreams. I hate sleeping because of this. I have nightmares, every single night, and I wake up in the same condition you saw me in that night. What you saw, is me every single night. Every. Single. Night. There is not a day that goes by. I don't take vacations because of it. I don't rest because of it. My only hope is to work myself to death until I can no longer see these things."

"It's hard to imagine that you're still alive if your life is as tragic as all that," she said. *I choose to believe you think yourself a murderer, but I don't!*

He showed his wrists. There were no scars. "There should be scars here from me cutting. They're gone. I've tried drowning, driving a car and locking myself in while driving into the ocean. I failed that. I tried hanging myself, and all I did was hang there until I passed through the damn noose!"

"Why don't you ask for help? Ted, you need it!"

"You don't understand! I'm not human!" he gritted his teeth. "I don't deserve help, besides, in the end who would want to help a monster like me?"

Then what are you, Ted? That I believe. God, just what did you put him through?

"What I told you that day, and you thought I was exaggerating, was the truth. Yeah, sure, I believe in God, a God of forgiveness and mercy, but so does the devil. I have killed too many people for Him to even consider forgiving."

"Te—"

"No!" he jabbed her in the chest with his finger. He grabbed his wallet and dropped a c-note on the table. "No, Sam! You know something, they told me the first kill was the only one that mattered. And it broke me! And they lied! They all fucking lied!" his knuckles struck the table, "The first one wasn't the only one that mattered. Every single one mattered. I remember every single face. Every face! And I was never given a choice. Not one! Sam, I know the monsters and demons aren't hiding in the closets or underneath our beds. I'd be lucky if they were that far away. No, they're running amuck in our heads. And they are restless," he stood up and started walking away.

"Ted!" Sam called, trying to grab his hand.

He snatched his hand away, raising his voice, "No, Sam! I'm not— I'm not worth saving." Warm tears streamed down his face. The ruckus of the bar ceased, and everyone turned. Jennifer put her drink on the bar and stood up, keeping her hands to her side. "I would like to believe," he choked on his tears. "That a person like me would be welcome into Heaven, because that's where I believe them to be. But I can't. I have too much blood on my hands. I'm not welcome there, and why should I be? I only have a handful of good memories, and what I wouldn't give to have that again, but the nightmares never stop. It haunts me when I'm awake, it haunts me when I'm asleep."

Sam looked deeply into his eyes. Finally, though she suspected as much, he admitted to the reason those bags exist. She took measured breaths, hoping to make them subtle enough. *Just listen, Sam. Just listen. That's all he needs. Just let it out!*

He continued, "I came into this world with nothing. I still have nothing. Everyone I have ever loved is dead. Everyone I ever trusted is either dead, dying, or betrayed me, and those that betrayed me I murdered. And I would do it all over again. I came in this world with nothing, and what little I had accumulated was ripped from me. I will die with nothing. I'm not even going to get a tombstone. None of them ever got a tomb stone. They served their country better and with more honor than anyone flashing that damn flag ever has and ever will and they were all thrown away for something they didn't do. If I could go back in time, I would, and I would get into those hospitals and strangle each of us so we wouldn't have to live and face the cruelty of this world. It would have bee—it would have been better had the thirty-two of us never been born.”

Is he referring to his friends? Thrown away for something they didn't do? Treason? Sam felt like there was a rock in her chest. *The truth finally came out.*

“There. Are you happy now? There's my heart. It's out in the open. Now why don't you do with it what you want and dissect it like the science project you think I am. I'm done!”

Turning away, gunfire and screams filled Ted's ears. He could feel the hot gun in his hands, ready to fire. The faces assaulted his mind again, the bleeding, and desecrated faces. He couldn't hear the swift footsteps of a weeping woman, sprinting behind him. He felt pressure on his chest as the woman wrapped her arms around him and held him as tight as she could.

Ted gasped, and he came to, realizing he was crying all this time inside the back bar of Teri Nation. There was no sound, except the deafening sobbing of this woman in front of him. He reluctantly scanned the room, sobbing, still. All eyes were on him, many people who have seen him in passing, many whom he didn't know, nor did he care to know. He looked down, and it was Jennifer who was holding him.

“Ha—how were we to know the pain you were in? The guilt, the shame, the hateful regret, despair and utter isolation. Any one of them can be as heavy as a mountain. And you bear all of them, your spirit is crushing underneath all of that weight!” Jennifer sobbed. “Why do you do this to yourself? Why? You can't—you can't keep living like this. You just can't! One mountain is enough to kill a man, crush his spirit. And you bear all of it. There's no need, none, to go at it alone."

She buried her face into his chest, feeling the warm tears down his shirt. He felt her embrace, her arms wrapped firmly around him, unwilling to let him go.

She continued, "You need to stop not wanting to burden yourself to others. I know you feel like we won't understand, because we don't know what you're going through. I know you feel like we would sooner stab you than help you. You can't keep living like this, Ted. Not when you have—you have friends to help. You may not see it, and you may not accept us as your friends, but here we are, trying to help you." His body was still, and firm like a petrified dead fish. "We want to help. You can't go through life like this alone. Let us help you!"

He gazed passively at the bar top, filled with another traumatic memory he found himself trapped inside. His eyes watered again; he saw something absolutely terrifying.

"I know you don't trust us, but we trust you to make the right decision," said Jennifer. Her hands clutched the back of his shirt.

"The—the last person who put trust in me died," he sobbed.

She looked up to him with sobbing, swollen eyes, and she smiled through the pain. "Then let us be a light that your darkness so desperately needs. Let us fill that empty hole. I will help you bear this burden, Ted. We all will. I will be your light and I mean it," she rubbed her tears on his chest again. "I will—I will help carry that pain. You don't need to do it alone anymore. You say you've lost everyone you cared about, but we're here. And you may not care about us, but that feeling isn't mutual."

She sobbed into his chest, still held onto it tightly. He tried to move his arms up to push her off him, but then the most peculiar thing happened. Even his will was not enough to move his arms, no matter how hard he tried. They just wouldn't move as if his very being refused to let go of this woman, who provided something to him.

She continued, "Even in the handful of times we've gotten the chance to hang out with you, your absence will not go unnoticed. You say you no longer have a family. Let us be that. I know you're in pain, and hate yourself for living, but damnit all, Ted, life is too short to be bitter about the past, give yourself a fighting chance to enjoy what little life you have left. Give yourself a fighting chance, if—if not for your sake, then for mine!"

She released him, only to wrap her arms around his neck. "This is—this is what you forgot: the world is filled with so much uncertainty. The world is filled with darkness, and is contaminated by the poisonous rot of humanity, and at times we may think that life is not worth living. But what is certain, is that while the darkness of the world may be like murky waters, and impossible to see through, behind the veil of darkness is light."

"But the darkness has a way of snuffing out the light. I don't want to do that to you," he stammered.

"If that is what it takes, I will gladly take that risk."

"No—"

"At the cost of my own light," she repeated.

Why does she talk like her? Damn it, why is she so much like her. I don't want this. Why can't I just die in peace? Why must I be flooded into ancient memories of the past that must be buried, and buried properly? Jennifer, if I let you in, I can never let go. Do I—do I even want to let it go? Slithers, you were always there. Slither's face crossed his mind. He could see her smiling at him with the sun radiating behind her, and that beautiful meadow with the ducklings crossing in the lake. *So cruel, forcing me to look into the past as real today as it was, but it is only a mask. It's not real, but does it—does it really matter?*

Seeing Slithers in Jennifer, he was emotionally overwhelmed, weeping as the strength of his arms returned to him and embraced Jennifer. He wept into her shoulders, berating her with all his pain, all his trauma, all his grief, all his depression, and all his isolation. Lord knew he had those in no short supply.

Sam's tears streamed down her face as she approached him from the side and hugged them both, her head was buried on Jennifer's shoulder. No one could hear the steps of Michael and Tim who made it to the other side. Tim hugged Ted from behind as Michael placed his hand on his back. Tim was much more affectionate than Michael.

Ted saw the bar began to empty. The citizens of the bar left, one by one, leaving the huddled mass of people just there, moving around like water on rocks. Some glanced at the crying mass but gave it no more thought than that of curiosity, not sharing a shred of care in the world for the broken man, the man who wanted nothing more than to die, but could never follow through with it, or else risk killing what remained of his squad's memory, his only true friends and family.

He saw one man walking right by him, and unlike the rest of the bar, he took notice of him, sternly peering into his eyes, daggers stabbing into him. He was a tall man, and like himself, seemed all alone in this world. Ted didn't recognize him.

Jennifer rubbed her face against his chest again. "Ted, will you come with us on Tuesday?"

"Yu—yes," he replied. "I'll come. I'll come. You don't need to find me. I'll be there. You don't need to call or text. I will be there.

Chapter 21

The Hunger

~Innocence was murdered that day. A true friend will kill his friend, because only a true friend would bear the burden for him. A true friend wouldn't let another friend live in rotting regret.

He remembered seeing the snow season four times, that isn't to say he could have seen it once or twice more.

It was a long week. He waited in the bright white room, sitting in a grey steel chair, watching the room with his ever-watchful eyes, listening with those sensitive ears. There was a large speaker in the ceiling, and a large one-way window. He sat at a white table, pristine, and without flaws. The door creaked open, and his brother was escorted into the room by a soldier, dressed in camouflage, walking proud and mighty like a hero. His brother was about his age, perhaps a little older, and just a little taller.

His brother was friendly. He didn't have a name yet. He was sat right in front of him. He was happily sitting down, turning his head and marveling at the bright lights with a large smile and beautiful brown eyes. He waved his feet forward and backwards, just waiting for whatever surprise they had next for them. They were all good kids. They earned some kind of reward. He looked at the boy's shirt, which had merely the number "2" written on it, not a name. He turned down to his, looking for something to identify himself with: "7".

"This is exciting!" Two said, clapping his hands with elation, like a child who knew without a doubt something good would happen. He could barely restrain his excitement. "Seven, what you think they gonna gif us?"

"I dunno," Seven shrugged, leaning forward, looking at the room suspiciously.

"Maybe ah, ah, ah, one of those thick brown things the rest of 'em eat. That looks good!" Said Two, who began drooling.

"Or maybe a glass of that white stuff," Seven replied.

Two's brown eyes glistened with elation, and his blond hair glimmered in the light. "Somethin' nice and sweet to wash it down!" he continued to clap his hands erratically.

Another soldier, his mother came in with her name tag on her right breast: J. Nakamura. She had the gold-bar insignia. Seven paid attention to this. She came in with a plate, a single plate carrying a piece of bread, just a slice. The white bread was browning, with green mold growing at the side of it, the bread was crumbling on the plate. Nakamura placed it in the middle of the table, directly in between the two.

Number two looked down at, sighing heavily into his hand as he covered his face. A moment passed before turning around in his chair. "Mom, is this it?"

"Yes, it is," she sneered.

"You dun feed us a week and this all we get?" his head was downtrodden.

"Affirmative. Now, do be good, sweet little boys and don't touch it until we say so," she replied. She closed the door behind her, locking the locks from the other side.

"Well, sucks this!" Two cried out, slamming both of his fists on the table. The reinforced table trembled. His face cringed and tears streamed down his face, his hands were grabbing his hair as he leaned forward on the table, "I hungry. Mom, I so hungry," his stomach growled.

Number Seven joined in, staring at the food. Even the mold looked good enough to eat. They were all hungry, he couldn't think how much longer he could wait. They were starving to the point where Seven, at least, would gladly eat dirt. He was not so sure of number Two.

The bright light went out. Both leaped from their chairs and backed into the walls. The red lights came on, flashing the room in that twirling bulb in the ceiling. They were both startled, their hearts pounding against their chest. They huddled close to the wall. The intercom came on, and the loud alarm went off, scratching the inside of their ears. They both screamed, tears streamed down their wide eyes, covering their ears tightly with their hands. Even their hands were not enough, the oppressive sound pushed them to the ground as their back slid down. They wept, crying, "Momma! Make it stop! Mom, stop it! Please!"

The alarm stopped, and the white lights were turned back on. The intercom clicked on again. "I think it's time we play a little game. How's that sound?" said the voice of Lieutenant Nakamura. "That sounds like fun."

Two and Seven were still stunned on the ground. They panted heavily.

"Don't be like that. Do I have to sound the alarm again?"

They immediately crawled to their chairs again, crawling like little children out of their pen, but then of course they were children. They pulled themselves up with relative ease. They sat straight in their chair, both scanning the room.

"So, do you want to play a game?"

"Yes!" As if he nearly forgot about the alarm, Two sounded elated yet again. *Why?*

"You see, the door is locked and will only open from the outside. You have a plate with one slice of bread on it. Only one of you can leave. Decide for yourselves. You can both starve or fight for the bread. This is a winner take all game. You've got this!" she exclaimed rather enthusiastically.

They both looked at each other in disbelief, "Se—seven, are they—are they makin' us fight?"

"I dun wanna," Seven protested. He crossed his arms and turned his body away from the bread. "I dun wanna!"

"That's the name of the game," Nakamura said over the intercom. "You live or you die."

Seven stared at the wall, pushing his legs back and forth in the chair, ignoring his hunger. He ignored the growling in his stomach, "Seven. I'm not doing it. I'm not."

"I'm not doing it either. Cross my heart hope to die," Seven replied.

"Then decided."

Two went into the other corner of the room and sat there. Seven moved from his seat and sat in the opposite corner. They smiled at each other from across the room.

Hours passed. Neither of them moved. The hunger from inside their tummies grew, eating away at their life like a tapeworm. Seven pulled his knees to his chest, propping his elbow on it. That hand scratched his cheek as his palm covered his mouth. Two did the same thing, as they breathed deeply by sucking through their teeth as they both kept their hands on their tummies, applying pressure in the hope that it would alleviate some discomfort.

They both were in so much pain, they couldn't fall asleep. All they could think about, was not fighting, and not eating that disgusting moldy bread. They both toppled to the side, curling themselves up with their knees to their chest: grimacing, and crying.

The intercom turned on. "Congratulations!" Nakamura exclaimed from the other end of the mirror. "You've passed. You both can leave. Just make sure to finish the bread first."

They both felt a new energy sweep over them. They crawled to the chair. They both sat in, and number Two excitedly took the piece of bread and ripped it in half. He held both pieces in his hand and told Seven, "It okay! I knew we do it. Here."

Seven smiled at him, taking the smaller piece. They both smiled and nodded as they ate the moldy bread. It was bitter, dry, and unbearable, but it was food. They could hear the door mechanisms come free. "Seven! We can leave!" They both got up from the table together, and went together, walking side by side. They reached for the handle of the door, smiling.

Click.

Two's eyes opened wide, as he exhaled heavily. The handle turned but the door wouldn't open. He grinded his teeth. "Hey! Momma! What gives? You says we can go!" he pounded on the door with both fists, "Let out!"

"You both are going to leave," Nakamura explained, in her sweet motherly voice. "You didn't think we'd just leave a body in there did you? Only one of you leaves alive. You can't leave until only one of you is standing. I wonder, who will make it out? Two, or Seven. You get to choose who leaves alive. Good luck!"

"Sucks this," Two said, he clenched his fists tightly in his hands, the fingernails cut into the palm of his hand, now bleeding and trembling at his side.

Number Seven moved away from the larger boy. He cowered in fear as he leaned against the wall. Number Two sighed, and turned to number Seven, raising his fists. "I need out," he sobbed. "Come here! I can't do dis anymore!"

Number Two charged at Number Seven. Number Seven raised his arms over his head to protect himself from the much larger boy who struck him with fists like rocks. He was kicked in the side; his face was slammed into the wall. Two then grabbed the hair of Seven and repeatedly knocked his face into the wall. He tripped Seven and started stamping his feet on his face until he stopped moving. He took his free foot and kicked the head into the ground, hoping for certain Seven was dead.

Number Two cried as he walked back to the door. He went to open it, and there was no click. He looked back to the mirror. "Momma! Open up. He dead, just like you wanted. He dead. Let me out!" he sobbed, moving his fists to his side. "LET ME OUT!"

"I said, only one of you leaves alive."

"I already told you! He dead!" he cried out. He cried into the camera monitoring the room, pointing with open hands where he thought Seven was laying.

"N—no. I not," said Seven. His face was bruised and swollen. He put his hands up, in defense position. "I do dis arr day. I can do dis arr day."

"Let me out!" Two cried as he swung at Seven.

There was a blue flash as the temperature dropped in the room. Blue veins lit up Seven's arms, lighting up the room. Seven's output of his Mana Veins was so much that he was surrounded by blue cackling light, burning parts of his own flesh. Seven punched Two repeatedly with lightning-fast jabs, the impact made a sound so large, that the mirror cracked. Seven grabbed hold of Two's throat with his hand. He clenched his teeth, barring them as he squeezed the air out of Two's lungs. The larger boy tried his hardest to rip himself free, but to no avail as the blue light burned at his throat, black smoke rising.

Crack!

Two's arms dropped down. Seven dropped him, and blood filling his mouth and his eyes seemed empty. Seven gasped as the mana veins receded into his body, and his hands stood still. He slowly, mechanically moved his head to look at Two, dead on the floor. His eyes squinted as he let out a screamless cry.

The lock from the door came undone. The door creaked open. Seven looked to it, looking at Lieutenant Nakamura coming in with a smile on her face, and a plastic zippy bag. She walked over to him, and kneeled, meeting him at eye level. She had a pleasant soft smile on her face as she stroked the side of his face with a soft caress. "Good job, number Seven. You are my sweet little boy. Good job. As a job well done, here," his mother pulled out a black pill from the zippy bag and a bottle of water from one of her pockets, handing them both to him, "Eat."

Hungrily, Seven took the pill, and washed it down with the water she provided.

"Good boy," she said, taking his hand in hers. "Come with me."

Seven followed her silently, coming out of the oppressive white room. He walked with her down empty corridors, with the occasional soldiers looking down on him with disgust.

His right hand started to tremble. Seven looked at his right hand, covered in Two's blood. He felt his heart beating from his chest, not from excitement, but guilt swept over him. He knew this wasn't a mere camping trip, no, Two would never see light again, he realized for certain, Two was dead, and *he* killed him. He didn't mean to do it. He was told to. He didn't want to. It was self-defense. But that didn't make it any easier, he still killed someone, his own brother. Breathing heavily, he tried to calm himself, but the vision of the room was just as vivid, and just as real, like he never truly left the room.

He let that sink in as he came to a large door. The gears and mechanisms in the door started to move, causing the metal to creak as it scraped against itself. Slowly it let in the welcoming moonlight, where he saw many of the other children outside, in a chain linked fence. Nakamura brought Seven to the fence and opened the door. She ushered him in and locked the door behind him.

He stifled a cry as his heart grew very heavy, turning around to look Nakamura in the eye. She smiled back at him, "I'll play with you later, my sweet little boy. Good job tonight. I knew you had it in you, Seven."

He watched her walk backwards, behind the vertical door as it closed in front of her. He looked up at the moon, and he could have sworn there were less stars in the sky. He looked down at the children in front of him. He counted them. One. Two. Three. Their faces were bruised, and he could have sworn the smaller red-headed girl had a black-eye. Four. Five. Six. They were nursing broken limbs: arms, legs, fingers. Seven. Eight. Nine. These three were coughing up red blood. The larger black—haired boy, coughed up some baby teeth. He wheezed heavily. Ten. Eleven. Twelve. These three had blood, not their own, smeared over their faces. Thirteen. Fourteen. Fifteen. These three were huddled in a corner, staring and clawing at the fence. And Seven made sixteen. This morning, there was thirty-two of them. Tonight, they were reduced by half.

He bit his bottom lip and clenched his fists at his side. He started wailing with tears streaming down his face, the guilt of his first kill took hold of him. It felt like someone was inside his chest, punching his heart repeatedly. His knees buckled and he caught himself with his arms, kneeling on all fours like the dirty dog he was. His hand was covered in the sand, and his tears made mud in front of him. He looked at the rest of them, as if they waited for someone to start, they all wailed in the air. Tears streamed down their faces.

Number twenty-seven, the thirteenth he counted, her glasses tilted down on her face, with blood smeared over both lenses. She raised her gaze over the sky, her mouth opened, and blood drooled out of it.

Next to her was a crying girl, brown hair tied up in a ponytail, with bangs on either side of her face. Her face cringed, and her teeth gritted against each other. She let out one squeal before she silenced herself, closing her mouth and letting her eyes scream with rolling tears into the ground like a puddle. She was number thirty-one.

Number thirteen, cried out loud, wiping his eyes with closed fists. His short dark hair was invisible in the darkness of the night. The blood got into his eyes as he collapsed to the ground, curling in the fetal position and held his hands together in a tight ball, cutting off his own circulation in his hands. He brought that ball to his face.

Not one of them had names. These three would be part of Seven's personal squad in the future: Ticker, Butcher, and Slithers. All of them wept hard that night, and before the sun rose, nearly every foot had a puddle of nothing but tears.

Chapter 22

That is Enough

~After it all, I'm falling apart and I don't want to be put back together, but you're putting me back together anyway.

Jennifer woke up in the early morning, gasping for breath. She sweat profusely. She mechanically turned her head to her alarm clock, which read 7:21 AM. She coughed, covering her mouth with her hand as she slowly rolled out of bed, striking the ground. She slowly pulled herself up, using her side table to support herself. Her joints trembled, filled with searing pain. Her bones to her felt as frail as thin glass. She pulled herself back on her bed and leaned forward, taking deep breaths. She felt like her chest was caving inside, the lungs bursting out at the seams of her ribs. She took numerous measured breaths.

She now felt at equilibrium. She leaned backwards, still breathing heavily with her hands rested on her chest. She looked up to the sky outside her window, the sun beamed down on her, glimmering with shadowy clouds slowly rolling in. She eased up on her breathing, and she felt her shortness of breath was stable, but her bones still felt like glass. She pulled out her cell phone and opened her email. Her fingers trembled as she rapidly typed up an email to her work to let them know she was sick and couldn't come in today.

She went into her contacts. She scrolled down to Doctor Korowitz; her thumb trembled. She clicked the green call icon. She clicked speaker as the phone rang. She placed her phone on the side table. It rang and was answered quickly,

"Doctor Nicolai Korowitz's office. This is John, how may I help you?"

"Hi, John. This is Jennifer Miller. I am one of Korowitz's patients. I woke up with a shortness of breath and I feel exhausted, and my joints are in searing pain. I woke up like this, in the morning. It was sudden. Is there anyway Doctor Korowitz can see me today?"

"Half a moment, Jennifer," Jennifer could hear the rapid typing away rapidly. *"What is your date of birth?"*

"Eight. Second. Eighty-nine," she answered. *Click. Clack. Click. Clack.*

"He has an opening at nine o'clock."

"Please," she said.

"See you at nine o'clock."

***

Jennifer sat in the waiting room in the clinical office. The office was empty this morning, apart from a man sitting in the corner, waiting for his turn to get into the office. John, the receptionist was typing away on his computer, making notes and appointments for the doctors in the office. She waited patiently, still feeling weak in the legs. She crossed her arms over her lap as she stared ahead, concerned with whatever was going on with her body. It was all sudden. She had shortness of breath before, but not with this severity.

"Jennifer?"

Jennifer looked up and smiled at Doctor Korowitz. The doctor had a thick Russian accent, and bright brown hair in his full lab coat. "Yes?"

"I will see you now."

Jennifer trembled as she stood up from the floor. Pain seared into her joints, and she put on a smile as she stood up. Korowitz frowned as he looked at her. He took her hand as she approached him, and he led her firmly to his patient room. She took a seat on the bed, and he took a seat on the stool, logging into his computer.

"How are you feeling?" he asked in a soft voice.

"I'm in pain. This morning, I woke up with a shortness of breath. By itself, it isn't unusual; however, this wasn't usual. It was far worse, and it hurts my chest. I felt like my chest was going to collapse. I barely made it back to my bed after I fell off. My bones, particularly my legs feel like glass," she grimaced, letting her tears stream down either side of her eyes. "I've never felt this way, at least, not with this severity."

He started to take her blood pressure. "Is this the first time you woke up like this?"

"Yes," was all she managed to say.

"Ease up on that arm," he instructed. His eyes angled at the machine, as if trying to piece together an age-old mystery. He wrote down the blood pressure. "Blood pressure is fine. Nothing to worry about there." He took a needle out and he drew her blood. "I'll be back," he placed a bandage on the spot where he drew blood and left her inside the empty room.

She wiped her tears with her hand. She took deep breaths. She felt a vibration in her pocket. She took her phone out of it. And she received a text from Ted. *Tedward. I wonder how you're doing. That was a serious breakdown, or breakthrough last night. I don't know what kind of pain you're going through, but it seems you and I will suffer together. Perhaps I'm being overdramatic. Yeah. That's it. I'm fine.*

She opened the text message:

Good morning, Jennifer. Words cannot express my feelings, sometimes I don't understand them myself. Do you want to come and feed ducks with me by the Gardens?

She sniffled, smiling at the text. She returned it quickly, *I don't know yet, Tedward. I would certainly love to. Can you do me a favor and call me later? Whenever you get off work tonight. I'd really appreciate it.*

Immediately, he returned the text. *I'll call you after 6 pm.*

She smiled. He was certainly quick to return a text, a swift response, and a response with utmost certainty. She had no doubts within her heart that he would call her at that time. She wiped more tears from her face as she put her phone back into her pocket.

The door swung open. Korowitz took out a medical document and handed it to her. She looked over it, while much of it was a lot of medical jargon, there were some things she did recognize. These were the results of her blood test; her CBC was alarming: three. Her eyes opened wide as the document trembled in her hand.

"We need to get you to the hospital. Did you drive here?"

"Yuh—yes," she stammered.

"We'll get the necessary call in-place for a biopsy to be certain, but it's possible you may be developing Leukemia," Korowitz took her hand. "Are you okay to walk right now?"

"Yes," was all she could say. *Leukemia?*

He took her hand. He led her out of the patient room and led her down the hall, leading her through the vestibule and down to a chair in the waiting room. He went back behind the door. Korowitz went behind the receptionist, saying something to him inaudibly, who started typing away, and sent something to the printer.

She sat; her hands trembled in front of her. She held back her tears, but her hands betrayed her feelings, for even the receptionist noticed the anxiety fueling her: wide eyed as the pupils trembled, streaming down reluctant tears and her uncontrollable quivering. She leaned forward, frowning into her trembling hand.

She took another deep breath and buried her face in her hands, and spoke into them, muffling her words to God, "Lord. Forgive me. I don't think I've faltered. I don't think I have, but perhaps I've been caught up with Ted, and paid too much attention to him, and not enough of you. An innocent mistake by our standards down here below, but you are a perfect God, and our standards are not yours, and by yours I've made a fatal error. I'm sorry. I've escaped death before, twice. If it is your will, it would be a third time, but if not, I understand. I've had one too many second chances already. If it is your will, I accept. But please, let this not be my time. Just, please let me have a little while longer. Perhaps, I haven't been as faithful as I think I have. Perhaps that is my fatal error. Lord, remove the callouses from my heart. Please. Please. *Please*."

***

Jennifer woke up from the anesthesia, finding herself in a white room while sitting up. She looked out the window, the sun was setting. She looked around herself, seeing the nurses and physician assistants walking back and forth, attending to various patients. She looked around, to see if she could find her own pants and her phone. She looked carefully, trying to find something to tell the time. She knew she wouldn't have the results from the biopsy for another seven to ten days. There was no use trying to worry about it.

She found her purse sitting by the side of her bed. She couldn't reach it. She looked back up and moved her braided ponytail off to her left shoulder. She looked for a free nurse and waved her down. The woman moved over to her swiftly and gave her a warm smile. Jennifer looked at the women's name tag, catching only the last name: McCurdy.

"Hi. Miss. Could you tell me what time it is?"

McCurdy looked at her watch. "Five-forty-seven," she answered.

"Oh, really. I guess I woke up just in time. Could you hand me my purse, I can't reach it, and I'm not sure if I should be moving around much yet, but I'm expecting an important call."

McCurdy reached for the side of Jennifer's purse to her. "Thank you very much. Would you happen to know when I am to be discharged?"

"Let me find out for you. Do you have someone to pick you up?"

"Not yet."

The nurse walked from her into the other halls. Jennifer looked at her phone and saw no notifications just yet. It wasn't like she received texts very often, especially not on a Wednesday. She scrolled through her contacts. She went to Sam's number and texted: *Please pray for me. I woke up ill. I'm being tested. Pray that it's negative.*

There was silence, except the constant walking of nurses, the rolling of wheelchairs, and the constant stamping of crutches and walkers. There was constant rolling of various machines filled with oxygen, and other medical accessories. She waited as the time passed by, waiting for that call. She was still certain he would call, despite the constant efforts of distancing he kept putting between them. She was certain that *he* really wanted to talk to her, even to discuss something mundane. Perhaps, he'll finally reveal something else, not traumatic, about himself. She heard the imaginary clock ticking inside her head, like a little lost dwarf hammering away at her cranium.

She looked down at her phone, still waiting for any kind of response from Sam, while she still waited for Ted's call, her notifications remained empty, and silent as the sounds of the hospital drowned out the ticking of her internal clock. She looked back out the window, staring at the streetlights outside, illumined the streets, which was still filled with lots of pedestrians, walking around with their phones to their ears, or their faces bowed down and typing or reading away aimlessly in them. Many others, children, seemed happy to be skipping along in the street with their parents, skipping away like little children. Many of those children were tugging on their parents' arms for attention. She couldn't help but smile.

She looked back to the end of the bed and looked at her feet. She wanted to know and feel if her bones still felt like breaking glass as they did this morning. She sucked in the air through her teeth, anticipating pain, as she lifted her left leg up, taking the cover underneath them. Her left leg trembled as it rose, but not so much from the pain, but rather with anticipation of pain. Her leg was growing defiant of her condition, however severe it may be. She put her left leg down and rose her right leg, which trembled as it rose. She smiled as she put her leg back down.

Buzz.

She looked down at her phone, smiling as Ted's name shone across the screen. She swiftly answered the call and brought it to her ear. "Tedward," her tone was filled with excitement as her lips rose from ear to ear.

"Jennifer," he spoke. His tone was not cheerful, nor did it seem grim or depressing. It was just there, empty.

"Tedward!" she exclaimed yet again. She smiled through the phone, not because of the empty monotone, but simply because his tone wasn't cheery. This time, he wasn't trying to hide anything. "Are you feeling okay? I mean, the other night, that was a lot to process. It couldn't have been easy."

"Well, I suppose I've seen worse," he replied. *"It is hard to say I've seen much better times in my life, but perhaps that was for the best. There's just only so much I can say."*

"I think we've all had our trials and faults. I think that it is not all you," she said, dropping her smile as she saw the nurse walking over to her. "I think part of it is on me, and Samantha. We did push hard on you when we had no right knowing anything, but we didn't want to see you alone. I recognize a fake smile, and while some fake smiles fade well into the crowd, yours stood out to me."

"I don't blame you. I don't. I find it difficult to express myself, even when you annoy me."

"Well, it was bound to happen. I annoy a lot of people. It is one of my quirks."

"You mean charms, don't you?" his tone was playful.

"You can be discharged if you have a way to get home," the nurse said to her.

Jennifer nodded, "I suppose it is one of my charms. You haven't ditched me yet, have you?"

"Discharged?" he asked.

"I'm in the hospital for a biopsy. I'm about to go home, somehow," she explained. "Nothing serious." *I hope.*

"Did you drive?"

"No," she answered. "I was delivered here by ambulance. My car is still at the doctor's office."

"Are you okay?" he said, even over the phone, his voice was monotonous, and seemed uncaring, but he was trying. She knew, otherwise he wouldn't have called.

"I'm sure I'll be fine. Hey, here's an idea. Why don't you pick me up and take me home? Sam's not getting back to me."

"Where are you?"

"The diseased manor," she answered.

There was silence on the other line. And then he laughed. *"There is no hospital with that name."*

"We can make it one," she joked, smirking with one curve of her lip rising higher than the other.

"Sure, so where am I picking you up?"

"Jameson's Hospital. Thirty second Broadway, Brookline. I think I'm on the fourth floor," she replied.

"Okay. I'll drive over. Give me about a half hour. I'm coming from Dedham."

"I'll see you soon!"

Click.

She looked back down at her phone, seeing a text message from Sam: *I will pray. Sorry for getting back so late. Work troubles. I hope you're doing well. Brunch on Saturday? Michael and Tim will be there. I don't want to invite Ted back just yet. I think he needs some time.*

She smiled down at the text, feeling accomplished. Not that she had Ted all to herself for the night, but the fact alone that he spoke to her without masking his emotions much. For tonight, maybe he will completely remove that mask. Perhaps finally, the iron heart *was* being softened, capable of being adjusted by a hard mallet.

She texted back: *I think I'll pass on brunch this week. I'll see you Sunday.*

Jennifer leaned back and looked up to the ceiling, placed both hands beneath her. She let out a deep breath, sighing into the air as an indescribably heavy burden was violently lifted from her chest.

"Lord, be with me," she prayed; she closed her eyes and crossed her hands over her chest. "Lord, thank you for the gift of modern medicine, and thank you for Doctor Nicolai Korowitz and his insight in catching this. I am content. Thank you for pushing me through my limits, through my dreams and aspirations. Forgive me Father, for even though I fall constantly, and fail to follow your laws. Please humble me when I am consumed by arrogance and pride," she opened her eyes at the room. She took a deep breath and tried to move her legs again. This time, she could move both legs up and down, and she did so, taking turns, not grimacing with any discomfort, for it seemed to have subsided, and she smiled. "Thank you for everything. Truly, I am grateful. I have more than enough, and more than I need. Thank you. Amen."

***

Ted walked through the doors into the hospital. He smiled as he walked in. No one here needed to know his *true* condition, or his *true* hatred. He noticed many people in wheelchairs, some amputees, many who's faces were void with sunken eyes, long and skinny faces, devoid of all personality, just like they were completely dead inside, much like himself, only they stopped caring enough to hide it from anyone. He smiled at the thought, being dead inside, if only his heart would stop beating. He went to the receptionist, waiting in line, still scanning the busy hallways, and the busy white floors, smeared with feces, and urine, just waiting to be cleaned up. A staff member, dressed in white, wearing gloves and a mask came by with a wet floor sign and a mop bucket, and started mopping away.

"Sir. Sir. Hello! Is anybody home?" the annoyed receptionist called out. Her spectacles hung by her chest with grey beads.

Ted jerked his head to her, catching a very unforgiving but friendly face out of the corner of his eyes. His fist clenched at his side as he removed his frown with a bright smile to the much older woman. "Sorry about that. My mind seemed to have slipped."

"Careful, or you'll end up slipping too. How can I help?"

"I'm sure. I'm actually here to pick up a patient, Jennifer Miller."

"What's your name?"

"Ted Anderson."

"I don't see your name here."

"Embarrassing," he chuckled nervously, as he was sure was the appropriate response. "I just got the call to pick her up. She does know me if you want to call her down, I'll take a seat somewhere."

The older woman motioned him to sit in a chair which was vacant.

"Thank you,"

Ted went and took a seat on the chair, waiting, and scanned the room. He continued to scan for the man he saw, the unforgivable man. The man still had that buzz cut, that sinister smile with his dog tags hiding underneath his lab coat. The man looked like a seriously joyful man, smiling cutely at other women who happened to walk by, as if encouraging niceties.

Doctor Adams. Are you really a medical doctor? It sickens me to think that you could actually care about people. I certainly never received such treatment from you. Not after you strapped me to that damn chair in leather straps, sending electrical currents all through my body until my pain receptors no longer worked. Adams, if I wasn't trying so damn hard to live a normal life, as normal as I can despite my own psychological deficiencies that you caused, I wouldn't hesitate to kill you.

Doctor Adams disappeared as he continued to walk down the end of the hall. Ted knew who and what it was that he saw, and frankly, out of all the painful memories and people in his past, he was sure this was real, and he wasn't merely having a psychotic episode in the end of the day.

Ted's hands relaxed as he pressed them against his pants, still scanning the hospital. He didn't feel safe here, not when there was a familiar face present, well, one that wasn't Jennifer's. For of all the things he knew, and it pained his heart, her smile, the least of all was genuine. He took a deep breath as he stared down the vestibule with a little nurse pushing a wheelchair, and in that wheelchair was Jennifer, holding her purse on her lap. She smiled as she waved her arm at him. She had a light blue medical gown over her clothes.

He smiled at her, breathing deeply as he stood up from his chair. He forgot abruptly that he just had a faint encounter with someone from his past, however one sided, as Doctor Adams didn't appear to recognize him, of course, why would he, it was eight years ago since when he last saw the bastard of a doctor. He turned his attention back to Jennifer, walking to meet the nurse.

"Hi, Tedward!" she smiled that foxlike smile of hers, there was something suspicious, but beautiful about it. As always, like she was playful, her eyes were half opened.

"Elizabeth," he gave a light smile.

"Well, is Mr. Darcy reading up on his Jane Austen for me? How romantic."

The nurse giggled behind her, "You got her?"

"I'll take her," Ted went into the back of the wheelchair to push her along.

"Onward! The chariot awaits!" She rose both her hands and kicked her feet out, "Weeee!"

"Well, I can't say I've had to be in a hospital before. But I don't think I would be in good spirits," Ted chuckled, pushing her out the door.

"Tedward," she leaned back into her seat as she looked up at him from below. Ted noticed her watchful eyes, watching him. He can't say he understood her true intention, but he felt vulnerable, almost like when Slither's broke him down after years of badgering to take her to go star gazing. "You need to learn to live a little. Life is too short to be miserable," she paused a moment. "I'm sorry. I know I can be overbearing at times." She sat back, all snugged in her little chair and hospital gown as Ted rolled her over the board walk, and carefully into the parking lot.

He awkwardly smiled down at her. "I see. Well, I suppose I've lived long enough to know how short life can be. Some lives may be long; others tragically short," his tone dropped.

"Ted," She looked back at him as he rolled her to his car. "I'm sorry. This isn't my way of trying to pry anything out of you. I just want your company."

"I understand," he wheeled her to the side of his black car. He opened the car door.

"Of course, what kind of friend would I be if I didn't desire to know something else about you?" she asked, sneering at him. She wobbled out of her seat and sat herself into the car. She smiled as she moved her feet into it.

"Is the chair yours or do I need to put it back into the hospital?"

"It goes back into the hospital. There should be a little depot right by the front doors, if I remember right." She gestured back to the hospital. "It's okay. I'll be here, waiting while you return it, Mr. Darcy."

"As you wish, Emma," he replied.

"Wrong Jane Austen novel! Emma was Mr. Knightly!" she snapped at him, pointing fingers at his chest. "Don't disrespect Jane!"

He snickered as he shut the door, and rolled the wheelchair back to the hospital, leaving Jennifer alone as she stared out the windshield. She fastened her seatbelt as she adjusted the seat, the bones inside her fragile legs trembled as she applied pressure to the floor of the car to push her seat back. She grimaced as pain filled her joints again. She leaned her head against the window to her left as she scanned the skies, the dark clouds reigning in overhead.

"Ted, I hope you find it soon. The storm is coming," a shiver went up her spine as the temperature appeared to drastically drop; she felt it from within the car. She started rubbing her shoulders and gazed back out the window and saw a woman, walking through the street, with crimson eyes, silver hair, and a youthful face as she skipped along. She seemed familiar of a sort, someone looking for adventure, or so she thought.

The girl disappeared behind a crowd, gone like a wisp.

The door on the other side opened. She sharply turned her head as Ted moved into the car, buckling his seatbelt. "Alright, Jennifer, let's get you home. Where did you leave your car?"

"It was at the doctor's office."

"I'll pick it up for you," he put his key into the ignition and started the engine.

Ted drove out of the parking lot, into the street, and started driving through the heavily congested roads of Boston as they drove towards the Seaport District. Jennifer moved in her seat, thinking about the tears Ted shared that night, on the night she would remember, the Fourth of July. She was certain he had every intention of wearing that mask, living in the façade of his own life, forgetting everything else that was important to him. This constant reminder of his condition she found most curious, and shameful of her own compulsive obsessiveness over him, but she couldn't not think about it. *But does he really have anything important to him?* Then an image flashed through the back of her mind, walking in the darkness of the night, the quiet stillness of College Ave when he broke down on all fours, weeping, crying, letting all the pain leave his body. But truly, there wasn't an outlet big enough to house all that pain to let it out at once.

The temperature dropped drastically that night, and light emitted in the air. An unnatural light that shouldn't have been shining, the light came directly from his body. Maybe it was something small enough, small enough to pry that he would remove a brick from that wall he keeps up.

"Ted?"

"Yes?" he replied, never taking his eyes off the road.

"That night, when you ran off," she began. She noticed he shifted uncomfortably in his seat. "I'm not going to ask your feelings or what you are going through, I'm not going to pry, but perhaps you can explain something to me that I am having a hard time trying to understand. I saw these lights coming from your body. What was that?"

His smile faded, and he let out a deep sigh, keeping his eyes on the road, maintaining his laser focus on the busy road. "I am the only person I know that has ever had them. I don't know what they are, but they are regrettably a part of me. I can't get rid of it. I've tried, but nothing works. I don't know what they are, nor do I truly understand what they do. All I know, is that when I use this organ, the temperature drops. It's really hard to describe. I've never had to describe it before. It is like breathing, but it's something other than air. It goes into these veinlike things and protrude out of me. It appears to change colors depending on what I'm breathing in. I don't know how else to explain it, no medical doctors knew what these were either. I first noticed it was a part of me during an especially difficult time in my life that I don't care to discuss right now."

"That is enough, Ted," she replied.

"Hmm?" he turned to her slightly.

"That is enough," she smiled to him, twiddling the loose ends in her braided ponytail with her right index finger. "Just to admit that, is enough. You don't have to explain any more than that. The fact alone that you trust me enough with that, is warming to my little frail heart. I want you to know, that even while it may be unnatural, I do not judge you for it, nor will I condemn you. I just want you to know that."

"Thanks," he answered before turning his head back to the road, his eyes angled with a sharp frown like he made a fatal mistake.

The streetlights shined brightly on the sidewalks. He parked his car in the back of the Seaport, a short walk away from her apartment. He turned the key off. "I don't think I asked, but maybe we can talk in your place. Do you need help getting up?"

"If you don't mind, Tedward," she smiled at him as she opened the door. "My legs are still a little weak."

"Hang on," he walked hastily around the front of the car to get to Jennifer on the other side. He took her hand and carefully helped her out of the car. She moved to the side, leaning against the side of the car for support. He closed the door and locked it.

He pulled her arm over his shoulders, pulling her closer to him. He held her close to him as they walked, using his strength so that she felt weightless, light, like a feather. He walked her across the street and into her big apartment building. He took her up the elevator and walked her down the hall. She breathed heavily with each breath, especially reaching for her keys in her purse. She opened the door, and it creaked open. Ted walked her in and brought her to her couch.

"Thank you," she said, smiling up at him.

"You're welcome. I've been meaning to ask you, and I don't know why I waited this long. Why were you in the hospital?" he asked empathetically.

She let out a sigh and patted the cushion next to her, "Take a seat," he looked suspiciously at the cushion before cautiously sitting down next to her. She looked up to the ceiling as if the answer to some unknown question was written on it. "Life, it is so fragile and ought to be protected. No matter how worthless it might seem, no matter how useless. All life has value, and I think sometimes I feel I take the life I have for granted. It became apparent to me today, when I woke up, gasping for breath like some devil was inside my chest. I am a survivor, Ted. I've survived a lot, and perhaps that is why I seem to be overbearing at times, so full of life because I have already been on my deathbed."

Ted actively listened to her, the small details, how her tone changed from sentence to sentence. It was clear to him, she wasn't stalling to tell him the reason, but she still hadn't processed everything just yet. Death was something he was all too familiar, and while deathbed wasn't an alien concept to him. There were times where he thought he would be on his death bed. Well, that was until he found out he couldn't die by normal means, it would seem. Those cursed veins prohibited it.

"I called the doctor's office and had a blood test, and my doctor seems to think I have a high chance of having Leukemia. I went to the hospital for a biopsy, and I did have some treatment to deal with the pain. I don't know if I have been confirmed for Leukemia, that is what the biopsy is for, and if I have it, it will determine the type of Leukemia I have."

"You seem to be in good spirits for someone who has potentially received her death sentence," he said grimly, turning his head away from her, not wanting to look into her eyes.

She took her hands and clasped them around his cheeks and turned them to her, so she could smile that faithful smile, filled with cheer. Despite the cruelty of her uncertain condition, she was full of it. Of course, Slithers would never do this, but it was warming all the same, "This world can be a dark place. It is filled with despair and hopelessness. It is filled with tragedy and loneliness. It is filled with gloom; however, I know where I will go. If it is my time, I will gladly accept my deliverance from this world, and be all the gladder because of it. I don't know where your faith lies, or if you have any in the Lord, but I wholeheartedly believe, and He gives me peace in all of this. I may be cheery now, but like many others, I will cry, but not yet."

"I didn't grow up in a church, I've heard telltale mentions of a God who is loving and good," he replied. "However, I find it hard to justify a loving and just God created this world with so much tragedy."

"I thought the same thing once. Many years ago," she sighed. "But no point in dwelling on this now, if you don't want to. I'm hungry."

"You're not in any condition to cook," he said.

"I don't want to cook, silly," she giggled as she released her grip from his face. "What do you like to eat?"

"I can't taste anything. I can't taste anything. I haven't been able to taste anything in over eight years."

"Well, that's boring," she sighed as she leaned back in the cushion. "So then, the baclava?"

"I couldn't taste it. I tried it and tossed the rest."

"Ted," her tone dropped. "I appreciate you being honest and showing me a part of you. It's like meeting a new person."

"You're welcome," he said flatly.

"I want Chinese food," she pointed to a brochure on her TV stand. "There is a menu right there. Can you grab that for me?"

"As you wish," he replied, getting up from his cushion to grab the menu. He brought it back to her. She looked at it. "Ted, I know you said you can't taste anything, but are you hungry?"

"I barely eat," he replied. "Only when necessary."

"I'll order you something," she dialed a number on her phone as she stared at the menu.

***

About an hour passed, and they sat at her dining room table, with the brown crunchy paper bags, and the sturdy white boxes with aluminum handles sprawled around with some paper plates. They were filled with fried rice, chicken fingers, and teriyaki. It smelled delicious as the steam from the steamed vegetables assaulted their noses with their sweet and delicate fragrances. Ted ate sparingly.

"Ted?"

"Yes?"

"Last night, at Teri Nation, you came back there, and hid away on a Tuesday night around the time we would have been there, which we were of course. Why did you come? I don't entirely understand why, if you were hell bent on avoiding us."

"I guess, you could say I was running away. I quit my job, fortunately I can still do that with my computer and not have to worry," his voice trailed off as soon as he realized how stupid that was. "I don't worry for money; I have plenty of it. It's much rather I worried about not having something to keep my mind occupied. I knew you all would be there. I wanted to say goodbye, to give that courtesy, but when the time came, I couldn't muster it up within myself to do it. So, I tried to leave, only, something else happened instead. Sam managed to find me there as I was finishing up some potatoes. Unfortunately, I am very good at hiding my own thoughts, my feelings."

"I know you don't wear your heart on your sleeves, but they came out bursting at the seams last night. Ted, forgive me, I know I said I wasn't going to pry, and I guess I won't, but I do want to know a little more about what happened to you. Would you be willing to share something?"

"I would be willing, but the question is what? A lot happened to me, and so much of it wasn't exactly legal," he let out a deep sigh as his eyes scanned the ceiling as if to study it. "You see, Jennifer, I was part of this group that was part of the U.S Army but the program itself was run by the CIA. They chose Thirty-two men and women to be part of this program, of which, I was one of them. I nearly didn't make the cut due to an earlier heart attack. We were all physically fit, and battle hardened by the time we started our series of deployments, lasting a total of four years. We barely slept. We barely ate at all during that time. For four years, we were up before the sun, and didn't sleep until the moon slept. One morning, we'd end up in Iraq, and fight a two-week fire fight. After we were done raising hell, we would go back to the Forward Operating Base to resupply. We wouldn't get a chance to go into our barracks, of course we had none, we didn't need them. We'd be on the next flight immediately to North Korea the following day. Repeat. Fly to Russia. Repeat. Fly to China. Repeat."

He stopped scanning the room, pausing briefly, waiting for Jennifer to respond. She chewed the food in her mouth slowly, peering into his eyes. She nodded her head, waiting for the rest of his story.

"The nations began to fear us, and rightly so. We learned their tactics and killed them in their sleep. Whenever there was a fight between America and any other opposing force, once it was known we were on the battlefield, the battle was already over. It didn't matter how many people they took with them; it was a matter of how fast they could arrange an organized retreat."

He paused again, biting his index finger, and looked down to the table, seeing a speck of dust. He took his free hand and brushed it off, on to the floor. He returned his gaze back to Jennifer who looked back at him, ignoring the fact that he just wiped dust on her floor.

"I too value life to the highest degree, but my actions tell a different story. You'd think that after killing so much I would become numb to it. I never did. I still see the blood on my hands, and I still see the light leave their eyes. I still see their faces and they never leave me, always staring at me like a murderer. Why shouldn't they look at me like that?" he choked up as he shed tears from both eyes, his heart was on the table, and it was opened. But this time it wasn't something that needed to be pried open, he willingly gave her the key. "I didn't have a choice. I didn't have a choice," he wiped his eyes with two fists, twisting them about.

He felt warm hands cover his, and softly pulled them away from his eyes, guiding them, palm upwards to the table. Her fingers caressed his wrists, and he saw she never once looked away, "We always have a choice. At times there may not seem to be any good options, but there is always a choice."

Seeing Ted was hyper focused on their hands, she removed hers from atop his, and laid it palm facing upwards next to both of his. She noticed his hands trembled before they flipped, holding her hands firmly on the table, and with that, she saw him with clenched teeth. His eyes turned towards her with watery eyes, shimmering from the ceiling's light. She was thankful, that another layer of his façade came undone. *If only he could bring it upon himself to seek help, and yet, as if some cruel fate or curse was laid upon his birth, he is compelled to do nothing and carry the burden of guilt alone. Ted, you didn't tell me everything, and I don't mean you to.*

He took a deep breath, sucking the air through his teeth, and let the air out through measured breath through his clenched teeth. "You're wrong," he spoke silently. "And I can't tell you why."

"Can you tell me why you can't tell me?" she asked.

There was a silence. Jennifer gripped onto his wrist a little more tightly. Finally, Ted slowly shook his head. She slowly nodded, never once letting her gaze escape his as she finally clasped his hand with her second free hand. "What you've said already, is enough. Like a shaken-up soda bottle, you need to release some of that built up tension before you can open it properly without it getting messy and blowing up all over the place. You have told me what I have asked, and I will ask for nothing more tonight, and Tedward, I want you to know that what you've told me is not going to leave my mouth, nor my lips tonight, tomorrow, or ever. I hope you believe me."

He nodded.

She scarfed down the rest of her food, "I could use a shower, but tonight has been a rough one. I think I'm going to turn in early."

"Good night."

She turned to get up, and her legs wobbled before she gained full composure of her legs. "Okay. It isn't that bad," she said to herself, hoping to use the placebo to stave off the pain. She started walking back towards the couch. "Ted, you are still in your house, right?"

"No. I sold it as soon as Sam started getting too close to me. I have an apartment in Waltham."

"Ted, I wouldn't normally do this," she said. *But I don't want to be alone, neither should you.* "But I do have an extra blanket if you want to spend the night here. The couch isn't all that big, but it does pull out into a spare bed. I don't want you to be alone tonight."

"I'll stay."

She smiled and tilted her head down as her eyelids drooped halfway down, "Now, Ted, does this mean I'll see you in the morning then?"

"Yes," he said slowly, and his volume dropped to a whisper.

She smiled as she went into the other room. Ted watched her, carefully monitoring her every step. He watched as each leg shifted, and her feet turned with each passing step. They were disorganized. Tonight, he felt an incredible weight lifted from upon him. It's been eight long years, at least, that is how he remembered it. Too bad. The memories won't go away. The nightmares won't stop.

She came back out of the room with a large blanket already folded up, walking into the living room, placing it on the coffee table. She removed the cushions from the couch and moved them to the side as she pulled out the folded bed from the couch. She set the blanket on top of the bed and started to tuck in the sheets.

"There you go," she said.

"Thank you," he spoke softly.

"Good night, Ted."

He nodded to her as she slowly closed the door to her room and walked to the futon.

Looking down at the soft futon, he let his arms drop to his side. For once in his life, a bed was made for him, not one that he was forced to make and remake over and over again with a single wrinkle on the sides. This bed was made perfectly, no wrinkles, nothing drooping too far from one side to the other. His hand reached for the blanket. The hand trembled abruptly as it touched the blanket, glaring, he found his hand pulled his nightmares again into his reality.

His hand, covered in crimson blood, lit by the burning flames. He saw iron and stone rubble in front of him, and the roar of the flames drowned everything else out. Covering his mouth as the awful scent of spilled petroleum assaulted his nose. His nightmare turned again into reality, and further smells assaulted his nostrils, burning flesh, and rotting corpses and other expiring fluids. The buzzing of the flies filled his ears. He covered his nose as he reached for the futon that was no longer there.

Kicking the side of the futon, he tripped over it, feeling the burning coals against his palms. Head, striking the pillow, coming back into the reality that was Jennifer's apartment, and he left the flames of regret behind him. He kicked off his shoes, taking numerous deep breaths. He stared at the blank empty ceiling as he rested his back against the futon, sprawling his limbs on the unnatural comfort of the bed.

"We trusted you, you know," came a voice out of the corner. Ted immediately sat up and scanned the room. To the corner of his eye, he found an all too familiar face, someone he forgot. She had glasses on her face, and her brown bangs framed it as the rest of her hair was tied back in a ponytail. To him she was wearing black pants and the green fatigues. Her arms crossed over each other.

"Roach," he said.

"Ghost," she said, disapprovingly. "Why are you here?"

"The same could be said of you."

"You know why I'm here. Why are you here, trying to make a life for yourself? It was what you always wanted, wasn't it? To live as a normal man, with a wife, maybe have some kids, a job, get a house, and yet, here you are just as miserable as you were when you were with us," she dropped her hands and tilted her head as she took two steps forward to him. She sneered at him, showing him her blood covered teeth. "You should be sacking Uncle Sam right now."

"You know how I feel about that."

"Ghost, don't give me that!" she snapped at him. "Everything we fought for was a lie. Everything we died for, was nothing more than a sham. There is no point in lives like ours! If you don't sack Uncle Sam, then there is no point in a life like yours!"

"I don't want to," his eyes angled to hers, and he frowned, clenching his fists at his side.

"You don't want to, but you need to, Ghost. Do you want to finally lay us to rest?" her tone softened.

"More than anything."

"Then you need to sack Uncle Sam. You know what all of us sacrificed for that! Do you want your nightmares to go away? Do you want to stop seeing these vivid dreams? Do you want to end it all? I know you do, and if you do, you need to sack Uncle Sam!" she aggressively pointed a finger at him.

"There is no point," his voice was stern. "Roach, even if I did, I know that the nightmares will only get worse. There is no closure for a monster like me. It won't mean a damn thing," he gritted his teeth.

"Then you've given up."

"You don't understand, Roach. The difference between you and me, is that your nightmare ended eight years ago. I wish mine ended that day. I go to sleep, and I see it all over again, and my nightmares refuse to end!"

"Ghost," she sighed as she took a step back and leaned against the back wall. "I know. I know. We all know that you don't have the damn guts to do it, and you're the only one of us who can," she sighed as she stared at the ceiling. "Well, I've got to go. This was useless. You're useless. Oh, and Ghost, don't blame yourself with what happened to us. It's not your fault. It's not your fault."

Ted's eyes glimmered, coated in tears again. He wept softly as he rolled his fists in his eyes.

"It's not your fault I died," Roach said coldly. Ted looked at her and he saw her as he left her. Her left arm was severed in her black uniform. Her right leg was completely torn off, and the stumps bled profusely on the floor. She removed her uniform with her one hand, revealing the cavity that was inside her chest: the bones were shattered inside. The right side of her face completely burned: the oil on her face still burned and he could smell the burning flesh. He could smell the soot of blowing gun powder. "The fault was entirely mine, for trusting my life in the hands of a wretch like you! I can't believe I trusted you to be able to protect me. You can't save anyone. How could you when you can't even save yourself."

He gasped as she shook her head in disappointment. The color in her body and blood began to slowly fade into transparency. The silence to him was deafening, but he knew it wasn't over. The demons and monsters were about to come out. He slowly went to lay back down as he started to choke on more tears. He grabbed one of the cushions and brought it closer to his head as his ears were filled with the unrelenting agonizing screams of men and women. It drowned out his thoughts completely as the room around him turned into a prison made from flesh and arms, and the tiles of the walls were faces, dead and dying with eyes still lively, seeking out his face.

Servicemen and women surrounded him, aiming their weapons, the screams of agony outweighed the sudden bursts of gunfire. He felt the vibrations in the air as bullets passed over his head. He silently wept, his eyes filled with tears and terror as he tried to drown out the noise by squeezing his ears with the cushion to no avail. He could still hear them as plain as day. These men swore in the languages of all the people he killed: English, French, German, Chinese, Russian, Polish, Italian, and Korean. He saw every last detail in all their faces, the scars, the malformities, every last one of them.

Because of him, he thought, he made countless widows and orphans. Because of him, there are families going without food. Because of him, there is going to be an emptiness in their lives, and those kids the parents left behind are going to think ill of him, and should they know who he was, for certain, they would seek his head. And who could blame them? If only, he thought, there was a way to achieve world peace without needless bloodshed, he could have found a purpose for his miserable existence. Roach was right. There really wasn't a point in a life like his.

***

Jennifer's eyes came open with a start as her ears rang with loud tormented screams. The temperature dropped drastically, and she pulled the covers off and hopped off her bed. She opened the door into the other room, peering behind from it. The room was filled with a light of rainbows. *Tedward.* She investigated the bed where Ted should be, and she found the cushions ripped from the sofa, laying to the side, and the blanket was disheveled. *Ted.* She moved out from her room, dragging her blanket with her. She put her hand out in front of her to shield her from the blinding light and she found Ted in a corner, huddled up with his knees to his chest with multiple-colored lights emitting from his body. These lights looked like human veins, and they covered his entire flesh from his fingertips to the top of his skull. The lights were beautiful like a rotating rainbow.

She looked at him carefully, tears streamed down his face, and he looked dead ahead, at nothing in particular, but as if he was in one of those horror movies and a monster just killed everyone he was with and he was next, and the monster was not far behind. He looked terrified as his hands clasped both sides of his face to cover his ears.

Just like before. How vivid are your nightmares? She knew he needed help, a shoulder, and certainly a therapist, but she knew already he would never see one. All she can do is listen and offer a shoulder, any more would undo all the work she and Sam accomplished with him. She walked towards him, maintaining eye contact with him, but his eyes didn't seem to react to her presence as the temperature continued to drop, seeing the white mist of her breath, she took each step with care, knowing full well her condition, albeit, maybe not as severe yet, but one can never be too careful. Her heart felt some strain on it, but not because of her condition, but merely because it hurt her inside to see anyone like this. *Ted, it is good you stayed. This was what worried me.*

She took another step beside him and leaned against the wall with him. She wrapped her arm around his shoulders and leaned into him. He jerked away as he stared into her eyes as if he didn't know her. She moved in front of him and placed her hands on his wrists ever so gently and removed his hands away from his ears. She cried tears with him, and they streamed off her face and into his lap as the strings of her heart were pulled. *I'm not a therapist! God, help me!*

"Ted. I can't hear what you hear. I can't see what you're seeing right now." She spoke softly and his hands dropped to her wrists. "I know you don't want to talk about it, and I'm not going to force you to. But at some point, you will need to talk about it, or you'll explode. I'm here when you want to talk about it."

She moved to the side of him and leaned into him again and wrapped the blanket around them. He started to take deep breaths as he wiped the tears from his eyes with his fists again, turning them in his eye sockets.

"Why?" he breathed.

"'Why'?" she replied, turning her face to his.

"Why are you and Sam so focused on me? I am filled with regret and guilt. I try so hard to function in the real world, but I just can't. These nightmares and phantoms simply won't let me. My nightmares don't end when I wake up. Every night. Every night when I try to sleep, I wake up screaming because I see ghosts. These ghosts are people I've killed. I remember their faces, every single one of them. I see those who I fought with and fought for. They're all dead, because of me. I couldn't save them. I can't save anyone. I couldn't save any of them because I just couldn't muster the strength in me to kill anyone anymore. I couldn't save anyone. Perhaps they were all right, and there really isn't a point in a life like mine."

She nodded, "You may feel that way. It is human, to believe in the sanctity of life, and while there are those that like to undermine it by defining life on their own terms, the truth remains the same, we all value life and when we take it away, we feel guilt and regret. We are told to value life at a young age, or at least I'd like to think so, and taking that life is enough to break us. Ted, even when we are not the one taking something away, we feel heartbroken by it. You remind me of my uncle, he came back from wartime, and he never expressed himself openly, like you, and he eventually took his own life. I don't want to see that happen to you."

She watched these veins on his body, shimmering the light on the ceiling and on her flesh. Despite the dropping temperature, the veins as they touched her, was like a frying pan. *What is this? God, what happened to him that made him like this? Surely, he wasn't born like this, was he?*

"Life can be hard, and like I said to you on Independence Day, life can be Hell. It's like that for everyone. We go through rough patches, and sometimes we feel like the light at the end of the tunnel is nothing more than where the last traveler fell, and what is left of his hope is burning in a lamp, stationary in a dead end. And sometimes we get to dance in the meadows and see the fireworks," she continued.

The lights from these veins started fading and was cooling down as the air around them warmed up. She didn't understand what was going on, or what exactly these veins were doing. Even Ted admitted he didn't know what these were, but that he was the only one who ever had them. She felt his body cease trembling, thinking he reached some level of homeostasis.

She continued, "It is no mistake to say I've become fond of you, even if I seem to know next to nothing about you. I know where you're from and that's about it. I know you served to protect our nation, and that whatever happened to you there is unforgiveable, whatever it was.

It sounds like what you went through was nothing short of betrayal and regret."

She was right. She knew nothing about him but was able to ascertain that much that everything that happened to him should never have happened to begin with. Could he trust her?

"Ted, do you trust me with your heart? I will never say anything to anyone that you don't want spoken aloud. But do you trust me?"

"No," he hesitated. "I don't trust you," he paused as he looked at her again. "But I am willing to try."

"That is enough."

Chapter 23

The Garden

~There was something I tried to run away from. But it won't leave me alone.

Jennifer woke up Saturday morning with the sun beaming on her face. She stretched out and yawned over the back of her bed. She looked at the clock, 9:32. *A tad early. No matter.* She leaped out of bed and put the covers back on to it. She looked at her phone, no messages yet, except there was a voicemail. She saw that it came from Doctor Korowitz's office. *Must be the test results.* She stared down at her phone and her hand trembled with anticipation. She felt much better these last few days, and even now, the pain in her bones had completely subsided. She took a deep breath as she opened her voicemail to listen:

Jennifer. This is Doctor Nicolai Korowitz calling. It is important that you call the office when you get a minute. Thanks.

She erased the voicemail and sat back down on her bed. She looked up at the sky, as if looking up to the Lord for her guidance. "Give me strength, Father. This is hard, but, not my will, but yours be done," she smiled with certainty. She scrolled through her phone to find the number for the Doctor's office. She dialed it.

"Korowitz's office. This is John, how may I help you?"

"Hi, John, this is Jennifer Miller. I'm returning a call from Doctor Korowitz," she replied.

"Sure thing. One moment."

She was immediately placed on hold, and she danced to the annoying hold music with the obnoxiously loud saxophone. The music stopped, and Nicolai's thick Russian accent filled the silence, *"Jennifer, are you feeling okay?"*

"I'm doing fine. The meds are keeping the pain down. I can walk without wobbling, and I don't feel dizzy."

"That's good. So, your test results came back. When can you come in for an appointment?"

"Monday?" she asked.

"Let me see," Jennifer could hear him typing heavily on the computer on the other end of the line, his heavy fingers hammering the keys, *"2:30 PM work for you?"*

"Yes. I'll put it on my calendar."

"I'll see you then," Click.

She exhaled heavily. *It's not serious, not yet. No point in worrying about it right now.* She exhaled deeply, letting the air decompress her lungs. Her hands relaxed as she held her phone. She went back into her phone and scrolled through to Ted's phone number. She dialed it.

"Jennifer?" he immediately picked up. If Jennifer didn't know any better, she would have thought he was staring at the phone waiting for her to call him, not that there was any reason she would.

"Tedward," she smiled into the phone, filled with an overwhelming sense of felicity. "Hey, so I am feeling much better. Are you still up to go feeding the ducks today?"

"Yes," he smiled through the phone. *"Do you need me to pick you up?"*

"Ted, you're farther than me. Let's just meet outside the T at Park Street station. We can walk to the Gardens after and feed the ducks there."

"Sounds like a plan. What time?"

"I was thinking noonish."

"I'll be there."

"Do you play Chess?"

"I used to play it frequently," his tone went low.

"I'll bring my mini chess board. I'll see you at noon!" *click.*

***

Jennifer walked down on the boardwalk, walking all the way from Seaport Boulevard, with her purse hanging from her side. She had her hair held back with a green headband and wore a modest yellow sundress and white sneakers. She walked briskly through the boardwalk, over the bridge, and crossed the sidewalk. She welcomed the warm gentle breeze caressing her hair as she made her way to the Boston Common. Of course, she could have just taken the T, but it was such a nice day outside with the bright sun shining down on her.

There were many people about at this hour, after all, tourist season was upon them, and there were many tourists, domestic and foreign walking the Freedom Trail, and exploring many small domestic shops and antique bookstores. She walked up through Winter Street, ignoring the heavy traffic of pedestrians and street performers in the street.

Winter street was dark as it had parallel to each other, tall skyscrapers. She welcomed the sunlight again as she walked across Tremont Street, welcoming the lovely view of Park Street Church on the right. She walked towards the T stop which was behind a concession stand ran by a woman, handing out cans of soda and bottles of water with the exchange of cash.

She looked around her, and found many people happily tossing frisbees, or playing with their dogs on the grounds. She saw the gathering area filled with many round tables and folding chairs which surrounded the big fountain there, still streaming water out of its various holes and into the makeshift pool at its base. She saw the many birds of the air chirping around her, fluttering their little wings about.

She heard the doors behind the T stop open and out came flooded people as they pushed themselves carelessly out the door, excited to see the lovely Boston Common, and all things of which it had to offer. And out of that same crowd came a man, modestly dressed in shorts, and dark hair with a plan T-shirt, holding a paper bag which had a large roll of bread.

She giggled and hid her smile behind a hand. With her other hand she waved at him. "Oh, Tedward, that's a rather big roll you have there. I think that might be too much bread for our little ducks."

"One never knows," he smiled his warm smile.

She reached out with her free hand. "Come on. We have ducks to see!"

Ted took her hand in his and she led him away from the hustle and bustle of the gathering area and down a path, leading upwards closer to some more of the dogs and frisbees. She led him enthusiastically down the path, skipping with her feet as they watched the squirrels scurrying up the trees with their acorns.

"Tedward," she said to him. "You have shared a lot with me, during the Fourth of July, and this week, I think it is time I tell you a little more," she smiled as he turned his head to look at her while they continued their little stroll. "You see, I got off the phone with my doctor this morning. I'm going over my results from the biopsy to confirm if I have Leukemia or not, and then go over any treatment plans with my oncologist. Maybe I don't have it," she let out a smile. "And it was just an isolated incident, maybe isn't related to Leukemia at all. If it is serious, I'll have to go for serious treatment for the long term. I just wanted you to know that."

"Information can be a dangerous thing, and so is trust. This was something I regrettably learned the hard way and thank you for sharing that with me," he said as he turned his face to something else that moved behind a tree, like eyes were watching him. "I'll try my best to not betray your trust in me."

Of course, he'd say that. Information is a tool to him, that's how he's lived his entire life.

"A paradox wouldn't you say," her eyes dropped to cover half of her eyeball as they walked, and finally reached the end of the common, to the entrance to the Boston Public Garden. The black gate was open and the pathway on the other side of the street was pleasantly shaded by trees. "You can trust me, but you don't."

"And you can't trust me, but you do," his eyes continued to scan the pathway.

"I knew you'd say something like that, but if that was the case you wouldn't have warned me of the potentially harmful nature of giving part of myself to you. Of course, I feel I know you much better after this week, and quite frankly, I don't think we've seen more of each other than this week at all. Seriously, Tedward, it is like pulling your teeth out to get you to hang out with me. Well, I must say, I am pleasantly surprised that you actually started this. Although, I did talk you into picking me up at the hospital."

"Yes, I am sorry. I'm trying to be better," he stared down at the ground.

"Don't try to be better, Tedward, try to be you. That's really all we can be."

"Right," his tone dropped.

"Tedward, I heard that." She snapped at him as the light changed and they proceeded to walk across the crosswalk.

"Hmm?" He turned his head towards her.

"Your tone dropped. What's wrong? You know what, Ted, I'm sorry. I shouldn't have asked. Eh. I take it back. I should be asking that question, but *please* don't feel pressured to answer."

He sighed as they entered through the gate. "No. You're right. I appreciate you asking. Just, that particular thing is something I struggle with, because I don't really know who I am. Part of my job was espionage. If you put me in Russia, Italy, or any other country, I have been able to assume identities."

"You know, you seem to be very experienced for being so young. How old did you say you were?"

"Twenty-five," he replied softly.

"Sam thought you might be twenty-three." She squeezed his hand tighter.

"Sorry. The truth is, I don't know how old I am. It's complicated. I don't know when I was born, or where. That is really all I can say about it."

"I see," she spoke softly as she tightened her grip on his hand. "How is the sleep?"

"Still the same. Only thirty minutes," he replied as they continued to walk through the gardens, watching the trees and the beautiful lake with flocks of ducks paddling about in the waters. "I still see the nightmares, and they aren't going away. I don't expect them to."

"They will. They will," she assured him as she drew him closer to the lake.

She found a bench and pulled him down to it so they could be closer to the water. He ripped off a piece of the bread roll and handed it to her. She sniffed the bread and started pulling a little piece off and tossed it on the ground. A small flock of ducks started waddling out of the lake. Ted ripped off a piece and tossed it to the flock.

"Did you have friends? In the service I mean," she ripped off a little piece and placed it in her hand and leaned down to some brown ducklings to feed off of.

"The only friends and family I had were those I immediately worked with. I didn't see much of anyone else. There were fifteen of us," sighing, he ripped off another piece of bread and tossed it a little closer to the bench as more ducklings flocked towards them. "One of them I got real close with, and I proposed. She died. They all did."

"Did you ever have closure with them and their families?" She exhaled heavily as she tore off little pieces of bread and littered over the ground.

"No. The only family any of us had was one another. I suppose you could say we were all picked up from the same cloth. We were never on speaking terms with our families, for good or ill," he kept tossing more bread to the ducks. "In many ways, we were the only family we ever had."

"And are you on speaking terms with your family now?" she turned to him as she continued to rip bread up in little pieces.

"No," his tone dropped.

"I'm sorry for probing," she placed her free hand on his shoulder.

She took her pieces and tossed it in the air and let them fall down like snow to the ducks. The flocks of ducks became larger around them. There were white ducks, brown ducks, mallards with their green heads as they picked up the bread from the ground and quacked, and waited for the next one.

"Why did you join?"

He sighed as he tossed aside his last piece of bread. "I suppose you could say I was forced into it. I was groomed you see, to fight and was pushed to pursue a career in the military. That's all I wish to say about that, but what I will say is why I continued to fight. I continued to fight, despite knowing full well what it was doing to me, with every life I took brought pain and regret as if my heart was being torn to pieces inside my chest. But I kept fighting because I was promised that if I kept doing it, the world would be safer once the foreign powers were left at bay. I killed, and I killed, and I killed. I killed without halting. I killed until at last, I stopped caring and became an empty hollow husk. And at last, my hope came true, there was peace for a time. Now, that doesn't seem to matter anymore with NATO disbanding and all that. All my hard work was worthless."

Of course. All the wars stopped a decade ago, and you are responsible for that, but then you should be older. To be responsible for global peace, and now, after all this time to watch it crumble must be a punch in the face.

"The world will be a darker place now because of it. That's certain," Jennifer replied. "But no one man should ever have to bear that burden alone. Not you, not anyone. No one should carry it by themselves. You should not have been held responsible for that, as you can see, that peace was very short lived. Don't get me wrong, the peace was great while it lasted, and I think you might be closer to my age, if not older than me, Ted. My entire adult life I've lived in world peace, and it is now crumbling, but knowing what I know now, no one man should be forced to carry that burden alone."

"Yeah. You're right, but unfortunately that doesn't change the past," his voice became barely audible.

"No, but we can move forward, and you aren't serving anymore. It's not your problem, nor your responsibility," she tossed her last piece of bread on the ground and leaned into his shoulder. "Tedward, who am I to you?"

He leaned his head atop hers, "My friend."

Chapter 24

Ted Anderson

~No matter what good you accomplish, there is no point in helping others. In the end, you will find that humans are selfish conniving little dastardly creatures that aren't worth saving.

Ted Anderson looked up into the sky, the red ashes floating up like reverse snowfall. His left arm had a sharp piece of metal impaled in it, and his warm blood streamed down his arm and into the hot Nevada sand. He pulled the knife out and let it drop through his fingers onto the ground. He breathed deeply as he walked away from the carnage, avoiding the stench of dead bodies piled up high in the sand. His right arm dragged his AR15, and his trigger finger rested on the side of his rifle, away from the trigger. His eyes drooped down, and his mouth was open wide as if to say something, but he couldn't muster up the courage to speak. He walked towards the FOB.

He smelled the burned-out oil and fuel; the rotting flesh assaulted his nose as flies buzzed around the dead. The Nevada sand was filled with blood after all of this. There were many other soldiers walking around with stretchers, trying to get the wounded out of the way, before starting the long arduous process of identifying the dead. The burning gunpowder still filled the air, and he could still hear the loud revving of truck engines, and the movement of the tanks as they were being driven away.

He looked at the desert sand and was haunted with the sight that would never leave his mind. Bodies littered the desert, so many, one wouldn't think there was a desert out there. Limbs strewn all over the place, the uniforms torn to shreds, and even helicopter parts were on fire, blown up out of the sky. There were numerous blown parts from missiles that littered the flaming sands.

He stepped over the bodies, looking at the numerous dog tags on the necks of his fallen comrades, many of which, their faces were unrecognizable. Many of them no longer had faces, and some missed their dog tags. Identifying this many was going to be damn near impossible without DNA testing for identity. And then, he found something most peculiar about many of them, not all of them had an American Flag on their emblem patch. Some wore the patch of Russia, Ukraine, France, Italy, and China.

What were they all doing here? He thought.

"Sergeant Anderson," said a soft but ragged voice.

He turned swiftly and saw none other than Lieutenant Nakamura. "Go get some rest. You need it."

"Yes, Ma'am," he walked over the corpses of the unnamed soldiers.

He continued to cover his mouth as the flies were beginning to buzz around him like they thought him dead. He found an angry platoon, dragging severed limbs and corpses, a small amount, of corpses into a pit. He watched them, and he was able to identify most of these individuals, man and woman alike. These were the corpses of Task Force Seven: every single one of them.

Two masked soldiers came from behind him holding large red plastic oil containers. They made it down to the pit with the bodies and dismembered limbs. Behind him was another man, an ensign, Ensign Malcom. He looked down, angrily at the bodies as the two soldiers poured gasoline on them. The ensign took out a match and lit them aflame. There was one still alive, her fair but dirty face began to scream in agony as her face caught on fire. Her fists barely clenched. "I'll kill you! I'll kill you! I'll kill you! I'll kill all of you!"

"Sir?" One of the masked men pointed his pistole at her screaming head.

"Negative. She'll be dead soon enough. No use in wasting another round. We've already used enough of those as it is."

"What did they do?" Anderson asked. "They didn't deserve this."

"Evidence was found on Ghost that he was colluding with Germany to stage a coup. They are traitors," the ensign answered. "Now, don't get yourself in too deep in all of this, Anderson. Much of this is need to know, and you don't need to know any more than you do now."

"Yes, sir," he about-faced. *Best stay out of it, Anderson.*

Anderson left it at that and continued dragging his weapon in the sand as bodies were being counted and collected, being sent to the medics for identification. The amount was staggering. He continued walking to the FOB. *Didn't we just broker international peace? Ghost, why would you do this? At least I, at least I can finally go home.*

The entire firefight was completely endless and over exhausting. Ted knew he had been sleepless for nearly two weeks, and he wasn't even present for half of it. His legs were heavy, his arms were weak, and his spirit felt like it was being shackled inside his chest as he took heavy breaths, his lungs expanding. "It's over," he said under his breath. "I don't know what this was all about, and I don't care anymore. At least, the world will be a little safer."

Sergeant Ted Anderson never questioned any of the orders given to him over the last two weeks.

***

Six months later, Ted went on leave for a full week before returning back to active duty. No new wars were declared, no recent terrorist activity, in the middle east, nor here in the United States. It looked like the military was about to do some downsizing or pushing people out of the service. There was now next to no need for an over abundant military force. The army was going to be cut first.

Ted was on base in Fort Bennington, Georgia. He was running his half marathon in the oppressive heat. He stopped towards the end, leaning against a Humvee, sweating profusely and inhaled the fresh scent of his own body odor. He went to the barracks and showered before heading back into his office to finish off some paperwork. He planned to resign today.

He was in his office, on the computer and printing out some paperwork for his discharge. There was a knock on the door. He looked up; it was Sergeant Hernandez. "Sergeant, you're wanted with Lieutenant Nakamura, immediately."

"Copy," he sighed as he got up from his chair. He followed the private down some lengthy halls through Georgia. He moved around and listened very closely to the conversations around the hallway, some small talk, others were more political in nature. He didn't care. *Today's the day.*

He was ushered into Nakamura's office. She held a clipboard and pointed to a chair, "Have a seat."

Hernandez closed the door behind him as he took the seat in the black chair.

"Anderson, you're being reassigned," she said, looking him in the eye with a soft glare, "Effective immediately, you are being shipped out to Germany."

Fantastic.

"How are you holding up over that little incident?" she leaned back in her chair, crossing her arms over her chest.

"All things considered, could be worse," he said. *You crazy bitch.*

"It was Hell on all of us. We're not going to recover from that," she sighed. "Many good men and women died."

"It's behind us. Are we done?"

"Yes. If you're psychologically fit, you are flying out at 0600 tomorrow."

"Thanks," Ted got up from his chair and went to the door, his hand touched the doorknob. He turned to her as she filed the paperwork away, "Nakamura."

"Anderson," she looked back at him from her desk.

"I'd tell you to go to Hell, but I think they would spit you back out," he told her coldly as his eyes angled down his nose.

"Excuse me?!" she glared at him.

"Hell is too good a place for you," Ted scowled. "Why did we kill them?"

"Treason," she gritted her teeth, leaning back in her chair.

"Horse! Shit!" Ted shot back. "I want the real reason, Nakamura. If I killed them, I want to know why. Now tell me!"

"Wars stopped. They made that happen. There's no need for them anymore," she answered.

"You could have discharged them! What the hell, Nakamura!" Ted was unsatisfied with the answer. He kept his voice down as to not draw attention from outside her office.

"Really?" she frowned. "Really, Anderson? You don't know all the details; you'd best leave it alone. Knowing all the details as I do, I know there was no chance in Hell they could integrate back into civie life. Besides, too much confidential information is on the line should they be released out in the world. You don't know the details; you don't need to know. Now get out of my office!" she stood up, pointed violently at the door behind him.

Unsatisfied, he swiftly jumped over her desk and tackled her to the ground before she could scream. The various items from her desk slid off to the floor. His hands clasped around her neck and pulled her up from the ground. She was striking him with her hand and tried to release his grip. "Hell is too good a place for you! What the hell were you thinking! What's wrong with you? They were just kids damnit! They were just kids! You know full well as I do, they did nothing to deserve any of it." *Crack!* Her arms immediately dropped down. He released her corpse to the floor as it tumbled.

He opened the door and briskly walked out of the room, closing it behind him. *Good riddance.*

Reflection

The story of "The Hedgehog" has seen a few drafts, here and there. The original concept was produced from one of the campaigns in a very popular First-Person Shooter game back in 2017. I outlined a draft of a tale, and started writing, and 40,000 words in, was since abandoned. Not because of time, but because of passion. I was writing a tale of convoluted plots and it was, ultimately a revenge story. I lost passion, and that manuscript with its characters in a doc, and it was sitting there.

A number of books, games, and anime later, I decided to pick it back up again; however, it was a new outline, I started elsewhere, not in the middle of some grand ceremony, but in the center of a horrific event, tossing you, my reader right in the middle of the action. This book ended where it started: unsettling. The tone of this novel is like a whiplash, moving myself, and hopefully you, in many different directions emotionally, and I will find that to be true the farther these tales take us.

As I was outlining this in the end of August of 2020, I was reflecting more about what story this was going to be: a tale of adventure, despair, magic, suffering, regret, or action, and I brought myself again to one of my favorite anime, which depicted a 15-year-old girl, coming back from the war who was viewed as nothing but a tool, and she valued herself as nothing more than a tool of war, needing orders to do anything, holding up a firm military and cold, distant social demeanor. She came back from the war, with two arms replaced with metallic instruments, and used them for her arms in way to write letters.

That was a tale about a veteran's struggles, retuning to integrate back into what they call, "Civie Life". "Civie" is short for Civilian, for those unaware. Most soldiers come back with some level of emotional baggage, suffering internally with a variety of stress, the most common one is PTSD, and others coming back with the inability to express oneself openly.

Circling back around that anime, it tells the story I elaborated upon just above, and in that, was a book I wanted to read. The book was a light novel, and upon doing a quick search, I was unable to find anything like that. There were no comparisons that popped up, and even trying to use the subject matter as a reference, all I was able to find were memoirs, and textbooks, both of which I was not looking for. I am assuming this may be the first fictitious novel exploring Veteran Integration, and confident in that. If I am wrong, please send them my way, I want to read them!

This story wouldn't have been written, (likely) if it wasn't for that anime, and revealing the elements on such subject material, and I might say, between this novel, and my first one, they are worlds apart in terms of quality. Reflecting upon this, reminds me of the times where the muse took over, and it was such a relaxing feeling. When the muse violently took over my fingers, my brain and mind went numb as I typed away at the computer screen not thinking about the words I typed. My fingers typed away without my brain cognitively thinking about what happened next.

This was truly a passion project, and I remember one night, it was a Friday night when I finished the first draft of this novel, I was listening to depressing music, (because, why not?) and I typed away for hours on end. I knew where I was going next, and knew the next line of words, so I elected that it was a good place to stop, and I could continue first thing in the morning. I shut down my laptop, and went in the shower, continuing to listen to said depressing music as I cleansed myself of mud and sadness.

What happened next, was awe inspiring, and funny. I went over the first part of the chapter in my head and when I got to the place where I stopped, my muse decided that I was not done yet. Damn you. I dictated the rest of the chapter as I finished the shower, and thought to myself, "I can't stop now. This was too good, and I will forget what I just said first thing in the morning."

So, I did what any normal person would do, hop out of the shower, dry myself, and put clothes on. Clothes are essential. I went in my room, and turned on the computer and finished the chapter, which was, at that time the end of the book. I clocked in 64,000 words; give or take, in two and a half weeks.

The editing process was time consuming, mentally exhausting, but the revisions needed to be made, and some changes were implemented to make the story fuller, and more justifiably a Fantasy Novel. Upon my last revisions, I got to the chapter which I detailed above, and had a little emotional breakdown. Not because I was getting towards the end of this bittersweet tale, but because the emotions that was invoked within me upon rereading it was raw, and I cried, and I could only mutter two words, "I'm sorry".

Eventually, I made it to the end of the chapter, and scanned the next chapter to see how long it might take me. Seeing how the next chapter was short, so I elected to keep going. Upon reading the first few lines, I immediately realized that was a dreadful mistake, saying to myself in the darkness of the night, "Oh, it's that, it's that chapter. Dear God! No! I can't freaking handle this right now!"

I know this novel is going to hit differently for different people, and for me, I spent countless nights crying, not just writing it, but editing it. While I know this will not please everyone, I know it will please others. I know not everyone, myself included, has seen what War looks like. I know not everyone has experienced the mental toll it can place on the mind, and especially those who were tossed aside, continue to fight the demons of war as they relive those wretched moments again, and again, and again.

This is one of the many real problems we face globally, and there are some who handle it better than others, but regrettably, like many problems, it still persists, and within the themes discussed in this novel, and ultimately this series, perhaps an idea can come about solving some of these larger social detriments plaguing our society, in whatever corner of the Earth we reside.

Triggers: Violence, murder, human trafficking, gore, and violence against children.

About the Author

Armanis Ar-feinial grew up in the backwoods of Maine, cultivating his love for the fresh scent of cut grass and pine trees. He now lives in Boston with his family and two dogs. He enjoys the board games of chess, tabletop rpgs, video games, Anime, Manga, books, and of course, Renaissance Fairs. You may find him at King Richard's Faire.

Other Titles include:

The Secrets of Terra Silenti; The Covenant; The Desecration of the World

Twitter: @sarcastic_elf

www.ingramcontent.com/pod-product-compliance
Lightning Source LLC
Chambersburg PA
CBHW020909110726
47900CB00001B/78